ATTICUS

S. Bennett

ISBN: 978-1-947212-05-3

Find Sawyer on the web!
sawyerbennett.com
twitter.com/bennettbooks
facebook.com/bennettbooks

DEDICATION

This novel has been a long time in the making. I've been wanting to write a book for years about my dog, Atticus. I've wanted to memorialize him because he is simply the world's most awesome dog ever (even if he is the world's worst behaved). When I first laid eyes on him as a puppy, I knew he was going to bring mayhem into my life and that's exactly why I chose him.

Everything in this book that the fictional Atticus did, has been done by the real Atticus.

No joking.

I have so many people to thank for helping me with this project. First to my friend and veterinarian, Laura Gaylord, and to Atti's vet, Anne Jones. They both helped me with some of the technical details on veterinary medicine.

Gentry Hogan, lawyer and good friend as well as an advocate for disabled veterans. He helped me understand more about PTSD within the military and its evolution.

To the Berner Gang—my girls MJ Lees May, Wendy Britton, and Valerie Yoffe and their dogs Mimi, Maggie, Sirius, and Kiera. We have the best puppy playdates.

To the Berner Community. So many friends we've made along the way. So many people who absolutely love this breed just as I do. Special shout out to Deb Schaeffer, Dorene McCune, Wendy Djang, Kimberly Perry and Atticus' original mom, Venus Slater.

A very special nod to Scout, my rescued Golden Retriever, who is as goofy and bad as Atticus. You came from a tough background bud, but you're loved by all of us so much.

Shout out to Kevin Peddicord—friend and amazing artist for the watercolor painting he did of Atticus when he was a puppy. To the best cover designer in the world, Hang Le, for taking that art and making my most favorite book cover ever.

To my Chief Officer of Everything, Lisa Kuhne… thank you for believing in me and this book. Oh, and for keeping my business running so I can write!!!

Mark Yoffe—as always, your oncology expertise has pushed me through many books, this one most importantly. More than anything, thank you for being a wonderful friend and one of the most caring doctors I've ever known. Thanks to your insight, I hope I did justice on how hard it is to watch a loved one die.

To my family—Shawn, Parker, Mom, Dave, Dad, Sue, Glenn—thank you for all the help and support you gave me while I wrote this book. I think it's one of my best, and that's partly due to y'all.

To Bernard—my real life homeless friend. You are admired and worried over.

To my dad, Jerry Leone and my father-in-law, Glenn Noble, who have both beaten colon cancer. Your strength and courage are inspiring.

Here's a PSA to all my readers: please get a colonoscopy when you reach the age that you should. I can tell you from personal experience (I've had two) that it is not bad at all. I swear it. Even the prep these days is easy, and the procedure itself completely forgettable (thank you, good drugs). Colon cancer is preventable, but you have to make the first move.

And finally... yes, finally. Thank you, Atticus, for enriching my life beyond measure. I would not trade one zany thing you've done over the years—

Wait! Scratch that. I would totally trade the surgeries after you ate my socks, but all the other things are bearable. I love you so much!!!!

Follow the real Atticus on Instagram at @atticuscrazydog or on Facebook at The Adventures of Atticus.

TABLE OF CONTENTS

PROLOGUE

Atticus

THINGS WERE FUZZY when I first came into the world. I remember a lot of scrambling and sometimes fighting to get at my mama's teat, but there was always enough room once we settled into our respective places and I never went hungry. It seems in those early days all I did was eat, sleep, poop, and pee. It was an easy life, but not very exciting.

I'm a curious sort of pup by nature, unlike my brothers and sisters. They're happy just wrestling around with each other or chewing on toys. I like to watch things.

Intensely observe the actions of others. Skillfully smell the air for the scents that help me to understand my world. I like to taste things, and the new grownup puppy food we started eating a few weeks ago is delicious.

I'm what you call a Bernese Mountain Dog. I'm not quite sure what I look like, but if I had to judge by my brothers and sisters, I'd say I'm black, brown, white, and really fluffy. Our owners are what you call breeders. My mama and daddy make baby puppies, and then people buy us.

Lately, people have been coming by to look at us. Prior to such an event, me and my siblings are brought out one by one to an outdoor bathtub where we are scrubbed with warm water and sweet-smelling soap. We're then toweled off before being placed into a makeshift outdoor pen made of interlocking panels. There we dry in the sun and chew on blades of grass or each other's tails. When the people come to look, we preen and act silly and look our adorable best.

If we're one of the lucky pups, people will ask to hold us. Our owners will pull us out of our little pen, then we get to play with people and get belly rubs. They exclaim over how cute we are and even if we're not chosen, there's a general air of excitement buzzing through the rest of us while we watch from our pen.

This is one such day. We're all bathed and smelling like flowers. It's chilly out, so our man owner pulled one of the cars outside of his big, two-car garage, and set up the pen beside the remaining car. He then opened the big door for the people to come look.

Because I'm always aware of my surroundings, it doesn't take me long to notice that one of the panels on the cage isn't fully locked, and there's a tiny gap at the bottom. While the other pups do somersaults and put their front paws on top of the cage to get the people's attention, I nudge my nose through the tiny opening.

Next my head.

Wiggle a bit to get my shoulders through.

Then it seems I'm sort of squirted through to the other side.

I look over my shoulder. All my sibs are still trying to get the people's attention and acting very foolish in my opinion.

I'm suddenly intrigued by a smoky sort of smell that's coming from somewhere outside the garage. I scramble underneath the car, then belly crawl quite stealthily to the other side. Without a moment's hesitation, I dash out and into what I call the big world. The minute the soft pads of my paws hit the crispy brown grass, a rush of jubilation over takes me.

I submit for a moment to the unmitigated exhilaration of freedom, running around in a tight circle for a few laps before flopping to my belly. The grass pricks at my skin because my fur isn't very thick there yet, and I hang out for a bit while watching the people ooh and ahh over my siblings. Not one of them turn to look at me, but I don't feel like I'm missing out on any important action.

The smoky smell hits my nose again, and my mouth waters. My tongue comes out and licks all around my snout as I lift my head to get a better sniff. It definitely makes me want to sneeze a bit, but there is a strong scent of some type of cooked meat underneath. I think I'll die if I don't get a taste of it.

It's from somewhere—my gaze moves to the back of the property—just over there.

A thick copse of pine trees stands strong and tall. I've never been back there and it looks dark and a bit scary, but I feel an adventure calling me.

Plus… that smell.

It's so delicious, and I can't resist checking it out.

PART I

"A journey of a thousand miles must begin with a single step."

—Lao Tzu

CHAPTER 1

Hazel

M<small>Y EYELIDS ARE</small> sealed shut with the type of nasty gunk that a hard night of partying leaves behind. The act of rubbing them with my fingers sends sharp bolts of pain reverberating throughout my skull. I believe my tongue is glued to the top of my mouth for a moment, but it comes free with a little bit of suction.

It's a typical Wednesday morning for me. I didn't have to work last night which meant I partied. It's what I do because if I don't put myself out there, how will I ever find what I need?

I manage to blink against the morning sun coming in through the living room blinds that are so worn and twisted they're completely nonfunctional.

Not my apartment though and since I'm essentially a freeloader, I have no right to say a word about it. I just accept that sleeping on a friend's couch means rising early no matter how hungover I am.

After freeing my feet from the ratty old afghan

Charmin's great-grandmother or some such person crocheted, I roll slightly toward the coffee table to root around for my pack of cigarettes. The bright sun has me keeping my eyes clamped tightly shut, so I'm going by instinct alone.

Which sucks because my hand lands inside of the overflowing ashtray. I immediately jerk it backward before making another attempt, grab air for a moment, and then stick my hand right back into the pile of stale cigarette butts and powdery cinders.

Squinting at my ash-covered fingertips, I realize it's nothing more than a metaphor for my life. Floundering around, landing in crap situations, not learning my lesson, and repeating.

Prying my eyes open further, I roll my head and zero in on the pack of cigarettes. I grab it, squeeze lightly, and determine it's empty.

"Shit," I mutter, tossing it down on the scarred wooden coffee table that's littered with beer cans, a bong, and an empty bag of Doritos. I vaguely remember partying last night with a few guys from the bar.

Even more vaguely, I remember Charmin and her boyfriend Chuck coming in. They joined us for a few bong hits before they took their own personal party to the bedroom. The headboard knocking against the wall and Chuck's oddly high-pitched yips of pleasure had me laughing so hard I was afraid I'd pee my pants.

Probably wouldn't have been as funny if I wasn't stoned, but any time I can laugh at Chuck behind his back is good times for me. The dude can't stand me, and the feeling is mutual.

I push into a sitting position on the couch, intent on getting all the way up and making my way to the bathroom. My head swims and my stomach rolls, so I just slump backward against the lumpy cushion. I drag my fingers through my hair, promptly getting them caught in a mass of brittle knots before letting out an audible sigh because now I have clean fingers but cigarette soot coating my scalp.

I'm a fucking mess.

My shoulders go tense when I hear the bedroom door creak open. I know it's the bedroom door because there are only two off the apartment's short hallway. There's the bathroom, which does not squeak but also does not close all the way because one of the hinges has been knocked loose.

And then there's the bedroom. Its hinges are secure but rusted, making it sound like a screeching eagle every time the door moves. I once sprayed some PAM cooking spray on it because it was driving me nuts every time Charmin or Chuck would enter or exit their room, but that just didn't have quite the lube power of WD-40. I wasn't about to buy a can as my funds are limited and precious to me. I'd live with the squeak as well as the bright light in the morning.

"Hope you're going to clean that shit up," Chuck says as he enters the living room.

My shoulders tighten even more. I've been staying at Charmin's apartment for almost three months now. It'd been a good deal for me as she was only charging me a hundred bucks a month plus half the utilities to squat on her uncomfortable couch. I couldn't afford anything more than that and on my part-time bartender's wages, it was a stretch as it was.

But she started dating Chuck last month, and he moved in after four days of wild, passionate, yipping sex. I have no room to judge her for pathetically latching onto the man so quickly, because I've been accused of doing the same. As of now, I'm on the prowl for the next Mr. Right Who Is Totally Wrong because I just do better when I have someone to help take care of me.

It's the way it's always been.

In fact, the three months I've been living at Charmin's since my husband kicked me out of our house is the longest I've ever been single in my fourteen years of adulthood. I feel so very lost and yet, I'm just wise enough to know how lame that makes me.

I don't bother giving Chuck my full attention as it's too much effort to roll my head his way. Besides, the dude grosses me out, strutting around in his saggy boxers with his hairy stomach rolling over the waistband.

Closing my eyes, I merely point out, "You could help clean it up. You didn't mind drinking the beer and taking hits off the bong last night."

"Wasn't your beer and dope, though, was it?" he replied.

Fair point. It wasn't mine, but it was the dudes I invited over to party last night. They were only casual acquaintances from the bar but given the fact they were providing the booze and drugs, they were my bestest buds last night.

I don't reply to Chuck. He's the type of person who has to have the last word anyway. The man has an ego that's overstretched and filled with a false sense of importance, meaning he's always right.

Because it would be more painful and nauseating to attempt a civil discourse with the man, I push from the couch and suck down the bile that wells up in my throat. I never bothered to take my shoes off last night before I passed out, so I'm almost ready to roll out of here.

Once in the bathroom, I take a much-needed pee. I try to ignore my reflection in the mirror as I scrub my hands and teeth, but there's no getting around the fact I look about as pathetic as I feel. My hair is a lank, dry mess and my roots are about three inches long, which corresponds quite nicely to the fact I haven't been able to afford a discount box of hair color from the drugstore since my husband kicked me to the curb.

Asshole.

I try to creep my way to the front door while Chuck roots around in the refrigerator.

"Hazel," Chuck yells as I open the front door. "You going to clean that mess up?"

"Later," I mutter as I step over the threshold.

"Later as in you'll clean it up later?" he presses, and I make the mistake of sliding my gaze over to him as I start to pull the door closed. I quickly snap my eyes shut, trying to block out the image of him exuberantly scratching himself between the legs.

Pivoting quickly, I call out just before I shoot out of the apartment, "I'll clean it up later."

Right now, I need cigarettes.

Maybe a cup of coffee.

Jamming my hand into the back pocket of my skinny jeans, which are falling off me because I'm not eating much these days, I pull out a crumpled pile of money. By the time I reach the sidewalk that runs along old Highway 17, I've got them smoothed out and determine I'm the proud owner of eight dollars. It's a good thing I'm working tonight because after I buy a pack of cigarettes and a cup of coffee, I'm broke until I can collect tips.

Old Highway 17 is different than the new Highway

17. It's just a small portion of the original that runs north and south through Jacksonville, North Carolina but was relegated to a service road once a new bypass was built last year. It's roughly a quarter mile long and from said service road you can access three bars, the ghetto-styled apartment complex where I now live, a pawn shop, and a convenience store. In the seventies and into the early eighties, this part of Jacksonville and a few more miles of Highway 17 were densely populated with bars, strip clubs, pawn shops, and tattoo parlors catering specifically to young marines who had just arrived at Camp Geiger to begin infantry school from boot camp. The drinking age wasn't raised to twenty-one until 1986, and those glory days made those types of business owners very rich.

It was the same on the north end of town where Camp Lejeune borders the stretch of Highway 24—also a multi-lane thoroughfare that was studded with all kinds of business that would provide mischief and mayhem to young marines recently graduated from Camp Geiger and moving over to the big base.

As the owner of the bar I currently work at tends to lament to me on a nightly basis, that all changed when the drinking age was raised. Highway 17 started to dry up and one by one, the businesses started going under. Those that hang on do so out of a sense of nostalgia and mostly because the bar owners have strong social ties to what few customers are left.

Plus, they like to drink a lot.

I walk south toward the 7-Eleven, rubbing my bare arms against the chilly morning air. The weather has been weird lately. We're four days into spring, but it's hardly breaking the forties in the early morning hours, which is definitely not typical of eastern North Carolina. I'd been so focused on getting out of Chuck's notice that I forgot my jacket.

Not a biggie.

The 7-Eleven would be warm, and I could enjoy a cup of coffee there while shooting the shit with whoever is on duty. I'm a frequent customer there to buy cigs and/or beer. If I wait it out for at least half an hour, Chuck would be gone to work by the time I got back.

As I walk past a large culvert a quarter filled with rainwater and months of accumulated trash, a barely perceptible sound reaches my ears through the early rush-hour traffic. On weekday mornings, there's a steady flow of cars filled with young jarheads heading to the Marine Corps Air Station. It's home to the loud helicopters and Ospreys that fly over Onslow County daily, and it's where most of my current bar patrons work since it takes up much of the southern part of Jacksonville.

My thoughts turning me away from whatever sound I thought I'd heard, I almost make it past the wide ditch before I hear it again. A tiny yip.

Completely different from Chuck's orgasmic coyote sounds, and far more pitiful.

I stop, leaning over the edge of the culvert that's probably a good three feet in depth and twice as wide. The wet bottom is lush with a weedy type of foliage, green grasses, and proud standing cattails, interspersed with empty McDonald's bags, cigarette butts, discarded lumber, and beer bottles.

Something moves among the greenery, and the slimy water ripples. I take a step back, because in my experience, I'm the type of down-and-out person who would get bit by a poisonous snake.

Another yip and my brain finally recognize it as distinctly canine.

My curiosity gets the better of me. I start a careful descent down toward the water, holding my arms out wide for balance. It only takes two steps before I go down onto one knee, the soft dirt and long blades of dewy grass causing my foot to slip out from under me.

"Shit," I curse, and get two resounding little barks back.

Keening, pleading cries for me to come even closer to take a look.

Resigned to the large, muddy wet spot on one knee and realizing I stand a good chance of toppling head-first into the brackish water if I continue down, I move closer to where I hear more whimpers.

Using my hands to peel back a curtain of long grass, I see the source of distress.

It's a puppy of indeterminate breed and color. It's covered in the blackish muck and struggling against a tangle of barbed wire wrapped around the lower half of its body that's nailed to a splintered piece of two-by-four. It looks like the puppy tried to squirm through a loop or something and got caught up.

Or even worse, someone intentionally wrapped that poor thing up like that and threw it in the ditch to die.

Despite its precarious situation, the little mud-slicked tail wags furiously for a moment as its head swings to me, fully revealing that the dog has one brown eye and one blue eye. That one crystal eye stands stark against the mud, almost colorless closer to the pupil and darkening to a faded denim on the outer edge. I wonder if it's blind in that eye as it seems rounder and wider than the other.

Perhaps it's just fear making it stand out that way, but it looks wild and desperate as well as insanely happy that someone has answered its calls for aid.

My entire body shivers, partly from the cold but partly from recognizing the terrible predicament this little creature is in. When my husband kicked me out of the house three months ago, I spent a few brutal nights freezing my ass off in my car because I had nowhere to go and no one to help me. It was a mere four days before Christmas.

I'd swallowed my pride, and begged Charmin for a spot on her couch. My car has since broken down and I can't afford to get it fixed, so I walk where I need to go. I muddle through my life working the measly hours I'm allotted at the bar because the owner doesn't want any of his bartenders getting close to a forty-hour workweek and God forbid asking him for overtime.

And so far… I've survived.

Twisting my neck, I tear my gaze away from the dog and glance back out to the edge of the culvert. Just a mere thirty yards away from a hot cup of coffee and a relaxing cigarette.

A deep shudder ripples up my spine, reminding me that my life is shit. I have no business helping this dog. Even if I free it, the damn thing will probably wander out onto the service road. If it doesn't get squashed by a lone car zooming by on this dead road, it'll most definitely be killed quickly once it ventures onto Highway 17. I'd be dooming it to certain death, whereas if I just leave it alone, it might work its way free of the wire and I can forget about it.

Heck… someone else might even come along at any minute to help the stupid thing.

Or… it could die from the elements, which would probably take a few days and promises to be an unbearably cruel and painful end to its life.

"Damn it," I mutter as I reach for the puppy. I'll get it loose from the wire, after which it can take its chances on the highway. At least if it gets hit by a car, it will be a quick death.

An easy end to its suffering.

It's the most I can do for the little pup.

CHAPTER 2

Atticus

I T WAS SWEET and utter relief when the woman freed me from that pokey-wire I'd gotten tangled up in. It had been many days since I'd left my brothers and sisters, in search of the smoky meat food. I never found it.

I did find that ditch, though, and my nose told me there was food down in there. It was way far down and there was water there, which I don't mind but it didn't look nice. Not like the clear water in our bathtubs with the sweet-smelling soap.

I found no food down there.

I have no clue how I'd gotten tangled up in that wire, but the more I tried to escape, the tighter it grabbed onto me.

When the woman appeared, I thought I would just die from pure happiness that someone had found me. She looked nice, although she smelled a little stale.

She also smelled… unhappy.

All I know is she had me out of that ditch and in her arms, walking down and eventually across a big scary road with lots of loud cars roaring by. I had ducked my head, pushing it into her armpit so I didn't have to look.

Now we're just sitting here in front of a building, and I'm so tired.

The woman has me on her lap, and she tries to blow warm air onto me. It feels good, but it doesn't last. I can't stop from shaking. My stomach makes rumbly noises and I close my eyes, thinking I'll dream of food and warm baths and chewing on my siblings' ears if I ever make it back to them. I haven't eaten since I left except for some grass I tried to chew, but it was yucky.

"It's okay, puppy," the woman says softly as she spreads her palms over me, ever so gently. It feels a bit warmer. I'm so tired I can barely open my eyes.

CHAPTER 3

Hazel

I GREW UP on the north side of Jacksonville—the complete opposite end of the city where I've made my current stomping grounds. My dad was stationed at Camp Lejeune in heavy motor transport and my mom was a salesclerk at Belk's, which was considered the cream of upscale shopping there. My upbringing was fairly normal except for the fact we moved around a lot because my dad was a marine. Sometimes he had to leave for extended periods of time when he was deployed to some far-flung corner of the world but the last seven years of his service were at Camp Lejeune. That meant Jacksonville became the place we lived together the longest as a family.

Just nine days after I turned eighteen, and three months shy of graduating from high school, I left home. I reasoned I was an adult who could make that important decision without my parents telling me how stupid it was.

Which they did.

Repetitively.

But what did they really know? I was in love with a marine who looked gorgeous in his uniform. He was two years older than me and had baby blue eyes that made me absolutely silly over the moon for him. I had absolutely no problem giving up my virginity.

It was true love.

Well, at least for a few months anyway.

Then I got pregnant, and he got twitchy.

It was a relatively peaceful time for the Marine Corp on the heels of the Gulf War ending but before 9/11 occurred, so I guess being married to a pregnant eighteen-year-old wasn't exciting enough for him. He broke up with me on the morning he left for a six-month med cruise, which isn't as glamorous as it sounds. It basically means he's stuck on an aircraft carrier cutting squares in the middle of the ocean for weeks and weeks on end.

Still, he wasn't afraid of the loneliness, nor did he need my letters of love, support, and encouragement. He didn't need me the way I needed him.

Perhaps he knew the future or perhaps he was just an asshole, but I miscarried less than a week after he left. I was too embarrassed to go home with my tail tucked between my legs, and thus started my career in bartending. It's funny, but I don't remember much about my first love. I believe I must have blocked out one of the biggest mistakes I've ever made. It was a whirlwind romance that ended so badly for me that it helped create the loser of a woman I am today. I do remember his name was Chris—the man who impregnated me and then broke my heart—but for the life of me, I can't remember his last name.

I just know my failure with him is part of what landed me where I am today.

My ass is falling asleep, and I adjust my weight to lean on my left cheek. The concrete stoop in front of Onslow Veterinary Hospital is freezing cold, and the wet pile of mud-soaked, bloody dog I'm holding on my lap isn't helping matters much. I'm shivering nearly as violently as the puppy.

Pulling my hand out from under the painfully gaunt animal, I'm dismayed to see more bright red on my palm. It was a lot harder to get the dog free of the barbed wire than I originally anticipated, since a few prongs were embedded pretty deep.

When I saw the blood, I knew I couldn't leave the dog to fend for itself. For some reason, seeing the puppy's life force all over my hands made me a bit more committed to its welfare.

Worse than the blood, its pitiful mewling and incessant shivering about tore my heart in two. We never had pets growing up, and I don't have much experience with them, but this wretched creature that's starved, broken, and bleeding speaks to me in a way that not much in life has before.

My game plan is thin on deep thought and motivated pretty much by emotion at this point.

I knew there was a small veterinary clinic about half a mile north, but on the other side of Highway 17. The half-mile walk wasn't daunting to me. I'd lived on the south side of Jacksonville for the last fourteen years of my life, and a small two mile stretch of this busy highway has been the center of my universe the entire time. Plenty of bars to work at, even if the good ones had all closed down, and I could walk wherever I needed which was beneficial in these carless times.

But getting to that vet clinic required crossing three southbound lanes of 17 during rush-hour traffic followed by a guardrail surrounding a wide, grass median, and then three north-bound lanes. Not impossible by any means, but it certainly wasn't pleasant while I was freezing and carrying a bloody, dying puppy in my arms.

It took me almost half an hour to get here, and I was dismayed to find the clinic closed. It's a small, square building of white-painted cinder block and a low-pitched tin roof reddened by rust. There's a thick glass door and two square windows to either side, which are darkened because no interior lights are on. I've passed by this building on several occasions over the years, but never gave it any thought.

Now I'm thinking I wish this vet would hurry up and open the damn door.

I have no clue what time it is since I don't have a cell phone or watch. I didn't bother looking at the clock on my quick exodus from the apartment today. By my hungover estimate, it's anywhere between eight and nine, although it could be earlier or it could be later. I try to ignore the fact the front door is stenciled with the hours of operation.

Monday-Thursday, Ten AM to four PM.

What kind of business has hours like that?

Especially when there are dying animals to treat?

My head tips down and I stare at the wet, cold mess in my lap. The mud is so thick and pervasive throughout the fur I can't tell what type of dog it is other than it's a long-haired breed. The dual-colored eyes suggest a mutt to me, but what do I know about dogs? Perhaps it's a trendy "thing" or maybe it's a mutant thing.

It shivers hard, and its breathing seems more labored. It hasn't opened its eyes since it settled wearily onto my lap once I sat down on the stoop. I can't even pet the damn thing because it's nothing but slime and mud, but I keep my palms spread across its sides to try to give it some measure of warmth.

Hunching my shoulders and leaning over the puppy, I bring my mouth closer to its head. I blow hot breath onto it, not even knowing if it's a boy or a girl at this point. It gives out a labored chuff as if it appreciates my efforts, but it seems entirely futile.

I blow on the dog again, but it doesn't move.

My heart sinks, and a cold hopelessness seeps into my veins.

The sound of tires crunching on the asphalt parking lot strewn with loose highway gravel has my head lifting, and I see an old car pulling in. It's one of those long ones that seem to take up a city block, and it's an olive green that's not used on new cars these days. It comes to a stop in front of the clinic and to my right, taking the one parking spot that has a handicapped logo in faded paint. The word Impala is on the side. There's an elderly man behind the wheel. He's staring at me from under bushy white eyebrows, but I don't see a handicapped sticker.

Probably the first scheduled appointment of the day and it gives me hope the doors will be opening soon.

I stare down at the puppy, thinking it certainly constitutes an emergency, and then back up to the old man sitting behind the wheel. He just stares at me with his lips pressed into a grim, flat line. Perhaps he's thinking I might ruin his schedule by preempting his time slot with my emergency.

With a slight shake of his head that seems more resignation than anything, he turns the car off and opens the driver's door. He rocks in his seat slightly as if he needs momentum to get out, one aged hand covered in brown spots grabbing onto the "oh shit" handle above the window. That's what my dad used to call them when we were little and he'd take a curve too fast.

"Grab hold of the 'oh shit' handles, kids, because the faster you go, the better you adhere to the road," he'd always yell out to me and my younger sister, Liz. "And I have a need for speed."

Liz and I would cackle, each grabbing onto the handles while Mom would shoot him disapproving glares from the front seat. It's one of the faint memories of my childhood that can make me smile, and then make me unbearably sad.

The old man is finally able to pull himself out of the car, only to shuffle around and lean back inside for something. It's only after he straightens and closes the door that I see he's leaning heavily on a cane. It's wooden and knobby, but befitting him for some reason. He wouldn't look right with one of those modern-day aluminum canes in pink or blue.

He has no cat, dog, lizard, or fish bowl with him so perhaps he's here to pick up his pet.

The man bends at the waist slightly, peering at the limp pile of misery I'm holding as if it's a specimen on a glass slide. Stabbing the end of his cane toward the puppy, he asks, "What do you have there?"

The man has a distinctive southern accent, so I peg him as a local.

"An injured dog," I answer, placing one palm on the concrete to help push myself to a standing position. I'm blocking the front door, which I assume will now be opening soon. My other hand goes under the cold belly, and I'm worried over how limp the animal has gone. "If you don't mind, I was hoping the vet could take a quick look at it when they open. It's kind of an emergency."

"I'll decide what's an emergency," the old man snaps with his thick, bush-like eyebrows drawn inward. His entire demeanor screams disapproval at me.

I'm all for respecting elders and stuff, but once people dispose of common courtesy to me, I'm pretty much done with them regardless of the age. "I think I'll leave that up to the vet to determine," I inform him prissily.

"I am the damn vet," he growls, hobbling toward the door. I'm forced to scramble out of the way before he runs me over. He moves awfully quick for a man with a cane and a pronounced limp.

I watch mutely as he loops the end of his cane over his forearm so he can unlock the front door. He sways back and forth unsteadily without the support, and if he goes down, I can't help. Not going to drop the puppy to help this jerk.

He doesn't say a word to me as he pushes his way inside the heavy swinging glass door, immediately using his cane to supplement his gait. The door whispers shut behind him, and I'm left standing beside the low stoop.

If not for the shallow breathing from the puppy I might have stood there for much longer, but I'm reminded this dog could very well be dying in my hands.

I move for the door and push it confidently open.

The lobby is small with only four plastic chairs on metal legs and one table with a browned plant on it. Several of its leaves have fallen off to litter the floor. There's a door to the right, one to the left, and a recessed window straight ahead behind which a receptionist might sit. It's dim, as the man hadn't bothered to turn on any lights, and I see neither hide nor hair of him.

"Hello," I call out as I walk to the window.

"Get back here and let me see what you got," his Scrooge-like southern voice demands of me through the door on the left.

I go through it, finding a small exam room. The vet is standing behind a metal table with a short counter behind him. It has a sink and some basic medical supplies. He's put on a white lab coat that says "Dr. Peele" written in blue embroidery, and has a stethoscope around his neck. He taps one hand impatiently on the

29

table; the other presses down onto the top of his cane as he leans his weight onto it.

Jerking his head toward the table, he impatiently gestures for me to put the puppy down.

I comply and the pitiful creature sort of splays out, legs going in four different directions and its head falling limply to the steel-colored top. My nose starts to tingle with emotion, and I hope to God I don't start blubbering like a baby. I'm a crier by nature.

"Get hit by a car?" the vet asks.

Shaking my head, I explain my morning and how I found it wrapped in barbed wire in a ditch. The puppy doesn't move at all, and I can't even tell if it's breathing anymore.

Even though the vet has an expression on his face like I just shit in his coffee or something, he jumps into action. Or rather, he moves very slowly and gingerly as he attempts to examine the puppy. Leaning his cane against the table, he presses his hip to the edge for balance and to free his hands. He deftly picks the dog up and feels gently around. His fingers come away covered in the same blood and mud that mine are. He lays the pup back down, then uses his stethoscope to listen for something.

Breathing?

Heart beat?

Any sign of life?

Lifting his head, the doctor glares at me. "I'm going to have to wash him off. He might need stitches, and I can't see what I'm working with. No clue if anything's broken. That would take x-rays, but right now its pulse is so weak I'm not sure it's worth the effort."

"But you have to try," I say, the overt begging tone in my voice startling me.

It's not that I don't beg, because I have before and often, but that was when I truly needed help. After so many times of trying to get it and not receiving it, I've let that tactic fall by the wayside. But this puppy shouldn't produce that type of reaction from me. I've never begged on anyone or anything's behalf before, and there's no reason to start now. I've got myself to worry about.

"I'll need a deposit of a hundred dollars," he replies with a stubborn tilt to his jaw. "And of course, it could be more than that if we have to do x-rays."

That's simply not going to work for me. "I have eight bucks in my back pocket. That's all I got."

"Then I can't treat the animal," he grouses. "I got to eat, too, you know."

"What am I supposed to do with it?" There's no hiding the panic now. I can't take this dog out of here to watch it die.

As if on cue, the puppy moves.

Actually lifts its head and opens those little eyes,

fixing me with one orb of chocolate and the other of ice. It chuffs and stares at me expectantly, as if it knows its entire existence is completely within my power.

I don't think I've ever felt more helpless.

I move my pleading gaze back to the vet. "Please… you have to help it."

"I will if you can pay for my services," he says stubbornly. "If I treated every sob story that walked in here for free, I'd be homeless."

"So what?" I demand. "You're just going to kick us out of here and let it suffer to death?"

"God no," he gasps indignantly, sincerely appalled I'd suggest such a thing. "I'd euthanize it. It's the humane thing to do."

"Oh, can you do that for eight dollars?" I retort sarcastically.

"I never charge for that," he returns in a miffed voice. "And I bury all the animals on my farm outside of town."

That mollifies me somewhat, but it's not good enough.

For some reason, there's only one thing that will occur here today to satisfy me, and that's for this dog to survive.

No, to thrive.

It's the only acceptable future I foresee right now. I have no clue what's going to become of me tomorrow, but this fucking dog is going to make it.

The little thing is still staring at me, head all wobbly and body shivering. It gives a pathetic onetime thump of its tail as if to say, "See... I'm a fighter. Give me a chance to live."

My gaze slides up to the vet, who seems as cold and standoffish as ever before. I take in a deep breath, let it out slowly. "Please... please help this dog. I don't have money now, but I'll find some way to pay you. I'll work for free. I'll dig graves on your farm. Anything you want, but please... save this dog. I'm begging you."

The old man stares at me, and I realize his eyes are blue, the same pale color as the dog's one eye. They're frosty—made even colder looking by his snowy white hair—and he's seemingly unmoved by my plea.

I brace myself for his refusal, which makes my legs almost give way as he points to the sink. "Bring the dog over there. Help me clean it up first."

A surge of hope explodes within me, and it's so vibrant I can almost see it. Golden and warm like rays of afternoon sunlight, chasing away every bit of coldness within me.

"Okay," I say with a tremulous smile. I swear I see a flash of gratitude in the dog's eyes before I pick it up.

CHAPTER 4

Hazel

THERE'S NO STRUGGLE from the dog as I hold it over the sink while Dr. Peele runs a gentle spray of warm water over it. Thick mud and slime starts to slither away before circling down the drain. Pink streams of watered-down blood wash away and little by little, black, brown, and white fur is revealed.

I move the puppy this way and that, carefully supporting his head like I would a newborn. Not that I have any experience with those, but I've seen it done on TV. This dog is like a brand-new baby just brought into the world. Actually, it's probably weaker. His rib bones feel too sharp under my fingers as I cradle him.

The entire time he washes the dog, Dr. Peele mutters curses—of the fairly tame variety—punctuated with condemning clauses for whoever landed this poor thing in that ditch.

What the holy hell is the matter with people?
Damn miscreants is what they are.

Take 'em out and shoot 'em is what I'd do.

Finally, after all the gunk is washed from the fur, he says in an almost reverent tone of voice, "I'll be damned… it's a Bernese Mountain Dog. A boy, too."

"A what?" I ask.

"A Bernese Mountain Dog. Not a very common breed and quite expensive. Originating in Bern, Switzerland, they're originally farm dogs, pulling carts and such."

"Never heard of it."

"See the distinctive coloring of its fur?" he says, pointing with his finger. "Mostly black with brown legs and white paws. White fur in the shape of a cross on its chest, white on the snout and top of head with some brown at the side of the face."

He points all of these areas out, sounding like a science professor giving a class lecture.

"And look at those eyebrows." He rubs a thumb over one of them.

I did. They're brown against the jet-black fur on the dog's face and I have to admit, they lend a certain amount of character.

"What about his blue eye? Is he blind?"

"Nah," the vet says with a corresponding shake of his head. "Just has a blue eye. But if you were to show this dog, it's not part of the standard so it makes the dog worthless."

"He's not worthless," I snap at him.

How could anything that cute be worthless?

"Well, it would be to someone trying to make a big buck off this dog. These sell upward of fifteen hundred, two thousand bucks."

"You're kidding?" I ask, startled. I had no clue dogs could cost that much money. Who would pay that much money for a dog?

"Want my guess as to what happened?" he asks, but he really doesn't care what my opinion is because he tells me without waiting for a response. "A breeder chucked this dog into the ditch rather than try to at least adopt it out or sell it for a nominal amount. Probably didn't want to have to list the dog as part of the litter and dilute the standard."

"That's awful," I murmur, but I have a hard time believing that theory. That puppy could have ended up in the ditch for any number of reasons.

"People are awful," he replies bitterly, and it makes me wonder ever so briefly what his story is.

I want him to be wrong about the ugly side of humanity, so I challenge him. "That's a pessimistic view."

The look he gives me tells me I'm a naive dumbass. "Trust me, missy, you live in this world long enough, you see there's more bad than good in your average human."

"Sounds like there's a story there," I observe softly.

"And my name is Hazel…Hazel Roundtree. Not missy."

Dr. Peele refuses to acknowledge my nosiness into his life and the given name I offered. Instead, he opens a cabinet above the sink to grab a towel. We both work to gently rub the wet fur, and I'm thrilled to see the puppy seems to have revived a bit. He's squirmy and lets out a few yips, although they are remarkably weak sounding. I think the warm bath helped to reinvigorate him, but he eventually goes limp again with what I'm betting is exhaustion, dehydration, and starvation.

Cradling the puppy inside the towel, I take him back over to the examination table upon the veterinarian's orders. His energy expended from the bath, the sick dog again flops onto his belly with his legs splaying outward and his chin resting on the cool metal.

"Hold him still," the vet orders as he grabs a pair of electric clippers from a drawer. He plugs it in and turns it on. I gently hold the puppy, lest he get freaked out from the buzzing, but he doesn't even move. He just watches with flat eyes. The vet efficiently shaves the areas around the small puncture wounds—a few on his sides over his rib area and one in his back haunch.

Next, Dr. Peele pours an antiseptic-type solution on each area. They've thankfully stopped oozing blood. He gently pats it dry with a gauze pad. "I'm going to leave these areas open rather than stitch them up."

"Why's that?"

He spares me a glance, but then goes back to his work dabbing the wounds dry. "No clue how long that pup was down in that ditch and what's inside those wounds. It's best to leave them open so they can be cleaned a few times a day. Also going to put him on an oral antibiotic to fight off any potential infection."

Sounds like a good plan to me, I guess. Not that I know a damn thing about dogs with puncture wounds.

"Good news is I don't think there's anything obviously broken so we could skip x-rays," he says briskly, yet his hands are incredibly gentle while he works. "He wasn't in any obvious pain as I was washing him."

I don't reply, just continue to stroke the puppy's head while the doc works. He's not going anywhere due to his pitiful state right now, but somehow, I feel he needs a comforting hand.

"But," Dr. Peele continues, his tone turning dire. "He's not in good shape. He's extremely malnourished. I estimate he's between eight and ten weeks old."

Picking the puppy up, he hobbles without his cane back to the counter where there's a small scale. Clucking his tongue and shaking his head, he pulls the dog back off. "Only nine pounds. He should be upward of fifteen at this point."

This doesn't surprise me. I've felt his bones through his skin. I've heard the sounds his tummy makes.

"Should we feed him?" I ask. "Like... does he need milk or something?"

"He's old enough to have been weaned."

I don't know what "weaned" means, but I suspect he doesn't need milk. This is confirmed as he continues. "You can buy a can of dog food off me with that eight dollars you have in your pocket." His tone is haughty, and no doubt meant to remind me nothing we're doing here is free.

Handing me the dog, Dr. Peele grabs his cane and hobbles over to the sink to wash his hands. "I've got my first appointment to get ready for. You can feed the dog."

I'm given a very quick tour of the rest of the clinic. There's a room that runs the length of the back of the building that seems to be multipurpose. There are storage racks filled with medical supplies, medicines, food, and even office supplies. The tile floor is scuffed and faded. There's a small bathroom at one end, a refrigerator, a table holding a microwave, and another table with two chairs. One wall has stacked wire kennels of various sizes and Dr. Peele tells me they were once for boarding, but he doesn't do that anymore.

"Too hard on my old bones to come here several times a day to care for them," he says bitterly.

I don't ask why he doesn't have employees. I just inherently sense this man's veterinary practice is dying a slow death, and it's related to the fact he's old as dirt and can't do what he once did. Plus, he's cranky as hell, which doesn't lend to a good customer experience.

He shows me where the food and bowls are. Provides me with a tiny collar for the puppy and a leash so I can take him out to the bathroom after. I'm pointed to a rear entrance door I'm to use that will have a small patch of grass he can do his business on.

And then I'm left alone with this little miracle dog that's not going to die today.

As his fur dries, it becomes fuzzy and puffs out all over the place. I open a can of dog food and per Dr. Peele's instructions, I sit on the floor and hand feed it to the dog, so he doesn't eat too much too fast and get sick.

At first, the little guy isn't all that interested, but once I push my finger in his mouth with a tiny bit of the disgusting-smelling meat concoction on it, it's like a light bulb goes on inside his head and he becomes ravenous.

Sharp puppy teeth bite into the pad of my finger before he starts to use his tongue. It's almost as if he forgot the mechanics of how to eat.

I pull him onto my lap and the more he eats off my fingers, the more his tail starts to wag. It's as if every tiny bite gives him strength and renewed purpose. Little growling sounds emit from him, but they don't sound ominous. They sound ridiculously happy, in fact.

After a few moments, I have a vague sensation… a cramping in my face. My cheeks are sore, and I realize I'm smiling like a damn fool.

Dipping the tip of my finger into the food again, I realize I've fed him much more than the quarter of a can Dr. Peele had instructed me to. He told me he'd want more, but that we needed to go slowly with him as his stomach would no doubt be incredibly shrunken.

"Shit," I say, wiping the dog food off on the lip of the bowl and then letting the pup lick the remainder off. He growls deep in his throat, asking for more.

I pick him up gently, aware of the puncture wounds from the barbed wire and hold him up so we can look eye to eye. Supporting him with one hand at his chest, I cradle him under his butt with the other. "Sorry, little man… have to take a break. I don't want you to barf up all that good nutrition."

He gives me a solemn look of understanding. I lean in, and his tongue comes out to lick the tip of my nose. A shiver runs through me as if my soul craved that brief kiss of gratitude.

The door to the storage/break/kennel room opens, and I guiltily jerk back from the puppy as if it's wrong to be having such a good time. Dr. Peele sticks his head in, his eyes going down to the food bowl. He makes no comment on the fact I've overfed his patient.

"Take him outside," he orders gruffly. "I'm getting ready to close up shop. No more appointments today."

CHAPTER 5

Atticus

THAT FOOD IS *delicious*!

I need more, more, more, more.

The girl called Hazel cradles me to her chest as she peers up at the grumpy old doctor. He was very gentle with me, but I could tell by the tone of his voice he's an unhappy man.

I feel a little icky in my belly and I think I need to poop, but I'm not about to do that while I sit on Hazel's lap. That would just be impolite.

I think I might throw up when Hazel sits me down on the floor, but it passes quickly. She stands up to face the man who gave me a bath and made me feel a little better.

"Be here tomorrow at ten so you can start working off your bill," the old doctor says to Hazel. I can tell he's a very no-nonsense type of person. "You can bring him back with you, and I'll check him out. No charge for that."

My ears perk slightly. Bring him back? Does that mean I'm leaving with Hazel?

"Wait," Hazel exclaims, and I don't like the sound of her voice. Instinctively, I pounce on her shoe and grab her laces in my teeth. I clamp my mouth shut and throw my head side to side, pulling on them so I get her attention. "I can't take him home with me," she adds.

"Why not?" the doctor asks as he leans heavily on his walking stick. I give him a glance while I attack her laces, and he seems very weary. He smells old, so I expect he's very tired.

Hazel starts telling the doctor all of her woes. "Well, Dr. Peele... I don't really have a home. I mean... I'm sleeping on a friend's couch for now."

He doesn't say a word. Just stares at her blankly while I growl in my throat, tugging, tugging, tugging on her shoestrings.

"I can't really afford my own place," Hazel explains.

Dr. Peele says nothing.

"My husband was cheating on me," Hazel says, and the tone of her voice is so desperate I go still. I don't like her sounding that way. "And I caught him. And demanded he stop. And, well, he didn't. He kicked me out and moved her in. I can't even take care of myself, much less a dog."

And now I'm sad because Hazel lost her happy. Whatever all that meant about a husband cheating and kicking her out sucks all of her joy away. I tug on her laces again, hoping she'll look down at me so I can convey I'll make her happy if she gives me the chance.

When Dr. Peele doesn't say anything to comfort Hazel, she starts talking again as if she can't stand the silence and what it means. "I'm a bartender for God's sake. I make less than minimum wage and shit tips. I can't afford a dog. I most certainly can't keep it at my friend's apartment. She'll kick me out."

"Not much of a friend," the doctor grumbles. "And why even bother bringing that poor dog here? All you did was get his hopes up for a better life."

I can feel something roll off Hazel. It's a vibe. Like I can touch her emotion. I don't know the word for it, but once I was wrestling with one of my sisters, and I grabbed her ear too hard. My owner was mad at me and yelled. It scared me, then it made me feel awful inside. I ducked my head and slunk away to the corner of the pen, weighed down by something heavy and wretched.

That's what I feel from Hazel. I stop tugging for a moment, trying to figure out what to do to bring her happy back.

"I thought maybe I could take him to a dog shelter or something," Hazel says.

"Nice," Dr. Peele says sarcastically. "You're a true angel."

"Don't judge me," Hazel snaps with the utmost offense.

"Oh, I am." The doctor sneers at her. "I'm totally judging you. Just like every young upstart around here that thinks the world is all about them."

"What the hell, old man?" Hazel snarls in such a way that it scares me. I try to dislodge the laces from my mouth, but my teeth are so sharp they stick. Hazel pivots for the door. She must have forgotten I'm attached to her foot, and I go sliding along the tile floor as my feet shoot out from under me. I can't help the tiny yip of fright. As I roll, the laces come free of my mouth.

"Oh, shit," Hazel moans in horror, falling to her knees on the cold tile floor. She holds her hand out, but for some reason my instinct says to back away. I thought Hazel was nice, but she was very angry just now and she sort of hurt me.

Hazel's face crumbles, her eyes getting a little wet. She holds her hand out and coos at me. "I'm so sorry. Come here, little guy. I won't hurt you. I'm sorry I wasn't paying attention."

And just like that, Hazel is back. The one who has been very good to me and wants me to get better. I decide to give her the full benefit of the doubt. My butt wags with happiness as I waddle up to her, my lips stretched wide and curving up my cheeks in a smile so she knows I'm not mad at her.

"Give him to me," Dr. Peele growls.

It's a mean sound, but Hazel just sighs as she scoops

me up from the floor. She pulls me in close, pressing me to her chest. My tail flaps back and forth on its own accord. It does that when I get giddy with excitement, and there's no controlling it.

"I'll try to find someone to adopt him," Dr. Peele says with such exhaustion marking every syllable that I now feel sorry for him, too. He's a very strange man. He smells old, mean, and sad, and I don't know how that makes me feel about him.

To my dismay, Hazel hands me over to the vet. He cradles me with an arm under my tummy and pulls me into him. I sense nothing but care and gentleness, knowing instinctively he would never hurt me, but when he talks to Hazel, he doesn't sound nice.

"Be here tomorrow at ten. You can start to work the bill off. It's $135, and I'll pay you $7.25 an hour. That's minimum wage. However long that takes you given your other obligations."

"Got it," she says curtly, and then turns toward the door.

I bark at her, but she doesn't even glance back at me. My heart sinks as I watch her disappear, and I start whining. It's the sound I used to make when I was a baby and really hungry for my mama's milk.

For a long time, Dr. Peele doesn't move. He just stares at the door, holding me close to him. My whines finally die down because I'm feeling tired again.

CHAPTER 6

Hazel

TIPSY MCBOOZERS HAS to be the dumbest name for a bar I've ever heard, and I know bars. The owner, Cary Boot, supposedly has Irish genes and perhaps thought to pay homage to that.

Cary's a nice enough guy. He used to be a shrimp boat captain, following in his father's footsteps, but rumor is he got seasick a lot and traded in the boat for a bar. At least Cary's not an overbearing boss. He's a barfly for sure, choosing to sit at a corner table with his old high school buddies from yesteryear, drinking cheap draft beer and playing darts. He's been in the bar business for almost four decades now, and I'd heard once had a knockout of a wife. She enjoyed the prosperous times before the drinking age was raised, but when the downward turn hit and money wasn't quite as good, she kicked him to the curb and married the owner of a tattoo parlor. One thing that never went out of popularity with the young marines were tattoos, and there was no age-limiting factor to cut into business revenues.

My shift is from seven PM to two AM every night but Tuesday and Sunday. It's early and dead right now, but it will pick up later. Even though the marines have to be on base and ready to work usually by seven, they're still able to party until the wee hours even on work nights. Granted, the weekends are busier, which means tips are better, but I'll make enough on a Wednesday night to keep me in cigarettes and 7-Eleven hot dogs. I'm thankful for the night shifts, especially Friday and Saturday, which usually provide enough in tips to at least cover my terrible smoking vice.

The only downside to working the weekend shifts is that I can't go out and have a good time. But ultimately, what does it matter? I have no close friends to share those evenings with. No man. I can't even fill my Sundays and Tuesdays off with interesting things because I have no hobbies and no ambition to have any.

Movement outside the bar door catches my attention. It's tinted glass, but it's still light enough outside I see Bernard getting ready to come in. I have his draft beer poured and waiting for him by the time he sits down on his regular stool. Last one on the end where the bar top meets the wall, which provides a semi-secluded corner for him.

Close to eighty percent of the customers at Tipsy

McBoozers are active-duty military. The bar sits on the southbound side of Highway 17, directly across from the entrance to the Air Station. The other twenty percent of patrons are comprised of bikers, locals with no direction in life other than to drink their nights away, retired military, and one homeless guy by the name of Bernard.

"Evenin', Hazel," he says as he sits his wiry frame down.

"Hey, Bernard."

He pulls some cash out of the front pocket of his lightweight camo utility jacket. The pile is thick, but I know that's because it's all one-dollar bills. He has it neatly smoothed and folded in half.

With precision, I watch as he counts out fifteen ones and pushes them across the chipped Formica—brown with some black streaks to make it look like real wood—to me.

"Four beers tonight," he says as he folds the rest of the money and stuffs it back into his pocket.

I pick up the cash, and Bernard takes the draft beer. After removing three dollars from the pile, I put it in my tip jar, sliding the remaining twelve dollars into the register. Bernard is budget conscious. Whatever he collects from panhandling during the day is carefully parceled out. Draft Busch is three bucks a pop so that meant the remaining three dollars he handed to me are intended to be a tip.

The first time I'd ever met Bernard was on my first day working here about a year ago. I had no clue he was homeless when he came in, but he advised me when he sat down on his stool that he paid for his beers in advance and no matter how much he might beg or plead, I was to cut him off after he finished his allotment. It's been tradition ever since.

Some months later, I found out Bernard was homeless. After he finished his beers, he always loitered around, but I didn't think anything of it. Conversation with him was always good. But one night, Cary chased him out because he was taking up real estate and not buying more beer.

When the door closed behind Bernard, Cary muttered, "Stupid fucking vagrant. I'm not running a hotel here."

I was stunned. Nothing about Bernard seemed vagrant-like. I found him to be intelligent and funny. Hell, the man always tips me and that does not scream homeless.

These days, if Bernard is drinking and paying, Cary doesn't care how long he sits on that stool. If he loiters more than fifteen minutes after draining his last beer, Cary is escorting him out. If Cary isn't here, I let Bernard stay as long as he wants.

"Dead in here," Bernard says after taking his first

sip, then setting the mug down. He cherishes his beer, even if it's crappy and cheap. He'll make the four beers last for a good hour to an hour and a half.

"Terrible for tips," I respond before moving down the bar to wait on two marines. I card them, note the IDs are completely fake, but serve them anyway. I do this not to put Cary's liquor license in jeopardy, but because I remember fondly the days I would bar hop up and down Highway 17, grateful for those bartenders who would turn a blind eye to my youth.

So yeah, paying it forward and all that.

After serving them Bud in the bottle—to which they offer me no tip—I do a quick scan of the other handful of customers in the bar. Assured no one needs a refill, I head back down to Bernard.

"What's wrong with you?" he asks pointedly.

Staring at him a moment, I take in his craggy features. I have no clue how old Bernard is, but his dark skin is heavily lined with age and his wiry hair is sprinkled liberally with gray. His eyes are filled with wisdom born of hardship and loneliness.

"What makes you think something's wrong?" I ask, curious as to the source of his intuition.

His gaze roams over me, and he shrugs. "Face is pinched, shoulders slumped. You look sad."

God, but I'm sad.

All I can think about is that stupid puppy I left

behind with Dr. Peele earlier today. I regret not glancing back at him just once more before I left. My arms actually ache with the desire to cuddle him. It's so very strange because while I'm a woman who needs security from others, I'm feeling a profound sense of loss not to be able to provide the same for that dog.

"It's a long story," I say hesitantly, not sure if Bernard cares to hear it. I find myself to be the most uninteresting type of person. Unlikeable at my core, which makes my loneliness even more profound because I don't even like myself.

"Got four beers to drink," he replies.

The breath of relief I blow out is huge, lifting my thin, dry bangs from my forehead. Leaning in, I rest my forearms on the bar, giving a quick check around the bar to make sure I'm not needed. When I focus back on Bernard, I tell him all about my morning adventure.

I pour out to him all the emotion I've had bottled up since I left the veterinary clinic. How sad and pathetic that little dog was, and I even admit to him shamefully that I felt the dog was me and I was the dog. Abandoned, needy, and hungry for a lot more than food. I talk to Bernard like he's my shrink and the bar I'm leaning against is the metaphorical couch in his office.

Bernard sips at his beer, listening to me without interruption. I talk and talk and talk about the sounds the puppy made when he was eating food from my fingertip, and how horrible I felt at leaving him behind. I ranted at him that no one has ever felt that way about me, and how scared I was that the puppy would always have vivid memories of me abandoning him.

It's utterly ridiculous and pathetic and by the time I wind down, I regret opening my mouth.

Bernard just gives a casual shrug when I fall silent, and says, "So go get the dog."

"I can't care for a dog," I say, jerking my chin inward at the preposterous suggestion. It's no less ludicrous than when Dr. Peele suggested it. "I can't even take care of myself."

One salt-and-pepper eyebrow rises skeptically. "Hazel... you hold a job, have a place to live, and food to eat. You take care of yourself just fine."

Easy for him to say. Three months ago, I lived in a house with a yard, had money to buy hair color, a car that worked, and someone to hold me in bed every night.

"But—"

Bernard holds up a hand. "Don't give me every excuse why you can't do it. I want to enjoy my beer. If you want to talk about it further, let's discuss solutions."

"It's just a stupid dog," I mutter.

"Then let it go," he replies.

"I can't," I wail, and then huff with frustration as

two customers walk in. I move down a few feet to meet them as they approach the bar. After serving them shots of bourbon with beer chasers, I thank them profusely for the generous tip they leave and then ignore Bernard for a bit while I step out from behind the bar to wipe the tables down and collect the empties as well as my thoughts.

When I finally make my way back to him, he's ready for his second draft. I pour it, slide it in front of him, and say, "I don't have a solution for my housing problem. I'm staying on a friend's couch. I don't have a place of my own, and she won't let me have a dog."

"Have you asked her?"

"Well, no. But her boyfriend's a douche, and he won't let me just because he hates me."

"So, get your own place," he suggests.

I roll my eyes. "I work thirty-five hours a week in a crappy bar. I can't afford my own place. It would take me forever to just save up for the deposit."

"I pay twenty-seven dollars a month for the storage unit I live in," he says nonchalantly.

I'm so startled by that revelation I do a double take. "You live in a storage unit?"

I'd just assumed he slept on a park bench or something. Isn't that what homeless people do?

Bernard chuckles then takes a sip of his beer. "Hazel… you know nothing of being resourceful, do you?"

That kind of offends me. I'm resourceful. I found a couch to sleep on when I became homeless. I talked a vet into saving a dog's life. That's resourceful.

"Look," Bernard says in a matter-of-fact tone, locking his eyes with mine. "The point is you have options. You plan on spending the rest of your life on a friend's couch? Make a plan and pull yourself out of the shit show you're starring in."

It sounds so simple.

It also sounds so very hard. I don't want to acknowledge the truth in his words, so I turn it back on him. "Maybe you should take your own advice. I'm sure there are better places for you than a storage shed."

Bernard shrugs. "The way I live my life is a choice I made a long time ago. I could change things if I wanted. I just don't want to."

And therein lies the difference between Bernard and me. I was like him just yesterday. But after pulling that puppy out of the culvert, I find I'm a slightly different person now.

I actually want my life to change.

CHAPTER 7

Hazel

"Y OU'RE LATE," DR. Peele says as I walk into the lobby of the clinic the next morning at five after ten. He's sitting behind the receptionist window glaring at me.

"I brought you some coffee," I reply, holding up one of the two Styrofoam cups I'm carrying.

"I drink tea," he says as he pushes up from the chair with a groan and grabs his cane. I know this is a lie because I could smell coffee on his breath while we huddled over the sink together yesterday, bathing the puppy.

Giving me his back, the old vet moves to a door that connects to the storage room/break area.

"All the more for me," I mutter. Sighing, I head through the examination room door to my left that will lead me back to him.

I'm vibrating with a nervous energy and an excitement I don't remember feeling since I was a kid on

Christmas morning. My parents always went all out for Christmas. Big tree, lights all over the outside of the house, and all the presents that could be afforded for Liz and me on a marine and retail clerk's salary.

When I enter the back room, my gaze sweeps around hungrily and I immediately find the prize. The puppy is in a small wire kennel stacked on top of a larger one. Dr. Peele has it lined with fluffy towels. The dog has his nose pressed against the door, tail wagging madly.

His eyes though are on Dr. Peele as he ambles into the room from the receptionist area.

"Hey, little dude," I say softly, setting both cups of coffee on a counter before moving toward the cage. The puppy spares me a glance before staring right back at the vet, as if he's the only living being on earth who is worthy of his notice.

That stabs me through the heart more than I'd like to admit. I'm the one who freed him from certain death, after all.

But you're also the one who left him behind, Hazel.

Dr. Peele walks up to the cage. Leaning most of his weight on his cane, he reaches a fingertip through the wire to let the puppy lick him.

My palms actually itch with the need to get the dog out and play with it, but that's all squashed when Dr. Peele says, "You can start by mopping all the floors.

Start in the exam rooms and make it quick. My first appointment should be here by ten thirty. Mop and bucket's in the utility room. Dump the dirty water out the back door so it doesn't clog the drains."

I tear my gaze from the dog. "And after that?"

Please say take the puppy for a walk.

"Then you can help me with my appointment. It's a Rottweiler with a nasty disposition."

"Are you serious?" I ask him incredulously.

"Don't worry," he replies, still staring at the puppy but with a sly smile curving his mouth that doesn't put me at ease. "I can prescribe you antibiotics if he bites you, and he's up to date on his shots."

"And after that," I clip out.

"You know anything about accounting?" he asks, turning his attention to me.

"Accounting?" The stupid expression on my face should give him his answer.

"Stuff like reconciling bank accounts."

I blink in surprise. "Yeah... actually I do. I mean, I did mine and my husband's account each month."

Ironically, it's how I found out he was cheating on me. The charges on our credit card to Victoria's Secret and the fact I'd not been presented with pretty lingerie in years had clued me in.

"I hate paperwork," he explains. "I'll let you take a crack at it."

He moves away from the cage and I take the opportunity to move in closer. The puppy turns his head my way, and stares at me blankly for a moment before his little butt starts to wiggle. I stick my finger in and he starts chewing on it, and the feeling of joy that sweeps through me is indescribable.

He still likes me.

Dr. Peele moves to a supply cabinet and opens it up, pulling various items out that I suppose he needs for his appointment. "Don't you have any staff?" I ask him.

"Not currently," he replies vaguely.

"Why not?"

Scoffing from deep in his throat, he cranes his neck to look at me over his shoulder. "Because I'm a small practice and it's hard to find one person—which is all I can afford—who can do everything I need. Besides, most people aren't dependable. No one knows how to work hard for an honest wage."

His words are bitter. It's obvious he doesn't want to hear me defend humanity in general, so I don't bother. Instead, I ask, "How did the puppy do last night?"

"Very well," he says. turning back to the supply cabinet. "Now get going on those floors. I want them finished and dried before Daisy gets here."

"Daisy?"

"The Rottweiler," he replies.

Oh, sure... a Rottweiler named Daisy. That makes

me feel loads better.

◆

"DO YOU NEED help with the next patient?" I ask Dr. Peele. I didn't get bit during Daisy's appointment—she was quite sweet but slobbery—and I was feeling accomplished. Daisy was very well behaved, and she followed her owner's command with complete obedience.

I'd finished reconciling the bank statements, which were quite easy mainly because Dr. Peele just doesn't have a lot of business and not many transactions to account for. I found in doing so that his full name is Oley W. Peele, but I have no clue what the "W" stands for, nor does it matter. He's Dr. Peele to me.

"Not unless you know how to express anal glands," he says. He rises from the small break table where he'd been eating a tuna fish sandwich he'd apparently brought with him for lunch.

"I do not," I say firmly. "Nor do I want to know how."

To my surprise, Dr. Peele chuckles as he grabs hold of his cane and ambles over to the sink to wash his hands. The cage where the puppy is sitting, watching us intently, catches my attention.

"Can I take him for a walk?" I ask.

"Suit yourself," he grumbles. "I've got nothing left

for you to do today. You can give him half a can of dog food, too."

A wave of adrenaline flows through me. A bolt of pure excitement makes my skin tingle. I practically lunge for the cage and when I pull the little guy out, it feels as if all is right in my world even though deep down I know it's not.

Cradling him in one arm, I move to grab the leash hanging on a hook by the door. "Have you found someone to adopt him yet?" I ask casually, but even I can hear the quaver in my voice.

Dr. Peele doesn't respond, and the silence is ominous to me.

I turn to look at him. He stares back at me uneasily.

"What's wrong?" I ask.

"I think I'm going to take him to the shelter," he finally says. His voice sounds brittle and frail. "I don't know anyone really, and besides... I'm sure they'll find a good home for him. I just can't keep him here anymore. I'm too old to keep coming back here to care for him while he's boarding. He's too active for me to take him home. He needs to go."

"You're taking him to the shelter?" I ask, my tongue feeling thick and heavy in my mouth as if the words are too much of a burden to even release.

"He'll be fine," he assures me with a false bravado. "They have like a seventy-percent adoption rate there, and most of those people are decent enough."

What the what? That leaves thirty percent that don't get adopted, which means…

"I'm not sure that's a good idea," I say carefully, cuddling the puppy in close to me. He rears his head back and licks my neck.

"It's the best I can do, Hazel," he says wearily and it's the first time he's called me by my name. Somehow, that makes what he's saying even more true. "He's a cute guy. Someone will want him."

Not like *I* want him, though.

CHAPTER 8

Atticus

HAZEL LAYS BACK on the grass, and I pounce on her. She laughs and pulls me onto her chest. I feel pretty good.

I'm not hungry, my cuts don't hurt, and Hazel is here playing with me.

I was so sad when she left yesterday, and I truly didn't think I'd see her again. When she walked in, I pretended to be a little mad and showed extra attention to Dr. Peele—who has been nice to me in Hazel's absence, so I really like him, too.

But then I couldn't contain it. She put her finger through the cage, and I went nuts trying to chew on it.

She really, really likes me.

Hazel takes one of my paws, lifts her head from the ground, and puts her nose against it. She inhales deeply and then says, "Did you know your foot smells just like Frito corn chips?"

I did not know that because I've never had a Frito

corn chip before, but that knowledge seems to delight Hazel so I bet they're yummy.

Her hands come under my front arms, thumbs to my chest, and she pulls me up to her face. She breathes in deeply again. "And your breath... I can't describe it. It's like sweetness and innocence and rambunctiousness all rolled into one."

I grin at her, my mouth opening and my tongue falling out the side. Hazel laughs at me, and the corners of my mouth pull way back to curve up the sides of my face.

I really, really like her too.

"You're a tough little dude, aren't you?" she murmurs as she rubs a knuckle behind my ear. I push my head against her, creating more friction which feels so good, my back leg starts shaking.

"God, you're so freaking cute," she blurts. She frames my face with her hands, pulling me in for a kiss to my wet snout. My tail wags so hard my entire butt starts jiggling.

The back door opens and Dr. Peele stands there, leaning against the doorjamb, his cane loose in his hand. Hazel rolls her head on the grass to look in his direction. My head tilts to the side, and I raise one of my eyebrows. Wonder what he wants?

"Time to go," he says. "I have to lock up."

Hazel's body goes tight, and it puts me on high

alert. But her hands come to my back, and she strokes down my spine in a soothing way. I relax slightly.

"I'm keeping him," she says, and I might not fully understand the implications of what she just said, but I can tell by the tone of her voice she just made a monumental decision that is going to make us both very happy.

"Say again?" Dr. Peele asks with surprise.

"I'm keeping him."

Oh, my puppy heavens. She's keeping me.

"Thought you couldn't?" the vet responds smugly.

"I'll find a way," she says confidently.

"It's a big responsibility," he cautions, but I can hear it in his voice… this is what he wanted all along. I can see it within his eyes, that old coot. He wanted Hazel to keep me, and I think he manipulated her into it.

Oh, that's very good, Dr. Peele.

"I can do it," she tells him as she pushes to a sitting position. After crossing her legs, she sets me down onto her lap where I decide to chew on her sleeve.

Dr. Peele stares at us a moment before saying, "You can bring him here tomorrow while you work if you want. And I'll sell you food at cost to save you some money."

Something rolls through Hazel's entire body, and I can feel it meld into mine. It's that feeling I get when I'm offered food. So very, very happy and humbled.

"Thank you," Hazel says.

"He'll need his shots. You can work that off if you want."

"That would be great," she murmurs as she stands up and takes me with her. She presses her face into my neck and I feel... loved.

"And you need to name him," Dr. Peele demands with a glare I think he thinks is intimidating, but he's done too many nice things to scare me. Hazel seems unfazed, too.

Hazel pulls her face back and studies me. "What should I call you? Thor?"

I tilt my head to the right. Thor? It sounds like a name that might be hard to live up to for some reason.

"Bear?"

At that moment, something tickles my nose and I sneeze. Hazel seems to take that as a "no" from me, because she says, "Bubba?"

Wait... Bear. I could work with that. Let's go back to Bear. I give a tiny bark, and Hazel laughs.

"Bubba is ridiculous," Dr. Peele scoffs, which I agree with. Hate it. "He needs a noble name as he's a noble breed."

"Do you have a suggestion?" Hazel asks in a way that seems to be poking fun at Dr. Peele.

"Atticus," he replies with a firm nod of his head.

That does indeed sound like a noble name. I think I could work with that, too. Back with my siblings, we didn't have names, but we were given different colors of ribbon around our neck to tell us apart. I was always called "orange," which wasn't a very good name.

"Atticus?" she asks, testing the sound of it out. It's a weird name for sure. Coming from her, though, it sounds pretty cool.

"After Atticus Finch," Dr. Peele says.

"Who?" Clearly, Hazel does not know this person.

"My God, don't they teach kids anything in school anymore?" he mutters while shaking his head. He thinks Hazel is very foolish. "From *To Kill A Mockingbird*. Didn't you read it in high school?"

"Not before I dropped out," she says.

Dr. Peele's face goes soft for a moment. For once, he looks really, really nice. His voice is certainly softer when he says, "He was a southern gentleman. A scholar and a lawyer. He fought for the underdog. He did unpopular things. He was a man of pure integrity. Read the book and learn something."

"Is there a movie?" Hazel teases.

"God help the human race." Dr. Peele sighs, then turns to walk back into the clinic. "Come on… I want to get home, so I can watch my soaps."

Snickering, Hazel holds me up so we're eye to eye. "What do you think? Do you like the name Atticus?"

I lick her nose while my butt wiggles exuberantly.

It appears I have a name.

CHAPTER 9

Hazel

I GAVE UP having Atticus walk the little more than a quarter mile back to Charmin's apartment. He doesn't understand the leash, nor does he like being restrained. On top of that, he gets sidetracked easily.

We're walking, walking along, and then ooh... a rock. Let me pick it up and chew on it.

Or walking along, making progress, and ooh... a bubble gum wrapper. Let me also pick that up and chew on it.

Mostly though, when we were about a hundred yards from the apartment building, he started lagging. Little tongue hanging out the side of his mouth and heavy panting made it clear he wasn't up for such strenuous activity. I don't know the little bugger's story, but he's clearly still a sick pup. He was only nine pounds when he should be fifteen, with saggy skin and knobby bones that could be felt through his fur.

It sickened me to think of not only the pain this

puppy was in when I found him, but also how starved he was.

So I picked him up and carried him the rest of the way. This was no picnic for me since nine pounds over a period of distance can seem like a hundred. Plus, I was carrying a plastic bag with four cans of dog food Dr. Peele had sold to me before I left.

Rather, he added them to the tab I owe him as I didn't have any change to spare. I used my tips from last night to buy cigarettes and a biscuit this morning, and diligently set aside the remainder for the upcoming rent I owe to Charmin. It's not due for four more days, but I'm very serious about budgeting. I can't afford to get kicked out on the street, especially now that I have another mouth to feed.

The apartment building I live in is two stories and built of red brick with black wrought-iron railing. It's nothing more than a long, rectangular unit with four apartments upstairs and four downstairs. It's so old it doesn't have central heat and air, but rather one air-conditioning unit the landlord splurged for in each living room window, which means a lot of time is spent in that one room in the summer. For the winter, it has baseboard heating that means furniture can't be up against the walls. The carpet is ancient and so thread-bare padding is visible in some areas, and the padding is so thin the sub-flooring underneath can be felt. For all this luxurious living, Charmin still has to pay six hundred a month in rent. The only reason she can afford this with some peace of mind is she works a part-time job on the side to supplement her income. It's really something I need to do, but the job market's not overly kind to people like me without a high school education and no experience other than bartending.

Before I reach apartment number three—which is on the bottom floor, third from the left—I put Atticus down to let him do any additional business he might need to. I can't have him pissing on Charmin's floor before I have a chance to plead my case to her.

I hold his leash loosely in my hand. The collar and leash were also added to the tab I have to work off, but that's fine. I've got the time in my schedule, and I've never wanted anything for free.

Atticus sniffs around and I've already learned this means he's searching for a place to go. Dr. Peele provided me some potty training advice before I left.

1. *Take him out frequently.*
2. *Take him out after eating or drinking.*
3. *Praise heavily when he goes.*
4. *Don't chastise or harsh him when he makes a mistake.*
5. *When I leave him alone, keep him in a crate.*

I could handle items one through four fairly easily,

although I can't promise not to curse under my breath if he pees or poops inside, but I can't afford a crate. Although Dr. Peele offered to sell me one of his, it's just not an expense I want added to my ledger of red already accruing with the man.

Atticus walks around almost aimlessly, nose pushing through the weedy grass. Finally, he seems to find what he wants. He circles around three times—which means I have to hold the leash up high so he doesn't get tangled—and then does his business.

I don't feel foolish in the slightest when I squat down to praise him like Dr. Peele instructed. "Good boy," I say in a high voice that makes his tail wag. I scratch his head. "You're such a good boy, Atticus. I'm so proud of you, little man."

His mouth opens, tongue falls out the side, and he grins at me while his body wiggles with excitement.

"Gah... you're so freaking cute I could eat you up."

He flops to his back, and grins bigger with his two bottom canine teeth poking out. He gets belly rubs and more praise before I tell him it's time to go inside and plead our case.

Standing straight, I give a gentle tug on the leash to get his attention. He rears backward, shakes his head left and then right trying to get free, and then sits his butt down on the ground. The look on his face says, *I'm not going anywhere with this thing attached to my neck.*

The little shit sometimes will walk fine on the leash, and at other times it's like I'm leading him to his doom.

"Atticus... come," I say sternly, and give another gentle tug—just as Dr. Peele instructed me.

His tail thumps, but he doesn't move. Those little brown eyebrows slant inward, and the expression on his face is one of pure stubborn refusal.

"Atticus," I say again in a firm voice. "Come."

The little dude pushes his front paws down into the grass, and digs his position in. His demeanor tells me we're at a standstill, and I don't know what to do.

With a sigh, I walk to him and mutter, "Okay... you win this round."

I pick him up, tuck him under my arm with my hand splayed to support his chest, and walk toward the apartment.

Charmin is usually home at this time of day. Luckily, Chuck will be at work. I had thought about trying to hide the puppy by just staying away during the day, but I knew it would eventually be futile. While I've not always told the truth and have lied like any other person in certain circumstances, I just feel in this instance I should lay everything out on the table and then prepare to beg.

I unlock the apartment door and walk in, locating Charmin immediately in the kitchen frying up some bologna. My mouth waters because I love fried bologna sandwiches. It's something my dad would often cook if he was in charge of dinner when Mom had to work late.

Charmin keeps her back to me, but says, "Hey," in greeting. She's still in the t-shirt she must have worn to bed, which comes down just below her butt. It's one of Chuck's, and she told me he likes her wearing his clothes at night.

"Hey," I say, setting the bag of dog food on the dinette table.

"Want a sandwich?" she offers, knowing I'll say no because I only eat breakfast on occasion, and then something substantial for dinner. She knows I'll say no because it's her food she's paid for and not mine, and while I could give her some money for the sandwich, I won't. Every dollar is important to me and accounted for, and because I'd much rather spend five bucks a day on cigarettes, I forego lunch.

"No thanks," I reply, and then bend my head to my put nose to Atticus' head. His fur smells clean and fresh from the bath he got yesterday, and I inhale to compose myself and garner strength.

I rub my cheek against him for just a moment, while I take a fortifying breath. "I have something important I need to talk to you about."

Charmin turns to me, worry in her eyes because my tone is so dire sounding. She sees the puppy in my arms, and the worry dissolves into a huge smile that spreads across her face. "Oh my God," she shrieks, making grabby hands for my dog.

She freezes for just a moment, whips around, and shuts the stove off before spinning back so fast, her bleached-blond hair flies around and smacks her in the face. She makes grabby hands again, silently beckoning for my dog.

My instinct is to take a step back, but I'm also surprised she's such a dog lover. I had no clue, and that bodes well for me.

"Where did you get that puppy?" Her hands open and close furiously in desperate need to hold him. "He's so cute. Let me hold him."

She gives me no choice, pulling Atticus from my grasp. I reach out and unhook the leash from his collar, then Charmin turns him so she's cradling him like a baby. She puts her face right up to his and starts baby talking. "Gosh, you're such a cutie. Look at those eyes. And those eyebrows. You're so soft and fuzzy wuzzy. I could just cuddle you for days, you little cutie patootie."

Atticus responds to her tone, his tail wagging furiously with excitement as he starts licking her face. A stab of jealousy spears me dead center.

Charmin pulls him in close to squeeze him, and I almost leap forward to pull him away. I restrain myself and instead tell her, "Be careful. He's got some cuts on him."

"Oh, you poor thing," Charmin says as she relaxes her hold on him. Her gaze lifts to me. "Whose puppy is this?"

"Mine," I say, my own eyes cutting away so I don't have to face immediate rejection.

"Yours?" she asks in confusion.

I have no choice but to face the music. Scratching at the back of my head, I nod. "Found him yesterday in a ditch, injured. Took him over to a vet and got him patched up."

"So you're going to keep him?" Every bit of exuberance over a cute puppy is now completely gone from her tone, although I note she's still cuddling him gently with one hand stroking his belly. Atticus' eyes roll around his head in ecstasy.

"That's what I wanted to talk to you about. I want to know if I can keep him here. He won't be a problem, I promise. I'll even pay you a little extra each month if you want."

"I've got a no-pet policy in my lease, Hazel," she reminds me.

"So does everyone in this complex, but they all still have pets," I counter. She knows this as well as I do. I then make a bold assertion. "If he damages anything, it's my responsibility. If we get caught, I'll get rid of him lickity split."

That last was a lie. There is no way I am getting rid

of Atticus.

Ever.

This was the first thing I felt truly committed to on such a deep, personal level that I know inherently failure would probably destroy me.

I would just make sure we never got caught.

Charmin swivels her head between Atticus and me.

I go ahead and throw everything I got at her. "He was in a ditch, Charmin. Wrapped in barbed wire and thrown out like used garbage. This dog deserves a chance. Please let me give it to him."

Her face morphs, and pure sympathy radiates from her very pores. "Oh, poor baby," she coos to Atticus. "Who would do such a thing?"

"Right?" I ask, incensed and offended all over again on my dog's behalf. "It's evil."

"Pure evil," she concurs.

"So can I keep him?" I ask. When she lifts her eyes to mine, I bat my eyelashes shamelessly while clutching my hands to my chest. "Please, please, please, Charmin."

She doesn't hesitate. "Of course you can keep him. Good thing Chuck likes dogs."

I barely restrain myself from rolling my eyes. I never speak bad about Chuck to her because even though Charmin and I are friends and coworkers, she's so far over the moon for him I know where her loyalties will lie.

CHAPTER 10

Atticus

HAZEL IS MY new owner, but she's more than that.

I didn't even know my other owners' names. They were just a man and a woman.

They didn't shower me with affection or call me nicknames like "Mister, Mister" or "Little Man". Heck... I didn't even have a name. I was just the "orange".

Yeah... Hazel is more. I had lots of love for my dog mama. She licked me a lot and never begrudged us all fighting over her. But she gave us all equal attention. None of us were overly special in her eyes.

I'm the only special one in Hazel's eyes, and that makes my insides tumble all over the place with glee.

After Hazel shows me around my new home where I'll be living with her, and her friend Charmin feeds me some fried bologna, we go outside.

It's not overly hot and the old winter grass is prickly under my feet, but I can see patches of softer green starting to grow.

Hazel plays with me for a really long time. I must delight her because she laughs a lot, especially when I start hopping all around, trying to pounce on a cricket.

She brought out an old sock and plays tug-o-war with me. She's way stronger than I am, so she really just holds it while I try to take it from her. I grab onto it hard, shake my head ferociously, and growl as I try to pull it away from her. Just when I think I can't pull any harder, Hazel lets it go and I fall to my butt.

She does this over and over again, laughing each time I tumble.

This time, I lunge for the sock, determined I'm going to succeed and I won't fall. Except I get so caught up in the game I don't pay attention, so when she lets go, I fall again. This time, something jabs me in my butt and it scares me so bad I yelp really loud. Hazel's face gets worried, and I run straight for her. She scoops me up and starts cooing nice things to me.

Truth be told, I feel a little foolish, but I'm not complaining about the way she fawns all over me.

When I'm too tired to play anymore, we lay in the grass. I roll to my back and show Hazel my belly. She understands me perfectly and starts to rub it.

My tail wags because it's the most perfect place to get scratches.

Hazel leans over me, and I smile up at her while she

pets me. "You're a good boy, aren't you, Atticus?"

Why yes. Yes, I am. I give a little woof of acknowledgment.

"I'll always take care of you," she promises, and I believe her. My chest swells, and I get so delirious with love for my new owner that I pee a little in excitement. If Hazel notices, she doesn't say anything. She just keeps rubbing my tummy.

Eventually, Hazel takes me inside. We lay on the couch for a little bit with me on her chest. She tries to watch some TV, which I don't like because that means she's not paying attention to me. I consider ways to get her to focus back my way, but then I get distracted by these shiny things hanging from her ears. They beckon to me, and I inch forward on her chest to check one out more closely.

I snuffle at her ear, and she bats me gently away. Laughing, she says, "Stop. That tickles."

But then her attention goes back to the TV.

Craning my neck outward, I get very close to the dangly thing hanging from her ear and grab ahold of it with my teeth. As I did with tug-o-war, I start to pull.

Hazel shrieks, flying upward off the couch. I instinctively release my hold on the dangly thing as I tumble onto the cushion, landing on my back.

Hazel looms over me, pointing her finger. "Bad dog. You don't pull on my earrings. That hurts."

I don't like the way she's talking to me. It makes me feel sad, and I'm not quite sure why she's doing this. My ears flatten down, and I turn my head so as not to look at her.

She doesn't say anything. I remain super still, knowing I'm in a vulnerable position with my belly and throat exposed to her.

"Hey, buddy," she says softly, and I feel her hand on my chest. My tail wags in response to her sweet tone, and I dare to take a peek. She's smiling, and her voice is gentle. "I didn't mean to scare you. You just caught me by surprise."

I'm elated and my tail wags harder. I bark at her, so she knows I'm not mad at her either.

"Come here, you silly thing," she says, and then I'm back on her chest while she cuddles me.

We end up taking a long nap together.

CHAPTER 11

Hazel

THERE'S A CHANCE I could be fired tonight.

There's a better chance I won't.

As long as Cary sticks to his routine and sits out with the general bar population, I should be good. He's a hands-off boss and if I'm serving his customers in a timely manner, keeping the bar clean, and doing it all with a generally nice disposition, he doesn't have much to say and he rarely even ventures behind the bar.

He almost never goes into the stockroom, which is where I currently have Atticus stowed.

Charmin agreeing to let me keep him at her place was shocking to say the least, and I can only credit it to the fact that she's a true animal lover and my dog is like the cutest thing ever. As I sat on the living room floor and played with my new pup, I listened in amazement as Charmin held her own with Chuck after she'd called him to let him know about the newest housemate. He didn't put up much of a fight so hopefully Atticus will be a non-issue in our living arrangements as long as the landlord remains ignorant.

My afternoon before I had to come into work was spent getting to know my dog. We sat outside in the sparse grass. I used an old sock of mine that was missing its mate, and we played a lot of tug of war. He makes the most amazing sounds from deep inside his chest. He tries to be so ferocious, but they sound more sweetly spunky than anything.

I wish I had a computer or a phone to research his breed. Maybe one day if I save some money, I can Uber across town and use one at the library, but for now I'll just have to pick Dr. Peele's brain. I spent time today studying Atticus. His fur is fuzzy, almost like it's frizzed from humidity, and it's so soft I can't stop touching him. His markings are absolutely perfect.

His legs are tricolored starting with white paws, before sharply changing over to a gorgeous rusty brown at mid-leg. Whereas the white and brown are sharply delineated, the brown then morphs into a midnight black up to his shoulders which extends over his back and sides.

When he went belly up on me the first time, I noticed the outside of his back haunches are black while the insides are brown.

His chest is snowy white and practically blinding. I foresee a lot of baths in this dog's future to keep him clean.

That face, though. Such a study and a tricolored patchwork. But those eyebrows… rust against coal-black that move constantly to change his expressions. When he gets mad—for example, when he can't tug the sock away from me—they knit closer together in both concentration and consternation.

When he's happy or chill, the eyebrows relax and open. His mouth parts, tongue falls out the side, bottom teeth poke out, and he just has the dopiest grin ever.

When he's inquisitive, his head tilts and the eyebrows raise just ever so slightly. I can actually read his expression. *Please tell me more, Mom.*

But when it's all said and done—and I get past the gorgeous markings and the softness of his hide—his eyes are what makes him unique. I know he's not the first dog with different-colored eyes, but I don't care about those other dogs. I only care about that blue eye that seems to see things that I can't.

At one point today, his gaze lifted, and that blue eye peered at something over my shoulder with such intensity the hair on the back of my neck stood up.

"What are you looking at?" I asked him after I looked over my shoulder and saw nothing.

His gaze came to mine. Just slid to me in a calm fashion, and he fixed that blue orb on me. So clear and almost humanlike in the wisdom it seemed to hold despite his youth. I labeled it a truth teller. In that moment, I felt it had the power over me to keep me honest. His expression said, *You can't lie to me, so don't even try.*

I've known Atticus for less than two days, yet I think I was meant to love him from the beginning of my life.

Such a different type of love, too.

With my parents and sister, that's sort of wired into the DNA. There's years of relationship building—and hurting—that goes into familial love.

With Darren, my husband, love was part of a contract. He promised to love and honor and protect me. He may have loved me at some point, but he failed on the other two—a fact I've still not been able to quite reconcile in my mind. That type of love was cyclical. I gave him love so he would give it back to me, and I desperately needed it.

But with Atticus—after two days of knowing this dog—I don't feel like it's remotely close to the other types of love I've felt. My love is new and I can imagine will only grow, but I give it to Atticus without expecting a single thing back from him. He doesn't need to offer me words of adoration, and he certainly can't help pay my bills or put food in my stomach. I don't need a single thing from this dog, and yet… I know he'll give me everything.

And this is what's odd. I'm a needy person. I've

always been. I get every bit of my self-worth from the way other people treat me. My husband tells me he loves me, then that means I'm worthy of love. My parents tell me they'll always support me, and that tells me that my endeavors have meaning.

With Atticus, I don't need him to make me feel good. I mean, he makes me feel good no doubt. I can't help but constantly smile and laugh around him, but I don't require it of him as a precursor to what I can give him back. I just know inherently I would give this dog everything no matter what he could potentially offer me.

So very weird and without any further scientific, religious, or cosmic explanation, I just have to accept Atticus is my fate.

"Hello… earth to Hazel, come in Hazel," I hear someone say, and then my eyes focus to find Bernard standing in front of me snapping his dry and cracked fingers. They make more of a rasping sound.

My lips curl upward, and I shake my head. "Sorry about that."

Bernard moves over to his stool while I pour his beer. When I sit it down in front of him, I'm stunned to see him push a crisp twenty dollar bill my way. "Four beers tonight, Hazel, and an eight-dollar tip for you."

"Where did you get that?" I ask, not even making a move for the money.

I glance down at the end of the bar, noting Charmin

can handle the early drinkers if I want to take a moment to talk to Bernard. It's Thursday night—the early beginning to the weekend—which is much busier than the earlier week nights, so Cary puts two bartenders on shift.

Charmin thought I was crazy as hell for bringing Atticus into work with us tonight, but I wasn't about to leave him at home alone with Chuck.

Bernard is a welcome sight. Truth be told, he's probably my favorite customer. I like how he listens to me, and the sometimes-sage advice he gives. He doesn't let me get away with bullshitting him, and in some respects, that makes him seem like a father figure to me.

I nod down at the twenty, and Bernard's eyes don't sparkle with any extra brilliance that amount of money might bring to him.

He just shrugs. "Had an unusually generous person give that to me up at the intersection of 17 and Maplehurst. So I'm enjoying a few beers and paying it forward to you with a good tip."

Snatching the twenty off the bar, I tell him over my shoulder. "I am not taking an eight-dollar tip for serving you four beers when the tap sits less than two feet from your bar stool."

I ring up his beer, take one dollar and stuff it in the tip jar, then hand him his change. Over the course of the rest of his beers, he'll push another dollar or two my way, but I'm not taking more than three.

Maybe four.

I really need the money, but I don't want to cheat him. Bernard really needs the money, too, and yes, I know he squanders some of it on beer when he shouldn't, but he's an adult. He's lived a long life. He should do what he wants to do.

"So," he drawls as he leans forward on his seat just a bit. "What were you daydreaming about? New beau?"

Chuckling, I put my forearms on the bar. "First, no one says the word 'beau' anymore, and second, I resent the use of the term daydreaming. I was multitasking in my head."

Bernard snorts and takes a long pull on his beer. It's relatively mild out tonight, so he won't linger long past his last once he drinks it. He usually only stays longer than Cary likes him to in the colder winter months.

I look down the bar at Charmin. She winks at me when I catch her eye. I look over to where Cary's sitting with his friends, where they are starting the first leg of their journey tonight toward getting shit faced.

When I focus back on Bernard, I tell him with an uncontained smile on my face. "I got the dog."

Grayed eyebrows fly upward, and it reminds me of Atticus' eyebrows. That makes me smile bigger. "And where are you keeping it?" he asks.

The corners of his lips are tipped up slightly and I

take that to mean that he's not only amused by my clear happiness over such a bold move in my life, but also because he might be a little proud over me doing something I didn't think I could.

"Charmin said I could keep it at the apartment, but tonight… I have him in the storeroom. I wish you could see him, Bernard. He's so damn cute. In fact, I need to go check on him soon and take him out for a quick pee behind the building."

"Cary let you do that?" he inquires skeptically.

A pointedly cocked eyebrow from me gives him his answer. "He never goes in the storeroom. What he doesn't know won't kill him."

"Just don't get caught." His warning isn't needed, but he's only saying it because he cares for me. "After I finish for the night, I'm going to go around the back of the building. I want to see that pup of yours."

"Are you serious?" I ask incredulously. I mean… we're friends, but we're just bar acquaintances. And yes, he gives off that benevolent-dad kind of vibe when we talk, but he's showing true interest in something I actually care about.

It's kind of humbling as well as confusing.

"Of course I want to see that dog," he says with a grin that's blinding against his black skin. "I love animals, and besides… I'd like to lay eyes on the thing that has the apparent power to change your life."

"My life hasn't changed that much," I respond drolly.

"You're wrong, Hazel. It's changed completely," he replies with such confidence I wouldn't be surprised if he lugged around a crystal ball in his old backpack.

Bernard and I chitchat over the few hours it takes him to drink his four beers. It's mostly about Atticus, and I feel like a dolt sometimes the way I gush over the dog. But Bernard humors me and listens attentively. He tells me stories about childhood dogs he had growing up in Philly, and that he had a beagle mix back when he was married that lived to be almost fifteen.

After his beers, he meets me around the back of the building. I let Atticus take a quick pee, and then Bernard gets in some quick cuddles. Atticus puts his paws on Bernard's scruffy cheeks and licks him with exuberance. Maybe this dog will like everyone it meets, or maybe he's just a good judge of character. I suspect it's the latter with Bernard.

When I head back into the bar and move to where Bernard was sitting to take his empty mug, I note he'd tucked a five-dollar bill under it. That big jerk gave me that eight-dollar tip, and it makes my eyes prick with tears over his generosity and kindness.

CHAPTER 12

Hazel

WHEN I WALK into the parking lot of Dr. Peele's clinic on Monday morning, I'm surprised to find him sitting in his car with the engine running. He rolls down the window as I approach with Atticus tucked under an arm and a layer of sweat on my face because he's feeling heavy as hell and the walk was long. But the minute he started lagging and showing fatigue on our hike, I picked him up.

Ideally, I would have stopped to let him rest a bit, but Dr. Peele made it clear he expects me to be on time. While I'm not going to be handed a paycheck for my time, I still treat this like a job. I may be weak in a lot of ways, but one of my strengths is my work ethic. I got that from my dad, straight up.

"Good morning," I say brightly.

"Get in the car," Dr. Peele orders me with that grouchy voice and a thin-lipped grimace he seems to wear a lot.

I don't think to question him and do as he says, putting Atticus on my lap and maneuver the seat belt around us both so he's protected, too. Just to be sure, I wrap my arms around him. He has absolutely no qualms about snuggling into me.

Yeah... we've become snugglers over the weekend.

I managed to work Thursday, Friday, and Saturday night with Atticus in the storeroom and Cary none the wiser. Charmin worked the same shifts as me, so she wasn't going to rat me out. The only perilous part was one night, Chuck came into the bar and got so drunk he was practically falling off his stool. He was also talking loudly and mentioned Atticus in the back room. Luckily, the music was loud enough Cary didn't hear him and Charmin did a good job of getting Chuck to quiet down.

As far as how Atticus did those evenings in the store-room, I'm kind of proud of the little guy. Sure, he likes to chew things, but I figure that's a puppy thing, right? So that first night, I made him a bed from an old towel, put his food and water bowl down, and left three toys for him to occupy himself with. I'm ashamed to say they were hand-me-downs from Amy in apartment number four that secrets away her bulldog from the landlord. We sometimes shared early morning pee meetings out on the front grass, and she offered up the toys when I told her that we were playing tug-of-war with socks.

Being able to check on my puppy frequently helped, and he also sleeps a lot because I assume he's still gaining strength. But a few times during my shifts, either from boredom or maybe even just curiosity as to how they tasted, Atticus chewed up the corners of some of the cases of beer. This wasn't a big deal since the empty cardboard cases went straight into the recycle bin, and he didn't seem to be ingesting the stuff.

The only rough part of this situation was I couldn't check on him frequently enough to prevent some accidents. Cleaning up dog piddle isn't that bad, but I have a weak stomach and his dog poop had me gagging hard. Charmin just kept telling me to breathe through my mouth and not my nose, but that grossed me out. I thought I could taste the shit on my tongue when I tried it.

Outside of those seven-hour shifts Thursday through Saturday, I spent all of my time and focus on Atticus. Amy taught me a few training tricks, and I bought a bag of cheap kibble and used the little pieces as reward treats. By Sunday afternoon, Atticus knew his name and had already mastered how to sit on command.

On top of that, he was starting to understand that he was to pee and poop outside. I think because I take him out every hour, and heavily praise him when he goes, going potty is a fun thing for him. He even started going to the door and pulling on his leash I kept looped over the doorknob when he wanted to go out. Because I was hypervigilant, I never missed one of his cues, and he has not had an accident in the apartment.

So far—knock on wood—this raising a puppy thing is a piece of cake.

"Where are we going?" I ask.

"House call," he replies curtly, shifting the car into reverse. He doesn't provide more detail, but I wait until we get out on the road so as not to distract him.

"What type of house call?" I ask, just wanting to make conversation. Perhaps crack his grumpy exterior. He's becoming sort of a challenge to me and since it will take me a few weeks to work off my debt to him, I might as well try to get to know the old man.

"One of my patients is at the end," he replies. He drives slowly with both hands gripped tight on the wheel.

"The end of what?" I ask.

"End of her life." His voice is gruff. It doesn't seem to be born from his killjoy demeanor, but more of emotion. "A little dachshund I've cared for since her owners brought her home. She's fourteen, and it's time."

I'm speechless for a moment. It's not until I've pulled Atticus into me extra tightly I realize this has more of an effect on me than I'd like. I just got my dog.

I'm not ready for him to die.

I'm also not ready to watch another dog die.

"How do you know when it's time?" I ask after a slight cough to clear the fear for my own dog out of my throat.

Dr. Peele spares a moment to give me a glance before turning back to the road. "It's personal. Some owners let it go on way too long, unable to let their friend go. Others do it too soon, because they don't want the expense or responsibility of caring for a sick animal. Others just know exactly when the right time is, because they are so in tune with their pet. Usually if there's pain involved, or if they lose the basic ability to move about freely. Someone who truly loves their animal can look into their eyes, and they just know."

As if on cue, Atticus throws his head back to look at me. There's no doubt in my mind that truth-teller eye will let me know. But all I see right now is a whole lot of puppy spirit and bright future staring back at me.

"How will you do it?" I ask, knowing animals are euthanized, but not sure how.

Without taking his eyes off the road, Dr. Peele describes a two-injection process through an IV catheter. The first medication to sedate, the second to stop the heart from beating.

"I call it killing them softly," he says, his voice so gentle and tender I can barely hear him. "It's a beautiful and peaceful way to die. It's an honor for me to help them make that transition."

My head snaps to the right where I stare out the window, furiously blinking back the tears from my eyes. For all the grouchy, assholish ways this man has treated me on most occasions, I just realized he may have one of the kindest hearts I've known.

♦

THAT WAS AN experience I hope to never have to repeat, although I know it's impossible for Atticus to live forever.

And Dr. Peele was right.

It was a beautiful way to die.

What I hated was the choking, palpable grief Bernice's owners were exhibiting. Giant fat tears and wracking sobs as they held onto each other. Bernie, as they affectionately called her, was like their child.

Their only child.

Gone was the grouch I'd known in Dr. Peele, and instead he was a calming influence on them. He explained clearly what he would do, and then encouraged Bernie's parents to get right down on the living room floor with her while he started the IV.

We'd left Atticus in the car with it running and the AC cranked even though it was still in the low sixties this morning. Dr. Peele offered no explanation, but I figured it out on my own. Why drag my cute, lovable dog in to these peoples' house when they were getting ready to suffer the loss of their own cute, lovable dog?

Yeah, I got it.

When Dr. Peele injected the sedative, Bernie gave a sigh of what I'd term relief and her eyes slowly closed as if she were drifting off to sleep. Bernie's dad made a choking sound as if he were trying to swallow his tears, and Bernie's mom wept with her hand stroking this little dog's back.

It was almost more than I could bear and when I felt the prickles in my nose indicating tears were coming next, I made myself think of my dad's funeral. I was filled with such pain over losing him, and yet I wouldn't let myself cry in front of everyone. Stuffing it down inside, I put a cork in it. I gritted my teeth to keep them from chattering over the effort of remaining stoic and detached. After all, I had to prove to everyone I was okay. That my life was everything I'd hoped it would be and more.

Watching Bernie die pulled up a lot of emotion, but I tamped it down so no one could see it. Besides, it wasn't my grief that was important. It was theirs.

The ride back to the clinic is silent. I'm processing what just happened, and Dr. Peele is in his own world. Perhaps he's sorrowful right now, or perhaps he's slipped back into curmudgeon mode. After Bernie's heart stopped beating, Dr. Peele didn't ask for any type of payment. They had chosen to keep Bernie to place her under her favorite oak tree rather than let Dr. Peele bury her on his farm, to which I was thankful. I imagine I would be digging a grave today if that were the case.

Dr. Peele pulls in parallel to the vet clinic and puts it in park. Groaning as he leans to the side which puts pressure on his bum hip, he pulls out a set of keys and hands them over to me. "Clean up the place."

"Excuse me?" I say as I take the keys. Atticus immediately lunges for them, thinking they're a toy because they make jingle-jangle sounds.

"Clean up."

I blink at him. "You're leaving?"

"Got no other appointments today, and I'm not feeling all that well. So yeah… I'm leaving."

"And what do you want me to do with the keys when I'm done?"

Dr. Peele raises his head dramatically upward as if beseeching God for someone smarter to deal with before looking back at me. "Why, you'll keep them, of course. And use them the next time you need to come to work that I don't feel like it. Not rocket science, Hazel."

"Okay," I snap back at him, angrily pushing the car door open. Clearly, it's a spare set. He could have just said that. I swing out, clutching Atticus and the keys.

"We'll weigh the pup tomorrow," he says out of the

blue, and in a way, I think because he's sorry he just pretty much called me an idiot. "Get his shots done, too, okay?"

"Okay." My voice is respectful but leery as I turn back to face him, bending so I can see inside the car to give him my attention. I don't know where I stand with this man so it's best to remain aloof. Trust doesn't come easy to me, and he's not helping matters.

"Okay," he says and nods at the car door in a silent command I close it.

I do, and he leaves.

Inside the clinic, I get to work. Because he rarely utilizes his space, there's not much to do. I'd swept and mopped on Friday, and the floors are still pristine. Still, I do it again and it's not much of a hardship. Atticus loves chasing after the mop. He grabs hold of the stringed ends and I pull him across the floor while he growls at it.

Just as I'm finishing the lobby, the phone starts ringing. I don't even think to ignore it, concerned Dr. Peele might miss a patient. I know the man could use the business.

I answer the phone in my most professional voice, which is never really utilized when serving beer. "Onslow Veterinary Hospital."

"Yes, hi," a woman says, sounding flustered. "I would like to make an appointment to see Dr. Peele as soon as possible."

"Are you a current patient?" I ask, searching around the desk top for a pad of paper to write on.

"I am," she replies. "He's been treating our animals for decades."

I spy a spiral-bound appointment calendar sitting on a shelfing unit next to the desk. Opening it up to today's date, I see Bernie written in shaky lettering during the ten-thirty slot. There's nothing listed after, just as Dr. Peele had said.

I flip to tomorrow's date, and it's completely empty. "Um… what time were you wanting to come in? Perhaps we can work you in."

I don't know why I said that when his calendar is completely empty, but I don't want this patient to know Dr. Peele doesn't have much of a thriving practice these days.

"Anytime," she says quickly. "I'll take any slot you have."

"I think I can fit you in tomorrow at eleven."

She gives a shriek of excitement. "Oh my God. That's wonderful. Praise Jesus."

Her overabundant enthusiasm worries me, and I'm afraid her animal might be in peril because she's so thankful, so I ask, "What seems to be the problem?"

"Oh, Granger has another hot spot, this time on his jaw. He gets them all the time. He got one last month, but Dr. Peele was completely booked and couldn't get us in. I had to go to another vet, and Granger was so nervous. It was just stressful, and we really want Dr. Peele to treat this."

The minute she said Granger had a hot spot last month, my fingers started flipping backward through the days on the calendar.

Day after day, mostly empty, with only an appointment here and there. I bet he saw on average maybe only five patients a week. He most certainly wasn't booked a month ago.

"Well, let's put you down for eleven tomorrow."

She gives me her name, which I carefully write next to the word "Granger" in the eleven o'clock slot. I also take her phone number because I have no clue if Dr. Peele is even going to show up tomorrow, so I might need to cancel her at the last moment.

After profusive thanks and proclamations that she couldn't wait to meet me tomorrow because I've been so nice, I hang up the phone. Atticus is curled into a little ball at my feet. He looks up at me from beneath those fuzzy brown eyebrows as if to say, *You're going to be in so much trouble for doing that.*

I shrug. If Dr. Peele yells at me, so be it. That's about all he can do to me.

CHAPTER 13

Hazel

A TTICUS AND I are already in the clinic by the time Dr. Peele shows up at fifteen till ten. He has no appointments scheduled—at least to his knowledge—so I have to wonder why he comes in at all. Certainly it's not to give me direction, but it could be to check up on me.

I would have called him to give him a head's-up about the appointment, but I don't know his home phone number and have no clue if he has a cell. A cursory look through the receptionist desk hadn't found his contact information.

Dr. Peele finds Atticus and me in the lobby waiting for him. He looks surprised to see us there, but quickly masks it by glaring at me. Atticus—who I have found is not fickle when it comes to humans—bolts straight to Dr. Peele for some attention. With a long-suffering groan, Dr. Peele bends over with an actual honest-to-God smile on his face and scratches my dog behind his ears. "Howdy-do, Mr. Finch," he says with a chuckle.

Atticus preens over his nickname or perhaps from the ear scratches, but he grins up at Dr. Peele with his tongue hanging out all dopey like.

Dr. Peele puts a hand to his lower back, groaning again as he straightens. He leans heavily onto his cane, which I note takes pressure off his left leg. "Why are you here so early?" he demands, the smile now gone from his face. I get I'm not as cute as Atticus, but geez… some basic nice manners would be good.

"Good morning to you, too," I say with a falsely sweet voice. I stand from the plastic chair I'd been waiting in, letting Atticus chew on the laces of my fake Chucks that are older than dirt. Atticus, oblivious to Dr. Peele's sour tone and my sarcastically saccharine words, puts his paws on Dr. Peele's knee and barks at him for attention.

"Atticus," I say firmly, and his head rolls my way. His tail is wagging, and he's still smiling big as only this dog can. "Sit."

His front paws hit the worn tile floor, followed by his butt in a completely obedient move. He's shaking with excitement, though. Atticus can't hold a sit for very long before he bursts out in joyful abandon, so I quickly praise him with a "That's a good boy".

"Impressive," Dr. Peele mutters, giving me the compliment even though he's staring at Atticus.

Big mistake. As soon as he makes eye contact with Atticus, my dog takes that as open invitation to jump on him because he has translated his expression into some type of promise of reciprocal adoration. He jumps up on Dr. Peele again, who locks his cane arm to hold himself steady.

"Atticus, down," I say, and he completely ignores me. I reach out, grab the back of his collar, and pull him back from Dr. Peele. "Atticus. Sit."

The butt hits the floor, holding for all of two seconds before he makes a lunge for Dr. Peele again. Somehow, I've made this a game to him. Obviously, I've done something wrong in my training.

"Atticus. Sit." Again, he ignores me, still wanting Dr. Peele's attention.

Shaking his head, the vet sidesteps us and ambles into the exam room on the left.

I follow behind after giving Atticus a harsh glare. "You made me look stupid," I chastise.

He barks at me, and it's so freaking adorable I can't help but laugh. "You're such a bad dog."

"What's this?" Dr. Peele calls out to me and I find him standing at the receptionist desk, reading the appointment calendar I'd left open.

"Granger has a hot spot," I say casually. "His owner called while I was cleaning yesterday, so I scheduled her. She couldn't come in until eleven." The tiny white lie is because I don't want to admit to him I doubted whether he'd even show up so I was padding the schedule.

"Call her back and cancel," he orders, then starts to walk away.

"I will not," I clip out, and he turns back in shock over my defiance. "That woman thinks you are the greatest vet in the world, and she wants only *you* to treat her dog."

Dr. Peele's expression is like the proverbial deer caught in the headlights. His face makes it clear he has no good reason to refuse this appointment, or at least not that he feels comfortable enough to share with me.

But I've gone ahead and drawn my line in the sand. I figure I'm going to get fired here in about three minutes after we duke this out, so I go all in.

"What are you so afraid of?" I ask with a bit of challenge in my voice. Because for all the confusion I've had over the mystery of why this man even bothers opening his doors each day, I know he's driven by fear.

I know it because I recognize what fear does to a person. It takes away their confidence and self-esteem. It makes people the opposite of ambitious.

Completely ordinary.

Dr. Peele goes deadly still, and just blinks at me. I brace, waiting for him to let loose on me but to my horror, his bottom lip starts to tremble. "I've lost control."

I gentle my voice as I pull out the chair from the reception desk. A swell of sympathy for this man I barely know—but who ultimately brought Atticus and me together—overwhelms me. This almost stuns me to inaction because I'm not the most empathetic person in the world. I tend to focus on my problems, believing I have no room for anybody else's. It's a selfish way to live, but I've got fourteen years of self-preservation under my belt, and it's so exhausting trying to feel good about my life that there's nothing left over.

"What's the problem?" I ask when he sits down with a sigh.

His gaze drops to the floor, both hands on top of his cane. They're shaking slightly, and I wonder if they've always done that. I hadn't really noticed before.

I perch on the edge of the desk, silently waiting for him to screw up enough courage to tell me what's going on. When he finally raises his head to look at me, it's a punch to the gut over the severe hopelessness I see within his blue eyes.

"I'm getting old," he says in a tone that sounds so fatigued it matches the heavy age lines creasing his face. "I'm seventy-two and my body is failing."

"You get around okay," I say kindly. Because to an extent... he does. He still drives, and he's mobile but not overly fast.

"I can't handle Granger today," he says wearily.

"He's a hundred-pound Golden Retriever that likes to jump up on me. He's not obedient like Daisy. I foresee a broken hip in my future."

And I have that *aha* moment when it becomes completely clear to me the source of his fear. The few dogs I've seen him treat have been small or very well behaved. He was confident around them. But I'm betting most of his clientele are rambunctious and more than a handful. He must have been steadily declining to reschedule those recurring patients over time, until his practice just withered away.

"You only take those pets that you can safely handle yourself," I say.

He nods. "And as I cut back on patients, the income dwindled until I couldn't afford to keep on staff. The practice just kept drying up, and I should close the damn thing down. I'm pretty worthless as a vet right now."

"That's not true." He blinks in surprise, as if he can't even imagine what I'm saying could have merit. "What you did yesterday for Bernie? That held tremendous worth to those people. It was priceless, and I know your kindness to them won't be forgotten. You made a terrible loss just a little more bearable to them."

Dr. Peele waves his hand in dismissal. "That was nothing."

"You're wrong," I assert firmly. "You're so very

wrong."

"I'm not," he says back with staunch conviction as he stands. He has his ornery mask back in place. "Now, call Granger's owner and cancel the appointment."

"I won't." We're back to where I'm probably now just seconds away from being fired from a job I don't really make money at. "But I'll help you with Granger. I'll hold him still, and I won't let him jump. It will be fine."

"It won't be," he argues.

"What do we need to get out to treat his hot spots?" I ask, completely refusing to argue over this.

Dr. Peele blows out a breath of annoyance before snapping, "I'll need the clippers to shave around the area and some Neo-Predef out of the cabinet above the exam sink. A few towels and some gauze."

"You watch Atticus while I go get everything ready," I order and point back to the chair. "And take a load off."

♦

I WALK MRS. Bush to the door, Granger prancing along, happily wearing a clear plastic cone of shame around his head. The hot spot was on his jaw and too easy to reach for a scratch with his back paw, so he has to wear it.

"Thank you, dear," Mrs. Bush says as I open the door. "You and Dr. Peele were just wonderful."

"It was all him," I say magnanimously, because really... I was just the muscle.

She gives me a quick hug that startles me, and then she's out the door.

I find Dr. Peele in the back room, taking Atticus out of the kennel he'd put him in while we handled Granger. He howled and barked the entire time we were in the exam room, and it about broke my heart.

When he sees me walk in, he about leaps out of Dr. Peele's arms, who is just spry enough to bend over so the puppy drops to the floor. His paws grasp for traction on the slick tile before he manages to bolt straight at me. I scoop him up, gladly accepting his kisses on my face.

"Not much longer and you won't be picking him up," Dr. Peele says, and then points back to the exam room. "Might as well get him weighed and let's give him his shots."

"How big will he get?" I ask as I take him to the large scale on the floor and place him on it. He's too squirmy to use the small one on the counter.

"Probably somewhere between seventy-five and ninety-five pounds," he says, and my eyebrows disappear into my hairline.

"That big?"

"Yup," is all he says, and then peers with squinty eyes at the numbers. "What does that say?"

Leaning to the side, I look at the screen. "Thirteen

pounds."

"Excellent," he says with a smile. "He's gaining weight nicely."

"Do you need glasses?" I ask.

For the first time since I've known this man, his skin flushes beet red. He stammers and stutters, and finally admits he hasn't had an eye appointment lately. He also admits he hasn't been able to put stitches in an animal for months because of it, so he's had to turn away emergency treatment.

"But you put that IV into Bernie," I point out.

"A lot of that was by feel and was a onetime-only stick."

"Who is your eye doctor? I'll call and make an appointment for you," I offer.

"You'll do no such thing." The indignation in his voice is palpable, and his chin is lifted proudly. "Now put Atticus on the table so we can get his shots done."

I let the eye thing go before sincerely offering a service I hope he accepts. "Your floors don't need mopped every day, and the place is pretty sparkly now. Why don't you accept some more patients over the next few weeks, and I'll help you out to work off my debt?"

Atticus is still sitting on the scale, head tilted and watching both of us carefully. It's like he knows this is a serious conversation, and he needs to be a good dog for a few minutes.

Dr. Peele doesn't say anything, giving his back to me while he hunts around in the cabinet over the sink. Finally, he mutters, "Come over here and find the vaccines. One will say 'diluent' on it and the other 'distemper adenovirus parainfluenza and parvovirus'. He'll get his rabies vaccine in about four weeks."

He moves aside, so I can look at the various bottles. I find them easy enough and close the cabinet. Dr. Peele hands me a plastic-wrapped syringe, and I take it cautiously. "I'll teach you how to prepare the syringe."

"But I'm not giving him the shot," I say with a tinge of panic in my voice. No way I can stick a needle in my pup.

"Of course not," he snaps. "But if you're going to help me out around here, you're going to have to learn some things."

"Oh, okay," I say softly, lowering my face so he can't see my satisfied smirk.

Dr. Peele is officially back in business as far as I'm concerned.

CHAPTER 14

Hazel

I TAKE A long drag off my cigarette, sucking it down to the filter until my fingertips burn, and then flick the butt off into the darkness. Exhaling a long stream of smoke, I think about lighting another. I've got a nice buzz going, and I always smoke way more than I should when I'm drunk.

It's Tuesday night.

My night off.

And I'm doing what I normally do on most of my nights off. I'm bar hopping, searching for… something. If I were braver, I'd flat out admit I'm looking for a man. I'm lonely for the type of comfort only a man can give.

I'm not talking about sex, although that can be nice.

I'm talking about validation of one's self, and what better way for that to happen for an insecure woman like me than to have a man lavish compliments and praise upon her? It's a sick need, but it's the dysfunctional fuel I need to keep going.

No one ever looked at Hazel Roundtree and said, "She's going to change the world one day."

No, Hazel Roundtree left that all behind when she dropped out of high school and ran off with the first man who ever paid attention to her. When I didn't get forever from him, I kept looking.

And looking.

And looking.

"Can I buy you a drink?" I hear someone say, and I turn toward the door that leads into Tipsy McBoozers. I'd been leaning up against the brick exterior enjoying my cigarette, contemplating another, but this seems like a good option. The man is tall and lanky, younger than me by I'd guess five years or so with short dark hair and even darker eyes. He's a marine. The haircut and bearing give it away.

"Sure," I say as I pull my pack of cigarettes out. "I'll be in after I smoke another one."

He nods with a charming smile and a hopeful light in his eyes that he'll get lucky tonight.

I've had four beers, and that's more than enough to get me on my way to being drunk. I'd only bought the first one, the others coming from potential suitors who want nothing more than to get in my pants.

I get it.

Guys like sex.

I know sex is a good way to keep a man around. That's just a fact, and I'm so hungry for an existence with true companionship I'll give it up again if I find someone I like.

After Chris but before I married Darren, I was on a merry-go-round of revolving men. I wasn't trying to be a slut, nor did I enjoy the thrill of getting a man's attention. I truly wanted something like what my parents had. A solid existence. A good job. A nice home. A partnership.

I wanted the romance, too. Someone who would look at me and say, "Hazel… you rock my entire world and without you, life would just suck."

Sometimes guys would say that to me, but I knew they didn't truly mean it. Not in the way I wanted them to.

Not in the most important way.

So what would usually happen is I'd fall for some-one and let him get in my pants, knowing it was the best trick in my book. I'd try overly hard to keep him interested in me, to the point I'd give up pieces of my dignity doing so. Then he'd get tired of me, or perhaps I was too overbearing, and I'd get dumped.

Darren Roundtree ended that vicious cycle I found myself repeating. He never told me I'd rocked his world, nor that without me in it his life would suck. But he did tell me he loved me and wanted to build a life with me, and it was the first time someone had said that to me since Chris—my biggest mistake.

I loved my husband. Maybe I'm not perfect, and I might be annoying at times, but I was a good wife. I kept our house clean, cooked yummy meals, and worked to help pay the bills. I let him have sex with me any time he wanted, and I did all the things he asked me to do.

Everything a good and devoted wife should do, I did. I watched my mom keep my dad happy that way, so I knew the formula worked.

I don't understand why he cheated on me with another woman, since I gave him what he asked for, whenever he asked for it.

The only thing I can conclude is I wasn't as good a wife as I thought myself to be. Maybe the sex was terrible, or maybe my cooking sucked. Maybe I whined too much, or I wasn't pretty enough. I begged him to tell me why, but he wouldn't. I demanded he stop the affair, but he wouldn't do that either.

When he told me that he loved her, and he wanted me to leave so she could move in, I knew that all the hard work I'd invested into the relationship had been nothing but wasted time on my part.

I came to the singular but very clear conclusion that love was a sham. It didn't exist, and because the myth had proved to be just that... a myth, that I was never going to be anything more than just Hazel Roundtree. A high school-dropout bartender.

Which makes me wonder why I'm at a bar, getting drunk, and looking for something I know doesn't exist. I'm not going to find the love of my life in there. That cute marine isn't going to buy me a few beers, take me back to his place for sex, and then miraculously fall in love with me. Nothing will happen other than I'll wake up tomorrow, disgusted with myself for believing in something that has no merit.

I tap out a cigarette from the soft pack and light it. The smoke burns my lungs because I'd cut down a lot. Dr. Peele told me the day I took Atticus home that Bernese Mountain Dogs had weak lungs, and were highly susceptible to infections that could lead to pneumonia and then death. He told me cigarette smoke could be detrimental to Atticus.

I have no clue if he was shitting me or not, but I haven't smoked a cigarette around my dog since then. That fear of killing him after I'd saved him from certain death left me barely any opportunity to smoke at all since Atticus was with me most of the time. I'd only be able to sneak one in if Charmin would watch Atticus for a few moments while I stepped outside.

Tonight, Atticus is at the apartment with Charmin and Chuck while I'm on the prowl.

It's a decision I'm still fretting about.

When I'd gotten home from the vet clinic—where I'm proud to say I helped Dr. Peele treat three patients—I had every intention of a low-key evening chilling with my dog on the couch. Atticus was feisty since he had to stay in the kennel when Dr. Peele had patients, and he got what I call the zoomies—where he'd just run around the couch in a tight circle cutting corners so sharply his body was at a forty-five-degree angle to the floor. It was adorable watching as his floppy ears bounced around and his tongue lolled from his mouth. Eyes all wide and bugging out, the bluer one appearing bigger than the brown one, although it really wasn't. I called it his "crazy Samuel L. Jackson" look.

By the time Charmin and Chuck came back to the apartment after dinner, Atticus had calmed down and was snoozing on my lap.

I was feeling restless and Charmin urged me to go out, taking full responsibility for my pup. I trusted Charmin, but not Chuck. Ultimately, I decided to go for it.

It's been a week today since I convinced Dr. Peele to take on additional patients with the promise I'd help him. This coming up Thursday will be two weeks since I brought Atticus home with me. My life has changed a great deal, and I'm essentially working two jobs. I have no clue what will come of the second job once my debt is paid off, but for right now, I have purpose.

Which again leads me to wonder why I left Atticus in Charmin and Chuck's care—while I'm getting drunk with strangers. Clearly something in me is still broken and stupidly wishing for a happily ever after, and I have no freaking idea where to find it.

I take a drag on my cigarette, eyeing the door of the bar. Is it in there?

Or am I just walking right into another bad pattern, destined to repeat my mistakes?

"Hazel..." Bernard calls my name.

Swinging my head toward the highway that borders the parking lot, I watch as he cuts through it, heading my way. I raise a hand in greeting. "Coming inside?"

I'm disappointed when he shakes his head. That disappointment tells me the young marine waiting inside really isn't what I want tonight. I want something genuine.

"Just heading home," he says, his words slightly slurred. He has a can of beer in his hand, but it's too dark to tell the brand. I just know it's cheap.

I glance back one more time to the door, knowing more beer and meaningless sex waits on the other side. When I focus back on Bernard, I say, "I'll walk with you. My apartment's just over that way."

"Want a beer?" he asks, letting his backpack start to slide from his shoulder.

"Sure," I reply and toss my cigarette while I wait for

him to pull a can out for me. It's Pabst Blue Ribbon and it's warm as piss, but I enjoy it anyway as we meander along the highway.

"What you been up to?" he asks. Bernard hasn't been inside Tipsy's in several days, but that's not unusual. He only springs for draft beer when he has a good haul panhandling. Otherwise, it's PBR from the grocery store.

"Same ol'," I reply but then I realize… that's just not true. "I got a second job."

"No kidding," he says, and I can hear the smile in his voice.

"At the vet clinic where I first took Atticus," I tell him, and then I proceed to fill him in on everything. I even tell him how Dr. Peele taught me how to express anal glands today, and how it was the grossest thing I'd ever done.

Bernard lets out a bark of laughter that dies off into chuckles. "Good for you, Hazel. And how is Mr. Finch?"

That startles me. "You know about Atticus Finch?"

"'Course I do," he says with another chuckle. "Was an inspiring hero to a lot of black people. One of the best books I've ever read."

"What's it about?" I ask, because I hadn't bothered to find out anything more about Atticus' namesake.

"How can you name your dog Atticus and not know

anything about the man and what he did?"

I shrug, take a drink of my beer, and swallow. "I don't know. I dropped out of high school. Wasn't much of a reader after that."

"Well, take the time and read the book. You won't regret it."

We make it to where the service road starts. "Well, I'm this way," I tell him as I point to the apartment building.

"And I'm that way." He points in the direction we'd been walking.

"Those storage units by the dry cleaners?" I ask.

"Number 127 if you ever want to stop by and borrow a cup of sugar," he says with a grin, white teeth flashing from the glare of headlights as cars speed past us.

I laugh, raising my beer to him. "Just might do that. Thanks for the beer, Bernard."

"See you 'round, Hazel," he says before ambling off.

I finish my beer, then toss it in the dumpster beside our complex. Despite that being my fifth beer, I feel pretty clearheaded. I'm guessing it's from the cool spring air I'd been walking in. I consider smoking another cigarette before I go in, but my lungs say it's a bad idea.

CHAPTER 15

Atticus

I COME OUT of a dead sleep, my ears perking when I hear the key in the lock. That can only mean one thing.

Hazel is home. Hazel is home. Hazel is home.

My head pops up from Charmin's lap where I'd fallen asleep while she watched TV, and I see Hazel walk in. I shoot off the couch, and barrel right into her legs. My paws go to her thighs and I hop up and down in excitement for her to acknowledge me.

She doesn't pick me up as often as she used to. When she does, she groans a lot from the effort. Instead, she's been coming down to my level like she does right now, so my paws can reach her chest. She wraps her arms around me for a hug, and then runs her fingers through the fur up and down my spine.

It. Feels. Amazing!

Hazel stands, cocking her head at Charmin. "What's wrong?" she whispers, and I swing back to Charmin.

She doesn't look happy.

I follow Hazel over to the couch and then jump on her lap, collapsing there with delight so she may pet me. I don't like that her body feels tight, and I know she's worried about something from Charmin.

"Um… Chuck's a little pissed at your dog." She whispers this, and I bet it's because she doesn't want Chuck to hear. But he's snoring in his bed, so I know it doesn't matter.

"Why?" Hazel whispers back.

"Well, honestly… he kind of turned into a little shit after you left tonight. Clawing at the front door and whining for you. He wouldn't settle down. Chuck was getting frustrated. He yelled at Atticus, and it scared him, so he peed on the floor. That really set Chuck off. He told me the dog had to go."

Yeah… I did pee on the floor. I didn't mean to, but Chuck scared me when he yelled. He's a jerk, and I know Hazel doesn't like him. She once said she'd like to "nut punch" him. I'm not sure what that means but I knew it would give her immense satisfaction. If my mom is happy, then I'm happy.

"Charmin," Hazel murmurs while her fingers work my fur. "This is your apartment. Not his. Do you want Atticus to go?"

While her voice sounds calm to my ears, I can feel the fear vibrating within her.

"Of course I don't want him to go," Charmin says, cutting eyes down the hallway to where Chuck is sound asleep. "But... well, he lives here too now, and I have to take into consideration his—"

"It won't happen again," Hazel cuts her off, whispering the words with desperate urgency. "I won't leave him again. He's been good since I brought him here. And he's just a puppy. If Chuck scared him, it wasn't his fault."

Charmin doesn't say anything, and I can feel Hazel practically vibrating with anxiety. I've never felt that from her before, and it makes me feel like I have to pee. But I'm a good boy... so I hold it.

"Charmin, please," Hazel begs.

"I'll talk to him," Charmin replies with a soft smile, and I can feel Hazel relax just a little. "I'm sure he'll cool down."

"Thank you," she says on a harsh exhale of breath that smells like beer and nasty cigarette smoke. I don't smell it often on her, but it's strong tonight. It makes me want to sneeze, so I just rub my nose on my paws to make it go away.

"I'm going to head to bed," Charmin says as she stands up.

Hazel doesn't reply, just pulls me up so she can bury her face in my neck. I can feel her breath through my fur, warm and smelling of cigarettes. That's okay. She's loving on me, so nothing else matters.

CHAPTER 16

Hazel

IT'S BEEN A lot, juggling the multiple balls of my current life.

Balancing two jobs. Raising a puppy. Hiding a puppy from my boss at night. Keeping peace between my puppy and Chuck, the asshole.

That's been the real problem. Ever since "The Incident"—as Chuck likes to dramatically refer to it—three days ago, he does nothing but yell and glare at Atticus whenever he can. If we're playing and Atticus dares to bark at me in giddy delight, Chuck yells at him, "Shut the fuck up."

Even if Atticus is quiet, Chuck will point a finger and snarl, "You better not pee in this apartment again, dog."

Atticus reacts like any being that's being bullied would react. He scrambles up on my lap, tail between his legs, and ducks his head so he can push it under my armpit to hide from Chuck. It pisses me off every time, but I don't say anything so as not to provoke things.

I should have known the balls would come tumbling down at some point.

"You should take the dog out," Chuck says from the kitchen table where he'd just finished eating some Sloppy Joes Charmin had made for them for dinner. She and I are working the Friday night shift at Tipsy's, and I'm making due with a Snickers.

He's looking pointedly at Atticus as he drinks from a water bowl I'd put near the back door of the apartment. It leads out onto a tiny enclosed concrete patio I'll sit out on if it's nice outside. There's an old wicker love seat that someone had set out by the dumpster. Charmin and I lugged it back to the apartment. She bought new cushions at Kmart and voila... outdoor seating.

Atticus freezes when he hears Chuck's voice, turning his head with wide eyes and eyebrows spread far apart with apprehension.

"He doesn't need to go out every time he drinks water," I snap from the couch where I'd been watching the news. I'm already ready for my shift as I only have a limited amount of shits to give about my appearance. Clean clothes, brushed hair, and a thin application of mascara. Charmin's in the bathroom primping, the sound of her hair dryer muffled by the closed door. It takes her almost an hour just to get prettied up to work behind a bar.

Of course, she often gets better tips than I do, which goes to show that beauty over customer service is what matters in this business.

"He just better not piss inside again," Chuck snarls. "Fucking stupid dog."

"What the hell is your problem?" I explode, launching up from the couch. "He's just a little puppy. He made one damn mistake and suddenly you've become a supreme asshole about it."

I hear the bathroom door open and Charmin calls, "What's going on out there?"

I hadn't realized how loud I'd just yelled at Chuck, but if Charmin heard that above her hair dryer, it must have been at max decibels.

"Nothing," I call back, but that doesn't stop her from stepping into the hallway and looking between Chuck and me with worry.

"Son of a fucking bitch, I'm going to kill that dog," Chuck booms in a voice so ferocious it causes my heart to skip a beat.

It's like everything goes into slow motion. My head turns slowly to look at Chuck. His gaze is pinned near the front door of the apartment. His fists are clenched, face mottled red. He takes a step toward where he's staring.

I spin—all slow-mo like—and see what Chuck does.

His tennis shoes sitting by the door where he always takes them off when he gets home… with Atticus squatting right over the left one.

Taking a dump inside it.

For a moment, I have a surge of enormous pride course through me. Even as scared as he is of Chuck, I believe my dog is shitting in his shoe because he yelled at me. It's Atticus' way of standing up for me.

Things go back to fast motion as Chuck storms across the small living room to reach my dog. I have horrific visions of him kicking Atticus like a football, a move that would most likely kill him.

Chuck passes right by me. Without thought or hesitation, I leap on his back and wrap an arm around his throat as tightly as I can while shrieking at the top of my lungs, "You stay the hell away from my dog."

Atticus takes off running down the hallway, disappearing from my sight. Chuck becomes focused on trying to reach a hand over his shoulder to grab me. I clamp my legs hard around him, then put my other hand to his hair where I start pulling viciously.

"Jesus Christ," Charmin screams. "Stop it right now."

"Not until he promises not to hurt my dog," I snarl, giving his hair a mighty yank.

"Damn it, you crazy bitch," Chuck cries before spinning around and slamming me into the wall. It seems like the entire apartment shakes, and my head flies backward, connecting with the drywall.

Doesn't even loosen me in the slightest. I've got rage and mama-bear type hormones coursing through me to protect Atticus.

"Hazel… get off him," Charmin yells.

Chuck somehow manages to get a hand lodged in my hair. He starts pulling hard, which hurts like a son of a bitch and wrenches my neck sideways.

"Chuck… let her go," Charmin yells.

And then Atticus is there again… standing at the edge of the hallway leading into the living room. Front legs spread wide, a mohawk of hair raised right along his spine, and his teeth bared at Chuck. The snarl he emits is adorably ferocious, yet so very pitiful at the same time. It reminds me of when Simba in *The Lion King* tries to roar at the hyenas, and it just comes out as a kitteny purr at best.

But there's no time to laugh, because right now my still-underweight twenty-five-pound pup who is at best three months old is facing off against a man who stands at least five-ten and weighs at least a hundred and eighty pounds.

He doesn't stand a chance.

I'm not a brawler. I've never been in a physical fight in my life, unless very rowdy pillow fights with my sister when we were little counts. My mind scrambles, trying to figure a way to take Chuck down before he can think to advance on Atticus.

Charmin reacts before any of us do.

She bends down and scoops Atticus up, bending her head to give him a quick kiss—perhaps in hopes of calming him down—then she runs him over to the enclosed patio and puts him out there. He immediately starts scratching at the door to get back in, howling in frustration that he's been separated from the fight.

Charmin spins and strides toward us with a really scary look on her face. In a deadly calm voice, she says, "You two break apart right now."

I loosen my hold around Chuck's neck, releasing my grip on his hair. When I unclamp my legs, Chuck unfists his hand from my hair and I slide off until my feet hit the floor.

He's the first to talk, turning to glare at Charmin. "That dog is gone. Either it goes, or I go."

Thumbing at me, he adds, "And that bitch owes me a new pair of shoes."

"Not fucking likely," I say, using my inside voice. I might just get Atticus to poop in *all* his shoes.

Chuck storms off down the hall. The bedroom door squeaks and then slams shut.

I turn to face Charmin, who is rubbing the bridge of her nose with her fingers. She finally opens her eyes, weariness apparent. "I'll go talk to him, Hazel. Maybe you can try to clean his shoe?"

I nod at her mutely, and then she disappears into the bedroom. Ignoring the shoe, I go to the patio door, opening it and letting Atticus inside. I scoop him up and hold him close, edging toward the hallway so I can try to hear what's going on.

My fingers scratch at the back of Atti's head—which has gotten really fuzzy as he gets older. His whole body is still sort of fuzzy, hair slightly frizzed and all one length. He looks like a giant black, brown, and white cotton ball or something.

"You were such a brave boy," I murmur while Charmin talks in a normal voice and Chuck yells obscenities.

The bedroom door squeaks open, and Atticus tenses in my arms as we both look that way. A tiny snarl rumbles in his chest, but when he sees Charmin step out, he goes still. He doesn't wiggle with excitement to see her as he normally does, and I think that means his loyalty to her is stretched right now because she was yelling at me, too.

I can read Charmin's face before she even opens her mouth. Still, it hurts when she says, "I'm really sorry, Hazel, but he won't budge. He wants Atticus out."

"Do you want Atticus out?" I ask, my throat suddenly parched with fear.

"Of course not," she assures me, but then her eyes

harden slightly with resolve. "But he's my boyfriend. I really think this is going to go the distance, and I have to make him a priority. Otherwise… well, it could cause trouble for us."

"You're serious?" I ask in disbelief. I know Charmin really likes Chuck, but I never thought she'd side with him on this. She's really come to love Atticus over the last few weeks of him living here.

She doesn't answer me directly, but instead replies, "Tomorrow morning. You can take him to a shelter. Or see if Dr. Peele can do something with him. Bring him to work tonight and I'll cover more breaks for you, so you can spend time with him. He can stay tonight at the apartment, but tomorrow morning, he has to go."

"Charmin," I beg. Just a single word… her name. Because I don't know what else to say to convince her.

"I'm sorry," she says and pivots on her heel, hurrying back to the bathroom.

I only stare at the closed door a moment before I look down at Atticus. His eyes meet mine, and he gives me a little head butt against my jaw, which has become his way of demanding my affection. I give him a hearty scratch along his back before bending over to put him on the floor.

"You're not going to a shelter, little man," I tell him distractedly as my mind whirs, seeking a potential solution. I'll try to talk to Charmin more tonight while we work. Maybe I can reason with her after everything has calmed down a bit.

Atticus walks over to Chuck's shoes, sniffing his handiwork. His head turns in my direction, waiting to see if I have any harsh words for him.

I don't. "Poop in the other one for all I care," I say.

He seems to consider it, turning back for another sniff. Then he lifts his head, tips his nose in the air as if saying Chuck's not worth the effort, and trots back to me.

I bend down to scratch him, promising, "I'll figure something out. It will be okay."

CHAPTER 17

Atticus

I DON'T KNOW what's going to happen, but I regret nothing.

Chuck had it coming.

That's all I have to say on that issue.

CHAPTER 18

Hazel

CHARMIN REFUSES TO talk to me about it. I've tried time and again tonight, but she cuts me off. She has generously given me more breaks, which of course I spend with my dog in the storeroom, going over various scenarios in my head.

I've got options.

I could move into a storage unit and live a life of freedom like Bernard, although that doesn't appeal to me at all. Running water and a toilet are priorities.

I could go home to my mother with my tail between my legs. Beg her to take us in. I'm not sure what her answer would be.

I could call Liz and ask for some money, but that would be extremely awkward. The last time we saw each other was not pleasant, and I've avoided her since, mainly because I'm extremely embarrassed by my behavior.

There are lots of options, and none of them are

good.

As the night wears on, my anxiety increases. I'm short-tempered with customers, which has a horrible impact on my tips. But I can't stop worrying about what's going to happen to us. I've been homeless before. Granted, it was just for a few days, but it was terrifying. At least then, I had a car to sleep in.

Now I have nothing but one little puppy that is now my sole responsibility to care for.

The door to Tipsy's opens, and my stomach tightens when I see Chuck walk in. He sort of struts, shaking hands with people and giving back slaps. He shoots a wink at Charmin with what I bet he thinks is a roguishly charming smile, but I think he looks like an idiot. I roll my eyes when she giggles and winks back at him.

He shoots a sidelong glance my way, smirks, and then turns toward Cary sitting at his usual table and about seven beers deep into drinking tonight.

My stomach clenches painfully tight and I rub at it, watching with worry as they talk. Bile rises in my throat when Cary leans to the right to see past Chuck, straight at me.

"Shit," I mutter, now feeling like I'm going to hurl.

Frozen, I watch as Cary gets up from his chair and strides to the swinging pass-through door at the end of the bar. A quick glance at Chuck and I find him grinning evilly at me. My eyes move to Charmin. Confusion coats her face as Cary steps behind the bar and brushes past her, moving straight for the storage door. I leap at him and yell, "Don't," but I know it's futile.

I've been ratted out.

Cary steps inside and I follow, closing the door behind me, shutting out the noise of the bar.

"I can explain," I say urgently when Atticus comes to greet a new friend. He jumps on Cary, putting his paws, which are getting a lot bigger each day, on his thighs.

Turning sideways, Cary dislodges Atticus and turns to glare at me. "You have to be kidding me, Hazel."

"I'm sorry. I know—"

"Just stop," he growls, his eyes glazed with beer and anger I'd been hiding a dog in his storeroom. "Do you know how many health violations you've caused?"

"You sell frozen pizza in a toaster oven," I point out rationally. "I don't think it's really affected."

"You lied to me," he continues, rolling right over me. "Kept an animal where food products are stored. It was probably pissing and shitting on everything."

"He didn't do that," I defend Atticus. "Well, a few times, but I cleaned it up really good."

"You're fired," he says bluntly as he turns for the door.

"What?" I cry out as I lunge for him. I grab his arm, forcing him back to look at me. "Just like that? No warning?"

"Just like that," he affirms with a nasty smile on his face. "Chuck's sister is looking for a job, and she's a lot better looking than you are. It's better for business."

With that, he goes back into the bar and slams the door behind him.

Mess with my dog for shitting in a shoe and I'll go Rambo on your ass.

Call me ugly, and I have no fight in me.

My shoulders hunch, and I swallow against the tide of emotion rising within me. I'd seen Darren's new girlfriend—she was there the day I moved out—and she's way prettier than I am. I know what it's like to have my looks work against me.

I push that aside, though, giving Atticus a tremulous smile. He whines in response because he knows there's nothing genuine in it. "Stay here. Be right back."

When I open the door and step in behind the bar, Charmin meets me there. She's wringing her hands with worry. The sympathy in her eyes does nothing for me.

"You sure know how to pick 'em, Charmin," I murmur softly as I push past her. I go over to the tip jar that covers my half of the bar, which is always pathetically less full than Charmin's, and pull the cash out.

I don't bother counting it right now, although I can

guesstimate I might have close to twenty dollars in ones in there.

I grab my purse from under the register and stomp to the storeroom, my gaze fixed on the floor so I can avoid Charmin.

She steps in my path. "I'm so sorry, Hazel."

Lifting my head, I lock my eyes on her. "Sorry enough to kick Chuck out and let me and Atticus stay rent free until I can find a job? Oh, and you'll have to buy his food, too, since I can't afford to now that your douche of a boyfriend got me fired."

Tears well in her eyes. I know she feels terrible, but she can't answer me.

But she's not my problem. She's one of the causes of my problems.

Pivoting, I head into the storeroom to grab my dog. I don't say goodbye, and I don't look back.

◆

BACK AT CHARMIN'S apartment, I find Chuck's tennis shoe that Atticus shit in on the front stoop. It still has the offending substance in it, and I can't help but feel satisfied it wasn't a solid dump. He'll never get that mess out completely.

After I unclip Atticus from his leash, I let him roam around while I get packed up. I don't even bother keeping an eye on him, not worried he'll have an accident. I hope he pees and poops all over the place.

My possessions are meager. When Darren had asked me to leave over four and a half months ago, I was so stricken with grief and terror that I wasn't thinking clearly. There was also a part of me that thought he'd come to his senses and tell me it was all a joke. As such, I only packed a few pairs of jeans, several shirts and sweaters, as well as a handful of underwear and bras. I threw these items in a trash bag along with some toiletries, making sure I took my good winter coat and a pair of high-heeled shoes, although I have no idea why. I didn't bring a single dress, and had nowhere to wear them.

Those are the same exact items I pack up tonight. The only additions are cans of Atti's dog food, his toys, and the kibble treats. I also pull out the money I'd stashed away for rent and utilities, then add it to my tips from tonight.

Throughout it all, Atticus sits and watches me stoically. He knows our life is changing tonight.

Before we leave, I decide to help myself to some food. It's the first time since I've been living here I've eaten any of Charmin's stuff. I pull the pack of bologna out and fry some up, eating it on thin white bread slathered with mayo, salt and pepper. I also place a few slices of cooled bologna on the floor for Atticus, and we have ourselves a goodbye feast.

When I'm done, I take one of Chuck's Mountain Dews out of the fridge and chug it. Atticus washes his bologna down with some water out of his bowl.

Wandering the small apartment one more time, I make sure I'm not leaving anything important behind. I even walk through Chuck and Charmin's bedroom, even though nothing of mine would be in there. Grumpily, I wonder if I can get Atticus to crap on command because I'd like to leave a pile behind on their bed.

As I'm walking out, I spy a photograph stuck into the edge of the dresser mirror. It's of Charmin and me. It was taken at Tipsy's, and I don't even remember the night. We both have beers in hand, which means it was either a Tuesday or a Sunday, and we have our arms wrapped around each other, heads tilted in and touching.

Like we're the best of friends.

Scoffing, I snatch the picture, tear it in two, and lay it on the dresser. That's my goodbye note.

Because the garbage bag I'd used to put all our stuff in is full, I put my winter coat on, which is fine. It's a chilly mid-April night, and the warmth feels good.

Because I anticipate an entire night of aimless wandering, carrying a heavy-ass garbage bag over my shoulder, I know it will come off before too long.

Atticus is very well behaved on his leash as we head

north on the southbound side of Highway 17. There's a lighted intersection about five hundred yards up, and we can cross over that way.

I have no clue where to go.

I have no idea if I will be safe once I finally decide on a destination.

It's only going to get colder tonight once I finally pick a spot for us to try to sleep, and I wonder if it's possible to freeze to death in April.

CHAPTER 19

Hazel

THE SOUND OF a door opening vaguely penetrates my sleep. The jangling keys sound familiar, too. I'm exhausted from the worst night of sleep in my life, so I try to put it out of my mind in the hopes I'll fall back under.

But Atticus stirs in my arms, and that causes my senses to fire. I crack an eye open, not understanding exactly where I am for a moment.

My left hip aches mightily as I roll to my back and stare at the speckled water-stained ceiling tiles above. Atticus starts bounding across the tiled floor, and that's when it hits me.

I'm at Dr. Peele's clinic, and that's him walking in the front door.

"Shit," I curse under my breath as I scramble from the floor. My hip screams with pain, and my left leg is slightly numb from laying on that side.

I bend over, snag the pile of towels I'd used as a

pillow last night, and hobble over to the big laundry bin tucked under a counter. Before I can make it, Dr. Peele is coming through the door that separates the exam room from the back supply area where I'd bedded down for the night.

Dr. Peele may be slow and hampered physically by age, but his mind is as sharp as they come. His gaze rakes over me, taking in my rumpled clothes, rat's nest hair, and the pile of towels in my arms.

"Did you sleep here last night, Hazel?" he asks with narrowed eyes.

I swallow hard. "Yes, sir."

It's the first and only time I've ever called him "sir," and I didn't think twice about it. I feel like a schoolkid standing before the principal who just got busted painting graffiti on the walls.

"But why?" he merely asks, locking his arm and giving his weight to his cane.

Turning to the laundry basket, I dump the towels in there and scrub my hands over my face. I use my fingers to clean the gunk out of my eyes before folding my arms across my chest and turning to face him. "I sort of had a bad night."

"You look it," he says pointedly.

"I got kicked out of my apartment because Atticus pooped in my roommate's boyfriend's shoe, and he gave her an ultimatum. Atticus had to leave, or he was leaving. She chose to keep the boyfriend and well, I wasn't about to get rid of Atticus, so I didn't have anywhere to stay. Then I went to work, and that same boyfriend came into the bar. He told the owner I had Atticus in the storeroom, and I had been keeping him there during my shifts. So I got fired from my actual paying job. I didn't know what to do last night, didn't know your phone number, and even if I did, I have no cell phone so I couldn't call you to ask your permission. I'm really sorry I stayed here."

After I finish that mouthful, Dr. Peele appears thoughtful. "Atticus pooped in his shoe?"

My head jerks back in surprise that he's focused on that. "Um… yeah."

"That doesn't make sense," he says, scratching at his head. "He's doing really well with potty training. I've seen how well you work with him here, and he consistently goes to the door to be let out. Were you ignoring him?"

"No," I say quickly since I'd rather Dr. Peele focus on this rather than the fact I squatted in his office building for the night. "In fact, I think he did it because he didn't like the guy. He sort of looked… calculating while he did it, and totally unrepentant after."

Dr. Peele's bushy eyebrows jack upward. "You're kidding?"

"I'm not," I assure him, because there's no doubt in

my mind Atticus was letting Chuck know he didn't like him. "And Chuck went after Atticus, and I went after Chuck, and then Atticus came after Chuck. It was crazy."

His mouth drops open, and his eyes widen in disbelief. "What happened?"

I shrug. "Nothing. My roommate, Charmin, got things calmed down before it could escalate anymore, and then well... she sided with Chuck and said Atticus had to go."

"So you were just planning on sleeping here at night?" he asks neutrally.

"Just for last night," I correct. "It was an emergency. It was close to midnight, and I didn't want to waste my money on a hotel. God knows when I'll get the money owed me for working this week at the bar. Between last night's tips and some money I'd set aside for rent and utilities I owed to Charmin, I've got about sixty bucks to my name."

"What was your plan for today?" he asks.

"Honestly?" I throw back at him.

"Always honestly, Hazel," he chastises.

"I was probably going to go rent a storage unit. Apparently, I can get one for twenty-seven dollars a month."

I wonder if I can be neighbors with Bernard.

Dr. Peele gasps, his head shaking in disbelief. "You

were going to do what?"

"I was going to rent a storage unit off Highway 17."

"Are you crazy?"

I defend my course of proposed action with indignation. "My friend Bernard lives there."

Dr. Peele's eyes practically bug out of his head. "You're friends with a vagrant who lives in a storage shed?"

"Well, he's not really a vagrant. He… well… panhandles and lives in the storage unit, but he's really nice and wise. You know… he just has this insight into life that many folks don't have, and…"

My words trail off as I realize Dr. Peele thinks I have lost my ever-loving mind.

"I'm doing the best I know how," I say in a soft voice, my gaze going down to Atticus. The puppy just patiently sits on his haunches at our feet. Mouth open, tongue hanging out the side. It's his dopey grin. "But I found this dog, and my life has just taken a turn I never expected. I thought my life was shitty before, you know… with my husband cheating on me and then kicking me out. But now I'm jobless and homeless. You'd think it doesn't get any worse than that, but actually… here's what's weird. My options are limited, my situation perilous, and yet… I'm happy. I have my dog and my health, and for the first time in my entire life, I'm trying to handle things on my own. I'm scared shitless, and yeah… still just happy. And it's all because of that dog."

I slowly lift my gaze up to Dr. Peele, ready for him to mock my silly words and aimlessness. Instead, he merely asks, "What time is my first appointment?"

"Eleven," I say cautiously. I've taken to scheduling his first of the day at eleven rather than right at ten when he opens, because some mornings he gets here before ten, and some mornings it's after. I suspect he has good days and bad days when getting out of bed in the morning.

"Come with me," he says and turns as gracefully as one can when needing a cane for balance. "And bring Atticus."

I snatch his leash off the hook on the wall, then clip it to his collar. He's taken to the leash, and we've been practicing. I know this is something I have to make sure he gets down because in another few months, I won't be able to hold him back if he gets a wild hair up his butt.

Atticus comes to a heel at my left foot, and we start off after Dr. Peele. As if Atticus senses we're on a grand adventure of sorts, he even puts a little prance in his step, throwing his front paws up high with his snowy-white chest puffed out.

I follow Dr. Peele out of the clinic. While he locks up, I walk Atticus to the side of the building so he can pee.

When we get in the big Impala, Atticus gets on my lap and I strap both of us in.

I don't ask where we're going because I'll learn soon enough. As long as it's not the shelter where he's going to try to force me to surrender Atticus, it can't be all that bad. Dr. Peele doesn't initiate any conversation on his end. The few glances I sneak at him, he appears to be deep in thought.

We head south out of town about three miles, cut over onto Dawson Cabin Road, and then take several turns onto smaller roads leading out into the deep country of Onslow County. I'm lost as I've never been out this way.

Finally, Dr. Peele slows and puts on his right blinker. We pull into a gravel driveway where a huge white farmhouse sits about two hundred yards off the road. Large oak trees provide a canopy as we drive up to a house that is worn with age but still spectacular. It has a blue tin roof, a sprawling front porch, and a double-car garage. There's a barn that sits off to the right and slightly behind the house, also with white clapboard siding and a blue tin roof. There's even a weather vane with a patinaed rooster sitting on top.

Dr. Peele stops his car in front of the garage, then turns it off. After we exit, I follow him around the side, taking in the lush landscape of the property. There's a pond out back with ducks floating in it, surrounded by marshy grasses and several pine trees. Beyond that, I see cows in a pasture separated off with wired fencing.

"Is this your place?" I ask as he starts climbing—with much difficulty, I might add—up a staircase that runs along the exterior wall of the garage. There's a door at the top, and we slowly—very slowly—ascend it. I've got Atticus' leash loose in my hand as he hops up the steps beside me, but hold my hands hovering right about butt height on Dr. Peele as he precedes me up, just in case he tumbles backward.

When he reaches the top, he's only huffing slightly, which means his endurance is pretty good, but he's got almost all his weight on his right leg. He unlocks the door, pushes it open, and motions me inside.

I enter a dim room that's sparsely furnished with a couch, a coffee table, and a side table with a lamp. There's a kitchen just behind that with a very short counter separating it from the living area. The kitchen has a really old refrigerator that's about half the height of a normal one, an older stove, and a small sink. There's an open door just off the kitchen and I can see it's a small bathroom with a standing shower.

Dr. Peele flips on the lights, then hobbles over to the windows overlooking the back of the property. He pulls the curtains open to let in more light. Puffs of dust waft off them, throwing hazy streaks through the air.

I close the door after Atticus trots in, but keep him

on the leash. I don't trust him enough to go exploring on his own.

"What do you think?" Dr. Peele asks.

"About what?" I'm not being dumb or stupid. I think I know why he brought me here, but I don't want to appear assuming in case I'm wrong.

"This apartment, Hazel," he grouses. "That couch pulls out into a bed. A lumpy bed, but it's better than a tile floor or a storage unit."

"You want me to live here?" I ask neutrally, but inside, I'm jumping up and down ready to accept.

"The rent will be two hundred dollars a month," he says, and my heart sinks. "And I'll start paying you a wage at the clinic. Still minimum wage until you can learn a few advanced things. I can only afford to pay you about twenty hours a week with the way the patient load is right now. But if we keep increasing, then I'll increase your hours."

"Oh, wow," I say, feeling slightly dizzy. Taking two steps back, I plop down onto the couch, staring at him hopefully. "Are you serious?"

Dr. Peele contemplates me, his eyes warmer than I'd ever seen them before. "You ever hear of the saying 'When one door closes, another opens'?"

"Sure. And here you are opening a door for me when one just closed on me last night," I reply, my voice getting a little choked up over his generosity.

"No, you opened a door for me," he corrects. "You pushed me to start taking patients again, and you gave me the support needed to do so. So now, I'm opening a door for you."

I can't help myself. I lean forward, put my face in my hands, and start crying. Atticus jumps to the couch and tries to push his head in between my hands. When I pull them away from my face, he starts licking at my tears. Dr. Peele sidles closer to me, and then pats me awkwardly on the shoulder.

It makes me cry harder, and it flusters Dr. Peele. "Now… this isn't anything to cry about. It's a happy moment, not a sad one."

I laugh and cry harder, peering at him through the pools of wetness in my eyes. Dashing the tears away with the back of my hand, I feel my smile widening. "Do you realize this is my first real job? I'm thirty-two years old, and I've never done anything but bartend. I feel like such a grownup right now."

Dr. Peele starts chuckling and ambles away, moving into the kitchen. I pull Atticus fully onto my lap, hugging him tight.

"You're going to have to give this place a good cleaning," he says as he opens the refrigerator to look inside. A light doesn't come on, so I assume it's either broken or unplugged. "I've got a bunch of cleaning stuff down in my utility room off my kitchen. Just borrow whatever you need."

"Thank you," I finally manage to get out the words that should have come immediately after he made me this wonderful offer. The amount of gratitude in my voice makes him pause to look at me. "It's seriously the nicest thing anyone has done for me in my life."

Dr. Peele's face flushes beet red from the compliment and he turns away, poking through the cabinets. Giving a slight cough to clear his throat, he says, "I suppose you could call me by my first name. Oley."

I knew that was his first name, but I didn't know how to pronounce it. He says it with a long "o".

Oh-lee.

I grin at Atticus and then at Dr. Peele, who is still giving me his back. I don't think he takes compliments well. "Okay. Thank you… Oley. I'll never let you regret this decision."

CHAPTER 20

Atticus

IT'S A PRETTY exciting day.

Last night, I was terribly worried about Hazel. We left what had been our home with Hazel carrying all our possessions over her shoulder. She trudged us through the late night until we came to Dr. Peele's office. I could feel the exhaustion rolling off Hazel.

I could smell her defeat.

What scared me the most was how terrified she was. After she laid down on the tile floor and pulled me into her arms, she was shaking so bad I couldn't fall asleep. I licked at her hand, but she kept telling me to "stop". I whined for a bit, but finally I was so sleepy I couldn't keep my eyes open anymore.

But today something monumental has happened. I have never felt such joy from Hazel. She even smells different... like belly rubs and tug-o-war, two things that make me deliriously happy.

We spend some of the day at the clinic, which I

don't like because I have to stay in a kennel. But the rest of the day is spent cleaning the new place we're going to live in. Hazel gives me a very stern lecture about the importance of not peeing or pooping inside. I make her a silent promise to be good, and I pay extra attention to when my bladder gets full.

Like right now. I give one bark and a scratch at the door. Hazel's head lifts from the kitchen floor she is scrubbing. and she smiles at me. She drops her scrub brush in the bucket, and then peels off the rubber gloves she was using to clean.

When she gets to the door with my leash in hand, she gives me a pat to the side of my head. "You're such a good boy, Mister Mister."

I wag my tail, but it makes me need to pee even worse. I sort of prance in place, hoping she understands the need is getting urgent.

She laughs at me and hooks me up. Within moments, I'm squatting over the grass in relief. I lift my nose into the air, sniffing all the wonderful smells.

My own pee, cows, ducks, winter hay, cherry trees, fresh mown grass, and pine pollen. That last one has me sneezing repetitively. I don't know why I do it but sometimes after I pee, my back legs kick outward, scratching at the grass. I do that a few times and feeling satisfied, I look up to Hazel.

She's just staring back at me with an expression on

her face that makes me want to lick her.

"Hazel," Oley calls out from his front porch. It's the name he told Hazel to start using.

We both turn his way, my tail wagging. I liked Oley before, but I really like him now. Not as much as Hazel, but way more than Charmin who let us down. He gave Hazel this new home and now Hazel feels safe, so he's next in line after her.

"What's up?" she calls back to him.

"Let's go into town," he replies, waving his car keys. "You're going to need some sheets for the pull-out bed and some towels. Plus, some food."

Food?

Yeah… I like Oley a lot.

For this trip, I sit in the backseat as Oley says I'm getting too big, and he can't see very well when trying to look out the passenger window. This is fine by me because I can run the length of the seat, peering out one window, then the other.

When we drive past cow pastures, I bark at them so ferociously my slobber flies everywhere. Hazel tells me to quiet down, but I can't.

I'm just so excited about our new life it makes me need to pee.

But I hold it.

I'm pretty sure it would be frowned upon to piddle in Oley's car.

PART II

"The greatest happiness of life is the conviction that we
are loved; loved for ourselves, or rather,
loved in spite of ourselves."

– Victor Hugo

CHAPTER 21

Hazel

"COME ON, ATTI," I say as I grab my thermos and purse from the counter.

Atticus raises his head, which at this age seems bigger than the rest of his body. He'll be roughly six months old tomorrow and he's nothing but head and paws, sort of like a gangly teenager. I weighed him last week and he was at sixty-one pounds, which Oley said was right where he needed to be.

Tomorrow is the Fourth of July and I'm going to have a combo Independence Day/birthday event. While we don't know Atticus' true age, I found him on the 28th of March. It's a date I'll never forget.

Atticus' Gotcha Day.

He was roughly ten weeks old then, so by my calculations, he's six months old tomorrow give or take a few.

"Let's go," I command, giving a slap of my palm to my thigh.

The mutt doesn't move a muscle, except for those

brown eyebrows that slant inward at a steep angle. His eyes are piercing and defiant.

I call it his "stubborn look". He's been giving it to me a lot over the last few months.

I suppose in dog years, he would be a teenager now.

Here's what I've figured out about my dog in the almost three months we've been living at Oley's farm.

He's batshit crazy.

Simple as that.

Okay, he's smart as hell. Like I can teach him a trick once with a treat as a reward, and he has it down. He was fully potty trained just about a week after I moved into this apartment. He's perfectly behaved on a leash, and we took a course and got his Canine Good Citizen award.

And all of that means exactly shit, because outside of those few behaviors, he's just plain bananas.

First, he's stubborn as hell. Many times, he won't do something I ask just for the sake of making me jump through hoops to get him to do it. I think it amuses him. Mostly, he's waiting for me to pull out a treat for doing something as basic as getting his ass off the couch so we can go somewhere.

On top of that stubborn streak that rears its head randomly, he's an absolute wrecking ball of a dog. I can't even begin to count the things he's chewed up in this apartment, but the highlights include a door casing, drywall, my lumpy mattress in the couch, a corner of carpet, and every roll of toilet paper that I leave within his reach.

I was horrified the first time this happened, which was the casing around the front door. I had left just for a few moments to run a casserole I'd made for Oley down to him. I couldn't have been gone more than five minutes, but that little shit chewed through the wood like a damn beaver.

Every additional "incident" was when I was gone or involved in something and not giving His Supreme Highness attention. Oley was a good sport about it, claiming the apartment was old and needed some updates. He'd said, "That's just what puppies do," but I seriously doubt that. If all puppies were this bad, the shelter would be full of them.

At any rate, I've been diligently setting money aside to make the repairs myself.

That problem has sort of been solved because Oley let me bring home a big wire kennel from the clinic. It takes up one wall of my living room and Atticus has to be crated when I leave now, unless he's staying with Oley.

Like this morning. "Come on, doofus," I say crossly with another palm slap to my thigh. "Because if you want to stay with Oley rather than in your crate, you best get a move on."

I get nothing back except that look that says, *Make me.*

"Want a treat?" I ask him in a falsetto voice.

His head tilts and his ears perk up. Suddenly, I have interest.

With a sigh, I head into the kitchen, open the chugging fridge that seems like it's ready to die any day now, and pull a small carrot from a baggie.

Atticus immediately jumps off the couch and runs into the kitchen, flopping his butt onto the linoleum and eyeing the carrot like he's starving. He's such a food-motivated dog, but joke's on him... he doesn't know the carrots are good for him.

I put the carrot in my fist, then hold it to my side. Atticus' nose bumps it in a silent plea for me to release it to him. I ignore him, heading to the door. He trots beside me, continually hitting my hand with his nose and follows me right out onto the staircase landing.

After I shut the door, I turn around to look at him. I spare a tiny smirk before popping the carrot into my own mouth. His expression transforms from expectation to pure confusion, so I explain it to him. "You don't get a treat just for coming outside, little man."

Reaching down, I give him a scratch on his head and he gives me a goofy grin in return while his tail thumps the small wooden deck. While he may be motivated by food, he loves physical affection the most.

Atticus and I trot down the stairs on our way to the back of the house. We've been able to hang up his leash around the farm as long as me or Oley are with him. If he catches a scent he wants to chase after, he'll stop in his tracks if we tell him to. I would not, however, trust him out here by himself. He'd be miles away if left to his own devices.

Atticus races up the steps to the back patio, and then has to wait for me to open one of the double french doors that lead right into Oley's kitchen.

He's at the table with a cup of coffee and the newspaper.

"Morning," I say brightly, heading over to the coffee pot to fill my thermos. He's got one of those old-fashioned percolators. It makes the best coffee, so I pilfer it from him. I snicker as I remember that morning I'd brought Oley coffee and he told me he drank tea.

Such a liar. He very much loves his java in the morning.

"Mornin'," he grumbles. Atticus jets right toward him, pushing his big head onto Oley's lap. He gets a few scratches before he gets shoved away. "Go lay down."

Atticus obeys completely, dropping right to the floor with a chuff of resignation. I chuckle over the way he's laying. I call it his "froggy position". The dog must be double jointed because his back legs splay out to the side and resemble frog legs. His two front legs are extended forward and he lays his head down on them, carefully watching me as I pour coffee into my thermos, then doctor it up with a lot of cream and sugar.

"Need anything else while I'm out?" I ask as I screw the cap back on.

I'm running out to pick up his new glasses that are ready at the optometrist's office—finally talked him into getting an updated eye exam—and to the grocery store for us both. I'd taken to doing errands for Oley when I can because I know it's difficult for him to walk long distances. I did suggest a scooter for him, and he bitched at me for about fifteen minutes that he wasn't an invalid and didn't need that.

"Not that I can think of," he replies without taking his eyes off the paper. "But I got something for you... There's a box by the microwave."

That something turns out to be a rectangular box with the Apple logo on the front. I hesitantly lift the top, gasping at the brand-new phone sitting there, all sleek and shiny.

My head pops up, my eyes rounded with shock as I gawk at Oley. "You got me an iPhone."

"Yup," he says, still scanning the paper. He picks up his coffee, takes a casual sip. When he lowers the cup, he says, "That way I can reach you while you're out if I need something."

"It's too much," I say, hands itching to pick it up.

I'd had cell phones in the past. Darren had even gotten me a lesser-model Android last year, but he turned off the service to it after he kicked me out. But I've never had something so… expensive. I know these things cost a crazy buttload of money.

So I repeat, "It's too much for a phone just to be able to call me with."

"I expensed it out under the business," he replies and finally turns to me for the first time this morning. "Besides… you deserve it."

He grimaces a little when he says that last bit. While Oley has warmed considerably to me over the last three months, he still has his grumpy ways. He's not big on handing out compliments either.

I've been busting my ass for him, helping him to build the clinic back up. Even when he could only pay me for twenty-five hours, I'd work thirty-five, some-times forty. It was a slow process, but Oley's at the point now he's got several patients a day and he's even considering opening back up on Fridays.

I also help Oley around the farm when I can. It's not a working farm, but it once was. Mostly there's a lot of land to maintain, so I help mow the grass and trim the weeds. He has a few pastures he leases out, which explains the cows I often seen grazing in the distance. I helped him plant flowers in front of the house—which basically meant I did the work and he directed where each flower was to go.

Then there's the pet cemetery to maintain. Oley offers to bury any animal he euthanizes out on his property. Many customers have taken him up on the offer. There's a corner of the farm that's dotted with tiny wooden crosses he makes for each one, where he burns the name of the pet on the horizontal piece. It's totally creepy and completely beautiful at the same time.

Oley's never once told me "good job," or that he appreciates my work. But he doesn't have to. I can feel his appreciation in other ways.

Like when he told me to just come on in his house whenever I wanted, including for coffee in the mornings.

Or when I was down with a sinus infection for a few days, and he trudged all the way up my staircase to bring me some chicken noodle soup he'd made.

Or that I could borrow his car anytime I wanted.

Oley isn't big on words as he's more of an action guy.

Like with this iPhone.

"Just… wow," I murmur. I pull it out of the packaging, oohing over the rose gold color. The screen is so big I could easily watch a movie on it. "Thank you, Oley."

He grunts an acknowledgment before returning to his paper. I've been forgotten.

After I put the phone back in the box, I shove it in

my purse. I'll have to figure out how to work it later. Right now, I've got errands to run.

Walking over to Atticus, I bend over and give him some rubs behind his ears. "You be a good boy for Oley."

Atticus gives me two thumps of his tail on the floor in acknowledgment.

"I'm outta here," I say as I snatch the keys off the ring by the door that leads into the garage.

Oley doesn't say goodbye, but he grunts at me again.

♦

I FOUND OUT that Oley's car was a 1970 Chevrolet Impala that he had restored and customized about fifteen years ago. Once upon a time, he was big into that kind of thing. It was his hobby away from the veterinary practice. He would even go to car shows and I've seen some of the pictures he's got around the house of him posing near a 1963 Corvette or a 1965 Pontiac GTO. I didn't really understand if these cars were a big deal or not as he was pointing them out one evening I brought some dinner down to him, but they looked pretty cool to me.

The Impala is a nightmare to drive. It's big, wide, and long. Like I have to take corners with an extra-wide turn, so I don't run up on the sidewalk type of monstrous. But admittedly, the more I drive it, the easier it gets.

I time my drive perfectly to arrive at the optometrist's office right as they open at nine. I'm out of there fifteen minutes later, and then I pick up the mail at the post office.

I'm well ahead of schedule to get back to the farm, pick up Oley, and get him to the clinic for his first appointment at eleven, so I decide to treat myself to an absolute luxury.

Starbucks.

In the three months I squatted on Charmin's couch, a luxury was being able to buy a pack of cigarettes and get enough food to keep me going.

These days are different. Thanks to Oley and his generosity, I've got money to pay bills and even occasionally get myself a treat. I've quit smoking completely because of that sneaky man telling me Berner's have weak lungs. With the help of Google, I eventually found out it was a lie, but when I confronted him about it, he just smirked and told me I should be thanking him for helping me quit a deadly habit.

I'm actually kind of grateful, but I'll never admit it to him.

I cruise up Highway 17, going straight through the city rather than the bypass and turn onto Western Boulevard. It's the main thoroughfare that connects

Highway 17 with Highway 24, where the big military base, Camp Lejeune, sits. On this road you can find dozens of restaurants, retail stores, the Jacksonville mall, and the hospital. It's the original hub of action in this town, but this place has grown so much it's not the biggest or best anymore.

It's a North Carolina summer morning. The sun is bright, and I've got the windows rolled down. The air is already humid. My hair is frizzy as hell from it, so I've got it pulled back into a tight ponytail. I pull the shade down and the minute the sun is blocked, I see him walking along Western Boulevard.

Bernard.

Without thought, I flip on the right turn signal, then pull into the parking lot of a Wendy's, right in front of him. I toot the horn, calling through the open passenger window, "Bernard."

He bends down, peers in, and then his mouth breaks into a wide, toothy grin. "Well, hello stranger."

"Want a ride?" I ask, having no clue where he's going. I didn't even know he hung out on this side of town.

"Sure enough," he says as he opens the door and slides in. He's wearing a pair of worn but clean jeans, work boots, and a navy t-shirt. His forehead is glistening with sweat, and he doesn't have his backpack that he always carries.

"Wow, it's good to see you," I say with a smile, then hit the gas, circling around the restaurant and pulling back onto Western Boulevard.

"It's been… what… two months?" he asks.

"Closer to three," I reply. I hadn't seen Bernard since that night we shared PBRs while walking home. There's no need for me to go over on that side of Highway 17 anymore. I sure have no desire to hit the bars over there.

My world is limited to the clinic, Oley, the farm, Atticus, and whatever errands need to be done.

"So where you headed?" I ask.

"Nowhere in particular," he says vaguely. "Just walking."

"Then come join me for a cup of coffee. My treat."

"It's too damn hot for coffee," he grumbles.

"It's never too hot for coffee," I disagree with a laugh. "But they have cool drinks, too."

"Like beer?"

"No beer," I reply with regret.

We make our way over to the Jacksonville Mall where they'd built a Starbucks in front of it, bordering Western Boulevard. I park in an angled slot, which are my favorite kind with this mammothlike car, and we make our way in.

I get a coffee Americano and Bernard settles on a bottle of water after saying the menu overwhelmed him.

I'm guessing he's never been in a Starbucks because he could probably buy a six pack of cheap beer for what one cup of coffee costs.

We sit at a corner table by the window. As he uncaps his water, he nods his chin at me. "Tell me everything. I had no clue where you'd up and went to. Went into Tipsy's one night and you were gone. Charmin told me what happened."

It takes me about fifteen minutes to fill Bernard in on everything that's happened in my life. He raises his eyebrows a lot. A few times, he says, "No kidding," but otherwise he listens attentively.

"When one door closes, another opens," Bernard says solemnly.

I blink at him in surprise. "That's exactly what Oley said when he showed me the apartment. He told me I'd opened a door for him."

"What good goes around comes around," he says knowingly.

"What about you?" I ask with a smile. "You still over in those storage sheds on 17?"

"Sure am," he says, scratching at his chin. "Got a nice setup there. Owner knows I'm living in there, and I sort of keep an eye on the place at night."

I have no clue why Bernard is homeless, or why he doesn't try to do something to pick himself up out of the gutter. I don't think it's the alcohol because he doesn't spend all his money on it. And he doesn't drink all the time. Right now, he's sober. He's taking care of himself, and I feel like if he just applied himself a bit more, he could do something… better for himself.

"Got any big plans tomorrow?" I ask.

"What's special about tomorrow?"

I roll my eyes. "It's the Fourth of July, but more importantly, it's Atticus' six-month birthday. I'm doing a thing. Barbeque chicken on the grill, corn on the cob, and strawberry shortcake. You in?"

Bernard just blinks as if what I said came out in a garbled mess.

"I'll pick you up at your storage unit at five. Okay?"

More blinking.

"Bernard." I snap my fingers in front of his face to get him to focus.

He blinks again, but then shakes his head, a wry smile on his face. "You sure you want me coming to your house?"

"Well, it's Oley's house. We're going to use his kitchen and grill, but yes… I'd love to have you come. You're a friend of mine, right?"

"I suppose," he replies hesitantly.

"No supposing about it. You're my friend, Bernard, and you're coming to celebrate the Fourth and Atticus' birthday with us. And that's that."

CHAPTER 22

Atticus

I REMEMBER BERNARD from what seems like long ago. He smells different than Hazel and Oley, but not in a bad way. He actually smells… wise. Like he knows what mystic forces make the world work.

He's a nice guy. Fed me bits of barbeque chicken under the table when no one was looking. Thankfully, Hazel didn't see as she would have told him to stop.

I'm not allowed to have table food. Hazel says it's to help teach me proper manners, since I seemingly wasn't born with "well-behaved genes".

Whatever that means.

There are lots of rules to remember, and I'm pretty good at many of them. But sometimes, the temptation to break the law is just too much for me to ignore. This is usually when there is food involved, or I'm feeling anxious for some reason.

Rule number one is an important one, but it's so hard for me to resist.

No counter surfing.

I am forbidden from putting my front paws on any counter, and it's a grave sin to take food from there. If I even walk near a counter and lift my nose to smell, I get a stern look from Hazel and a, "Don't you even think about it, Mister." There was an incident with a pork loin a few weeks ago that landed me in the crate for a few hours.

But seriously… they can't leave a yummy, savory, pork-smelly piece of food out and think I've got the willpower to resist. Hazel had it in a pan while the oven was pre-heating.

She went to the bathroom… and the opportunity presented itself.

Now normally when Hazel uses the bathroom, I'm right in there with her. She always tries to push me out, but I like to be close to her. Besides, her on the toilet puts her almost face to face with me. I can push my head right up into her business, forcing some type of scratches around that area.

Her first clue I was up to mischief should have been in the fact I didn't follow her in to watch her potty. She didn't even leave the door cracked to keep an eye on me.

I swear, I don't know where that woman's head was at, but there was nothing I could do.

It didn't take long for Hazel to take a pee. She squats just like I do, which is cool. But it was just enough time for me to snatch that pork loin out of the pan, and then run it into the living room. It was a three biter. I wolfed it down as fast as I could because I knew if she caught me, she was diving in after whatever remained.

I was licking my lips when she came out of the bathroom. She gave me a sweet smile because she loves me so much, and then she went into the kitchen.

Let's just say she unloaded every imaginable curse word on me when she saw the empty pan. Awful, mean jabs that were meant to shame and humiliate me for eating her dinner. I just cocked my head to the side, watching her with a curious expression on my face.

Listen… I know if I would just "act" like I've been duly chastised, she'd get over it a lot faster. But it's not within my nature to do so.

I live by the motto "I regret nothing". I learned that little philosophy when I pooped in Chuck's shoe, and I knew Hazel respected it.

Now she expects me to change my ways, and that's just not going to happen.

Like tonight for example. It's my birthday, and I'm feeling especially impish. Anything could happen.

CHAPTER 23

Hazel

I WASN'T SURE how Oley and Bernard would get along, but my worries were for naught. The two men kept up a running banter throughout dinner, argued over who has the best baseball team, and discussed politics in a sane, rational manner, which really shocked me since they lean in opposite directions.

I think Oley was expecting something different in Bernard, in that he'd stereotyped him, which is just human nature. Until I'd gotten to know Bernard over countless beers at Tipsy's, I'll admit my view of the homeless—especially those who beg for money—was jaundiced.

Bernard showed up wearing a nice button-down shirt with dress pants, although his scruffy work boots sort of made it a weird combo.

He'd even shaved the scruff off his face, and I couldn't help but ask on the drive out to the farm after I'd picked him up, "Bernard... can I ask you a personal question?"

"Shoot," he replied.

"Where do you… you know, get cleaned up and stuff? It's not like you have running water in your storage shed."

Bernard chuckled. "There are lots of ways. Just have to be smart about it. I've washed up in public restrooms before, but currently, I got a membership to that cheap gym, Muscles. Fifteen bucks a month. They have showers."

My mouth dropped open in astonishment, and I took my eyes off the road to look at him. He smirked and went on to tell me that he washes his clothes while in the shower. He explained that he has a line stretched in his unit where he lets them dry. Bernard pointed out he'd just gotten his current outfit at the Goodwill. He said he'd tried to find some nice shoes to go with the outfit, but they didn't have any his size.

Currently, we're all sitting on the back patio in rocking chairs. July and August are the hottest months in North Carolina, but as the sun sets and the fireflies come out, Oley's outdoor thermometer has us sitting at a comfortable—but still humid—seventy-five degrees. The outdoor ceiling fans generate a gentle, cooling waft of air around us so it's more than bearable.

The only one not out here with us is Atticus. He's in the kitchen, sleeping on the cool tile floor. I'd made him a doggie friendly cake, and had taken a lot of pictures of him wearing a birthday party hat.

But given he's a mountain dog and would rather be neck deep in snow I'm sure, he prefers the air conditioning. If I had the same amount of fur he has, I'd be right there beside him. I periodically check on him through the double french doors, but he's out like a light. Turning six months old is hard work apparently.

"Dinner was excellent," Oley says to me—although he's staring out across the pastures when he says it. Still a rare compliment from the man, but he doesn't look as pained when he gives them.

I noticed a funny thing about Oley over the past few months. When he's not being grumpy and is fully relaxed, he's actually got a courtly southern accent when he talks. It's like his words come out a little slower... and a lot gentler. Definitely thicker, but more refined. He seems like he'd be more at home in a seersucker suit or something.

"Sure was," Bernard echoes Oley's praise. "I don't get many home-cooked meals these days unless it's in a shelter or something."

While I'd often tiptoed around the subject of Bernard's homelessness because it is what it is, Oley has no such qualms asking blunt questions.

"Bernard," Oley drawls, as he holds his sweetened ice tea I'd made in his hand. Bernard and I are drinking beer, although I'm limiting myself to two since I have to drive him home. "If you don't mind me asking, you seem like a smart fellow and you're clearly able to take care of yourself, so why exactly are you homeless?"

"Oley," I blurt out in surprise. That just seems to cross a politeness line, although Oley didn't have an ounce of condescension in his voice when he asked it. He's genuinely curious—the way I am—about Bernard, but I've been too afraid to ask.

I couldn't be more stunned over Bernard's answer, though. "It's an easy way to live."

"Pardon me?" Oley says. Straightening up in his rocker, he turns to face Bernard. "How can your situation be easy?"

Bernard gives a quick smile to Oley before turning his head to scan the pasture. He's totally relaxed with his third beer in hand. The rocker gently sways as he rests his head against the back.

He doesn't say anything for what seems like an eternity. I can feel my face flushing with embarrassment over the situation, but then he says in a very simple and matter-of-fact way, "It's easier than *real* life."

That simple answer seems to paralyze Oley and me, as we just stare at Bernard in confusion. When we don't say anything, he tilts his head to regard first Oley, then me. A low rumble of laughter comes out, and he shakes his head in amusement.

Sitting forward in his chair, he puts his elbows on his knees, loosely holding his beer. He stares back out at the dancing fireflies. "What's real life? Job, wife, kids. Mortgage payment and unforeseen dental bills. Arguing with the neighbor because his dog keeps crapping on my lawn. I don't deal with any of that. I beg for a little money to put a tin roof over my head and a few beers in my gut."

I don't even know the appropriate response to that. Yeah... life is hard, but there's positive to it too, right? Something strikes me about what he just said, "Do you have a family?"

Bernard's eyes go a little glassy as a short bark of laughter comes out, as if mocking the term "family". So I'm surprised when he says in a voice filled with yearning, "Yeah... wife and son. He just turned thirty-seven not long ago."

A gust of surprised air blows out of my lungs.

"Why aren't you with them?" Oley asks.

Bernard settles defeated eyes on Oley. "Because I cause more trouble than good for them."

"No way," I blurt out. I don't know Bernard all that well, but he's a genuinely nice guy.

I get Bernard's gaze now, and his smile is sympathetic to my disbelief. "This has been a pattern with me for a long time, Hazel. I don't deal well with pressures, so I take off."

"And just live in a storage unit, until… what… you decide to go back home to your family?" I ask.

"I haven't been home for a couple of years now," he says softly, but there's no undercurrent of self-pity in that fact.

"I don't understand why," I say, pressing him for a better answer. As someone who was kicked out of her home just over seven months ago, and has had two brushes with being homeless, I can't fathom it.

"You know about the Beirut Bombing?" he asks.

"Of course I do." I can't remember what year it was—somewhere around the early eighties—but when the marine barracks there were bombed a lot of people died. We even have a memorial here in Jacksonville although I've never been to it.

"That was in 1983," Bernard says with a nod of his head. "I was in that building and I was one of the few who survived. We lost a lot of marines. I didn't handle it all that well when I got home."

"So you have… PTSD?" I ask gingerly. Now things are getting personal. I hadn't expected to learn something like this about Bernard.

He shrugs. "PTSD wasn't a diagnosis back then. It was called anti-social personality disorder. Before that, it was called shellshock or battle fatigue. I came back from Beirut, and I couldn't stand to be in crowds. I was hypervigilant all the time. Couldn't sit with my back to a door. Loud noises terrified me. I drank to self-medicate. Had a short temper with my wife and kid. At work, I'd mouth off to superiors and I'm sure you know that doesn't work in the Marine Corps."

"Did you get medically discharged?" Oley asks.

Bernard shoots him a glance. "Yeah."

Oley nods as if it all makes sense to him, but it doesn't to me. I don't get how someone leaves their family. As someone who had her husband discard her like used trash, I can't fathom it.

"Don't you miss them?" I ask. I cringe internally over the slight condescension in my voice.

Bernard's tone is chastising. "Of course I do. Don't think my refusal to be there has anything to do with a lack of love for them. But I've screwed things up with them. Put them through the ringer with my drinking and by leaving for long stretches of time. Coming home when I'm lonely, only to do it all over again. They've moved on from me, and I need to let them have that peace. I stay away because of how much I love them."

That shuts me up as I realize the old adage "there are two sides to every story" is true. I can't presume to know what's right for Bernard or his family. Maybe they *are* better off without him. Maybe he is giving them peace.

Or maybe what he said is a big ol' crock of shit.

"You'd be getting disability money from the government," Oley observes. "Why do you beg?"

"That money goes to my wife. She uses it to supplement her retirement. Puts some into a college fund for the grandkids."

"You have grandkids?" I ask, wondering if Bernard will ever quit shocking me tonight.

His smile goes from troubled to nonexistent, and it's clear I've hit on a very sensitive nerve. Slapping a palm to his thigh, he makes to stand up from his rocker. "Well, it's getting late. Would you mind giving me a ride back to town?"

I feel horrible for chasing him away with my questions. He's shared a lot tonight, and I should have backed off.

So I lighten things up. "Absolutely I will, but first we're having my strawberry shortcake. I made the pound cake to go with it from scratch."

A wave of relief washes over Bernard's entire body, and he sinks back into his chair. I can see it in his eyes, the relaxing of his jaw and the droop of his shoulders. I had clearly stressed him out with my poking around, and I feel wretched about it.

He knows I feel bad because he gives me a bright smile to bring me out of it. "Strawberry shortcake sounds delicious."

I smile back as I put my half-empty beer on the small patio table and stand up.

"Just a small piece for me," Oley says. "I'm afraid I

ate too much of your potato salad."

Another roundabout-Oley-compliment. I beam at him.

As I'm opening the french door to head into the kitchen, I hear Oley say to Bernard, "The Pirates are playing the Indians tonight if you want to stick around and watch."

My chest swells with fondness for Oley. For making Bernard feel so welcome, and for redirecting him onto less stressful topics. The fact he's opening his home up to Bernard says a lot about the man.

But then again, Oley's also a lonely person. He's been by himself here for over twenty years. His wife died when she was fifty-two, and their kids had already flown the nest and moved to other parts of the state. Oley has a daughter over in Raleigh and a son in Charlotte. He has grandkids, too, but he rarely sees any of them because, in his words, "They're always so busy they don't have time for me".

In fact, he rarely talks about them at all. I realize Oley totally understands Bernard's family issues. They have something very important in common.

Well, and baseball, too.

When I step into the kitchen, Atticus—who is laying on his side—opens his blue eye to stare at me. His tail thumps, but he makes no move to get up. He ate quite a bit of the dog cake so he's in lazy, sleepy mode right now.

"Don't get up on my account," I tease. Of course, he doesn't understand my words, but he always understands my tone, which makes his tail pound the tile harder.

I move to the counter where I'd set the pan of pound cake I'd left earlier. For a moment, I'm utterly confused. I'd put it back into the L-shaped corner where the counter meets the wall because I know Atti's propensity to counter surf. He's so damn fast, too, but I don't think he could have reached it.

Besides... the pan itself—which is made of heavy ceramic—is gone.

I did bring it down from my apartment, didn't I?

Yes, I absolutely remember bringing it down. I had covered it with tinfoil, set the bowl of strawberries on top, and carefully walked down the steep stairs.

I turn around to scan the counter with the kitchen sink that overlooks the backyard. Perhaps Oley moved it.

No pan.

I look to the kitchen table.

No pan.

The stove.

No pan.

"What in the hell?" I mutter, feeling like I'm in the twilight zone.

I check inside the fridge, the oven, and the microwave. No pan.

And then, a bell goes off.

I slowly turn toward Atticus. He sure looks innocent enough. I had been keeping an eye on him through the double doors while we sat on the patio, but I didn't keep my eyes on him one hundred percent of the time.

But there's no way he's involved because the entire freaking pan is gone. I know damn well he didn't eat ceramic.

Spinning around in circles, I keep thinking I'm just overlooking it. In frustration, I decide to check the living room because maybe I'm just totally losing it and I put it in there. Or maybe Oley's playing a trick on me.

I move around the kitchen island. When I clear the corner, I see it.

The ceramic dish on the tile floor. The tinfoil cover is beside it. And the pound cake is nowhere to be seen. Oh, there are crumbs left. Some pieces in the corner that were perhaps too difficult for a huge Berner mouth to get at, but—

"Atticus," I shriek in frustration as I wheel back around to face him.

The little asshole doesn't even move, but his tail thumps harder and the corners of his mouth pull back to smile at me in defiance.

The door to the patio opens and Bernard comes

rushing through, followed by Oley hobbling as fast as he can. Both men look from Atticus to me to Atticus, wondering what in the hell he's done.

I point a shaky finger at my dog, who just lays there on his side with that truth-teller eye staring at me. His mouth is curled into a lazy smile that says he's content with the outcome of the pound cake. "That… that… monster," I manage to sputter as I glare at my dog. "Ate the entire pound cake."

Bernard blinks in surprise, but Oley snickers. He knows how bad my dog can be.

Turning for a moment, I bend over and snatch the pan off the floor, holding it out for them to see it. "This is all that's left."

"Whoa," Bernard says in awe.

"Wait a minute," Oley says as his eyebrows furrow inward. "That pan was on the floor? Is that where you'd left it?"

I roll my eyes and snap, "Of course not. I had it on the counter, pushed to the back. Besides, I had my eye on Atticus the whole time he was in here."

Oley shakes his head in disbelief and chuckles. "Do you realize that means he got up on that counter, lifted a heavy ceramic pan filled with cake with his mouth, and gently set it on the floor. If he'd pushed it off or let it drop, that pan would have shattered. Talk about smart dog."

"He is not smart," I growl. "He's an asshole."

"Language," Oley reprimands with his eyes narrowed behind his glasses.

"Asshole," I mutter under my breath.

Bernard's eyes are sparkling, his hand covering his mouth as he tries not to laugh. He makes a choking sort of sound, and then it just comes out. A deep, rumbling belly laugh that makes him double over and hold his stomach. That gets Oley laughing right along with him.

I just stare at the two old farts in disbelief. My dog ate our dessert, and they're laughing. Atticus' tail thumps harder, and I glare at him.

Still smiling with not an ounce of apology in his expression.

"Asshole," I mutter again as I set the empty cake pan on the counter.

Admittedly, I am now slightly marveling in hindsight over the fact Atticus had to have picked that damn thing off the counter and set it on the floor before eating it.

My voice is tight and clipped when I tell the men, "Looks like we're just having strawberries and whip cream for dessert."

Both laugh harder over my obvious distress. I'm sure I'll laugh about it later, too, once I get done being pissed off at my dog.

Good thing he's cute, or I'd have shot him by now.

CHAPTER 24

Hazel

HOLY HELL IT'S hot today. It was in the mid-nineties all day, and I was thankful I have an inside job working with Oley. But when we left this afternoon and locked up, the heat radiating off the asphalt felt like it would melt my shoes.

As soon as we get back to the farm, I'll race up the stairs to my apartment to let Atticus out. I'd stopped taking him to the clinic with us because he couldn't stand to be separated from me for any length of time and made quite a fuss. If I had to help Oley with a patient, Atticus would scratch and scratch at the exam room door to get in. We tried to kennel him, but he'd just howl and bark and make such a ruckus Oley and I determined he should stay back at the apartment. Of course, because he's a puppy and still quite destructive, he has to be crated.

We had a busy day packed with patients, and I even assisted Oley neuter a seven-month-old Great Dane.

With his new glasses, Oley can now see to do detailed work. Stitches and cutting balls off are a piece of cake for him. He told me it was a very simple surgery, and it really was. I didn't even get sick watching. And that's about all I did. Even though I say I assisted, I pretty much just shaved the dog after it was under anesthesia and Oley did the rest. It took no more than half an hour, and the castration was complete.

Poor Atti. I need to schedule his soon. Oley says he thinks some time in between six and nine months is the sweet spot. I have to admit I was hesitant to have Oley do it until I saw how much his new glasses improved his vision. He's sharp minded and steady handed, but I want him to be able to see what he's doing if he's going to be cutting on my little boy.

And now I hate I doubted him, but that will be my secret to keep.

I'm covered in sweat just from that jog up the stairs. Even at four-thirty, it's still brutally hot. Atticus barks from inside, an exuberant bellow that goes high pitched when I put the keys in the door. When I open it, he starts clawing the plastic tray at the bottom of his kennel, paws moving furiously fast. He's not trying to get out but rather doing his "happy dance" to see his mom. His barks turned into whines as he starts batting the wire door with his paw.

It's the same routine.

I pull the latch back but before I open it, I say, "Sit."

Atticus vibrates with pure energy and excitement. He ignores my command.

"Sit," I repeat again and reluctantly, he obeys me. His butt drops ever so slowly to the ground.

"Stay," I drawl slowly, holding my hand up, palm out toward him. I repeat the command again, because Atticus is stubborn and hardheaded. "Stay."

His gaze zips back and forth between my face and my hand poised to open the kennel. I brace myself and say again, "Stay."

I slowly open the door, still holding a palm up to him. Atticus trembles, and it reminds me of the way big rockets sort of rumble and shake in place before they lift up from the launch pad.

And like a rocket, I brace for Atticus to explode out.

"At ease," I tell him, which is his release command.

Shooting out of the kennel, he charges me in a blur of fur and tongue flopping out the side of his mouth. There's not time to give a command for him to stop, and it wouldn't do any good anyway. I've yet to be able to control this part of his enthusiasm over me coming home.

He goes to his hind legs, front paws to my shoulders, and he starts jumping as if he wants to land right in my arms. I put my arms around him, turning it into a bear hug. He whines and slaps at me with his tongue, and when I finally push him off, he jumps at me again.

This starts a series of more "sits," which he ignores, another jump at me I try to turn away from, and his paw rakes over my back, scratching grooves into my skin that hurt like hell. At six and a half months old and sixty-seven pounds, it's clear Atticus is going to be a big boy. I should do a better job of getting him calmer once he's out of the kennel, but there's a part of me that secretly likes this onslaught.

Never in my life has anyone been so happy to see me.

"Come on," I say after I push him down for the third time. "Let's go get potties."

Atti's ears perk forward and he prances toward the door, looking at me to ensure I'm coming, too. He has to pee, but he doesn't want me to be out of his sight either.

It takes less than half an hour for me to take care of Atticus, which includes his dinner, then change my clothes and drop him off with Oley in his living room so he can watch the early news. He's cocked back in his recliner, and I know his hip has to be hurting him. I've been trying to get Oley to see a doctor about it, but he says it's arthritis and there's nothing they can do.

"You're leaving already?" Oley asks in surprise as he looks away from the TV. Atticus jumps on the couch, making himself right at home. The first time he did it, I yelled at him to get off, but Oley was fine with it. He told me all the dogs he'd had over his lifetime were always welcome on furniture.

"I'm going to stop by Charmin's," I say.

He nods in understanding.

"Okay… I'll be back by six thirty with Bernard and pizza in hand," I tell him. "Anything else you want?"

"I'm good," Oley says, settling his attention back on the TV.

This has become our Friday night tradition since Bernard came to join us for 4th of July a few weeks ago. The two men got along well, bonding in their shared hilarity over Atticus eating the pound cake. They both share a love of baseball—Oley follows the Braves and Bernard the Phillies as he's from Philadelphia original- ly—but they'll watch any game. So regardless of who is playing on Friday night, I'll go pick Bernard up, grab a pizza, and come back to the farm where we'll all watch baseball.

Rather, they'll watch baseball and I'll play around on my phone. I'm deep into Angry Birds and deter- mined to get three stars on every level.

As I maneuver the country roads that will lead me out to Highway 17, I consider what I learned about Charmin and contemplate my struggle with going to see her. Bernard told me last week as we were munching on pizza and drinking PBR—Oley stuck with iced tea—

that she told him to tell me hello. I grimaced when he said that, because I'm obviously still sore at her.

Bernard regarded me with those dark eyes. "She's really sorry about what happened, Hazel."

"I'm sure she is," I clipped out, flinging a yellow triangle-shaped bird at the horde of green pigs mocking me on my phone.

"She broke up with Chuck the week after you left," he added.

"Good for her," I said vaguely. "He was a douche."

"Language," Oley chastised, but we both ignored him.

"I witnessed the breakup," Bernard said and that got my attention. I looked up from my screen. "It was very loud and very public, right there in Tipsy's. She pretty much broke up with him because of what he did to you and Atticus."

That mollified me a bit, and I've been stewing on it since. I was really hurt Charmin hadn't stood up to Chuck when he said Atticus had to go, especially since she knew it meant I'd have to go, too.

But there's a part of me that absolutely gets why Charmin sided with Chuck. She's a lot like me... sees her value tied up with a man. As much as it shames me to admit it, it's perhaps something I might have done if this situation were reversed.

What really made up my mind, though, is one simple undeniable truth. What happened to me that night Chuck said I had to go, and me subsequently getting fired, was actually one of the best things that has ever happened to me. These past months working for Oley have given me confidence. It's built up my badly wounded self-esteem. I've realized I'm worth more than just the title of "wife" to a man who didn't value me.

In addition, as I discover ways in which I'm changing for the better, I'm realizing the people I surrounded myself with tended to change me for the worse. I'm not sure at what point in my life I became an absolute doormat, but I know I let it happen.

But more than all of these new realizations about myself is the one thing that changed it all.

Atticus.

Having responsibility for him gave me purpose. Seeing the way he loves me for who I am and nothing more makes me realize there are many types of love in this world, and I wasn't searching for the right type.

The unconditional type.

So yeah… how can I still be mad at Charmin when I am right where I'm supposed to be and I'm loving my life right now?

Or, another way to look at it… had Charmin stood up for me that night, I'd probably still be sleeping on her couch and working a dead-end job while I hid my dog in the storeroom.

I make it to Charmin's apartment by six. She'll be getting ready for her shift at Tipsy's, so I won't stay long. She doesn't have much room in her primp schedule for an extended visit.

She opens the door, greeting me with a bashful, surprised smile.

"Hey," I say casually with my hands shoved into the front pockets of my shorts.

"Hey," she says, gaze briefly going to our feet before popping back up. And then she gushes, "I am so sorry, Hazel. Chuck was such an ass, and I can't believe I ever even thought I was in love with that guy. I kicked him out."

"Bernard told me," I say with a nod. We just stand there and stare at each other. Finally, I say, "Going to let me in?"

Charmin slaps her palm to her forehead. "Sure."

She steps back, and I enter the apartment where I'd lived for a while. My first step in pulling myself up after Darren knocked me down low.

"Want something to drink?" she asks. She's in her bathrobe, her hair wet.

I shake my head and motion to the couch. "I know you've got to get ready for work, but why don't we just sit and chat a bit?"

"Okay," she says nervously.

We situate ourselves on opposite ends of the

couch—also known as my former bed. Charmin tucks her legs underneath herself, warily eyeing me.

I give her a comforting smile. "It's okay, Charmin. About what happened. I just wanted you to know I'm not mad about it, and I get it. And honestly... I have never been happier in my life."

Charmin practically sags in relief, her face lighting up. "Bernard told me you were a veterinary assistant."

I laugh at the title. "Something like that. I pretty much do whatever my boss needs, but I'm definitely learning about veterinary medicine."

"And how is Atticus?" she asks, her voice sentimentally soft.

"Oh, my God," I gush as I pull my phone out and unlock it. "He's so big now. Sixty-seven pounds."

"Holy shit," she exclaims, sliding closer to sit next to me as I pull my photos up. I start scrolling through, catching her up on everything Atticus.

They're in reverse order, and I give her a little explanation.

"I just took this one this morning. Look how big his paws are."

"Oh, here's the one where he ate our freaking pound cake a few weeks ago. Took the heavy pan right off the counter and set it on the floor before he gorged. Asshole dog."

Even though I was mad at him, I still took pictures

of him to memorialize how unrepentant he was.

"And look at this… the way he sleeps in bed on his back."

I flip to another picture. "This is a good one… sitting at the fence of the cow pasture, watching the cows. He never even barks at them."

I go on and on, and Charmin oohs and aahs. She laughs at my stories when I tell her how destructive he's been. We both agree it was probably a good thing Chuck kicked us out when he did.

Slyly, she says, "In hindsight, I'm glad he took a shit in Chuck's shoe. I hope it still stinks."

My wicked smile tops her sly look. I tell her in a conspiratorial voice despite the fact no one can hear us, "I swear to God, Charmin… he did it on purpose. He knew how to scratch at the door to go out and poop. I saw the look on his face, and I'm not kidding… he knew what he was doing."

We both crack up laughing.

Then Charmin sobers a bit, takes my hand, and squeezes it. "If Atticus knew what he was doing, then he surely knew it would get you two booted. Maybe Atticus was put in your life so that exact scenario would happen to force you into a new life. One you were meant to have."

"You mean like fate or something?" I ask. As loony as that sounds, it also sounds… right.

Charmin shrugs. "I don't understand that philosophical shit. I just think you are in a good place because of that dog."

"Agreed." The time on my phone catches my attention. "Shit… I've really overstayed. I have to get going."

"Okay." We both rise from the couch, and she walks me to the door. Before I reach for the knob, she touches my shoulder. "There's something you need to know, Hazel."

I turn to face her. "What's that?"

"Darren has been by a few times looking for you," she says, and my stomach pitches slightly. I'd like to say I don't think of Darren anymore, but that would be a lie. There's always something that makes me think of him on a daily basis.

"What does he want?" I ask.

"He never said. And I didn't tell him where you were. I knew you were working at the clinic because Bernard told me, but I didn't know if you wanted to see him or not."

"He probably wants to serve me with divorce papers or something," I say thoughtfully. I realize… it doesn't make me sad.

Doesn't make me happy either, but I'm not crushed by the imminent end of my marriage. I think that's definite validation that my self-esteem has become strong and stable.

"I better give him a call," I say. "Might as well get this all over with."

She nods, and then surprises me with a hard hug. I squeeze her back. "Want to get together sometime? Maybe dinner?"

"Sure," I reply. "That would be nice."

And it would. I've forgiven her, and she's still very much my friend.

CHAPTER 25

Hazel

A RIVULET OF sweat trickles down my back to disappear under the band of my shorts. Droplets fall from my forehead and splash onto my hands as I pull weeds out of the flower bed that borders the front porch of Oley's house. It's barely ten in the morning, but it's already hotter than the burning fires of hell.

The front door opens first, then the screen with a loud squeak. Atticus comes barreling out with Oley hobbling on his cane behind him. His limp has seemed worse the last few days.

Atticus bounds down the three porch steps to me with tail wagging and eyes rolling. He'd been enjoying the cool air conditioning with Oley while I got my yard chores done. Atticus starts licking my face, more from enjoyment of the salty sweat than any true affection. He's a dog that will give a kiss or two in greeting when he's excited to see me, but this continual licking that now extends to my neck and left shoulder is going too far.

"Get off, you big doofus," I say as I swat him away. He ignores me and lunges his head forward, his big rough tongue catching me along my nose. I go from my hands and knees to my haunches, which gives me better leverage to push Atticus away.

He finally takes the hint, running onto the porch where the shade is minutely cooler. I consider forcing him back inside since it's so hot out here, but a few minutes won't overheat him, and I'm almost done with my task. With the back of my hand, I wipe off my sweaty face, wincing at the feel of the gritty dirt I'm leaving behind. After a few unsteady steps, Oley sits heavily in one of the rockers right in front of the flower bed I'm working on.

Oley has never made the extra work I do for him around here a condition of me being able to live here so cheaply. The only price he ever requested was the two hundred a month he originally set. But I know he's giving me such a good bargain that I don't mind doing this stuff for him. There's no way in hell a man at his age, with his physical limitations, can get down here in the dirt and pull weeds. Plus, I know that the pretty flowers neatly maintained bring him joy, so this is what I do every Saturday morning.

"Looks good," Oley observes as he starts a slow rock in the chair. Atticus flops down beside him, and Oley drapes his non-cane arm over to scratch his back for a few minutes.

"If I do it weekly, it's not so hard," I say as I go back to pulling weeds. I toss them over my shoulder onto the grass. I'll rake them up when I'm done, and then take them out to the burn pile. The first time I'd raked up grass clippings for Oley and asked where his waste bags were so we could set them out by the road for pickup, he laughed at me.

"That's not how we do things in the country," he'd said with an almost imperious look down his nose at me. "We burn things."

And truthfully, it's really fun to burn things, so I never mind adding to the burn pile.

"How'd things go with Charmin last night?" he asks. He hadn't had a chance to ask me when we'd returned with the pizza. We all ate, then him and Bernard watched the game. I'd fallen asleep on the couch, waking up to find the game over and Oley's car gone. He must have taken Bernard home.

"It was good." I look up briefly, giving him a smile before going back to my work. "We're going to try to get together some time soon."

Oley doesn't ask anything further. He's not nosy and all up in my business. Never has been.

Doesn't mean I don't volunteer some stuff because let's face it... Oley's my closest friend and he's given me a lot of wise counsel in the past.

"She told me Darren's been looking for me." Pausing my weeding, I sit back on my haunches, peeking at him through the porch rails. "I guess to serve divorce papers or something."

"How's that make you feel?" he asks, gauging the impact it's having on me before he offers anything.

I shrug. "I don't feel much of anything about it."

"If that's truly the case, then just give him a call and get it done with."

"Well, yeah… that's the easy thing to do except it's not easy," I reply as I go back to the weeding. "I mean… we were married for six years."

"And he cheated on you and kicked you out," he reminds me pointedly.

I wince. It still hurts to be reminded of it. But it also makes my blood boil, and my head snaps up to look at Oley. "You know what… I do feel something. I feel pissed off, and don't call me on my language."

Oley chuckles. "Give him hell when you call him, Hazel… but sign the papers. You don't need him."

"That's the truth." I give him a saucy wink before I get back down to it. I start yanking weeds with more vigor, imagining Darren's head in the middle of each one I rip from the ground.

"Tara called a bit ago," Oley says hesitantly. When I look up at him, he's got his head turned and gaze focused over the side yard rather than at me. That tells me whatever he's getting ready to say is causing him some difficulty. Like most humans, we have a hard time looking others in the eye when things get tough.

"Oh, yeah?" I ask lightly.

Tara is his daughter. She's a yoga instructor in Raleigh and her husband Will is an attorney. They have a seventeen-year-old daughter named Abigail, which was Oley's wife's middle name. I've not met them yet. In the three months I've been living here, Tara and her family haven't come to visit even though Raleigh is just a few hours away.

I try not to let that color my opinion about Oley's daughter, but it kills me when I hear Oley talking to her on the phone and he'll hopefully ask, "Think y'all could come for a visit one weekend?"

Then he'll remain silent for several minutes while Tara tells him exactly how busy their lives are and how they can't. She'll then offer for him to come to Raleigh to visit them, to which Oley declines. I'm not sure if he just can't make the trip on his own, or if he's just discouraged.

"She wanted to let me know they're doing Thanksgiving at Cameron's house this year, and wanted to make sure I put it on the calendar."

"Huh," I say noncommittally, and his gaze comes back to mine. Cameron is Oley's son. He's some bigwig at a bank in Charlotte, and his wife spends her days playing tennis at the country club. He talks to his father less than Tara does.

"I told her I couldn't make that type of trip on my own." He says that casually... in a matter-of-fact manner. Oddly, his eyes don't appear troubled at all. Perhaps I misjudged the difficulty of this conversation.

Oley doesn't offer anything else.

But I do. "Would you like me to drive you there?" I ask hesitantly. Charlotte is a good five-plus hours away.

I expect relief to overtake his expression. Instead, he cuts his gaze back out to the side yard, pointedly refusing to look me in the eye.

I don't have time for this. My back is aching, I'm hot and sweaty, and little stones are digging in my knees. "What's wrong, Oley?"

"Nothing's wrong," he snaps. "I just thought... that perhaps we could do Thanksgiving here at the house if you didn't have any plans. Invite Bernard, of course."

My jaw drops open, but I hurriedly close it again. My lips curve upward into a smile. "I think that's a great idea. I can cook a turkey, and we'll have all the classic sides. But... are you sure you don't want to go spend it with your kids?"

Oley shakes his head, and his eyes turn a little sad. "They don't bother to come visit me, so why should I bother to go visit them?"

It's a fair point. Plus, Oley's not in the greatest of

health. Driving that distance would be hard on him.

"I wasn't sure if perhaps you had plans with your family," he says uneasily. That's when I realize the source of his uncertainty over Thanksgiving. He has no clue if my family is in play or not.

Standing from the flower bed, I brush dirt and bits of mulch off my knees, remove the gardening gloves, and place them on the porch railing that separates me from Oley. "Why would you think I had plans with my family?"

"I wasn't sure," he says cautiously. "You never talk about them. You told me early on your dad was dead and your mom and sister live around the area, but that you're not close. I didn't bother to ask more, because well… not all families are close. Look at my kids, who can't even be bothered to come visit me to make sure I'm okay or not."

I nod in understanding, suffering from the guilt that I live less than fifteen minutes from my mom, but I don't go see her. My sister lives a bit further north of town, but it's not prohibitive to me if I wanted to visit her. I just… can't.

Putting them out of my mind because it makes me feel wretched to think about them, I brush off Oley's worry. "They wouldn't expect me there, so I'd love to cook for you and Bernard. Can we invite Charmin, too?"

"Of course we can," Oley assures me. "Would you

like to invite your mom and sister?"

I scratch at the back of my head, focusing on Atticus. "They wouldn't want to."

"Why not?" he asks, leaning forward in the rocking chair.

I don't answer.

Can't for that matter.

My throat has a lump of guilt and embarrassment preventing any words.

Oley raps the end of his cane against the railing. "Why not, Hazel?" he pushes.

I guess he's decided to poke all up in my business.

Atticus is almost eye level with me through the porch rails. He's watching with interest from underneath those brown eyebrows. His eyes are pinned on me now, the blue truth teller lasering into me. I feel like he'd know if I lied. Oley might not, but even though dogs can't understand much of the English language, I still think he'd know.

With a sigh, I step out of the flower bed and head up to the porch. I step over my dog to take the rocker to Oley's left. He shifts his weight and turns to look at me.

Atticus pushes up from his spot on the other side of Oley to sit right before me. He pushes his head into my stomach, demanding I pet him.

Which I do because he's like my security blanket.

My zen.

My doggie Xanax.

CHAPTER 26

Atticus

I MIGHT NOT understand the full language Hazel and Oley speak, but coupled with facial expressions, tone, and body language, I know a lot more than they give me credit for.

My human needs me, so I give her my head to pet. It's hot as blazes out here and the air conditioning inside calls to me, but this is more important right now.

Hazel blows out a hard breath that gusts warmly over the top of my head. "My dad died three years ago. It was sudden… a brain aneurysm. I hadn't talked to him for almost seven months before he died. Not because I hated him, or he was a bad person, or a horrible father. But because he was disappointed in how I turned out, and I couldn't stand to see it in his eyes."

Right there… not sure the deeper meaning behind what Hazel just said, but I sense sadness and guilt. Her fingers work behind my ears, not because I need it but because she does.

"I'm not following, Hazel," Oley says gently.

Hazel leans back in her chair which frees my face that had been pressed into her. She stares down at me while she rubs behind my ears in a way that makes my back legs shake. I return her look, feeling no pressure or compulsion to blink away the sadness gazing back at me. I could stare at her for hours, but my preference would be for her to happy.

She turns her head to look at Oley, her fingers still digging down into those little muscles right behind my ears. "I left home when I turned eighteen, three months shy of graduating high school. I was boy crazy... well, over a certain boy, you understand. My parents were horrified I'd dropped out of school. Tremendously disappointed in me. They ranted and yelled, telling me I was stupid to do something like that and I'd regret it one day. That a boy wasn't more important than finishing school."

"But you didn't listen to them?" he surmises.

"Nope," she replies with a grimace, and I can feel the self-hatred radiating off her. It makes me whine just a little. She spares me just a brief glance, a little smile to reassure me, and continues. "And of course, they were right. Without getting into the details of how I continually messed up, let's just say I went from bad relationship to bad relationship with no direction or aim in life other than to just be needed by a man. I worked in bars and partied."

"But you still had some type of relationship with them," Oley guesses. "I mean… you left school what… thirteen years ago? But you said your dad died three years ago, and you'd talked to him seven months prior."

"I left home fourteen years ago," she corrects. "And yes… I still had a relationship with my parents and sister. It was very tenuous, and I often didn't show up on their doorstep unless I needed money or something. My parents always opened the door to me, though. They were disappointed and wished for better things for me, but they loved me no less. I know that, which just makes me feel even more guilty for the poor choices I made."

"Doesn't mean you can't get it back," Oley suggests. "If they love you, the door will still be open."

"It would be," Hazel replies confidently. It's the tone of voice I hear from her most often these days, and I like it. "If I went to my mom's house right now, she'd open that door wide to let me in."

"But—" Oley prods.

"But," Hazel says with a sad smile, her eyes getting wet. I smell the salt in them before I see it, and it makes me sad. Jumping on her, I put my forearms on her thighs. I lick at her face, making those tears go away.

Hazel chuckles and gives me a hard hug, probably just to stop the licking. Then she pushes me back down to a sit before her.

She looks to Oley. "I can't. I just can't do it. When my dad died, and I sat down and did the math... that it had been seven months since I'd bothered to talk to any of them, I was so ashamed of myself. For my selfishness, that I would go about life as if they didn't matter, and for how horribly I took them for granted. I was so worthless as a daughter and a sister that I didn't deserve to be with them. In a way, I think a lot like Bernard... that they're better off without me."

"Hazel," Oley says softly, his eyes pools of sorrow and empathy. I wait for the wetness to come to his eyes, poised ready to jump and lick if necessary.

"I made my bed," Hazel says resolutely. "I've accepted the consequences of how I treated them."

"What about your sister?" he asks.

My other senses kick in, and I swear I can feel the heat coming off Hazel as her face turns red. My body quivers with the unmistakable need to jump on her. Cover her up. Chase away the pure shame I'm feeling radiating off her. There are not many times I feel guilty about the bad things I do, but on those infrequent occasions when I know I really let Hazel down with my antics, it's not a pleasant feeling to have.

Hazel clears her throat. "Liz gave birth last year to my nephew, Benji. It was her first child. Her husband is a marine."

Oley nods as he leans a little more out of his chair and closer to Hazel. This must be very important, so I drop my head and lay it on her thighs. Her hand automatically comes to my head, where she just rests it there.

For support.

Just as I meant her to.

"I showed up at the hospital drunk," she says in a quiet voice lesser canines wouldn't be able to hear. "Stoned, too, for that matter. I'd been partying with some friends when my mom called to tell me Liz had the baby. She could tell I wasn't sober and asked me not to come to the hospital. To make a long story short, I didn't listen. I showed up and made an ugly scene when Liz wouldn't let me near the baby. I haven't talked to her since."

"Not because you're angry at her, but because you're ashamed of how you behaved," Oley says, his voice very un-Oley like in its tenderness.

I love Oley.

Hazel nods, but I can tell she doesn't want to meet Oley's eyes. So she grabs onto the fur at the sides of my head, just below my jaw, and gives me a gentle tug to pull my attention to her. Little does she know but my attention was never anywhere else.

I give her my best smile—the one where my tongue hangs out the side of my mouth and my bottom teeth peek out.

Hazel laughs, and that makes me feel good.

"You're not that person now," Oley states.

Hazel meets his gaze, but only for a moment. When she looks back at me, she leans in close and seems to be staring at just my left eye. "I'm not ready to seek their forgiveness. I am different, but I'm just not ready."

Oley nods, leaning over and patting Hazel on the shoulder. "I get it. But don't wait too long. Life is too short."

I can feel Hazel's pain over what Oley just said. Feel it bloom within her chest and it makes my chest hurt. I whine to let her know I feel her emotions very much, and I don't like it at all.

She gives me a smile before pressing her lips to the top of my snout.

CHAPTER 27

Hazel

IN ABOUT THREE months—October 27th to be exact—it will be my seventh wedding anniversary with Darren. It's when Hazel Marie Milton became Hazel Marie Roundtree. I'd known him all of about three weeks before he asked me to marry him, and I said yes. I didn't know it then, but I know it now.

I was so damn stupid.

Twenty-five years old and agreeing to marry someone I hardly knew.

But in fairness to me, Darren *was* different than the others. It's humiliating to think about it, especially given the fact he was unfaithful to me, but Darren and I met when we were both "with someone else".

Mine was not a serious relationship, although I wanted it to be. His name was John—Johnny—or was it Jim? I liked him a lot. I saw a future with him.

Just like I did with every guy that gave me a measure of affection and attention.

Because I wasn't getting enough from John/Johnny/Jim and because it had become my pattern to look for love everywhere and all the time, Darren's attention had an impact on me.

It was real attention. He came into the bar where I was working at the time, and he'd sit there for hours just for the chance to talk to me for a few minutes here and there when I could take the time. He didn't just talk about himself. He asked questions about me that seemed ridiculous, but showed he wanted all the details.

Hazel, do you prefer walnuts or pecans in your brownies?

What's the worst nightmare you ever had?

What would your dream job be?

After two weeks of getting to know each other through silly questions and snatches of conversation while I bartended, Darren offered to drive me home one night. John/Johnny/Jim was out with the boys, and I accepted.

I had sex with Darren that night, and it was amazing. He cuddled me, and we talked for a long time. He told me he had been seeing another woman, but that he was going to call it off. He wanted me to do the same.

Yes, so very shameful I cheated on someone to be with Darren, and I have to think that means I deserved the same at some point, right? It's about the only way I can reconcile why Darren did this to me.

I had it coming.

Which is why I'm also reconciled to get this meeting over with, so I can move on completely. I'd called Darren a week ago last Saturday. It was right after I'd finished weeding Oley's flower bed and we'd had our "cleansing" sort of talk about my family. It felt good to get that off my chest, and to tell him about what a terrible daughter and sister I was.

Ironically, the only other person who really understood how fucked up my relationship with my family is was Darren. But he was my husband, after all. He deserved to know my secrets.

Darren was hesitant and uncomfortable during our short phone talk. He wouldn't come right out and say why he wanted to see me. I assume it's because he's a coward, and he just doesn't have the guts to say he wants the divorce.

Regardless I agreed to meet him for coffee this morning at Starbucks. We would have met sooner, but he was out of town on a work assignment. He's a subcontractor for the cable company doing commercial installations, so he goes wherever they tell him to.

As was typical in our marriage, I'm five minutes early and I know Darren will be ten minutes late. I sip at my coffee, scrolling through Instagram. Charmin had told me I simply had to create an account to post pictures of Atticus and all of his shenanigans.

I admit... he's turning into a seriously beautiful Bernese Mountain Dog. He clearly comes from very good stock. I don't necessarily buy Oley's thought he was dumped by the breeder because of a tiny flaw such as bi-colored eyes. He's simply too beautiful otherwise. Besides, I can't imagine people who go to the trouble of breeding could ever be that cruel to animals.

At least that's my new way of thinking. Old, pessimistic Hazel would have believed Atticus had been dumped, but these days I like to believe in the good of things.

I scan through some of my photos of Atticus. There are hundreds and hundreds, all of them seeming to convey something different. It's those damn brown eyebrows against velvety black that can create such a mimicry of human expression.

The day I'd created his Instagram account was the day of The Great Toilet Paper Incident. I should have known not to leave him alone, not even for the sixty seconds it took me to run down to Oley's kitchen to borrow some—as cliché as it sounds—sugar. I was making another pound cake.

Sixty seconds.

Might have been even shorter. And besides, he'd been really good for a few weeks. Obedient and less stubborn. I thought perhaps he was maturing.

When I walked back into the apartment, I realized

my dog would always be an unruly child. I couldn't even believe what I was seeing. Toilet paper everywhere. Streams and streams, but I saw no end or beginning. Ribbons of it leading from the bathroom into the living room, where it was all over the floor in a circular pattern, over the coffee table, and right to… Atticus.

Standing on the couch, mischief and mayhem blazing in his eyes. His tail wagging, his mouth grinning, and the end of the toilet paper roll in his mouth.

My first reaction?

I snagged my phone, whipped the camera out, and took pictures of it all while laughing my ass off. Atticus grinned and wagged his tail, elated that he delighted me with his bad behavior. If there's a reason why I can't teach him to be good all the time is because most of the time, I can't chastise him because I'm laughing too hard.

Yes, after The Great Toilet Paper Incident, the Instagram account @atticuscrazydog was born.

I flip through some of the more recent photos I'd posted. His various facial expressions. Some of his destruction—an old pillow on the couch he chewed to pieces just last week when I'd fallen asleep for a nap. He's an absolute menace, and I've decided to embrace it rather than fight it. I still work on his obedience, and he proves time and again he's got a brilliant mind.

But I've also accepted he has his own mind, and it's stubborn, mischievous, and ornery. He does what he wants, when he wants.

No regrets.

"Hazel..." It's Darren's voice, and my head lifts slowly. I can't say he ever made my blood race with excitement or passion, but my heart does squeeze in sorrow because he fulfilled my need to be loved.

"Hey," I say as I sit my phone down on the table I'd chosen in a corner. He's empty handed, so I politely offer, "Would you like some coffee or something?"

He shakes his head, pulling the chair out opposite of me. His gaze comes to mine, and he just stares at me for a long, thoughtful moment.

"You look good," he finally says.

It's a compliment he would have given me in the past, causing me to fluff my hair and give him a shy smile while saying, "No, I don't," so he'd be forced to repeat the words to assure me I did. It was an awful game I used to play to help build my confidence.

My hands remain steady and lightly clasped on the table. With a smile, I cut to the chase. "So why did you want to meet?"

"I wanted to see how you were doing." His gaze never wavers, which means he's telling the truth. Darren, like many, can't look me in the eye when he lies.

When I confronted him about the woman he was screwing behind my back, he immediately dropped his eyes to stare at the floor and said, "I swear it's not true."

"I'm doing very well. And how are you?"

He sort of jerks a little, perhaps caught off guard by my bland politeness. Maybe he came braced to receive tears and pleading from me. Our eyes lock, and I don't let myself blink.

Darren gives a sigh, his gaze cutting out the window for a moment before coming back to me. "Actually... I'm not doing well at all. I miss you."

Okay... so now I blink.

A lot.

And my mouth parts in surprise. "Excuse me?"

"I miss you," he repeats, reaching across the table to grab my hand in his. "I want you to come home, Hazel. I made a terrible mistake, and I want to fix our marriage."

Pulling my hand free of his, I put it on my lap with my other. I do this not only so he can't hold my hand, but also so he can't see he's rattled me so much they are now shaking.

"I don't understand." My voice comes out thick and raspy.

"What's not to understand?" His voice is slightly teasing, a roguish smile playing at his lips. It's how he first ensnared me.

That smile of his.

I don't smile back. "What I mean is you cheated on

me... kicked me out of our home... chose another woman over me, and now... you say you miss me?"

Darren's face flushes red but to his credit, his gaze never wavers. "And I'll never be able to apologize enough for it, Hazel. It was a stupid, cowardly, and asinine thing to do. I wish I had an excuse to offer you, but I don't. I can only offer my apology, which is from the deepest part of my heart. I love you, Hazel, and I'm just so sorry."

I'm stunned into silence. Of all the things I thought would go down here today, Darren apologizing and telling me he missed me isn't one of them.

"I've learned one thing over these past months," he continues, and his additional words put me on edge. I learned stuff, too, but I'm not sure I want to know what his enlightenment is all about. I'm afraid it would diminish mine in some way.

When I don't respond... don't give him any indication I'm on the edge of my seat to hear his wisdom, he gives me a sad smile. "Don't you want to know what I learned?"

"I'm not sure," I croak, and then immediately pick up my coffee to take a sip. Something to unclog the dryness of my throat.

Darren gives a tiny, sardonic laugh as his eyes roam over my face. "Christ, Hazel... you look like a scared rabbit ready to bolt. Did I break you that much?"

There was a day I was a meek, scared rabbit.

There was also a time he had broken me. I remember the feel of the first crack, when I slept in my car the night I found myself kicked out of my home.

I lift my chin. "I'm not scared. And yes, Darren. You broke me. But I'm rebuilt now, and I don't need your apologies."

"Yes, you do," he replies softly as he rubs his hand over his scruffy face. He always looked best when he didn't shave for a few days. "You need them and more than that, you deserve them. What you do with them is up to you."

"Well, thank you," I say primly as my hands circle around my coffee cup. "That was big of you."

"You *are* rebuilt," he says appreciatively, eyes once again roaming all over me. "You look like the same, Hazel, but you are absolutely different. What have you been doing?"

"I've been learning to survive, Darren," I snap. "I have survived. Without you."

His words are soft and melancholy. "I can see that."

The conversation stalls, and we both focus out the window so we don't have to acknowledge the heavy emotion in each other's eyes. I'm not sure what his absolute end game is, and I don't have all day for him to get up the courage to tell me.

"I really need to get going.'" I pull my cup into me

while grabbing my phone with my other hand.

"Can I see you again?" he blurts.

"Why?" I ask bluntly.

"Do you not feel anything for me at all, Hazel?"

That didn't answer my question, so I just wait him out. I'm not ready to admit to myself, much less to him, that yes... I still feel something. All the same insecurities that were an innate part of me rise, swell, and almost choke me. I'm having a hard time remembering I don't need Darren to make me feel better about myself.

He sighs when he realizes I won't give him anything. Leaning forward slightly, he focuses on my face, his eyes piercing. "I want you back, plain and simple."

That's interesting. It begs the question... "Where is *she*?"

Another bright red flush of embarrassment coats Darren's face. He swallows hard. "We're not together anymore."

"When?" I demand, because I'll be damned if I'm going to be a rebound for him. That would be almost more insulting than him cheating on me and kicking me out of our house.

"Almost three months ago," he says quietly, causing my entire body to jerk in surprise. That was not long after I'd moved into Oley's apartment.

"Three months?"

He nods. "I asked her to leave."

"Say her name," I demand.

His cheeks burn with redness. "Delia."

"You asked Delia to leave three months ago?" I ask for clarification.

"Yes."

"Did you move anyone else in?"

"No."

My brows furrow inward. "Why didn't you try to find me then?"

Darren gives a mirthless laugh. "Come on, Hazel. You know what it's like to be so ashamed of yourself that you're not willing to put yourself out there to others. It's why you don't see your mom or sister."

Now my face is the one flushed hot with humiliation. He's right about that, and I can understand him keeping distance from me.

"Then why now?" I need to understand his motivations.

There's a moment where I think he might not answer, or that he might let his gaze drop from mine, which will mean he's lying. But he gives me the courtesy of responding while keeping eye contact. "Because I'm tired of missing you. Tired of feeling guilty. At the very least, I had to make sure you were okay."

"Well, I am," I assure him quickly.

"I can see that," he acknowledges. "Do you think we could get together to talk again sometime? At your convenience? It can be for coffee again, or I could take you out to dinner. We could drive to the beach and walk. Remember how much we loved to do that?"

"Don't," I whisper as I stand up from the table, palming my phone and ignoring my coffee. "Don't try to bring up memories to me. I've moved on."

"Then friends," he says as he stands up and tucks his hand in his pockets. "Can we get coffee sometime... as friends?"

"That's probably not a good idea." Nervously, I reach into my pocket and pull out the Impala's keys.

"Think about it?" he asks, stepping into my path so I can't move from the corner we're in. "Please, Hazel. You don't owe me a damn thing but a slap in the face or a kick in the balls, and I'll be glad to let you do both. But will you please just think about having coffee with me some time in the future at your convenience?"

I stare at him, taking internal stock of how I'm feeling in this moment. There's no hate or love. No sadness or joy. No unrelenting need to make him suffer, and certainly no desire on my part to hear pretty words from him.

I could walk away right now and not look back.

Which is why I totally don't understand when I say, "I'll think about it."

CHAPTER 28

Hazel

"**A**RE YOU SURE you want to do this?" Charmin asks hesitantly as she stands behind me in her bathroom. She's slightly taller than I am, so she easily can see my reflection from the mirror over the sink.

Reaching up, I pull a long lock of hair away from my face and hold it out. About six inches of brown followed by another six inches of blonde. When I'd been with Darren, he'd preferred me as a blonde and so... I was a blonde.

When he kicked me out, there was no room for the luxury of hair lightening products. Not even the cheap bleaches, and besides... I really didn't care what I looked like for a long period of time. The past six months, I've worn my hair in a ponytail, often doubled under so not much of the brittle blonde showed.

I examine the box of color I'd picked up at the drug store. Charmin helped me, and I think we picked one as close to my natural color as possible.

Atticus is laying in the hallway in his froggy position with his head resting on his front paws. He watches us with interest, wondering if perhaps there's a treat in the box I'm holding.

"You know women pay a lot of money for this look," Charmin says as she eyeballs my reflection critically. "They call it ombre."

I snort. "It looks ghetto."

Charmin gives me a cocked eyebrow. "Are you doing this for Darren?"

Pivoting to face her so fast my hair swings out and slaps her in the face, I assure her, "Absolutely not."

"That's an awful big protest your lodging," she teases.

I shove the box into her chest, and she grabs it while snickering at me.

I glare. "Just shut up and color my hair. And besides… Darren liked me blonde."

Charmin takes me into the kitchen, making me sit me down at the table as the bathroom is too tight and confined. Atticus flops down over near the window air conditioner, now dubiously regarding the bottle of formula Charmin's putting in my hair. He gave it a sniff when she opened it, sneezed six times, and then staked a position away from the nasty-smelling stuff.

"What's going on with Darren?" Charmin asks as she works the locks of my hair, using gloved hands to protect herself and a towel around my shoulders for the same. "Are you going to go out with him?"

"I don't know. He's been awful persistent, that's for sure."

Since our meeting for coffee just two weeks ago, he's sent me flowers four times and has texted me nonstop, always in the morning to say he hopes I have a wonderful day. The cards with the flowers have been benign and not overtly pressuring. Things like "Because you deserve these," and "Hope these brighten your day."

He texts me random questions, trying to learn more about the new Hazel. I want to ignore it all, but it's hard to.

Darren is trying to court me, something he never had to do before. We fell into lust, then love, much of our early relationship fueled by booze and pot. Twice he's asked me out for coffee, and twice I've declined. Politely, of course.

It's not that I'm not interested, because there is some interest. He's my husband, and he made a mistake. We have a history, and there was love. He's apologized, and I think he's truly regretful. I've even accepted his apology. The interest I have is in being with a life partner again. Someone to share burdens and laughter with. Someone who has my back.

It would be very, very easy to go back to that. Sure, I'd lose a little bit of self-respect, but no one ever said marriage was easy.

But then I focus on that self-respect thing, and it's a big deal for me. I've only learned how to respect myself in the past several months. It's so new I don't want to fall back into old habits. Every day I wake up, I wonder how I can better myself and my life. I work every day to make it happen.

"What do you think I should do?" I ask.

"Honestly?"

"No," I reply with a heavy dose of sarcasm in my tone. "I want you to lie to me."

"Then I'd tell you to take him back."

We both laugh for a moment, but then she adds, "I think you're doing very well by yourself, and I get you're a forgiving person, Hazel. But I'm sorry... he kicked you out and moved another woman in. He broke your heart, not even giving a damn whether you were surviving. I get he had some quick remorse and realized the mistake, but in my opinion, that's not something you can ever overcome. I think your marriage will always be marred by it to such an extent that it's going to fail at some point."

"That's kind of how I feel." I'd been thinking about this a lot because Darren was doing such an impressive job of getting my attention with the flowers and texts. "But I don't want to miss something either. That one possibility that if I'd just give it a chance, maybe something great could come of it. Like maybe we could talk about having kids or something."

She clucks her tongue chidingly. "Zebras don't change their stripes, Hazel."

"I know," I mutter.

Darren never wanted kids, and it's something I've always dreamed of. I guess I assumed he'd change his mind over time, but he never did.

"What do Oley and Bernard think?" she asks.

Funny that she should bring it up. We had a huge discussion about it this past Friday over baseball and pizza. Charmin hasn't had the privilege of joining us on Friday nights since she works, but she proclaimed that during football season, we were doing tacos and football at Oley's house. I haven't told him and Bernard about it, but I like the idea and I don't want to lose what good we've built with Bernard. He's actually developing a routine with friends.

"Bernard says I should cut ties and run." While she doesn't know him the way I do, I've filled her in a bit on Bernard and his background.

"I could see that."

Yeah, it's what I would have expected of a man who walked out on his family because life got hard for him. I know that's a harsh view of Bernard's situation, and I am not without sympathy, but I see how Bernard is with me, Oley, and other people he interacts with. He has so much to offer his family. I know he doesn't think so, but he's so very wrong about it.

"And Oley?" Charmin prods.

"He's more traditional." When I asked Oley his opinion, he stroked his chin a good long while contemplating his answer to me. I know the fact I asked his advice was important to him, and he wanted to make sure that what he told me wouldn't be a bunch of hot air. "He doesn't see the harm in giving it a shot. But he says I should ease into it slowly, and perhaps just date for a bit."

"So you've been given three opinions." I can feel her gathering my hair up, wrapping it in a wet, thick bun on top of my head. She secures it with a clip. "But what do you think you should do?"

"There's no easy answer."

"There is… it's called listening to your gut," she challenges.

"That's not so easy to do when you doubt yourself."

◆

CHARMIN DID A great job. She even gave me a quick haircut. Taking a few inches off did wonders for the bounce in my hair. I have to resist looking at myself in the rearview mirror on multiple occasions, having forgotten what it was like to have nice hair. After Charmin rinsed out my hair, she insisted on drying it, cutting the dead ends off, and curling it. She then pulled out her makeup basket. I'd forgotten what makeup did for my looks, so I settled in to let her play around on me while Atticus moved to the couch for a long nap.

Sometimes that goofy dog will curl into a tight ball while he sleeps, which given his size still takes up an entire cushion, but today he went to his back, which is his preferred method. Those double-jointed hips or whatever he's got going on that lets him do his froggy position on his stomach makes it so his back legs fall completely open. It would be lewd in a way if it wasn't for his long fur, which covers most of his boy parts. Hilariously, the pattern of colors on his body ended up so the hair covering one of his balls is white and the other is black. I've taken to calling them salt-and-pepper balls.

Speaking of salt-and-pepper balls, it's why I decided to take Atticus to PetSmart after Charmin finished my hair for a new toy and some decadent treats. Tomorrow he's getting neutered, and I'm already feeling guilt over the pain he's going to be in.

I'm also strangely sad he's losing his nub-nubs. Oley explained the importance of it for health benefits, and I know I'm making the right decision.

But I love my dog the way he is. The good and the bad. The wily behavior and destructiveness. The unrepentant spirit when he's bad, and the way he looks completely satisfied when I laugh at his antics. I don't want anything to change his personality, but Oley told me that was not a particular worry with this procedure.

I pull the Impala through a parking spot into another, so I can go straight out rather than have to back up. Atticus has taken to wearing a chest harness, and I clip his lead to the ring on the front.

He's a perfect gentleman, settling at my left leg in a nice trot, front paws raising extremely high as he prances into the sliding doors of PetSmart.

I knew Atticus was a special dog when I saw him tangled up in barbed wire and covered in mud, but it's disconcerting to me how much attention he garners. Yes, the Bernese Mountain Dog is a beautiful breed and they're not very common. Their striking colors and luxurious long fur causes eyes to turn.

But Atticus has something else about him that makes people stare. Maybe it is the way he holds his head high like he's royalty, or the way he trots like a show horse with chest all puffed out and fluffy tail in a perfect arch over his back. But if people see past all the pretty and look him right in the eye, they see the mischief and unfettered joy to be alive. Maybe that's why they gravitate to him.

The downside to his breed is that he is generally wary of strangers. It's not as noticeable in a public place like this, but if someone he doesn't know comes to my apartment or Oley's house, then he'll go completely defensive. He barks… loud booming noises that vibrate my body. If the person is invited into the house, Atti will continue to bark but will do so while backing a safe distance away.

He'll then quiet and observe for a bit, still at a distance. We usually tell visitors to ignore him. He's definitely all bark.

And that's when it gets interesting. Atticus doesn't like to be ignored by anyone, so if he determines the person is cool, he's going to come right in and get all friendly with crotch sniffs and stuff. But if there's something he doesn't like—and I'm not sure if that's by scent or perhaps doggie intuition—he goes over to his favorite spot to lay down and merely watches our guest very, very carefully.

I don't bother with a cart once we enter the store, because we're only going to get one toy and one bag of treats. I keep repeating that to myself over and over again. Sometimes I have a hard time limiting myself, and now that I'm working a solid forty hours a week at the clinic, I can afford this stuff for Atticus.

We head over to the toy aisles. I let Atticus stick his face into the bins on the bottom shelf and check out the ones hanging up he can reach. We walk up and down, letting him explore thoroughly. Finally, he settles on a thick braided rope with a rubber ball attached to the end. He loves to play tug-of-war and to chase things, but he's not that great at catching. Maybe he thinks the rope end will help him out or something.

After his choice is made, we head over to the treats. I'm fairly particular about what type of food he gets, and I do my usual perusal of the ingredients and where the product is made. Atticus gets bored, flopping to the tiled floor with a doggy sigh.

"Just give me a few more minutes, little man," I say as I read the ingredients on a bag of bison jerky. "Then we'll head home, play a little outside, and I'll make you a fantastic dinner."

"You in the habit of talking to your dog?" a deep male voice says from my left.

My head snaps that way, and my face flushes when I see a tall and extremely good-looking man with a large bag of dog food propped up on one shoulder. He's not military, and it's his longish blond hair and goatee that give it away. He's got on faded jeans, work boots, and a t-shirt that doesn't fit him at all. Maybe two sizes too small, which given how well built he is, is a very, very good thing.

The responding laugh I give is nervous. "Well, he can't back talk or disagree, so yes… I talk to him a lot."

The man throws his head back and laughs, exposing perfectly straight white teeth. Like so nice, he could be a model for toothpaste or something.

He nods toward the general direction of where Atticus had been laying. "Your dog is gorgeous, and his owner is equally so. Could I interest you in some coffee right now?"

I stare stupidly at the man, not sure if I heard him right. It's been so long since I've had someone pay me a compliment, so I almost doubt the veracity.

I'm so embarrassed over my inability to even respond that I turn to look at Atticus for help. I find he's gotten to his feet at some point and has backed a few paces away. He doesn't normally bark in public places, but he's got that look on his face like he totally wants to bark at this dude. Moreover, I can read his expression.

He doesn't like this guy at all.

I sigh inwardly, take a deep breath, and turn to face the man. He watches me expectantly, an easy smile on his face.

My smile back is genuine. "I really appreciate it, but I'm going to have to decline. Thank you, though."

The man doesn't look crushed, but he does seem slightly disappointed. He nods his head. "Sure thing. Have a great day."

"You too," I murmur as he turns and walks away.

Turning to Atticus, I bend over and scratch his head. "Okay... tell me honestly. Was he like a serial killer or something? Were you sensing some weird perversion?"

Atticus grins back at me, eyes closing halfway in pleasure from my head rubs.

"Or…" I ponder as I consider my dog and his penchant for mischief. "Or are you just threatened by someone paying attention to me, and thus taking attention from you?"

Atticus chuffs in response, and I'm not sure what that means.

If I had to take a guess, I would go with the latter. He enjoys being my sole focus of attention a little too much.

CHAPTER 29

Atticus

SOMETIMES I TRY to remember my family before Hazel. It's getting foggier, but I remember full bellies of Mama's milk and tussling with my brothers and sisters. I remember my owners were nice, and I know I probably caused them worry when I escaped.

But it all seems so long ago, almost as if it was a dream.

I ponder these deep thoughts while I lie beside Hazel on our couch-bed. She bought a new mattress for it since I chewed a hole right in the middle of the old one. That was one of those rare occasions when I was slightly contrite when she yelled at me. It was the earlier, puppier days where she wasn't as forgiving of my antics, convinced she could train the ornery out of me.

She's since been a good pupil and learned otherwise.

Hazel is propped up on some pillows, and I'm on my back in my favorite position. My neck is curved so I can lay my head on her thighs. She idly strokes the side of my face, and that feels really nice. I can feel my eyes getting heavy with sleep.

"So tomorrow's kind of a big day," Hazel says, and my eyes pop open.

Immediately, I roll to my stomach and turn my head so we're staring at each other, eye to eye. Oley once told Hazel it was unnatural for a dog to stare as intently as I do. He did an experiment one day where he timed how long I'd stare at Hazel. He stopped the timer at two minutes as Hazel and I held eye contact, barely blinking. Oley just shook his head in amazement while Hazel laughed and hugged me.

I like listening to Hazel talk, and she talks to me a lot. I think I'm her secret keeper because I can always feel her emotions as she confides, and they are often deep and painful.

Because I know it makes her feel good to talk to me, I always give her my full focused attention.

I cock my head and perk my ears up extra high. Because they are large and floppy and fall forward, the difference between a "regular perk" and a "high perk" is minute, but I like to think Hazel recognizes it.

"I've invited my ex-husband over tomorrow night," she goes on.

I don't know what an ex-husband is, but I don't like the uneasy vibes rolling of my mom. She's worried, so that makes me worried.

"He wants to give our marriage another shot," she says. "I feel like I need to at least introduce him to my new world... see how he fits in it. Because I'm not going back to that world I once lived in."

Hazel's words are fierce. If she were a dog, I imagine she'd have a deep growl ushered in behind them for emphasis.

"I wonder if you'll like Darren," she muses.

That still provides no clarity on what an ex-husband-Darren is, but if he's anything like the man at the pet store earlier this week, I will not like him.

That man had weird vibes rolling off him. And I could smell something on him that wasn't right. It's like he wanted all of Hazel's attention, and that isn't something I can be on board with.

More than that, I could tell he was interested in her because she was woman. No one in our lives has been interested in Hazel that way. Oley and Bernard love her because she's a friend. Same with Charmin. They're smart people, and they realize they come below me in the pecking order.

I don't think the man at the pet store would let me take top dog spot. He'd want to be, and yeah... just not going to work for me.

So I made sure Hazel knew I didn't like him. She's a smart woman. She took my advice and sent him on his way.

I wonder if I'll need to do that with this ex-husband-Darren person.

I guess it will depend on what he smells like and how he sounds. I'm prepared to chase him away if necessary.

If worst came to worst, I have no problems with biting him so he gets the message.

We will just have to see how this plays out.

CHAPTER 30

Hazel

I PACE THE foyer of Oley's house with a nervousness I had not expected. This was the logical thing for me to do, I was sure of it.

Peeking into the living room, I see Bernard slipping Atticus some pepperoni off his pizza slice. "Don't give him that," I snap irritably. "You did that last week, and he burped and farted pepperoni smell for two days after."

Oley laughs, and Bernard gives Atticus a speculative look, but he doesn't offer any more of his pizza to my dog.

The knock on the door has me spinning that way. I wipe my sweaty hands on the front of my shorts.

Oley calls softly in his gentle, southern voice. "It will be fine."

"Sure it will," I mutter under my breath.

Atticus starts his booming barks, but Bernard says in a firm voice, "Sit. Stay." The barks continue, but Atticus doesn't come flying into the foyer. "Quit barking, you daft dog. Here… have some pepperoni," I hear him say.

The barking stops and I take two steps to open the door, putting a smile on my face. Darren stands there with a bouquet of flowers in his hand—not surprising—and a bright smile of his own. His dark hair is washed and styled in a loose, wavy sort of way I always loved, and he shaved. He's wearing pressed khaki pants and a polo shirt. He doesn't have many clothes that are considered dressy as he hates wearing them, so it sends a message to me that he was making an effort.

Darren's gaze rakes over me appreciatively, spending extra time on my hair. I didn't bother doing much… just letting it hang casually over my shoulders and the most makeup I have on is a small coating of mascara. I'm wearing shorts and a tank top because it was another scorcher. Besides… it's pizza and baseball night and one doesn't dress up for such functions.

"You look beautiful, Hazel," Darren says.

"Thanks," I say, resisting the urge to duck my head and hide my eyes. I also don't need to hear him repeat that or add additional compliments like I used to crave. That relieves me greatly.

"Here… these are for you." He holds the bouquet of white roses to me. I've never liked roses much, but Darren doesn't know that. Out of all the hundreds of questions he ever asked to get to know me, he never asked what my favorite flower was. Perhaps that's just not something that's important to relationships. He certainly wasn't a flower giver during our marriage.

"Thanks," I say again, and reach for the flowers before beckoning him inside.

When I invited Darren over tonight for beer and baseball, I had to fill him in a little bit on what to expect. I didn't offer much… just that I was living in the apartment above my employer's house and we had a Friday night tradition. I didn't want to accept a "date" from Darren, and I didn't really want to be alone with him.

But I did want to be in his presence—to see if I could get my gut to talk to me about what I should do. I wanted to talk to him in an easy environment, and this provided the perfect way to do it. Oley and Bernard were on board as well.

I lead Darren into the living room, noting both Bernard and Oley are standing to welcome him. Atticus comes immediately to my side. This is unusual as he normally will back away from strangers.

Darren ignores my dog but moves to shake hands with the other men as I make the quick introductions.

"And this is Atticus," I say, resting my palm on top of his head. He's tall enough now that I don't even need to lean over to do this.

Atticus doesn't bark or move back from Darren.

Instead, he presses his side into my leg. His ears are perked as he watches Darren and his eyes are unblinking in a hypervigilant way.

"You have a dog?" Darren asks in surprise.

"I do," I tell him with a level of pride in my voice I don't think I've ever shared with him before. Which means I never had pride in much of anything when I was with Darren. "I rescued him when he was a puppy."

"He's cute," Darren says offhandedly before his head cuts to the TV. "What's the score?"

I can't help but smile to myself as I turn for the kitchen, so I can put the flowers in some water and get Darren something to drink. Atticus follows behind me.

He's cute?

That's all he had to say about the most awesome dog that ever existed?

My gut was starting to talk to me.

♦

GRANTED, WATCHING THE baseball game with Darren, Oley, and Bernard was fun. Darren's a completely outgoing guy and has never met a stranger. He fit in well with the other two men, and they were very polite to him even though I know they don't like what he did to me.

For my part, I observed, nibbled on pizza, and reassured Atticus. He insisted on sitting on my lap for most of the time. Let me say, having a seventy-plus-pound dog sit on my lap isn't the most comfortable or ideal situation, but I'm so used to it now I'm able to manage pizza while petting him.

Darren barely spared Atticus a glance unless he was trying to engage me in conversation.

After the game, Oley runs Bernard to his storage unit. I invite Darren out on the front porch so Atticus can do his business before we call it a night, and I *am* ready to call it a night.

We sit in the chairs and start rocking while Atticus sniffs around the flower beds. He squats to pee, and it's a distinct possibility he will do that for the rest of his life. His neuter on Monday went fantastic and he hardly seems to know he lost his balls. I took the cone of shame off him after the second day when he hadn't shown any interest in licking himself down there, probably because I was incessantly feeding him those yummy treats I'd bought him.

"So what's the story with the dog?" Darren asks with actual interest in his voice. It's not lost on me that he's already forgotten Atti's name.

"I found him in a ditch," I say as we watch him do his business. "Discarded. Broken. Abandoned. Hurt."

Darren's head slowly turns, and his eyes fix on me. His mouth is set in a grim line. It's obvious he understands I'm not just talking about Atticus right now.

"I'm sorry," he says in a rough voice, but I also hear a little frustration that he has to apologize again.

"I know you are," I say as I gently put a hand on his forearm. "And I appreciate it and accept it."

"But…" he drawls, sensing there is indeed a "but".

"But…" I reply with a smile as I withdraw my arm. Atticus has found a stick, and he's lying in the dewy grass to chew it while we talk. It's like he knows to give us privacy, so I can focus my attention solely on letting Darren down. "I have changed so much these last several months. I'm not the same woman you married."

"Of course you are."

I shake my head. "No. I'm not."

My gaze turns toward Atticus, and my heart swells just looking at him. "That dog changed me. For the very better. And though I accept your apology, and I even forgive you, Darren…" I turn back to face him, letting him see the truth on my face as well as in my words. "Our marriage is over."

"Are you sure?" he asks quietly, but I can hear he's already accepted defeat in his tone. My refusal to let him back in my life was given with too much confidence for him to fight.

I nod. "Yeah. I'm sure. I mean… had you found me before I found Atticus, I'd have gone back to you. But I'm stronger and value myself in a different way now."

"I know I should hate that dog, but that's good,

Hazel," he says, and I'm relieved to see a smile. "Are you really happy here?"

"I am. Very happy."

"Are you sure you can't be happy back in our home? You could obviously bring Atticus."

"I think," I tell him thoughtfully, "that I still need to be alone for a while. This ability to love myself is pretty new to me, and I've still got growing to do."

Darren stands up from his rocker, and I do the same. Atticus raises his head from his stick to watch us with interest.

"Well," he drawls in resignation, taking both of my hands in his. "Take care of yourself, okay?"

"I will." I give him a slight squeeze in reassurance.

Darren leans in to kiss me on the cheek. When he pulls back, he stares deeply into my eyes as if he'll see something within that he can use to change my mind.

Another sad smile from him when he realizes there's nothing there but resolve.

Later that night, after Darren leaves and I clean up from the pizza party, after Oley returns and heads to bed, I sit up in my apartment with Atticus. I run a brush through his fur, pulling it in straight lines down his spine. He shudders with every stroke as he stands before my perch on the couch. Sometimes if feels so good to him, his back legs shake in ecstasy.

"You like that, huh?" I ask, running it down his

back again.

Both legs quiver in response. I stop brushing him, only to have him swing that big head of his and push it into my chest, demanding more.

I laugh and resume my strokes. His coat is getting so pretty the older he gets. It's getting longer and glossier. It's not as wavy as some pictures of Bernese Mountain Dogs I've seen, and he still hasn't quite grown into the big pouf of hair on the very top of his head. It's longer than the rest of his hair and spiky, like Tina Turner's.

I pull the brush through Atticus' coat, running my other hand in its wake, reveling in the softness of his fur. It's the same fur I eat about a pound of a week because it still gets all over the place and most mornings I wake up with my face buried in it somehow.

"Darren didn't put up much of a fight," I say to Atticus pensively. "I think that was very telling."

Atticus looks over his shoulder at me, one eyebrow raised.

So I explain. "If he really missed me… if he really wanted to make the marriage work… he wouldn't have accepted what I told him so easily. That told me a lot. It told me that I did a good job listening to my gut. He wasn't a man who would ever value me in the right way, and I deserve better than that."

Atticus chuffs in agreement.

Laughing, I pull his head into me, so I can kiss the

top. I give him a few scratches under his chin before resuming the brush strokes.

"Besides," I add for his benefit only. "You're the only man I need in my life."

Atticus gives a bark of agreement.

I had planned to take off to the beach tomorrow after I did some yard work around the house. Oley said he had no plans, so I was free to use the car. I've yet to take Atticus there, and it seems silly not to take advantage of the huge playground where he can run free. It's forecasted to be cloudy with a chance of some late afternoon showers. It means the beach will be cooler than normal and mostly deserted except for those wanting to get some fishing in.

But tonight was monumental. I pretty much declared my almost seven-year marriage to Darren over, signaling to the world I'm a stronger, more secure Hazel Roundtree.

It gives me the confidence to confront the shame I've been carrying around over my estrangement from my family.

I think rather than a day at the beach tomorrow, I'm going to go see my mother.

It's long overdue.

CHAPTER 31

Hazel

I PULL INTO Oley's driveway and put the Impala in park. He'd felt like getting out of the house this morning, so he ran up to the clinic with me to feed and exercise two boarders. Turning to face Oley as he undoes the passenger seat belt, I pick up the green folder that was on the seat between us. Handing it to him I say, "So… um… If you get a few minutes, could you review this?"

Atticus—who has been sitting nicely in the back—hangs his head over the front seat to look at it with interest. Oley's eyes drop down for a brief glance without opening the folder and then back to me. "This better not be your resignation."

A soft smile plays at my lips and it's another way that Oley shows me how valued I am. Shaking my head, I say, "I actually did a new business and marketing plan for you. I've been working on it in the evenings. I pretty much had to Google how to do it, but I feel like you're in a position to expand the practice."

Oley blinks in surprise. "You're kidding."

"I'm not." I've been working on this for a few months, actually. While there are some things Oley just can't do, like complicated surgeries because he can't stand that long, he could expand other areas to make up for it. One of my big recommendations is to expand the boarding side of the business because I can come out during off hours to care for the animals. In going through his books, this used to be a significant stream of revenue. I think it can be again if we get the word out.

Oley and I stare at each other a moment, and he finally nods. "I'll look at it this afternoon while you're visiting your mom."

That's good enough for me and I watch silently as Oley gets out of the car, using his cane for leverage to hoist himself out. He doesn't say goodbye, but merely closes the door.

I wait for Oley to make it inside his house before I put the Impala in reverse. Atticus and I head to my mom's house.

I grew up in a three-bedroom brick home on the north side of Jacksonville. It was closer to Camp Lejeune as well as my mom's part time job at the mall. It sits in one of those neighborhoods that hovers somewhere between lower and middle class. Some of the homes are well maintained and some of them look like the Griswolds live there.

She was a mom first and foremost, but Alicia Milton is a hell of a gardener and so our yard was always beautifully blooming with some type of pretty flower or bush. While my father was responsible for mowing the lawn and trimming, she took care of all the ornamental flowers and perennials that made our house shine. My father's praise never came easy, but when he would tell my mom her flower beds were the prettiest in town, she would bat her eyelashes and say, "Oh, Peter... stop exaggerating."

Despite her humble words, it was obvious the praise meant the world to her because she'd strut around like a peacock and hum love songs while doing the household chores. As a kid, it always made me giggle, but as an adult, I realize how much my mom needed approval from my father.

Before I turn the car off, I throw my arm over the back of the seat and crane my neck to look at Atticus.

I give him a stern glare. "You have to be on your best behavior today. I need the Atticus who knows all the obedience commands and does them without needing a treat in return. Furthermore, if my mom has any food out on the counter or table, you are to absolutely leave it alone. Are we clear?"

Atticus shoves his face in mine, giving me a big slurp of his tongue up my cheek. I immediately wipe it off on my shoulder, proclaiming, "That is so gross."

We exit the car, and Atticus walks beside me at a perfect heel on leash. Before I knock on the front door, I glance down at the summery dress I had chosen to wear. I wanted to look nice for my mom. I'm walking in with many years of preconceived notions she has about me and most of them are well deserved.

As I was putting my hair back in a barrette while getting ready, I took a moment to marvel over how much I had physically changed in the past several months. Overall, I just look happier in my face. I don't look as old. I think some of that may have to do with the fact I quit smoking, but I think most of it comes from inside me.

Moreover, I've been eating regular meals because I can afford to now, and I've put some weight on. I hadn't realized how sickly I'd looked until my face actually filled out a bit. I swear it's shaved ten years off my appearance.

Lifting my head, I knock sharply on the door. When it opens, my mother is standing there with a multi-layered expression on her face. Mostly just genuine shock to see me since it's been well over three years—not since my dad's funeral. But there's more hidden deep in her eyes. Her gaze roams all over me in a hungry way... a mother starved to see her child. It shreds my heart to know the pain I've caused her. I see the relief on her face that I actually look healthy.

She sees what I saw in the mirror earlier. Glowing skin, clear eyes, and healthy curves.

"Hazel," my mother breathes out in relief. Her eyes mist up, and she clutches her hands to her chest. "You're here."

I nod, ignoring the lump in my throat. "I'm here."

My mom's gaze drops down to Atticus, the pup sitting quietly by my side. The minute they lock eyes, his tail starts thumping against the concrete porch. "Who do we have here?"

I look down at my furry love with pride and open affection. "This is Atticus. I rescued him when he was a little puppy back in March."

"He is absolutely gorgeous, Hazel. And he looks to be a very good boy."

My mom bends over and holds her hand out to him to sniff. He immediately gives it a lick and then ducks his head, brings it underneath her palm and giving her a hard nudge to indicate she should quit wasting time and start scratching him. My mom laughs in delight, putting both hands to his head to give him serious rubs behind his ears. I guarantee Atticus is a much better prospect on her front porch than some of the losers I used to parade around back in my younger, wilder days.

"Well, both of you come on in," she says as she steps back over the threshold and pushes the door open further for us to enter. I don't question my mother's seemingly easy acceptance of letting a big dog into her house. We never had animals growing up, so I have no clue what my mom thinks of them, per se. But I suspect she is not going to do anything to prohibit my entrance into her home when she has been craving this for a long time.

I take in my surroundings. Nothing has changed. The living room looks the same. Same furniture, same pictures on the mantle, same everything.

Except... I see pictures of Liz, her husband Trey, and her son Benji mixed among the others. They look beautifully happy, and my nephew is utterly adorable. My chest squeezes over the time I've lost with him.

My mom has certainly changed, though. She looks older. And of course, she is. But in the three years since my father's funeral, she has stopped caring about her appearance. Her hair is liberally peppered with gray, something she would have always chased away with color when my dad was alive. Her facial skin looks saggy, and she looks far too skinny.

I wonder if I'm the cause of these changes or if my father's death is, or perhaps a combination of the two.

"Come on into the kitchen," my mother says as she heads that way. "I just brewed some sweet tea."

I unclip Atticus from his lead, and we both follow my mom.

"Sit down." My mom points at the kitchen table that holds only four chairs. I do as she asks, and Atticus comes to dutifully lay at my feet. I'm not sure if he made the same perusal I did of the kitchen when I walked in, but there is absolutely no food left out for him to pilfer. Either he made that same determination, or he is just being good like I asked him to.

My mom bustles about filling glasses with ice and pouring dark, syrupy tea over it before adding lemon slices. She makes nervous chitchat, telling me how she was not scheduled to work today so she was having a lazy day by herself, watching her soaps.

When she sits down, placing both glasses on the table, she places her hands nervously in her lap and stares at me in a way that makes it clear she's afraid I might bolt at any minute. Her voice quavers when she says, "It's just so good to see you again, Hazel."

"It's good to see you, too, Mom."

"You look fantastic," she says, raking her gaze over me again. "You look… happy."

I give a wry smile. "Does that mean I looked unhappy when I used to visit before?"

My mom's face sobers, and her smile slips away. "Yes. I think you were a very unhappy woman."

With mine still in place, I nod in agreement. "I don't think I realized I was unhappy until my circumstances forced me to change."

My mom's eyes glitter with satisfaction that her child is potentially succeeding at life. For the past years, at least since I was eighteen, I've been a great mystery to my mother. Would Hazel continue down a path of minimal satisfaction in life or would she finally get her crap together?

I fill my mom in on everything that happened from the moment Darren kicked me out of our house until I told him it was over for good.

My mother's expression went from enraged to sorrowful tears as I told her of those miserable three months after Darren kicked me out. When I tell her about finding Atticus in the ditch, she leans over and scratches him on the head again. I bet she'd lay down a ribeye steak for him if she had one.

I tell her all of it. About Oley and my new career as his assistant, and about my good friend Bernard. Mostly, I talk about Atticus. Pulling out my phone, I show her all the pictures I posted on Instagram. I tell her about how bad he is and how completely wonderful he is. She listens to it all as she's realizing I am probably going to be okay in life, and it seems the years start melting off her. She sits a little straighter in her chair, and she smiles a hell of a lot as I fill her in on the past few months of my life.

When I finish, my mom leans over and again pets Atticus. "I love dogs. Always wanted to have one, but your dad didn't like them."

I blink in surprise. "Really?"

"Oh, yeah," she says with a fond smile. "Your dad didn't like the hair. You know what a neat freak he was, and you also know your father's word was law."

We both laugh. A lot of that was the military in my dad, which we understood.

A lot of that was why I am the way I am. My mother deferred to my father in all matters. She was unsure of herself, always needed his approval, and couldn't make a decision on her own. She was utterly dependent on him to not only provide a roof over her head, but also to validate her as a wife and mother, and I suddenly realize how alone and scared she must be since he died.

It's how I felt when Darren kicked me out.

I am my mother's daughter.

I aspired to have what she had because she was happy. She had a distinct role in our household, and my father had his. From her, I learned the man was the strength of the unit. He was the wise leader and the physical provider. I watched my mom preen with love from the sparse praise he handed out, as if they were the greatest moments of her life.

It's no wonder the minute the first guy crooked his finger at me that I went running. I was ready for it. It's what I was unknowingly taught. While there was absolutely nothing wrong with the way my mom chose to live her life and love her man, it made an impact on me. My mom didn't often have an independent thought of her own that she could exercise and then have someone validate. Perhaps she was afraid to even go there, or maybe she did unbeknownst to me and my father shot her down.

My parents were good to me, and they loved me. But I was never given the skills to think for myself within our family unit. I wasn't encouraged to have independence. Rather, I watched my mother flourish in a relationship that was built around her husband and all the wonderful things he did for her.

My mom lucked out. She found a good man in my father. I didn't find that good man, and I kept trying and trying and trying, eventually changing myself into someone I wasn't to become what someone could love. It was a horrific failure of a social experiment I'd been running throughout my life.

A vicious cycle that wouldn't have been broken if not for Atticus.

"Why did you stop coming around, Hazel?" my mom asks, and the abrupt change of subject to something so serious has me reeling. I knew we needed to talk about this, but it's still uncomfortable.

I really want to tell my mom, *I stopped coming around because of the way you made me feel. Like such a failure. Granted, it was subtle. It may be how your face pinched when I talked about tending bar, or maybe that you were never quite polite to the men I'd dated, or the way you gushed about how proud you were about Liz but never me.*

But I will never say that to her because it just doesn't matter right now. It would only serve to hurt her, and that I will not do.

What does matter is that I acknowledge my error, so I can absolve myself of the guilt for making my parents suffer under the terrible way I treated them for so long. "It was me, Mom. I was just messed up in the head for a long time. Couldn't see things for what they were, and I was too afraid to be different. I'm sorry for all the pain I've caused you."

"You didn't—" she rushes to assure me, but I cut her off.

"I did," I say firmly as I reach across the table. I hold my hand out, palm up. She doesn't hesitate and puts hers in mine. "I'd like to make up for it, though. I missed the chance with Dad, and I don't want those regrets with you."

She opens her mouth to argue. Perhaps to tell me it's not necessary. She's being a protective mom and that warms me, but I squeeze her hand and shake my head at her. "Let me own this, Mom. I need to."

Her cheeks turn pink over the gentle admonishment in my voice, but she gives a tiny nod. "Okay."

"Okay," I repeat with a big smile.

We share misty gazes across the table, and I'm incredibly happy I took this step. But my mom's face clouds slightly and I brace.

"Are you going to reach out to Liz?" she asks hesitantly.

My guts burn with shame, for as much as it was horrible the way I've been absent from my parents, it was unforgiveable what I'd done to Liz when Benji was born. When I'd shown up drunk, stoned, and belligerent at the hospital, ruining what should have been a beautiful celebration of new life. It's something that absolutely bonds Bernard and I together, as we both know how the power of alcohol and selfishness can hurt the ones we love the most.

I cough to clear my throat, nodding with a smile. "Yeah. But um… I've got to work up the courage to do that. It's a hard apology to make."

"She told me about what happened at the hospital," my mom murmurs.

"It was unforgiveable." I pull my hand away and lace my fingers in my lap. My gaze drops there because it's too hard to meet my mom's eyes. Atticus senses my distress, pushing from the floor with a grunt. He shoves his big head into my lap, burrowing his nose right under my hands so they're forced to go to his head. It always seems like a selfish move on his part to make me pet him, but he knows it's a calming therapy for me.

"It's not unforgivable, Hazel. Your sister loves you, and you should reach out to her."

My head lifts to meet my mom's gaze. It's soft and tender, full of understanding for her wayward daughter.

"I will," I assure her.

I'm just not sure when.

CHAPTER 32

Hazel

I LOVE OCTOBER in North Carolina because it's when the humidity starts to ease up and the torture of Hades-hot days starts to end. It doesn't mean there can't be warm days in October because eighty degrees and wearing shorts while trick-or-treating has been known to occur. But for the most part, October signifies that fall is coming. Granted, the "feel of it" may not fully get here until the end of November but at least we see it on the horizon.

My life has morphed into a series of scheduled standing events that define much of who I am these days. We still have Friday night baseball and pizza at Oley's house. That will continue through the World Series. Because Oley and Bernard are both Carolina Panthers fans, we have added Sunday football to the mix. It doesn't matter if the game is at one, four or eight, Bernard comes over to watch it. The only exception is if the Panthers play on a Monday night or one of those weird Thursday night games.

Another night has also been added to the social agenda, and that is taco night on Wednesdays. Charmin and I started that since it's her night off and we were sort of doing a single ladies solidarity type thing. We made the tacos in my apartment the very first night and invited Oley up. He gladly accepted and then proclaimed that taco nights would happen down in his kitchen because it was too much for him to climb the stairs. I readily agreed to this because Oley's kitchen is a lot nicer and bigger than mine.

For the last month and a half since I showed up on her doorstep, Saturday mornings have become the time for me and my mother to reconnect. I drive over to her place, sometimes bringing Atticus or sometimes leaving him behind. If my mom hasn't made a big breakfast, I will often take her out and treat her. It's something I've never been able to do before, not for lack of money, but for lack of wanting to put myself out there.

Sometimes we'll hit up The Waffle House or Central Café, which makes the best SOS in town—otherwise known by marines everywhere as "shit on a shingle". If we're feeling fancy, we'll head over to the Cracker Barrel and gorge on Mama's Pancake Breakfast.

I have yet to talk to my sister Liz, and my mom pesters me about it every Saturday. Sometimes it makes the eggs in my stomach curdle because it's something that needs to be done, yet I'm terrified.

Of course, my mom told Liz about our reunion. Mom then passed on that Liz would very much like to see me.

I want to see her, too. Very, very much. But I just don't know how.

The scene that played out in Liz's hospital room was far uglier than my mother could have ever imagined, despite what my sister may have told her. My stomach cramps up into painful knots, and my face flushes as hot as a summer sunburn when I think about that day. Compounding the shame is the fact I was so drunk and stoned I don't remember exact details. I just remember pieces. Hazy, dream like snatches of time which could potentially mean it was way worse than what my mind thinks happened.

I remember the room being filled with Liz's husband's family, everyone gaping me as if I were a carnival oddity.

The expression on Liz's face as she held her newborn son in the hospital bed, horrified at the way I was staggering around.

Her refusal to let me hold Benji, culminating in my drunken rant that she was a stuck-up snob who thought she was too good for the likes of me.

A security guard escorting me out of the hospital while I cursed and struggled and made an ass of myself.

It makes me shudder when I think about it. It is without a doubt the worst thing I've ever done in my entire life, and I am not sure how to move past it. I keep putting my mother off with one excuse or another why I haven't contacted Liz but the truth of it is, I can't even bear to think about looking at my sister because I am so ashamed and humiliated.

Because most days of the week are taken with me spending quality time with my friends and family, I carefully plan out the rest of my days. It's Thursday now and I have no obligations after I get off work.

But I do have a mission I choose to go on.

I borrowed the car from Oley. When he asked me where I was going, I point blank lied and said I was going shopping at the mall. I did this because if he knew where I was going, he would have moved hell and high water to talk me out of it, and I don't want to be talked out of it. He'd have preached to me in a fiery brimstone sort of way to make his point. He probably would have talked me out of it, and I don't want to be dissuaded.

I owe it to Bernard to try.

It's funny to think Bernard has become one of my closest friends in the world. He's not quite as dear to me as Oley is, but I feel closer to him than I do Charmin. The more time I spend around the man, the more I've come to love him. I have never seen anything from Bernard but genuine kindness and humility. He has given me good advice—some of it even fatherly—over the months.

Yes… I love him.

It's why I'm going to put myself all up in his business today by going to go talk to his wife.

Over the months that Bernard, Oley, and I have been hanging out for Friday night baseball and pizza, I have come to learn a lot about him. While he tends to talk more when he drinks, he has genuinely opened up to Oley and me. Some of that has to do with the fact we can be relentless in our questions to him.

We've learned that Bernard's last name is Jackson. He's sixty-two, joined the Marine Corps at eighteen right after graduating high school in Philly, he spent some time in Vietnam—he insists there was nothing traumatizing about that—yeah, right—and that he wanted to make a military career for himself. He would have retired after twenty years of service in 1988, but sadly received a medical discharge two years after the bombing that robbed him of some of his sanity.

He was thirty-two when two suicide bombers drove their trucks into the barracks he lived in at the time. He was on his bunk reading a magazine when the explosion hit. Two hundred and forty-one U.S. personnel died, but Bernard was one of the lucky ones. He escaped with only a broken leg and a slight concussion that got him shipped back home immediately. His leg got better, but his head never quite recovered.

Because we're nosy and we pry a lot, Bernard over time talked more openly about what it was like after he returned. The mood swings, the self-medication with booze, the irrational spikes in temper he said he often took out on his family, and the extreme paranoia that a bomber would be coming after him again. I was horrified to learn that he never got any type of psychological treatment, medication, or counseling, but rather was handed a medical discharge without the military offering much in the way of a helpful solution for him. His condition eventually became legitimately recognized as PTSD, but by the time the Veteran's Administration had a handle on the depth of the problem they were facing with our troops, Bernard was long lost to a life of alcohol, depression, and eventually periods of intermittent homelessness that has seemingly become permanent.

I'm not willing to accept that.

I'd also learned Bernard's wife's name is Wanda. He doesn't talk about her much because I think things really had deteriorated between them as a husband and a wife. But he does talk a lot about the son their son Tyrone, who he affectionately calls Ty-Ty. Tyrone, in turn, has a wife and two small children of his own. Bernard rarely talks about his grandkids, but I think it's because he just knows so little about them.

The last thing I learned about Bernard was that he and I are like two peas in a pod when it comes to being incapacitated with contrition and self-disgust. He is so convinced he's ruined his family's lives and deserves nothing from them that he won't even put himself out there to see if it's actually true. After repeating a pattern for years of returning home only to leave again for months or years at a time, he told me that the last time he left, Wanda begged him not to ever come back.

It absolutely broke my heart to hear that, but I can also understand where she's coming from. There comes a time where it's very easy to give up hope.

After much stewing, fretting, and even some praying about whether I was doing the right thing, I tracked Wanda down and decided to go visit her. When I looked her address up on Google, I was surprised to find that she lived in the neighborhood not far from that Wendy's parking lot off Western Boulevard where I had picked up Bernard all those months ago. I often wondered why he was on that side of town when it was such a lengthy walk for him, but I can only surmise that perhaps he was walking by his old house because he wanted to check in on Wanda. Or maybe it was purely nostalgia.

I did take it to mean that Bernard still very much cared for that part of his life.

I don't know what to expect as I pull up in front of

the small house with mint-green cement board siding. There is one car in the driveway, and I know that she lives alone.

Or at least that's what Bernard says, but I don't know how current his information is.

My hands are sweating by the time I make it up to the front door. I have an unbearable aching need for Atticus, who is always my puppy Xanax, but he would have been too much of a distraction and this is too important not to give my full attention.

I knock and after just a few seconds, a woman opens the door. She's average height and on the plump side, but I immediately don't take her for Bernard's wife because she looks like she's in her mid-to-late forties, and his wife is the same age as Bernard as they were high school sweethearts.

"Can I help you?" she asks politely, curiosity filling her dark eyes as she watches me through the screen door.

"Um… yes. I'm looking for Wanda Jackson," I say with a hesitant smile.

"I'm Wanda," she replies, and my jaw drops open. Her dark skin is creamy and completely unlined. She looks twenty years younger than Bernard, and I can't figure out if she has really good genes or Bernard's hard life aged him more than a sixty-two-year-old should look.

"Oh… um… I'm sorry. That just caught me really off guard." My stammering doesn't do anything to put her at ease. Her politeness ebbs away, leaving her expression cool and aloof.

I hold up my hands in a lame attempt to convey my apologies as I clear my throat. "I'm sorry. It's just… you look so much younger than Bernard."

"Is he okay?" she blurts out, her face now a mask of worry and fear.

"God, yes," I exclaim and then start stammering my apologies. "I didn't mean to freak you out. Let me start again. My name is Hazel Roundtree and well… I've become a good friend to your husband over this past year."

Assured that Bernard is not dead or in peril, her gaze becomes cool again. "And why are you here?"

I take a deep breath. "Because I can't stand to see him homeless when he has a family so close by."

"You think this is our fault?" she practically hisses through the screen door, and then starts to close the inner door on my face.

"No," I say quickly. "Please… I'm sorry. That's not what I meant by that, nor do I think this is your fault at all. Bernard knows this is all on him. He's so terribly ashamed of what he's done to his family that he's just… well, he's broken. His shame is what keeps him away, not his mental condition."

"You're a psychiatrist, huh? You know the inner workings of his demons?"

"Not at all," I murmur. "I just listen to him talk, and I know how he feels."

For a moment, I can see utter confusion take over her face as she understands a younger white girl is on her doorstep saying she's good friend with her sixty-two-year-old homeless husband, and she can't quite fathom how something like that occurs.

"I used to be a bartender, and Bernard would sometimes come in for a few beers," I explain.

Her eyes go frosty again. "Yes. He always loved his beer a lot more than his family."

"I don't think that's true," I say, and there's no hiding the admonishment in my voice that she would be so judgmental. "He medicates himself that way."

Wanda has the grace to look chastised, and her eyes cut guiltily away from mine.

"Look… I don't bartend anymore. I manage a veterinary clinic and my boss, Dr. Oley Peele, and I… well, we hang out with Bernard a few times a week. He comes out to Oley's farm, and we watch sports and talk. Like I said… he's become a dear friend to me, and I just… I just wanted to see if there was any way to reunite him with his family."

Wanda stares at me a moment, and I can see her debating whether to open the door to let me in or slam it in my face. To my relief, she relents and invites me inside.

Once she has us seated in the kitchen with cups of coffee for each of us, she says very bluntly. "My marriage with Bernard is over. I wouldn't let him come back here even if he wanted to."

I'm not prepared for the little stab of pain in my chest over that sentiment, and my face must reflect it.

"You must think me very coldhearted," she mumbles as she looks down to her coffee.

"Not at all," I assure her, and her eyes come back to me hesitantly. "Bernard has not ever held anything back regarding the hell he put you and Tyrone through. He told me that when he left the last time, you asked him not to come back. He understands that. I understand that, and I'm not sure he would come back even if he could. Bernard is a very strange person. He lives an absolutely simple and meager life, yet it suits him. It's like he's taking from life just about all that he can handle. He lives in a very narrow world, and I think that keeps his demons mostly at bay."

Wanda's eyes fill with tears. "I tried so hard over the years to get him help. I put demands and ultimatums on him, but he ignored them all. I have to tell you... that first time he left, I was a little relieved. There was finally peace in this house. Tyrone was only eleven, and he had no clue what was going on. Couldn't even understand it. The remainder of Tyrone's childhood was almost a game... when would Daddy come home for good? The last time Bernard went missing was on Tyrone's thirty-third birthday. That was four years ago. We haven't heard from him in four years. That's twenty-two years total of him putting us through that crap, so yes... the last time he left, I told him not to come back."

"I think you did the best you could, Wanda," I reassure her. "Bernard thinks so, too."

"Lord, I wish you hadn't told me that," she says with a watery laugh, dabbing at her eyes with a napkin. "Makes me want to take the fool back."

That makes me laugh, and we share a sad smile.

"Why are you really here?" she asks.

I shrug. "I just feel so bad for everyone involved. I don't know that there's a mainstream place for Bernard anymore. He doesn't do well with pressures and crowds. He has a hard time battling his guilt for failing his family. But maybe I was hoping there could be something... a reconnection maybe. If the marriage is over in your eyes, I respect that, but I know Bernard really misses Tyrone and I think he has major regrets where his grandkids are concerned. I just thought maybe there could be something, even if it's small."

Wanda smiles. It's wan and brittle, but it's genuine. "You seem like a really nice woman, Hazel. And I admire what you're doing for your friend. I care for

Bernard because he's the father of my son, but I've moved on. I'm actually seeing someone now."

"Oh," I say in surprise, then I give a hard shake of my head. "Well… why wouldn't you? You deserve to be happy and find love."

Wanda's eyes fill with tears. She doesn't check them, letting them slide right down her face. "Thank you for understanding."

My hand reaches out and takes hers. When I squeeze it, she starts sobbing. I end up staying at her house for a very long time.

CHAPTER 33

Atticus

I'M NOT SURE what's going on today, but Hazel and Oley brought me to the clinic. I rarely get to go these days because apparently, I make too much of a fuss when I can't see Hazel. It drives me nuts when she's in another room, with another dog or one of those stinky cats. So yeah... I make a bit of a ruckus. When she comes back to me, I sniff her all up and down. She smells of disloyalty and cat dander. I try to ignore her for a little bit, but that never quite works because I love her too much.

So far, there hasn't been any animals coming in today. Hazel and Oley are in the room that has all the cages and supplies. They're pulling everything out of cabinets. Then there's a lot of counting, sometimes discarding, and making lists. Oley called it "inventory-ing".

I'm currently lounging in the corner, enjoying the cool tile on my belly while I gnaw on a deer antler. It's pretty tasty, and it presents a challenge as it's not very chewable.

I got this deer antler at the pet store yesterday. Mom took me there, then bought me more toys and chew things than ever before. She told me I needed more stuff to keep me "occupied" and "out of trouble."

As if I'm actually "trouble".

She loves me just the way I am.

But I get her worry. I was really sick last night, and it freaked her out.

It started with me doing something really bad. I ate one of her socks, and it made my tummy hurt bad. It took me forever to throw it up. I gagged and wretched while Hazel cried.

She cried harder when it came up, this time in relief. Oley had told Hazel I'm lucky it didn't obstruct my bowels, which would have required surgery and could be really dangerous. He suggested I needed more stuff to keep me occupied.

So I got deer antlers, Kong's, and food puzzles I have to solve to get treats. All great stuff for sure, but that sock was tasty going down.

Oley and Hazel spent some time talking about why I do the things I do, and the truth is… I have no clue why I do. It's just that I see opportunity and seize it.

Also, I have very little willpower.

But in this instance, there were certain factors that

played into the sock incident. Some of it's Hazel's fault. For example, she keeps all the toilet paper locked up tight. She also bought a garbage can with a lid I can't pry open, which I find to be scandalous. She puts the pillows up in the tiny linen closet as soon as we get out of bed in the morning which is downright insulting. And last week, after I'd chewed just a tiny bit on the leg of the coffee table, she smeared something really hot on it to discourage me from doing it again. I had to taste it, though. It burned like fire and made me sneeze a lot. I've stayed away from the coffee table since.

She takes all my joy away and so, when I saw the sock that must have fallen out of her laundry basket as she was putting her clothes away, I seized the opportunity to try something new. At first, I thought about just chewing and shredding it, because that's what I normally do with non-food items that hold no nutritional value. But the next thing I know, I'm swallowing it right down.

It just seemed... natural to me.

While I am grateful for all the new toys and things to chew on, I'm pretty sure I'll leave socks alone now. When it was all said and done and yacked up, it just wasn't a fun experience.

"Oley," Hazel says as he goes through medicine vials, keeping some and throwing others away. I stop chewing my antler and raise my head to listen, because the tone of Hazel's voice speaks to me clearly. She's nervous, and I need to be poised to offer comfort.

"Yeah?" he replies without looking up from his work.

"I have something I need to tell you." I start to stand up. Hazel sounds terribly nervous now and she's wringing her hands as she faces Oley with an apologetic expression on her face.

Oley must sense it too, as he straightens and turns to face her. "What is it?"

"Maybe you better sit down," she hedges.

"Spit it out, Hazel," Oley grouses. He's not a patient man.

Hazel takes a deep breath, and I pad over to her side. A hand drops and goes right to my head where it starts rubbing. I try not to get lost in the sensation because it feels really, really good. I need to be vigilant, so I can support Hazel as needed.

"Okay… I know you're going to be really mad, and I just want you to take some calming breaths before—"

"Spit. It. Out," Oley orders.

Hazel jumps, and it makes me want to growl at Oley. I don't because I remember he's kind and loves Hazel like I do. He must just be a little grumpy, which happens on occasion with Oley.

"I went to see Bernard's wife on Monday," she blurts out.

Oley's bushy eyebrows fly up. He sounds completely scandalized. "You did what?"

Hazel nods effusively. "I tracked her down and went to see her. I wanted to know if there was any way I could help reconcile their family."

Oley's face remains impassive as he stares at Hazel.

"And… I spent a lot of time with Wanda. I'm sad to report there's no reconciliation that's going to happen there. I'm sure that won't be surprising to Bernard, of course."

Hazel doesn't say anything but just looks at Oley expectantly.

Oley sort of blinks and grumbles, "Well… that's not that bad. I mean, I don't think you should have interfered but doesn't sound like any harm done."

"His son Tyrone is going to come over to join us for pizza and baseball," Hazel blurts out, and she does it quickly because it's hard to unleash them.

"Jesus Christ," Oley says quite loudly.

Not sure the meaning of those words, but they must be bad because Hazel gasps in surprise.

"Have you told Bernard this?" Oley asks, but he doesn't wait for Hazel to answer. Instead, he holds his hand up and shakes his head. "No, of course you didn't. Otherwise you wouldn't be standing here in front of me looking guilty as hell for interfering in something extremely personal. I can't imagine the shit storm this is going to cause."

Hazel doesn't reply. She just stares at Oley with wide eyes.

"Oh… now you have nothing to say?" Oley demands.

Hazel's hand rubs my head furiously and my back leg starts shaking. "It's just… I've never heard you cuss before. And you took the Lord's name in vain."

"Focus, Hazel," Oley snaps. I want to growl again, but somewhere deep inside, I think Hazel might be deserving of his wrath right now, so I remain neutral.

"Wanda called Tyrone during my visit, and he came over and talked to me. Wanda doesn't want anything to do with Bernard anymore other than a fond concern for his welfare. She's actually seeing someone. I'm not sure how Bernard will take that, but Tyrone says he'll let his father know."

"He'll let his father know?" Oley repeats.

"Tonight. When he comes over."

"And you're just going to spring this on Bernard?" Oley asks.

"Well… I don't know. That's why I'm telling you now. I've been fretting over it all week, and I don't know what to do. Tyrone really wants to see his dad. He wants some type of relationship with him, even if it's not a deep one. He's willing to take whatever Bernard can give. He's a really great guy, Oley. You're going to like him a lot."

Oley sighs heavily, and his gaze drops to the floor. He scratches his hands through his white hair. I wonder if it feels as good as when Hazel scratches my head, but I don't see his leg shaking, so I doubt it.

When he looks back up to Hazel, the reproach is gone from his eyes. I think he's just accepting of the "shit storm" that Hazel has apparently created. "What do you think Bernard would do if we told him about it ahead of time?"

"Go AWOL," Hazel says without hesitation. "He'll hide. He's too ashamed of himself to see his son."

Oley suddenly looks extremely weary as he nods. "I think you're right. I suggest you don't tell him and be prepared for that storm tonight."

CHAPTER 34

Hazel

IF BERNARD FEELS the tension in the air around us, he hasn't said a word. But it's thick, and Oley keeps shooting worried glances my way.

I'd picked Bernard up like usual, and we grabbed a pizza. Luckily, he was chatty enough for the both of us that he didn't notice my reserved nature in the car. When we got to the farm, Oley helped contribute to the conversation.

But we're nervous. Tyrone will be showing up at any time now, and it's going to totally blindside Bernard. I figure there's going to be one of three outcomes.

Bernard is either going to be deliriously happy to see his son.

Bernard is going to be pissed at me for interfering.

Bernard is going to be happy to see his son but is going to be pissed at me for interfering.

My hands are currently rubbing Atti's neck—giving

more of a massage than a scratch—as he lays across my lap, intermittently burping pepperoni in my face. I saw Bernard "sneaking" it to him, but I didn't even tell him to stop. I was feeling too guilty about being a busybody that I let Bernard have his way.

The baseball game—the Cardinals and the Reds tonight—fades off to a commercial and where there is normally conversation between us during this time, usually about non-baseball stuff, it's utterly silent.

"What in the hell is going on?" Bernard demands as he looks from me to Oley. He's sitting on the opposite end of the couch from me, scratching Atticus' butt. Atti had his eyes half closed in ecstasy from the dual ministrations he was receiving from me and Bernard, but they fly open.

"What do you mean?" Oley asks in a voice that quavers slightly.

Bernard throws a hand my way. "This one is acting weird. She hardly said anything on the way over here, and I know damn well she saw me giving Atticus pepperoni, but she didn't say a word."

I stare back at him guiltily, face flushed.

"And you," Bernard says, turning his attention to Oley. "You didn't argue when I said the Braves needed to trade Lowe. I mean… what the hell, man?"

Oley averts his eyes, completely called out.

"Now something's going on and I want to know

what it is," Bernard concludes.

Oley won't look at Bernard or me, his focus going to the TV and a commercial for laundry detergent.

My arms circle around Atticus' neck, whose head had swung Bernard's way. He immediately gives me his full attention, bumping his head gently against the side of my face before pulling back. His crystal blue truth teller focuses intently on me.

I give my dog a smile before bracing myself. On an exhale, I say, "I went to see Wanda on Monday."

Bernard's jaw locks, but he says nothing.

"I wanted to do something to bring your family back together," I say without breaking eye contact. I even lift my chin a little because I've decided I'll regret nothing just like Atticus when he's bad. What I did was done out of love. "I also talked to Tyrone. He really wants to see you, so I invited him over tonight."

Bernard explodes off the couch, causing Atticus to yelp and try to climb up my shoulders. I push him all the way off the couch, then stand up to face Bernard.

"Goddamn you, Hazel," Bernard yells with fists clenched. "Goddamn your meddling. What gives you the right to decide what I want in my life?"

"You miss your family," I tell him, keeping my voice low and gentle. "I wanted to help give them back to you in some way if I could."

"That's not for you to decide," Bernard snaps.

"That's my life your fucking with."

It's not the first time Bernard's dropped an "F" bomb in front of me. He holds that language in reserve around Oley, though, so I know he's pissed.

"I'm sorry this upsets you," I say in an attempt to alleviate his anger. "I only did it out of love for—"

"Don't even go there, Hazel," Bernard interrupts me. "Because if you cared for me, you would have exercised a little more regard for my feelings."

I feel like such a shit right now, and perhaps I am regretting my actions. But before I can try to defend myself further, there's a knock on the door. Bernard's eyes go round and wild looking, as if he's having a panic attack.

"It's your son, Bernard," I state, trying to calm him. "And he loves and misses you. He won't put any pressure on you. He doesn't blame you for anything. He understands. You need to give him a chance to have something with you."

Oley pushes up from the recliner, grabbing his cane. "I'll get the door," he murmurs.

Bernard and I stare at each other. His chest is rising and falling deeply, and he rubs his hand over his face as his gaze cuts to the TV a moment, then back to me with a glare.

And then Tyrone is standing in the entryway to the living room, with Oley standing behind him with a sadness etching the lines on his face deeper. I know this is the worst way this could have gone down.

Bernard's shoulders hunch inward as he slowly turns to face his son. He looks utterly terrified.

Tyrone isn't going to let him feel that way, though. I spent about an hour with him at Wanda's house. In that short time period, I learned just how empathetic he is toward his father's situation. He'd done a lot of research into PTSD, and he chooses to rise above his bitterness about his father's abandonment.

Without a word being said between the two, Tyrone rounds the couch and practically walks right into his father. He pulls his dad in hard to him for a big bear hug. Bernard only hesitates a second before putting his arms around his son and burying his face into Tyrone's shoulder.

Oley jerks his head toward the kitchen in a silent command to give them privacy. I turn to look for Atticus, stunned to find him standing by the hugging men. He actually pushes his big head in between them as if he's a crucial part of the reunion. Bernard's hand drops, and he strokes Atti's neck.

I'm further stunned when I realize Atticus didn't even bark when Tyrone knocked on the door. He didn't back away from him until he could figure Tyrone out. It's like he must have known that the man coming inside was good people and so barking and wariness was not needed.

I decide to let Atticus stay with them, and I follow Oley into the kitchen.

Silently, I fix Oley and me some sweet tea. We can hear some low murmuring from the living room, which means we're not giving them enough privacy. We head out onto the back patio.

It's chilly outside but not too terrible. Probably low sixties. I have on jeans and a long-sleeve t-shirt. Oley's wearing short sleeves because the day was warm, so I sneak back inside quickly to the mudroom that sits off the kitchen and grab his jacket for him.

When we settle into the chairs, Oley says, "Well... that went about how I expected it would go."

"Yeah," I admit glumly as I stare out into the darkness. "Me too."

There's a few minutes of silence then Oley says, "You did a good thing, Hazel."

"Really?" I ask, my head turning to look at him with unmitigated hope.

He doesn't return the look, staring out into the night as I had been doing. But he reaffirms. "Yeah... no matter what Bernard says, it was a good thing. At least for Tyrone, who gets to see his dad."

◆

WE'RE NOT SITTING outside but maybe fifteen minutes

before the back french door opens, and Bernard is standing there. Atticus slips by him, runs out into the darkness to do his business.

"Oley," Bernard says in a hoarse voice. "Mind giving me a ride home?"

"Not at all," Oley says as he struggles out of his chair.

I stand up, unsure of what to say. I'm stunned they only talked for fifteen minutes and this doesn't bode well. The mere fact Bernard is standing there and Tyrone isn't tells me he's gone already.

"I can take you," I offer lamely, looking from Bernard to Oley who now has his cane under him for support.

"I'd rather Oley," Bernard says curtly. "No offense, Hazel… but I'm too pissed at you."

"Will you ever stop being mad at me?" I ask him, my hands wringing together with fear that I might have lost my friend. And then Atticus is there, pushing his head into my hands.

Sweet dog.

"I'll let you know in a few days how I feel," Bernard mutters, and that's better than telling me to go to hell for all time.

Oley shoots me a reassuring look before following Bernard back into the house. I sit down, Atticus coming to stand between my legs. I rub behind his ears and stare into his beautiful face with my nose almost touching his.

"What do you think, Atticus?" I ask him bluntly. "Did I do a bad thing or a good thing?"

My dog responds with a huge lick of his coarse tongue up one cheek. I wrinkle my nose, not from the slobber, which is par for the course, but from the smell.

It's rank and... smells like dog shit.

"Oh my God," I yell as I push Atticus away from me. "Did you just go out and eat your own poop?"

Atticus backs away a few feet and flops to his butt, grinning at me. I can't smell his breath now that he's put distance between us.

I jump up, run to the french door, and throw it open. Reaching inside, I turn the patio light on. I beckon my dog closer with extreme apprehension after I return to my seat.

"Come here," I say as I open my arms. He trots forward, and I put one hand under his head and use the other to pull his lip upward.

And oh my freaking God... there's poop stuck all in between his teeth. I smell it again and gag.

"God, Atticus," I exclaim as I push him away again. He thinks it's a game, so he tries to jump up at me. I push again. "Get away."

I bolt out of the chair and run into the kitchen. Atticus follows behind. I head to Oley's refrigerator to search for something short of Clorox bleach to clean my dog's mouth. Atticus pushes his head into the fridge, looking around.

I see a bag of carrots and grab it.

He eats three of them before I determine that the poop has been cleared away. My stomach is queasy the entire time, and I tell him how disgusting that behavior is and how he better not do it again.

Atticus thinks it's awesome, though, because he loves carrots. And I'm pretty damn sure he thinks they are some type of "reward" for eating poop. I'm going to have to talk to Oley about this to find out what in the ever-loving hell is wrong with my dog.

CHAPTER 35

Hazel

NOVEMBER 7TH.

It's my thirty-third birthday, and I'm strangely excited. No major plans at all, but I'm more thrilled to have a birthday where I'm not mired in self-pity and self-loathing for my poor choices in life.

It just so happens my birthday falls on a Wednesday this year, which means it's Taco Night and that's my favorite food in the world. Charmin's bringing a "surprise," which I am assuming means a birthday cake. I made sure she knew my favorite was chocolate with vanilla icing, and they make a really good one at Food Lion.

Oley, of course, will be there like he has been for all Taco Nights. Bernard is an unknown although Oley made sure to invite him when he was over on Sunday for the football game.

I've been staying out of Bernard's way per his request. I went to his storage unit the next day after

Tyrone came to see him, but he wasn't in a forgiving mood.

His exact words. "I'll let you know when I'm ready to talk to you."

I truly didn't expect it to go on this long. Bernard is a good human being. He understands people's faults. I thought he'd be able to forgive my butting into his life a lot quicker than he has, but perhaps he won't at all.

If this has taught me anything at all, it's that I need to consider the potential consequences of my actions a lot more carefully before I commit them. I've also learned that what I think is good for someone may not actually be what's good for them.

The good news is that Oley and Bernard's friendship is still intact, as it should be. Oley had nothing to do with it and couldn't have stopped it. I insisted that Oley let Bernard know that I'd stay out of his way, so he could continue to enjoy Friday night baseball and Sunday football with Oley. He'd never been part of our Taco Nights on Wednesday, but it doesn't mean I've given up hope that Bernard will decide to forgive me on my birthday. That would be the best present of all.

Ironically, I've become friends with Tyrone through all of this. He called me after he got home that night he came to see his dad and filled me in on that very short, fifteen-minute conversation. Tyrone has his father's genetic wisdom of sorts, although Bernard's is much more refined given his life experiences.

Bernard was cool and aloof with Tyrone, but Tyrone understood this was born of his father's own fears and shame. He told me he'd kept the conversation light. Updated his dad on his grandchildren, Monica who is four, and Tyrone Bernard, Junior who also has the nickname Ty-Ty. He told his father he'd like to see him again, if and when he was ready.

Bernard was non-committal, but Tyrone told me he isn't giving up hope. He is, however, giving his father a bit of space just as I am.

Since then, Tyrone and I have stayed in touch. I even went to have lunch with him and his wife, Carina one day last week. She's as kind and accepting of Bernard's faults as her husband is, and their determination to make something work with him gives me hope. I just know that it will take some time.

The exam room door opens, and Oley's last patient of the day comes out. Mr. Gorham and his poodle, Peaches. It was time for Peaches rabies vaccination and overall health screening.

Mr. Gorham comes up to the receptionist window, where I work a great deal of the time dealing with the business affairs of the clinic, which includes checking patients out and accepting payment. I only assist Oley on the bigger animals.

Atticus is at my feet. He got to come in today because there were no large patients, and he could stay with me in the reception area. Also, I wanted to weigh him.

Ten and a half months old and eighty-nine pounds. I was relieved when Oley told me that he was almost done growing, but that he might hit ninety-five pounds before it's all said and done.

I smile at Mr. Gorham as he cradles Peaches in one arm and pulls his wallet out with the other. "And how did Peaches do today?"

Atticus doesn't move. He doesn't have much interest in other animals and there's a wall with just a cut-out window between Mr. Gorham and me, so I guess that makes Atti feel less threatened. He continues to snooze in his froggy position beside my desk chair.

The big man grins at me. He's in the marine corps, built like a Mack truck and looks utterly ridiculous with that little poodle in his beefy arms. "She was a superstar," he says proudly. "I'd also like to book Peaches for some boarding at Thanksgiving if you have any openings. I'm going home to Arkansas for the holiday, and I don't want to travel with her."

"Of course," I say as I pull up the boarding schedule on the computer. I've moved Oley from a paper calendar to the 21st century.

After I get Peaches scheduled for her stay with us over Thanksgiving and accept his payment for today's visit, I bid them farewell and head into the storage room to find Oley sitting at the break table. There's an envelope sitting on the table in front of him.

"We're almost filled up for the Thanksgiving holiday," I tell him proudly. Opening for boarding was one of my better ideas. It means I have to come back to the clinic in the evening and early morning if we have guests, but I don't mind. The income it produces has been a game changer, and Oley gave me a huge raise to twelve dollars an hour. It's more money than I've ever made in my life.

"That's good," Oley says with a smile. He then nods to the chair opposite him. "Sit down a minute."

His voice sounds grave, and my heart starts to flutter with nervousness. I do as bid and take my seat, folding my hands on top of the table with a ramrod straight spine.

Oley notices my posture and starts chuckling. "Relax, Hazel. I just want to give you your birthday present."

"Oh," I breathe out in relief before shooting him a lopsided grin. "Sorry."

Oley smiles back, then places his fingertips on the envelope in front of him. He pushes it across the table toward me with a nod.

I hold his gaze a moment before it drops. It's a standard envelope, white with no writing on it. When I pick it up, I see it's not sealed. I reach inside and pull out two items. The first is a check, and the second is a folded-up piece of paper.

When I turn the check over, I gasp as I read it. It's made out from Dr. Oley Peele to Hazel Roundtree for the sum of one thousand dollars.

My eyes snap up and lock with his. "What's this for?"

"For your birthday," he says with a roll of his eyes. "Start a savings account with it, buy Atticus all the toys in the world, or get yourself something pretty."

"It's too much," I say, shaking my head in disbelief.

Oley snorts, but refuses to engage with me over the generosity of his gift. Instead, he says blandly, "You're welcome."

And it's here where I do something very uncharacteristic of our relationship. He's my employer and my closest friend in the world, yet I've never hugged the man.

I do so now, flying out of my chair and rounding the table on him. His eyes bug out for a moment, then I'm bending over and throwing my arms around his neck. He gives a surprised grunt as I squeeze him tight. "Thank you, Oley. That's overly generous and totally unexpected and I'm not quite sure what I did to deserve it, but I'll put the money to good use. I promise."

Oley pats my back awkwardly until I release him.

We stare at each other a moment, and I try to memorize the soft expression on his face. I've never seen it before, and it's beautiful.

Clearing his throat, Oley nods back to the piece of paper that was also in the envelope.

Backing away from him, I sit back down in the chair and unfold the paper. It's a promotional flyer from a college in Raleigh for their veterinary technician program. My brows furrow, completely confused as to why he's giving this to me.

"You'll need to get your GED first," he says, and my gaze lifts to meet his. "You can actually take the GED test without any type of prep course. I'll pay for it. If you pass, great. If not, I'll pay for a course you can take. You get your GED, and I'll pay for your associates degree to become a vet tech."

My mouth opens in surprise. I want to say something, but nothing comes out.

"But only if you want to," he adds on hastily. "I'm not forcing you. But if you want the opportunity, I'll pay for it all."

"I don't... I never considered..." I stammer as Oley smiles at me. "I never dared to dream about something like this."

"No reason you shouldn't," Oley replies. "At the very least, go get your GED, Hazel. You're a smart cookie. Correct that mistake you made dropping out of high school."

"Yeah," I say softly, looking back down at the paper in my hands. "I can totally do that."

"At any rate," Oley says as he pushes from the table and grabs his cane from where it rests against the wall. "I wanted to give that to you in private. I don't like money being anyone's business."

I stand up and grin. "I totally get that. And Oley... thank you."

"Happy birthday, Hazel."

"No... thank you for believing in me. You're the only person who has ever truly done that."

Oley's face flushes, but he's saved from replying when the bells on the front door to the clinic jingle. Atticus lets out a weak bark from the reception area, which means the sound woke him up from a deep sleep. He comes trotting into the storage room, eyes glazed.

"I'll go see who that is," I tell Oley as I put the paper down on the table next to the check.

I walk to the door that separates the storage room from the exam room, which leads to the lobby. I give a short, "Stay," to Atticus. He'll be fine as long as Oley is around, and he can see him. Otherwise, the big baby would have to walk with me.

When I step into the lobby, I freeze as I take in the woman standing there.

My sister, Liz.

She smiles and says, "Happy birthday, Hazel."

Oley's footsteps clomp in. I look over my shoulder to find his eyes twinkling at me. "You're not the only one who can meddle," he says with a smirk.

Turning back, I look at Liz. I still have not been able to bring myself to reach out to her even despite my mom assuring me it will be fine. I want to glare at Oley, but I can't. It's not fair to be mad at Oley when he simply took a meddling page out of my book.

Atticus comes pushing past both me and Oley, who wobbles a bit when my dog's significant bulk bumps against his legs. I want to harsh Atticus a bit because his bumbling ways could hurt Oley if he's not careful, but I'm still too stunned to see my sister standing there.

There's no barking or wariness. Atticus goes right up to Liz, and he starts sniffing at her legs. She stares at him a little bug eyed, but murmurs, "You must be Atticus. I've heard all about you."

Hearing his name, Atticus shoots his eyes up to look at Liz, takes it as pure fact she must want a hug, and starts to rear up on his back legs to do so.

I halt him before he can jump by lunging forward and grabbing his collar. "Oh no, you don't, Mister Mister."

I then order him to, "Sit."

To my relief, he does and grins up at Liz with his mouth parted and tongue flopping out.

"You two get out of here," Oley orders with a pointed nod toward the door. "Liz can take you out to the farm, so you can have some time together before we start Taco Night. I'll close up and bring Atticus home."

"Sounds like a great idea." Liz beams at Oley before turning for the door. I feel I have no choice but to follow.

After grabbing my purse and giving Atticus kisses goodbye, I head out to where Liz is waiting for me. I didn't bother trying to chastise Oley for bringing about something I was convinced I wasn't ready for, because he'd tell me the story about the pot calling the kettle black.

Liz is driving a nondescript silver four door. There's a child seat in the back on the passenger side, and I wonder where Benji is.

The car is idling and overly warm when I slide in, but I think that's more my internal temperature rising from nerves.

"Where to?" she asks pleasantly as I put my seat belt on and she puts the car in reverse.

She hasn't changed much over the years. She's two years younger than me and much prettier I always thought, and I don't mean that in a "woe is me" sort of way. I mean it genuinely. Liz was born with my dad's waviness to her hair and his dimples. She's always looked like the proverbial college girl with the face that doesn't need makeup and a confidence in her bearing that proves it.

I've never begrudged her any of it because I've always loved my sister very much.

"Where to, Hazel?" she asks again, her voice light and airy as if there's no ugly past between us.

But there is.

"Can we just talk a minute?" I ask, unable to proceed any further. I can't take a leisurely drive through the country out to the farm with her right now, pretending that everything is okay.

"Of course," she says simply and slides the car back into park.

When I reach out to the dashboard to turn the heater down, I find it's not even on. I resist the urge to fan myself.

"Let's talk about the hospital," Liz suggests. My eyes snap to hers, and my gut rolls. "I forgive you."

My face burns, and my throat feels like it's coated with sandpaper. I manage to croak out, "I haven't even apologized yet."

Liz gives me a sweet smile—filled with empathy and sisterly love. "Mom's told me so much about you the past few weeks. I've been waiting and waiting for you to reach out, because I would have thought you knew that as your sister, I will always forgive anything you do that might be wayward."

"I'm so embarrassed," I mutter as I look down to my lap where my hands are clenched tightly. "I figured you hated me. I'm sure Trey can't stand me."

"None of it true," Liz says adamantly. "Granted... Trey's family is fascinated that our family has a black sheep story that's fairly juicy. That biker you brought to the hospital was purely scandalous to them, but it's nothing that should ever keep you away from here on out."

I dare to risk a glance up at her. She reaches over to pull one of my hands away from the death grip they have on each other. I get a light squeeze from her. "It's done, Hazel. It's in the past. We're starting over again right now... today... on your birthday. And we're not looking back, okay?"

The lump in my throat makes it impossible for me to reply, so I just nod at her as my eyes fill with tears.

Her eyes do the same, then we're hugging over the center console of her car, and it feels so damn good I doubt I'll ever let go.

"Love you, Haze," she says, her childhood nickname for me I used to hate but now I hope she always uses.

"Love you too, Dizzy Lizzy," I murmur back as I squeeze her extra hard. I realize that's the first time I've said the "L" word to a human being in well over a year, and it doesn't feel awkward in the slightest.

CHAPTER 36

Atticus

I'M NOT SURE what the heck is going on, but this could potentially be one of the best days of my life.

It's Hazel's birthday, so first and foremost I'm celebrating the day she was born. Without such a purely awesome event, I wouldn't be the dog I am today. Hazel is my everything.

But it's more than just "a birthday".

It's the day that I've never seen Hazel happier. She radiates a joy so bright it almost hurts to look at it.

Okay, that's a lie. It's awesome to look at.

When Oley and I get to the farm, we find Hazel and Liz sitting out on the back patio talking. I immediately take stock of the situation, open my senses, and gauge my human. I get none of the apprehension I felt when her sister showed up at the clinic earlier.

Hazel feels… light.

As if she doesn't have a worry in the world, and I've not felt that from her before. She's always carried around something a bit heavy in her heart that I couldn't quite put my paw on, and I conclude it must have had to do with Liz.

Whatever it was is gone.

I make welcome to Liz, who I don't think quite knows what to think of me yet. I'm a bold, brash, and in-your-face type of dog, which is how most people like me, but Liz gets a wild look in her eyes when I approach.

Hazel gently tugs me away by my color, telling me, "Give her some space, Atti."

Normally, this would just be nothing more than a challenge issued for me to get even more up in a person's space, but I don't want to do anything to ruin Hazel's mood. I give a baleful look at Liz, who I very much want to like me, and trot off into the yard to take a whiz.

I do my thing, squatting low to the ground and kicking my back feet out when I'm done. I get distracted by a smell, which leads me to some orange flowers Hazel had planted a few weeks ago. She called them mums, and they're sort of peppery to my nose.

When I hear Hazel scream, I jump into high alert, the hair along my backbone standing straight up on end. My head whips to the patio, but then I immediately relax.

It's just Alicia, Hazel's mom. She has a box in her

hand with brightly colored paper wrapped around it, and I wonder if she's brought me a treat.

Bounding up the patio steps, I barrel into Alicia. I like her a lot, a lot. She always coos over me like I'm a baby, which some would think would threaten my impending adulthood, but I really love it. When she pulls out that sweet voice on me, I always go belly up on her without a second thought.

And it's a secret I'll take to the grave, but she gives better belly scratches than Hazel does, although Hazel gives the best ear rubbins.

I push my way through the hug that Hazel's giving her mom, vaguely hearing her say, "I'm so glad you came." Liz takes a wary step back as I bump my head right into Alicia's belly. She releases Hazel and bends over to pay sole attention to me for a bit.

I accept her scratches while keeping a hopeful eye on the gift she has in her hand. Maybe it's a new bag of sweet potato chips like she feeds me when we're at her house.

If she doesn't reveal it to me soon, I'll just have to pry open the box and find out for myself.

CHAPTER 37

Hazel

BEST BIRTHDAY EVER.

I hug my mom and Liz more than once as they're making their way out the door. I know I owe Oley a hug for pushing me to reconcile with Liz. She made it so easy on me, which makes me love her more.

"We're on for Saturday, right?" Liz asks hesitantly after pulling away from my last hug. She invited me to dinner at her house, so I could meet Benji.

I try to keep the tears of sweet happiness at bay. "I can't wait."

"And you can bring Atticus, too," she says nervously, which makes me laugh so hard I almost double over. Liz, if anything, is not quite comfortable with my dog. I can't imagine how she'd feel to have him around her child who just started walking within the last few months.

"I'll leave him home," I say, then laugh harder when I see the look of relief on her face. I'm sure, over time, she'll get used to him. I hope there will be a day Atticus and Benji can play out on the farm together.

We engage in one last hug, and then I give my mom another. When I pull back from her, I apologize again. "Sorry Atticus ripped into the present you got for me."

My mom rolls her eyes. "He didn't harm anything but the paper."

That's true. He demolished it when we were all eating tacos, and had been halfway through the box that held a beautiful glass hummingbird. I used to collect glass figurines when I was a young teenager, but had forgotten all about it. It brought more tears to my eyes, which were par for the course this evening. Mom told me that all the ones I'd collected were at her house packed safely away when I wanted them.

One more hug.

Why not?

Then I'm waving goodbye to Mom and Liz as they get into their respective cars to leave. The early November air is chilly but feels great on my skin. Atticus sits beside me, head pushed into my hip and my hand scratching idly at his head.

I look down at him. "Good birthday, huh, buddy?"

He chuffs and pushes his head into me harder, demanding more rubs.

"Spoiled," I mutter as I push him away and we head back into the house.

Oley's stretched out in his recliner to take some pressure of his hip. He's had a long day between work and hosting my birthday party.

"Want anything?" I ask as I walk by on the way back to the kitchen to help Charmin clean up. She took on main hostess duties by cooking and serving. Plus, she brought the yummiest homemade chocolate cake with vanilla icing I know I'll have one more piece of before bed tonight. We made sure to lock it away in the fridge lest a wayward Berner decided to help himself.

"I'm good," Oley says without taking his eyes off the TV. He's been binge watching old *Law and Order* episodes on Netflix. He told me once his first career choice when he'd been younger was to be a police officer. I asked him what changed, and he went on to tell me the saddest story about how one of his dogs got hit by a car and there wasn't anything he could do to save it. He decided then to become a vet.

Such a common occurrence, particularly out in the country. I wonder how many other boys and girls had something similar happen, and had it lead to their desire to become an animal doctor. I bet there were many.

I step up to the kitchen sink, grabbing a towel to help dry the dishes. Charmin tries to shoo me away, telling me the birthday girl doesn't have to do a thing, but I insist. I still have way too much energy from the excitement of the day to just sit still.

The only thing to mar the perfectness of the day is Bernard's absence. I know Oley invited him but my hopes for mending my relationship with Bernard were crushed when Oley walked in the door with only Atticus this evening.

Charmin chatters away about a date she has set for Sunday. She's been dating a lot, but to my relief she's being choosy. I think perhaps she's grown over the last several months, and she's realized she should hold out for something a lot better than what she's had.

I wonder when I'll start dating. It's not something I'm interested in right now, although I've had some offers here and there. But I'm still married to Darren, so it doesn't feel right to open a new door to another man without making sure the other one is solidly closed, locked, and the key thrown away. We'll be eligible to file for divorce in less than four weeks as couples have to be separated and living apart for twelve months in North Carolina before allowed to petition the court for divorce. I've not talked to Darren at all since he came over that one night back in August. I suppose I'll need to contact him soon enough to figure out the best way to get this done. I know I'm entitled to things... half the possessions we accumulated together in our six-year marriage... but I really don't want anything.

There's a knock on the front door, and Atticus leaps up from the kitchen floor where he'd flopped down. He starts barking, which is not unusual in and of its self, but the nature of his barks is quite different than normal.

Where they are normally loud and defensive, they come out high pitched with childish excitement. He starts prancing in place, staring at me for a moment, then to the hall that leads to the foyer.

Frowning, I throw the towel down and call out so Oley doesn't bother getting up, "I'll get it."

Atticus bolts out of the kitchen and goes tearing down the hall, his nails scrabbling for traction on the slick hardwood floor once he hits it. I follow him to the door, which has a thick frosted oval cut into the center of it. With the porchlight on, I can see two figures standing on the other side.

Jumping at the door, Atticus yips and barks with such frenzy I'm afraid he's going to pee on himself. I don't know what's on the other side, but I know whatever it is has to be good because Atticus thinks so.

Grabbing his collar, I pull him back and put him in a "sit". It takes three times for him to actually put his ass on the floor and stay, which by this time, Oley comes hobbling into the foyer with curiosity filling his eyes.

Oley puts a gentle hand on Atticus head coupled with his own low command. "Stay". For whatever reason, Atticus listens to Oley better than he does me, which certainly can chafe at times.

However, this affords me safe opportunity to unlock the door and pull it open to see who is on the other side.

I breathe out a huge, relieved sigh when I see Bernard standing there.

Tyrone is right beside him.

They each have a wrapped birthday present in hand.

Tyrone grins at me, all teeth and happiness. Bernard's face is blank and emotionless. I recognize it for what it is… an uncertainty as to how I'll react when I see him after weeks of silence.

I merely lunge for my friend, throwing my arms around his neck and practically strangling him while I gush, "Oh my God. I'm so happy to see you. You came for my birthday."

Bernard returns my hug hard, almost knocking the breath out of me. "Wasn't going to miss it, Hazel."

"Sorry we're late," Tyrone adds. "I couldn't get out of work early today."

I get knocked backward by Atticus butting his way in between me and Bernard. He hasn't seen Bernard in weeks either, which explains his frantic exuberance when he heard the knock on the door.

Giving Atticus his due, I step over and hug Tyrone. "It's good to see you."

"Happy birthday," he says as he gives me a short squeeze.

When I pull back, I find Bernard squatted down to

give Atticus attention, balancing his present for me in one hand. Atticus makes a lunge at it, teeth all bared and prepared to take a bite at the wrapping paper, but I manage to grab his collar to pull him back.

"Get inside, everyone," Oley orders from the threshold with a grin on his face. "I was just wanting another piece of cake."

"Actually," Bernard says. "I'd like a moment alone with Hazel."

"Take your time," Tyrone says, giving a squeeze to his dad's shoulder and following Oley inside. Atticus trots alongside him, nipping at the birthday gift Tyrone is carrying.

I have no clue what led to Tyrone and Bernard being together, but that's just as important to me as the fact that Bernard is here. Tyrone had settled on possibly waiting forever for his dad to want a relationship, so something happened and I'm dying to find out what.

After they're gone and the door is closed, I turn to face Bernard. He hands the present to me.

"Thank you," I say as I accept it, even without knowing what it is.

Bernard nods at it. "I wanted to get you something with meaning. I knew exactly what I wanted to get, but it was over at the mall. It was going to be a long damn walk, so I called Tyrone and asked him for a ride."

My lips split apart into what's perhaps the widest

smile that has ever graced my face. I understand exactly what he's conveying to me. He wanted to reach out to Tyrone and was still fearful, despite the fact Tyrone made it about as easy on him as humanly possible.

Bernard simply used my birthday and his desire to get me something as the catalyst to force him to reach out to Tyrone.

Now that right there is the best present ever.

"Open it," he orders.

"Okay," I say with a chuckle, ripping into the paper. I peel back a large chunk before I realize it's a book.

To Kill A Mockingbird by Harper Lee.

"Figured it was about time you read it," he says by way of explanation. "I wanted you to have the hardback version, which was why I needed to get to the bookstore at the mall. A book that special you should have in hardback."

Tears prick my eyes over the thoughtfulness of his gesture, not just in the journey he made there and reaching out to his son, but that he wanted the book to be a real treasure to me. I know how little money Bernard actually has, so this purchase is a major thing.

"Oh, Bernard," I murmur as I run my fingers along the spine of the book. It's got a glossy jacket that shimmers in the porch light. I haven't read a book in years, but I can't wait for everyone to go home so I can start. Looking up to him, I say, "This really means a lot."

He scratches at his head with a sheepish smile. "And I'm sorry. For being such a jerk to you. I should have never said the things I did."

"I deserved it," I say with a halting hand raised.

"No, you didn't. You are my dear friend, and I know you were only doing it from a position of love. And I want you to know… I'm grateful. I have my son back in my life now, and I don't think I knew how much I actually needed it."

"I do love you, Bernard," I tell him sincerely. "You're a very important part of my life, and I would never intentionally hurt you."

"Love you too, kiddo," he says gruffly.

"Want some cake?" I ask with a grin.

"Oh yeah," he says with a laugh. "And a beer if you got one."

"I can arrange that," I reply as I loop my arm through his.

Truly the best birthday ever.

CHAPTER 38

Atticus

I'M FASCINATED BY that tiny human sitting on Liz's lap.

He smells amazing, especially his butt. I watched earlier as Hazel tried to help Liz change a poopy diaper. My mouth watered, and Hazel gagged.

The dirty diaper went into a plastic bag, sealed, and then dropped into Oley's garbage can that also comes equipped with one of those lids I can't pry open.

Still, my belly's not complaining. Hazel made a turkey and a ham for Thanksgiving, and I've had plenty of both. I've just now digested enough that I can push myself up from the cool floor and amble over to the baby they call Benji.

I can tell Liz is nervous, but I show her my very best behavior. I don't jump, lunge, bark, or even slobber. Slowly, I approach.

Liz's husband Trey likes me. He had dogs growing up is what he said when we were first introduced. He watches me with an easy smile. Liz's eyes come to me, and she tenses just slightly.

I pause.

She stares at me.

Finally, I get a tiny smile and a nod from her. "Want to see Benji, Atticus?"

Oh boy, did I ever. I want an up-close smell.

I approach little by little, tail wagging and head ducked down so as not to intimidate the little thing. He smiles and waves his arms. When I'm within striking distance, his little hands go into the fur on top of my head. They fist and grab tight, but it doesn't hurt.

Still, Liz says, "Easy, Benji. Don't want to hurt the puppy."

"Puh-puh," Benji says, and I think we're going to be good friends.

A soft clinking sound resonates, and my head swings that way.

Hazel stands up from the long dining table, tapping a spoon to her wineglass. She surveys the people around the table with such fullness in her heart I can feel it.

Turning away from the little human who is certainly fascinating but in no way compares to Hazel, I pad over to her and sit my rump down by her feet.

She grins at me before clearing her throat. "I just want to thank everyone for coming to Oley's for Thanksgiving. I have so much to be thankful for this year, and this is the absolute best time to make sure I'm vocal about it to those I love the most."

Hazel takes a moment to connect eyes with everyone around the table—our family. Oley on the end, because he's king of the castle. Next to him is Bernard, then Charmin, then Alicia. On the other end, is Trey, not king of this castle but a cool dude all the same. To his left, Liz with Benji on her lap and then me.

Tyrone is coming later with his wife and kids as they were lucky enough to have a first Thanksgiving dinner somewhere else. I'm excited to see more tiny humans.

"The beginning of this year was extremely difficult for me," Hazel continues, and I cock my head to watch her. There's a touch of sadness in her eyes as she remembers the days before me when her life was bad. "I was at my lowest point in my life. I didn't know the meaning of family or true friendship."

I glance around the table, seeing everyone stare back at Hazel with such love that it makes me feel gooey inside.

"And then I found this little monster," she says affectionately as her hand comes to my head to give me a scratch. "He opened up a new life for me. And bit by bit, my life became more enriched. I developed close friendships and reconnected with family. I worked hard to be a better person to others, but mostly to myself. I just want to say I can't imagine a better life, and I'm so thankful for every last one of you sitting here. So… here's to all of you. I love you very much."

Her last words come out sort of choked up, and there are a few misty eyes around the table. Hazel holds her glass of wine up. Everyone else does the same, their own salute back to her that she's pretty freaking awesome in her own right.

Hazel sits back down in her chair, and conversation flows freely with lots of laughter in between. Reaching to her plate, Hazel picks up a piece of ham and holds it out to me.

My tail thumps involuntarily, and I reach out with my mouth just a tiny bit open to accept the treat.

It's delicious… salty and sweet.

We should have Thanksgiving every day as far as I'm concerned.

PART III

"Life is the art of drawing without an eraser."

– John Gardner

CHAPTER 39

Hazel

I COMPLETED THE checkout process for Mr. Tibbles, a Siamese cat that's mean as hell. He's a new patient to our clinic, and I assigned him to Dr. Gilroy since she's a cat person. While Oley is wonderful with all animals, Dr. Gilroy has some kind of magical touch when it comes to hissing, spitting mad cats.

Marsha Gilroy has been a blessing since we added her to the practice last year. She had been working for one of the big veterinary hospitals in town, but had no chance for upward mobility. She wanted to be not only a veterinarian but also a business owner as well.

Oley is on the downswing of his practice and I don't know how many years he has left in him. Maybe twenty, maybe two. At his age it's hard to know, so we better be prepared. I talked to him about coming up with a game plan to sell his practice out. He can't leave it for his kids as they aren't veterinarians, and I didn't want to see a profitable clinic go to waste. As his business increased, I suggested we look for another veterinarian to bring on board who would be interested in buying out Oley's practice when he was ready to fully retire.

Marsha—who just hit the big 4-0 last week—wanders into the reception area, using gauze to dab at a cut on the back of her hand. I smell alcohol wafting from it.

Smirking, I say, "Mr. Tibbles got you, didn't he?"

She grins back at me. "I must be losing my touch."

"Your next appointment called to say they would be about ten minutes late. It's fine since you have some room in your schedule."

"Thanks Hazel," Marsha replies. "That gives me a chance to eat my lunch I didn't get to eat two hours ago."

She walks behind my desk, then heads into the storage room where Oley has had to buy a bigger table to house the new additions to his practice. In addition to Marsha coming on as the second veterinarian, we've hired two vet technicians and a part-time worker to help with the boarders.

Plus, there's me. Hazel Roundtree, office manager.

The past four years since I met Oley have been amazing, but none more so than helping him to build up a thriving and profitable business that has given the man himself extra life and vitality. Outside of his bum hip, he's actually doing better health-wise than ever.

He's lost a bit of weight, and he's far more active around the farm. I credit this with the boost his self-esteem has taken over being able to work again without many limitations. As long as someone can help him with the more unruly patients, Oley's practically unstoppable in the clinic.

The one opportunity I passed on was Oley's offer to go to school to become a veterinary technician. I did take my GED—passing on the first try without any review course—and then promptly got my associates in business at the local community college. While I like working with the animals, I really have a passion for helping Oley in the operations, marketing, and human resources. I'm very close to finishing an online bachelor's degree, and then I'll consider whether to do an MBA. Whatever I do, it has to be done online because I'm too instrumental to the clinic and Oley to go to school full time somewhere else.

To this day, I'm still not sure why Oley gave me so much free rein to help build his veterinary clinic up. He didn't have much of a practice at all when I first met him but then again, he hadn't needed it. Over his decades of work, he had been very wise with his money and could now easily retire if he wanted to without a monetary care in the world.

I suppose his being able to work more has been giving him a sense of renewed life. It seems to have made him healthier and happier to keep working. Granted, the bum hip lets him work only about thirty hours max a week, which means Marsha does most of the heavy hitting these days.

"Hey," Marsha says just before she opens the door to the storage room. "Aren't you supposed to be leaving early today?"

My eyes drop down to the clock on my computer screen, and I grimace when I see how late it has gotten. I keep tapping away on my keyboard while I answer. "Yeah... But I have to finish the payroll."

"Anything I can do to help?" she asks.

"Not today," I answer with a quick glance over my shoulder at her. "But we really need to sit down so I can show you the payroll program soon."

Oley has no plans to retire anytime soon, but given his age, we have decided we need to train Marsha on as many of the business aspects of the practice we can, so she could step in if—God forbid—something happened to Oley.

"Then I'll leave you alone so you can finish that since you have important business to attend to," Marsha says with a laugh.

I throw my hand up over my shoulder to give a short wave in acknowledgment, because I do indeed have important things to do today. As soon as I finish the payroll, I'm heading out of here to grab Atticus.

It's an important day today.

The most important holiday I celebrate.

It's Atticus's fourth Gotcha Day.

Four years ago today, on March 28th, I found him in a ditch on death's door. I may not have been as physically beat up as he was, but my emotional psyche was comparative to his dire situation. From the start, we needed each other.

Four years later, we are still a dynamic duo. I'm pretty sure everything that is great in my life is due to this one very important day.

Granted, there have been other enrichments in my life. Oley, Bernard and his family, Liz and my mom, and let's not forget a wonderful new career.

But none of that would've ever been set into motion had I not pulled that muddy, slimy, bleeding puppy out of that culvert.

On Atti's second Gotcha Day, I decided it needed to be a solo and personal event between the two of us. We always had his birthday party on the Fourth of July where I would throw a big party and make a big deal over my little boy. But today is just for me and him.

♦

AFTER LEAVING THE clinic, I race out to the farm so I can change and get my dog. I still live in the apartment above Oley's garage even though I could afford to get a bigger, nicer place on my own. I still only pay him two hundred dollars a month, though I've tried to get him to take more. To assuage my guilt over such a great deal, I've made a lot of upgrades to the apartment over the last four years, including new carpet, paint, and some appliances. The real reason I stay here is because I want to keep a close eye on Oley. He's almost seventy-six, and I feel much better being close just in case something was to happen.

I pull a pair of jeans and a long-sleeved flannel shirt out of my closet. It's one of those early spring days where the weather is chilly in the morning, warm in the afternoon, and will be chilly by the time early evening hits. Since I'm taking Atticus to the beach, I want to be prepared for it to be even cooler with the ocean winds.

I think Atti senses my excitement and knows today is very special. I told him it was his Gotcha Day when we woke up this morning, but I don't pretend to think my dog understands English. Rather, he is an excellent reader of emotions and he picks up on mine very easily. He prances in place while I throw on my clothes, then we race down the stairs with his leash and harness in my hand. We take just a moment for him to get potties, and then he's jumping in the backseat of my Jeep.

My slightly used, but completely awesome rag-top Jeep Wrangler in an electric blue color. It's the first vehicle I've ever owned all by myself that I paid for all by myself. I make a lot more than twelve dollars an hour these days working as Oley's office manager.

Atticus loves riding in the back when the top is off, but it's going to be just a little too cold for me heading to the beach. "Sorry, buddy. Top stays on today."

Atticus just grins from the backseat with that tongue hanging out the side. I do crank down the windows for him, though, and he periodically puts his face out. I watch him in my side mirror with his jowls and ears flapping all around. His eyes are halfway closed against the rush of air. He looks wild and free and happy.

It's how I feel right now.

We stop for vanilla frozen yogurt before we hit the high-rise bridge that connects the mainland over the intercoastal waterway to Topsail Island.

I take the first left and head north up the island, pulling into the first public access parking lot I come to. It's only about half full, and I bet most of the people are fishing.

After attaching Atticus to his chest harness and lead, I let him jump out of my Jeep. I lock it up, carrying only my keys and phone down onto the beach.

It's funny that I bring Atticus to the beach to celebrate his Gotcha Day as it's not his favorite place in the world. He's not a big fan of the waves crashing in, which intimidate him a little, but he certainly likes to take long walks on the hard-packed sand. I'm not necessarily a beach girl either, preferring the mountains as a getaway destination. But I like being able to walk a long straight path with my dog for as long as we want just so we can spend some quality time together.

When we get down to the beach, it's mostly dotted with surf fishermen and a few other walkers. Atti walks at a heel on my left side. We stay away from the tide, so we can avoid getting caught up in fishing lines.

"What do you think I ought to make for dinner tonight?" I ask him, without expecting a response, of course.

One of my most treasured things about Atticus is that he's been my sounding board over the years. I can talk to him about stupid stuff, funny stuff, or serious stuff. I can try to figure out what's on the dinner menu, or how I'm going to budget in a pair of expensive running shoes I've been wanting to buy, or how I'm worried about Oley if he gets a cold. My dog listens to it all and as weird as it sounds, he manages to give me the appropriate support I need back. This means if I'm talking about something that stirs emotion within me, Atticus is there for me to pet and love upon.

If I'm down in the dumps, he'll without fail do something silly to make me laugh. If I'm getting too complacent with life, he'll do something really bad to keep me on my toes.

So we walk along, and I keep talking and he keeps

listening as we head further north up the island.

"Benji loves spaghetti so I'll probably make that, but maybe I'll grill up a few steaks for you and me. What do you think about that buddy?"

I swear Atticus' ears perk when I say the word steak. Of course he's getting steak for dinner. It's his Gotcha Day.

I'm babysitting Benji tonight so Liz and Trey can go out on a date. They've been struggling in their marriage over the last few years, and I think part of it was because Liz devoted one hundred percent of her time and attention to Benji without anything left over for her husband. I know motherhood is extremely difficult and taxing, but I get the sense she was going overboard in her attentions on her son. At least, that's sort of what she concluded after she and Trey did some heavy-duty counseling. One of the suggestions was they take one night a week and do something together. It didn't have to be for very long, and it was often only a dinner date. But that meant I got to see my nephew a lot more, who—at almost five years old—was a hell of a lot more fun now than he was as a baby.

My phone rings, and I nab it from my back pocket. I can't help the smile that comes to my face when I see Charmin's name on my screen. I connect the call, put the phone to my ear, and say, "And how is my sweet little mama-to-be?"

Charmin laughs, and I can't help but be amazed by the absolute peace and joy in her voice. "Your sweet little mama has a sore back. Carrying around an extra twenty pounds is no joke."

Charmin is five months pregnant. She's also happily married and living in Raleigh. Sometimes it seems like yesterday when we were schlepping beers together at Tipsy's. Both of us were terribly unlucky in love and always seemed to pick the wrong guys.

Charmin, however, has basically been living an actual real-life fairy tale the last couple of years. She was working one night at Tipsy's when an incredibly dashing man came into the bar. He was absolutely out of place wearing a three-piece suit and a two-hundred-dollar haircut.

Turns out, he was an attorney from Raleigh who was in Jacksonville on business doing depositions. He had just finished up for the day and wanted a beer. Tipsy's was the first bar he came to. His name is Shane Nicholson, and he shamelessly flirted with Charmin all night. He gave her a ride home, and didn't even try kiss her.

After that night, Shane was so taken with Charmin he came back to Jacksonville every Sunday for the next two months to take her out on a date. Within just a few months of that, he had convinced her to stop working at Tipsy's and move into his over-four-thousand-square-foot house on a golf course in Raleigh. They wed just a year after that, and immediately got started on making a baby.

"When are you and Atticus going to come visit me?" she whines into the phone.

"Why?" I tease. "Tired of hanging out with all your new country-club friends?"

She snorts. If there's one area of her new magical fairy tale she's not quite sold on yet, it's blending in with Shane's crowd of peeps. They're all wealthy, educated, and some are slightly snobbish.

"Maybe weekend after next?" I ask. "I'll see if Oley wants to ride up with me to see Tara."

Charmin doesn't say anything in response to that, but I know what she's thinking. Fat chance Oley's daughter will have time for him. Over the years, I've come to have a better understanding of his relationship with his kids.

And it's pretty clear they don't give many shits about their father.

He provided them a very good life growing up, since he made plenty of money with his successful veterinarian practice. They were kind of spoiled—Oley's words, not mine—and when they decided to leave the nest, they didn't really look back. Granted, they had busy, successful lives. But they were also self-absorbed enough to think calling their father once a week was all that was needed at his age.

"That would be perfect with me," Charmin says. "We're still working on the nursery, and I was hoping to go shopping for bed linens. You can help me with that."

I roll my eyes. Shopping is my least favorite thing in the world, but I'll never balk at doing it with a pregnant Charmin. This is sort of an epic deal for us both since she's asked me to be godmother.

"So what are you doing to celebrate Atti's Gotcha Day?" she asks.

I can't help but smile. She knows what an important day this is for me, and that's actually why she's calling. "We're at the beach right now. I bought him a vanilla frozen yogurt, and I'll make him steak tonight. I'm babysitting Benji but after he leaves, Atti and I will just chill out and play. Lots of belly rubs for sure."

"Sounds absolutely perfect," she says.

And I couldn't agree more.

"Perfect" is a word that pretty much sums up my life these days.

"Are you ever going to bother telling me how your date with that marine helicopter pilot went?" she asks coyly.

"I wouldn't even waste your time," I reply dryly as I glance at Atticus. He's plodding along beside me with his nose hovering over the sand.

"Bummer," she murmurs.

Yeah, bummer. He seemed nice at first, but then I found out he was one of those men who just likes to hear himself talk. He could be talking about piloting a helicopter in combat or about the brand of toilet bowl cleaner he uses, and trust me... I heard about both and so much more. On and on and on... blah, blah, blah. I don't think he asked me one question about myself.

What's even worse is he seemed genuinely surprised when he asked me out again, and I declined. He thought he was so interesting and such a great catch that I wouldn't possibly say no.

Sorry, but *bye Felicia*. I don't do self-absorbed any-more.

Actually, I don't do much of anyone these days. Since my divorce from Darren a little over three years ago, I've tried dating. But it's hard and stressful. Maybe I'm just too damn picky. I know exactly what I don't want, but finding out what I do is proving to be troublesome. I think part of the problem is I've found out I can be completely happy on my own. My life is so rich and fulfilled I don't feel like I'm lacking.

Okay... the sex is lacking and I miss that, but past that, I'm completely fine staying single.

Like I said... my life is pretty near to perfect as can be.

CHAPTER 40

Atticus

BENJI IS STILL a little human, but he is far more mobile these days than when he was a little baby.

He definitely doesn't smell as interesting as he did, mainly because he doesn't wear a diaper anymore. My favorite thing to do with him—outside of him throwing me food from the table—is to play tug-of-war. Sometimes, though, I get a little too rough. Hazel constantly reminds me I am over ninety pounds and Benji is half my size. This makes perfect sense to me, and it's why he is so easy to drag around Hazel's apartment. But that's his fault. He won't let go of the rope and once I pull him off his feet, there's no way I can resist the impulse to drag him across the living room floor. Hazel yells at me, but it's all good because Benji laughs when I do it.

Today, Hazel celebrated my Gotcha Day with me. She explained to me it was the day she found me in a ditch. I don't have very good memories of that, but Hazel does and she always reminds me once a year when we celebrate our time together. I know she calls it my Gotcha Day, but it's hers as well.

It's the day I got her in return.

These days, I'm a pretty good boy. I finally stopped eating socks, but that only occurred after I couldn't throw one up and had to have a surgery to get it out. That was not fun. It hurt a lot and they put these metal things in my stomach after they cut it out that itched like crazy. I wanted to lick at them so bad, but I wasn't allowed to. I had to wear the stupid cone of shame around my neck, and it was absolutely humiliating because I would bump into walls and furniture all the time. It also prevented me from putting my face up near Hazel's for kisses.

I've also eased up on the chewing of furniture, drywall, pillows, and such. While I still have great moments of rambunctious excitement that will overwhelm me at times, I don't mind just snoozing for a good chunk of the day. Hazel was brushing me the other day when she frowned and said, "Atticus… you're starting to get some gray hairs in your face."

I'm not sure what exactly that meant, but Hazel's tone was sad. That, in turn, made me sad.

Just because I'm slowing down a bit and perhaps maturing into a wiser sort of canine doesn't mean I don't still like to play. Every day, Hazel and I will either go on long walks around the farm or she'll throw a ball for me to chase. Sometimes we have doggy play dates with Marsha's boxer, Rex. He's a young pup and a complete goofball. He tries to hump me a lot, but I growl and remind him who's top dog.

That would be me.

Always me.

I heard Hazel tell Marsha the other day she was thinking about getting another dog, but I'm not sure I like that. I don't like sharing Hazel's time with anyone. I mean, it's cool if it's for a small amount of time like when she watches Benji for a little bit. That makes her happy, which makes me happy.

But when he leaves, I'm even happier. That means I have Hazel all back to myself. It's sort of like the men Hazel dates on occasion.

Personally, I have not liked a single one of them. I'm also pretty obvious about it. While I have not gone as far as to poop in one of their shoes—because that's reserved for real jerks like Chuck, and Hazel is far too smart to date someone like him—I can be ornery with them. Occasionally, I'll growl in a really vicious type of way just so I can scare them. That always surprises Hazel as well as embarrasses her, because I'm really a nice dog.

But those men don't know that.

One time, Hazel was watching a movie on the couch with one of the guys she'd been seeing, and I had a lot of gas. I mean... my butt smelled B-A-D.

I acted all nice and casually moseyed over to his side of the couch, where I laid down at his feet. He even reached down to pat me on the head before I let loose on the poor man. Hazel was embarrassed again, and the guy didn't stay for the whole movie.

I don't plan on changing my ways. Hazel is just fine without a man, and she has me for anything she could possibly need. But even if I felt they could give her something I couldn't, they would have to meet some very high standards I've set.

Any man who wants my Hazel would have to make her as happy as I've seen on a very rare few occasions where she shines from the inside out with euphoric joy. I can remember a few of those times... like when Oley let her stay in the apartment above his garage. When she reunited with her sister. Or even when we sit down with family and friends on that one day each year I get to eat unlimited amounts of turkey and ham.

Yes... if a man would ever give that to Hazel on a consistent basis, I might just have to give him a chance.

CHAPTER 41

Hazel

W HEN I PULL into the Hidden Valley Estates, I do as I always do.

I snicker over the name of the trailer park Bernard has chosen to live because I can't help but think of salad dressing every single time.

Calling it an "estate" is a generous term as it's nothing but a single dirt road with eight trailers on each side. Bernard's is the last one down on the right.

I'm not the only one who has had big changes in their life over the last four years. Bernard has moved out of his storage unit and into a single-wide trailer not too far from Oley's farm, but also within easy and safe walking distance of Highway 17 so he can get around.

His decision to move came after a lot of poking and pushing by me, Tyrone, and Oley, but occurred only after Wanda asked him for a divorce. If he was upset by her request, I never saw it. He stoically agreed and wished Wanda well with the rest of her life. Personally, I think Bernard accepted the marriage was over the last time he walked out on her and she begged him never to come back.

Wanda has found herself a new man. According to Tyrone, he's a pretty good guy. I've only met him once when I dropped by while over on that side of town to say hello to her. She appeared to be very happy.

Wanda knew what she was giving up when she decided to be free of Bernard for good. With marital ties legally severed, Bernard now had his disability benefits, which he had previously been letting his wife have.

After that, it didn't take a lot of convincing to get him to rent a place with running water and electricity. Bernard didn't want much, and an old single wide trailer was practically like a luxury hotel compared to where he had been living.

Since moving in, Bernard looks healthier and happier. He's put on a few pounds because he can afford decent food. But I think the real reason this works for Bernard doesn't have a damn thing to do with having money to support himself, but rather he doesn't have the same familial pressures that had previously stressed him out.

These days, he has a relaxed relationship with Tyrone and his family. He has neighbors who ignore him, and he ignores them back. He has no obligations unless our standing get-togethers at Oley's count. All of this means he leads a relatively peaceful existence with a solid roof over his head and better food in his stomach.

Granted, Bernard still likes his beer. He also doesn't want a car, and he doesn't mind walking to wherever he needs to go, although Oley and I try to give him a ride whenever we can. Tyrone also visits his dad regularly, and Bernard sometimes goes over to Tyrone's house for family dinners and to visit his grandkids.

It's amazing to me how much has changed for Bernard. It seems like a lifetime ago he was loitering in Tipsy's and panhandling for his daily beer and food.

I pull into the front yard of Bernard's trailer because there isn't a driveway. Just a sparse patch of brown grass bordering the equally brown dirt road. I get out and grab the casserole dish, bumping the car door closed with my hip.

Bernard had been sick the last week with a nasty case of the flu. At least I think it was the flu as he stubbornly refused to go to the doctor to get tested. This makes no sense to me since he has free medical care for the rest of his life. Maybe it's because he's a former marine and wants to be all tough about it, but I came by every day unless Tyrone did, and we kept him stocked in chicken noodle soup, Gatorade, and medicine. Yesterday, he looked almost normal when I stopped by after work, so today I decided he needed a good, hearty meal since he had not been eating much. I made his favorite tuna fish casserole and a double batch at that.

Bernard is opening the front door for me before my foot even hits the first step of the little wooden staircase bolted to the side of the tin trailer that's turning green with mildew.

His white teeth flash at me in welcome. "What you got there?"

I grin up at him, noting his gaze lingers hungrily on the dish in my hand. "Your favorite."

Bernard gives a dramatic rub over his belly and groans. "I was hoping you would say that."

He beckons me inside, and I head straight for the kitchen. I know my way around this little trailer well. The front door enters the living room and the kitchen is to the right. It's nothing more than a small U-shaped countered area with a stove, sink and refrigerator. There's only enough room for a small table that sits two people near the window and a small utility closet. His living room is sparsely furnished with just a couch and a recliner. There's a rickety old TV stand, but it holds a forty-two inch, high-definition flat screen Tyrone gave him for Christmas.

On the other side of the living room there's a narrow hall that runs along the backside of the trailer that leads to two bedrooms with a tiny bathroom in between. The bedrooms can't be any bigger than ten-by-ten, but they are more than what Bernard needs. He sleeps on a single mattress on the floor of the back bedroom and refuses Tyrone's offer to buy him an actual set of furniture, insisting this is far more than he had before and he's satisfied with it.

I suspect the next major holiday might just yield some furniture, though, and Bernard will accept it. I mean, he was totally against having a TV until Tyrone showed up with one, and he didn't decline the gift.

Regardless, Bernard has lifted himself up and is a much happier person for it. I credit most of that with his ability to reconnect with his son and to also forge a new and sweetly gratifying relationship with his two grandchildren. As long as Bernard's life will never get any more complicated than what it is right now, I expect he's going to die a happy man.

Hopefully that won't be for a long time, though.

"Would you like a plate of it now?" I ask as I set the casserole dish on the counter.

He follows in behind me and sits down at the table. "You know I do. Will you join me?"

I shoot a quick smile to him. "Of course I'll join you. It's always better to eat with company."

I know exactly which cupboards holds Bernard's dinnerware. He has a cheap plastic four-piece service set that he bought at Walmart when he first moved in. Not that he would actually have four people over for dinner at any one time, but it's there if he needs it.

I dish up the casserole onto two plates, grateful it's still quite warm. Bernard doesn't have a microwave. I snag two forks from one of the drawers, and then set the plates on the table. Bernard doesn't even wait for me to sit down before he digs in, but I go to his fridge and pull out two Pabst Blue Ribbon beers. When I settle back down, I open the cans and slide one over to Bernard. He swallows a mouthful of tuna fish casserole and picks his beer up, holding it up for me to tap mine against his.

We give a silent toast and take sips of our cheap brew.

"How come you didn't bring Atticus with you?" Bernard asks.

I wrinkle my nose and grimace. "The little turd wasn't invited. I'm mad at him."

Bernard rolls his eyes because even if I was mad at him before I left Oley's, I wouldn't still be mad. I just can't hold any enmity toward my pup.

"What did he do?" he asks.

"Little shit figured out how to open my upper cabinets," I say with disgust. "He's figured out he's just tall enough now on his back legs that he can grab the handle with his mouth. He ate an entire bag of chocolate chip cookies I had up there."

"Oh, my God," Bernard chortles, banging his fist on the table. He chokes on his laughter, then has to chug his beer to clear his throat. "That dog."

"Yeah, that dog scared the shit out of me. Chocolate can be toxic to dogs."

"Assuming Oley checked him out?" Bernard asks, punching his fork back down into the casserole.

I nod. "He's fine. Said that given the amount of chocolate compared to his weight, it wasn't enough to worry about."

"That's good."

"Actually, I did invite Atticus to come, but he was content to stay with Oley. Was laying on the couch, pretending he was interested in the news while Oley was watching it, which is ridiculous."

"I wouldn't put it past your dog to be interested in the news," Bernard remarks as he points his fork at me. "He's smart, that one. Like deviously smart. Sometimes I find myself watching what I say around him so as not to be a bad influence."

That makes me burst out laughing, not only because it's ridiculous but because sometimes I've thought that myself.

"I think it was more due to the fact he'd just eaten an entire bag of cookies, and he wanted to take a nap."

"Your dog is getting lazy," Bernard says with a laugh.

That's part of it for sure. But he's also getting older and losing some of his energy. I don't say this to Bernard because I don't want to incite a discussion about it. This is a part of my dog's life I'd like to blissfully ignore as long as I can.

Atticus is going to be four and a half years old in July. It may not seem like a lot of years, but it can be for large breed dogs. Bernese Mountain Dogs have an average life expectancy of only six to eight years, which means Atticus has lived most of his life already.

My eyes actually prick with tears. It always happens when I think about my dog dying, so I do what I usually do and think of something else.

"Atticus actually has a paying gig this weekend," I say.

He's chewing on a huge mouthful of food, so he just nods at me to continue.

"Some TV producer called about a show they are filming in Wilmington. They want some dog extras, and they saw Atticus on Instagram."

Bernard nods more effusively and with understanding. Atticus has become somewhat of an Instagram star over the last few years. That account I had started back when he was a puppy gained an intense following after I started posting about his crazy antics.

Atticus tears into a feather pillow...

Did I chastise him?

No. I grabbed my phone and videoed him lying in the middle of a cloud of feathers. I posted it for the world to see and as expected, most people were charmed and amused by his lack of contrition. He would stare into the camera after doing something bad, and people would fall for that absolutely unrepentant expression on his face that said he regretted nothing.

Astoundingly, he has over two hundred thousand followers. That kind of attention gets the notice of retailers and various companies specializing in dog friendly products have contacted me over the years. Atticus has actually been offered money and free stuff if he will endorse them. It basically means I take a picture with whatever the product is, and then I post it to his huge Instagram following. It's usually just a couple of hundred bucks here and there, or a huge supply of whatever product he's endorsing. Nothing that's ever going to make my dog rich, but it's a lot of fun.

"So you're going to take the boy to Wilmington to be a movie star?" Bernard says with a chuckle after he washes his food down with another long pull of his beer.

"It's a TV show, not a movie, and they only want him as an audience extra, whatever that means. I seriously doubt he's going to become a star."

Bernard snorts. "That boy already is a star."

True enough.

"What are your big plans for the weekend?" I ask.

Bernard shrugs. "Tyrone is taking the family down to Georgia to see his Carina's family. I was thinking about seeing if Oley wanted to do something."

I keep my smirk to myself. Those two men hanging out on the weekend means either watching sports or old Western movies. Maybe I'll make a nice pot roast for dinner for all of us since I'd much rather be hanging out with these two old guys and cuddling my dog than anything else.

CHAPTER 42

Hazel

I'M NOT QUITE sure what I was expecting for the filming of a TV show, but it wasn't this. I had thought it would perhaps be in a studio—the type that has a stage and stadium seating for the audience like on the *Ellen DeGeneres Show* or *Saturday Night Live*.

Instead, it's being filmed outdoors on the back end of the production lot. Wilmington has been a micro movie and TV film hub for years, most notably filming the TV series *Dawson's Creek* and *One Tree Hill*, as well as the movie *Iron Man 3*.

The show that invited Atticus on as an audience extra is actually about dog behavior, and it consists of a panel of experts ranging from veterinarians to trainers to dog psychics who help with problem animals.

They are working in an outdoor set today to show how occupying dogs with interesting activity can help to curb bad behavior. They have a huge agility course set up, which I imagine will be used with the guest animals.

I wonder, compared to Atticus, how bad are the guest animals going to be? Sometimes it's impossible for me to imagine there's another dog in the entire universe that's as obstinate and free spirited—translation really, really bad—as mine, although strangely, I wouldn't want him any other way.

Which is why I'm glad Atticus is just an audience extra rather than one of the actual guests who will be given some training. It's not that my dog can't learn. I'd stack him up against any dog here for brains.

It's more along the lines he only wants to learn what interests him. He only wants to exercise his knowledge when he feels like it.

Atticus and I mill about while they finish preparations for filming. There are several other people here with dogs of all varieties. So far, I've seen a Doberman, dachshund, Shar-Pei, lab, Rottweiler, German Shepherd, Newfoundland, Beagle, Shih Tzu, Pomeranian, and the list goes on and on...

I've never had any big aspirations that my dog was the most special, beautiful, and talented dog in the world. It's enough for me that he's the most special dog to me.

But I do get a kick out of people's reactions to Atticus, and he's garnering a lot of attention here. When he reached about two years old, he had finally and fully grown into his body as well as his fur. He's topped out at ninety-three pounds with a thick straight coat with long feathers at his haunches and forearms. His raven-colored tail is lustrously full and perfectly tipped white on the end. As always, his most interesting feature, that by far draws the most compliments, are his eyes and his eyebrows, which lend a human-like character to his face. With just one short glance at him, it's obvious he is one smartly mischievous dog that walks to the beat of his own drum.

"Hazel Roundtree…" I hear my name being called, so I go up to my tiptoes to try to see over the crowd to who it is. Unable to see anything because I'm not the tallest person, I make my way through the throng of animals and their owners, making sure to keep a short lead on Atticus.

"Hazel Roundtree," I hear again. I finally break through a group of people to see a beautiful blonde woman with a clipboard in her hand. She's looking around expectantly.

Right here," I call as I trot up to her, Atticus high stepping right beside me.

She gives me a wide smile, but then her eyes drop to my dog and it goes even bigger. "Oh, he is absolutely gorgeous."

"Thank you," I say as her gaze comes back up to mine.

"I bet you get that a lot."

I laugh. "All the time."

She holds her hand out for me to shake. "I'm Aubrey Stewart. I run the media division of LWW Enterprises."

Trying not to blink in surprise, I give her hand a firm shake. She's not who I spoke to on the phone when they first called. "Pleased to meet you. And thank you for inviting us here."

When we release hands, Aubrey drops down into a squat to get face to face with Atticus. She puts her hand under his chin, starting to scratch before turning to look up at me. "I'm a big fan of your dog. I follow him on Instagram, and I put one of my producers on the hunt to contact you."

My eyebrows shoot upward in surprise. I knew someone from this company had spotted Atticus on Instagram, but I had no idea it was actually the head of their media department. "He could be a superstar, you know?" she adds.

He is a superstar. To me. Still, I always downplay my dog's greatness. "Oh, don't let him hear you say that. His head will get bigger than it already is."

Aubrey tips her head back, spilling blonde hair down her back as she laughs. She stands straight again and places a hand on my shoulder, still chuckling. "I bet for every bad story you posted about Atticus on Instagram, you probably have ten more, don't you?"

"Guilty," I admit to her. Just this morning he grabbed a jar of peanut butter off my counter. It's not something I bothered to put away because it had a lid on it I had secured tightly.

Turns out, that's not a barrier. He just chewed the damn plastic top off to get to the peanut butter, which was not amusing because he also cut his gums on it.

Someone calls out to take places on the set, and Aubrey's head turns to look that way for a moment. When she looks back to me she says, "If you have a few minutes after filming, I would actually like to chat about an opportunity we'd like to present to you."

My heart skips a beat at this unexpected surprise. "Okay. Sure."

She beams another wide smile at me, inclining her head almost regally. Then she's turning away and melting into the crowd. Someone is calling out once again for everyone to take their positions on set and for the extras—dogs and humans—to line the edge of the agility area.

I follow the crowd, and we manage to form a fairly straight perimeter. Production assistants walk around, moving some of us here and there.

The experts—four in all—take their spots and are checked to make sure they're wired up correctly. Someone from makeup comes in and dusts a few of the faces. Cameras on rolling platforms move in and everything gets quiet as a man—presumably the director—starts barking orders.

They start rolling the film, and the panel experts do an introduction that's light and funny and clearly well scripted. I can tell the star of the show—if the show is actually going to be successful—is the dog psychic. The woman has a beehive hairdo, dramatically artistic makeup in bold colors, and she's wearing a flowing caftan dress I personally think isn't very conducive to training dogs. But she's definitely the one who has the magnetism and charm out of the group.

We basically sit there and watch as they bring on bad dog after bad dog to receive training. The owners are showed how to take their dogs through the agility course with the emphasis on making it fun for their dogs. They analyze how the dogs do, then give advice and training to the owners as well.

Honestly, it's a little boring, but I think that might just have to do with the fact these dogs all seem pretty well behaved compared to Atticus.

The last dog to come on is a beautiful male golden retriever that is tall and lanky. My eyes only touch on the animal a moment before going to its owner. I know because my dog is ornery, mischievous, and the biggest troublemaker ever, people judge me—wondering why I can't control my dog.

Today, I'm prepared to look down my nose at the

poor schmucks who can't control their dogs but in reality, I'm not judging them at all. I'm actually relieved there are owners out there who might have less control of their dogs than I do.

All thoughts of judgment fly out of my head though when I see the golden retriever's owner. He's one of those men who make girls go silly in the head. Tall and well-built to almost a cliché, he's dressed casually in a pair of jeans and a t-shirt. Currently, he's spending a great deal of effort trying to get his dog to sit, which I'm not ashamed to say makes me notice the way his biceps bulge slightly as he does so. I'd like to be all judgey about the way he's pushing on his dog's butt to make him sit down, but I admittedly get sidetracked by how handsome he is with shaggy brown hair and bright blue eyes.

I give a hard shake to my head. I tell myself, *Hazel Roundtree does not go gaga over hot men.*

Cute dogs? Of course.

Production assistants filter back in and powder faces. The panel of experts willfully ignore the man trying to get his golden retriever to sit, I'm assuming not giving a damn about training him until the cameras are rolling. The more the poor man tries to control his wily golden retriever, the spunkier the dog seems to get with him.

He thinks it's a game, and I know this because he's wearing that same naughty grin Atticus wears when he's being playful and stubbornly refusing to listen to me.

The golden retriever jumps away from his owner and stretches his forearms out on the ground, while raising his butt into the air with tail wagging furiously. It's a playful pose I've seen dogs employ—my own included—where they beckon others to join them in their frivolity. I can't help but chuckle over the dog's antics and over the fact the owner himself is amused, as evidenced by the way his lips are curved into a slight smile.

I can't help but laugh when the retriever springs up on his hind feet—barking exuberantly and really, really loudly—and launches himself at his owner. His paws go to the man's chest, and he starts jumping with wild and joyful abandon as if he wants to leap right into his arms.

Rather than get pissed off at his dog, he throws his head back and laughs, wrapping his arms around his furry friend's torso to give him a hug. I don't know how many times over Atticus' life I've done the same thing to him. It makes my respect for the man increase tenfold.

I'm startled when Atticus gives an excited yip beside me, and I barely have time to look down at him. He's watching the golden retriever with a dopey grin on his face, hell-raising fire in his eyes and a tail that's wagging furiously. I'm totally caught off guard when Atticus bolts forward, his leash pulling straight out of my hand to leave a slight rope burn behind.

"Shit," I exclaim.

He jets toward the retriever at a full-on run I'm terrified is going to result in a collision that could do some damage to the dogs.

"Atticus," I scream, but as is par for the course… he ignores me.

CHAPTER 43

Atticus

M ANY MAY NOT know this, but animals can throw off emotions just as clearly, if not more so, than humans do. Whereas the tone of human words can tell me a lot, I have to rely more on pure actions and scent when it comes to my canine compadres.

This golden retriever, for example, is insanely happy to be with his human today. I get the sense that perhaps they don't get to spend a lot of time together, and it's incredibly special for them to be out and about today. While the yellow dog is more than aware his human wants him to do something very specific—that distasteful notion of being good and obedient—I can tell he's just as wily and stubborn as I am when Hazel tries to control me.

Furthermore, this furry yellow creature—who is actually a little bit bigger than I am in height but not as stocky through the chest—wants to cause some havoc. I got that the minute he started barking. While the other dogs are standing by idly dumb and with little intuition for the adventure presenting itself, I answer the call of the retriever.

For a fleeting moment, I consider Hazel's wrath, but let's be honest. I'll get a stern lecture from her, and that's not so bad.

Decision made, I bolt. Hazel makes no move to hold me back, and I take that as tacit permission to go forward. I stretch my legs and fly toward the yellow dog, giving him a barking reply of acceptance as to his offer to cause mayhem.

He turns his big shaggy head my way, tongue lolling out the side of his mouth. His tail wags hard, and he's pushing himself away from his human.

I vaguely hear Hazel call my name but choose to ignore it, harsh lecture be damned.

The retriever has just enough time to turn my way, coil his body tightly before he's launching himself at me. His human says a bad word, followed by what I think might be the retriever's name. "Scout."

None of it matters.

Scout and I collide, rearing to our back legs with front paws scrabbling at each other. We drop to the ground, and I take a playful grab at his neck. He spins so fast his butt slams into my shoulder and knocks me sideways. I lose my balance for but a moment before I'm springing back at him where we once again go to our hindlegs to wrestle while standing tall.

"Atticus," Hazel yells, and then I'm being jerked backward by my harness.

The golden dog, Scout, is also being pulled back by his owner, who looks somewhat mad, but like Hazel, I can see a tiny twinkle in his eyes. Besides, the crowd around us is laughing enthusiastically so I know what we did wasn't all that bad.

"I am so sorry," Hazel says to Scout's human dad. I'm in an obedient sit, and I throw my head back to look at her. Her face is flushed red, which often happens when she gets mad at me, but she's got a weird smile on her face as she talks to the man.

The man laughs in response. I have to admit it's a good laugh. Easygoing and genuine. I don't sense any yucky vibes from this dude.

"Don't apologize," he tells Hazel. "Looks like our dogs might be twins separated at birth, I'm thinking. Figuratively, of course."

"There's no way your dog could be worse than mine," Hazel says with a coy laugh. She tucks her hair behind her ears, which is not something I've ever seen her do before.

That man just smiles back at her, as if he really didn't hear what she just said.

She keeps smiling, not seeming to care he doesn't bother saying anything.

I shoot a glance at Scout. He's watching this play out, and I sense confusion from him as well.

"I'm Jack," the man finally says, sticking his hand out.

Hazel takes it, and they shake. Which is cool, I guess. "Hazel. And this is Atticus."

I make sure to grin as I look up to Jack. He gives me a pat on the head and points at his dog. "Scout."

"Oh my God," Hazel exclaims.

At the same exact time, Jack says with a laugh, "You got to be kidding me."

My head swings back and forth between the two of them as I have no clue what's so interesting.

They both start talking about a book called *To Kill A Mockingbird*, and I tune out.

Bored now.

I take a tentative step toward Scout, and his head turns to me with a mischievous sparkle to his eye. Round two of wrestling ready to commence.

"Okay, take your places on the set, everyone," someone yells out.

Hazel and Jack go quiet. He seems disappointed. Hazel looks flustered.

None of it matters as someone is now pulling Jack and Scout away from us. Hazel watches them for a moment, but then that blonde woman named Aubrey she was talking to a bit ago comes up.

"That was hilarious," she tells Hazel, to which Hazel gives one last, longing look at Jack and Scout.

She turns to the woman and shrugs. "Such is my life with this dog."

"Which is what I want to talk to you about," she says as she hooks her arm through Hazel's.

CHAPTER 44

Hazel

"**D**ID YOU NOT like the pot roast?" I ask Oley as I watch him push food around on his plate. I personally think it turned out fine, and Bernard's had two helpings so far.

"It's good, Hazel," Oley says. He gives me a reassuring smile. "Just not overly hungry tonight, I guess."

My eyes narrow at him. "You haven't been eating much the last few days now that I think about it. Are you feeling okay?"

As has become the routine, I cook all meals for Oley. It's not because he can't, but why shouldn't I? I've got to eat, and it's hard as hell to cook for one person. It only makes sense we eat dinner together each night. It only makes sense when I pack my lunch for work the next day, I do the same for Oley. Neither of us are big breakfast eaters, so it's usually a small bowl of cereal or some fruit before we head out for the day.

I'm not sure when we morphed into an old married

couple who share meals and have separate sleeping arrangements, but it works out wonderfully for both of us.

"I'm fine," Oley says, and his voice sure seems confident. He's got great energy during the day and his color looks good.

But I have noticed he seems to be napping a lot lately. Not that that means anything, because at his age, he deserves to nap whenever he wants.

What's probably going on is I just don't want to face the truth. Oley's getting older and just like Atticus, I don't want to think about inevitable ends.

"So how did it go down in Wilmington today?" Bernard asks.

I'd already filled Oley in when I returned, but I don't mind repeating the story to Bernard. He laughs and shakes his head when I tell him about Atticus charging after Scout just before they started filming.

I do not, however, tell him anything about Scout's owner, Jack.

That's for my private memory vault. Besides, I've never much liked talking about men with Bernard and Oley. They're like my surrogate dads and grandpa's all rolled into one, and it's just icky to talk about men with them.

I did, however, call Charmin on the way back to Jacksonville today after I left the film lot and told her all about that handsome man and how our dogs brought us together if only for a few flirty seconds.

Charmin, of course, made the leap that we were going to go out on a date, but I had to tell her that after I finished talking to Aubrey Stewart, Jack and Scout were sadly done filming and had apparently already left.

It was a total bummer because I don't quite remember meeting someone so spontaneously who I felt an intense attraction and connection to. We spoke barely a handful of words to each other but for those few moments, there was no hesitation. No fumbling words. No talking over each other. Just an easy, funny back and forth I wish could have gone on a lot longer.

Oh, well.

Got all I need right here.

As if he could read my mind and was given a cue, Atticus pushes from the floor beside my chair and tries to stick his head under my arm which would put him within licking distance of my plate. I know without a doubt if Oley, Bernard, and I were to turn our heads away from the table for just a nanosecond, he'd be at that pot roast and have it downed before we could turn back.

"Get away," I say as I put a hand to his chest and push. He holds strong for a moment, but I give him a stern look and sterner voice. "Sit, Atticus."

For a moment, I can see in his expression he's going

to defy me.

I point at the floor. "Sit," I say again.

Atticus throws his head back and gives a woo-wooooo of a howl to show he doesn't like this command, but then flops to the floor with a big sigh.

"Drama queen," I mutter and turn back to my pot roast.

"So is Atticus going to be a star?" Bernard asks.

"Not from the show that was filmed today," I tell him. "But Atticus was given a pretty cool opportunity while we were there."

My gaze cuts over to Oley and he levels me with a proud smile. I'd already told him this earlier today.

"What's that?" Bernard asks, reaching out to the platter of pot roast for another slice. Oley pushes his plate away, then leans back in his chair to listen to my story again.

"So this woman approached me, and she heads up a big media production company in New York. She follows Atticus on Instagram. Anyway, the show we were on was her company's, but she flew down here just to meet Atticus and me. She got one of her producers to invite me out, but it was just the pretense so she could observe us firsthand."

Bernard's eyebrows furrow in, his knife and fork hovering over his plate. "That seems kind of… underhanded."

"Probably," I agree with a shrug. "At any rate, she wants Atticus and me to write a travel blog for one of their magazines. She wants us to go around the country and review pet friendly resorts. All expenses paid and even a salary."

"What kind of salary?" Bernard asks nosily.

"The kind that could feed Atticus in beef tenderloin every night," I say with a pointed look.

Bernard whistles appreciatively.

"I told her she should do it," Oley interjects. "It's for one year, and it sounds like the opportunity of a lifetime."

The look I give Oley is affectionate and frustrated at the same time. He and I had words about this today, and we don't see eye to eye.

Bernard turns to look back at me. "You don't want to do it?"

"It's just not a good time," I tell him. "I've got just one more year to finish up my bachelor's degree and of course, keeping the clinic running."

"Those are all things that can wait one damn year," Oley mutters. The fact he said the word "damn" means he's serious about this.

"Maybe it's just not my dream to travel around," I snap.

Which is absolutely untrue. I'd love to travel around the United States, and one day maybe even to other countries. Doing it with Atticus would be a dream I could never hope to fulfill.

But the real reason is I'm not sure Oley could do without me. I feed him, take care of him, work around the farm. I set up the clinic and the well-oiled machine it is today is because of me. I know how to operate the new computer system that maintains patient records, and I'm the one that knows how to pay the bills, manage vendors, and handle payroll.

It's just the right opportunity at the very wrong time. I told Aubrey that, and she was disappointed. She left me with her card, and told me if I ever changed my mind, I should give her a call.

Oley's phone rings, cutting into the conversation. It's coming from the living room and after almost four years with this man, I know it's Tara's ringtone.

"Want me to get it?" I ask.

He shakes his head. "It's dinnertime. I don't like being interrupted while I'm eating."

"Then I suggest you eat," I say with a pointed nod down to his plate. He picks his fork up, and then takes a small bite of potato.

Eventually, Oley's phone quiets. He looks at me and says, "In three... two... one..."

On cue, my phone starts to ring. I don't have separate ringtones for people, but I don't need to look down to know it's Oley's daughter.

This has become a cycle lately. Tara calls to talk to her dad. He doesn't feel like talking to her, and I can understand that. It's been the same stilted, uninspiring, one-sided conversation he's been having with her for years.

Then Tara will call me, and she's not at all frustrated by not being able to talk to her father. If anything, I know she's relieved when I answer, so she can do her duty to see how her dad is and not have to talk to him, which could eventually lead to an awkward discussion about how they never come to visit him.

I shouldn't say "never" because over the four years I've been living on the farm, they've been a handful of times. The stays are short—overnight only—and they are miserable. Oley's granddaughter Abigail is in her last year of college, and she's more interested in texting her friends while here. Tara's husband Will brings work and sits at the kitchen table the whole time immersed in legal documents. And Tara sits out on the porch doing yoga or talking on the phone with her friends most of the time, while Oley and I hang out doing stuff around the farm. It's completely futile, and it pisses me off.

I answer Tara's call, because it's expected of me and it takes the pressure off Oley to have to talk to her. Bernard watches while eating pot roast, and Oley stabs a carrot but only looks at it.

"Hey, Tara," I answer in a friendly tone.

She and I get along fine. I mean, we have absolutely nothing in common and she treats me as her father's caretaker and employee rather than as his friend, but whatever. If I can be a buffer for Oley, then I'll gladly do it.

"Hazel," she replies in greeting. "Just called Dad to say hello and check in on him. Got his voice mail again."

I cut my eyes to Oley, who's completely enamored of his carrot.

"Yeah," I reply. "No clue what he's up to tonight."

Bernard snickers softly as he chews his dinner, clearly enjoying the show.

"So," Tara drawls. "How is he?"

"He's doing well," I tell her. It's what I say every time she calls. "Work is going great. Hip still sore, but he gets around really well."

I don't tell her that he's not been eating well because I doubt Oley really wants her to know, but more importantly, it would result in her jabbering for ten minutes about how he should do a detox cleanse on his system.

"Well, that's good," she says in such a way I seriously doubt she was listening to me. Of course, she doesn't need to. It's the same thing I told her last time. "Well, let him know I called and if he wants to give me a call back, that would be great. Otherwise, I'm sure we'll catch up with each other soon."

"Sure will," I assure her.

"Bye, Hazel," she replies, and then disconnects without waiting for me to say it back to her.

I set my phone down and in an overly dramatic robotic voice, I say. "Your daughter says hello. You should call her if you'd like."

Oley gives me a mock glare, and Bernard laughs.

"Seriously though, Oley," I chastise him gently. "You should talk to her."

"Why?" he demands, sounding a little more cranky than normal. "She doesn't really care. She'd rather talk to you and make sure she has nothing to feel guilty over for not giving a damn about her dad."

This is usually a bit more than Oley shares about his feelings for his kids. This pattern with Tara is practically the same with Cameron except Cameron will leave an actual voice mail for his dad that he was calling to check in rather than call me. He does this knowing Oley won't call back.

"I just don't want you to have any regrets," I tell him firmly. "God forbid something would happen to one of your kids or something."

Oley scoffs. "I think I'm much more likely to die before they will. They're the ones who will have regrets."

Sadly, this is probably true. And I can't really condemn Oley for his choices. He had no relationship with his kids long before I came along. Granted, I think the divide widened once I moved in, as his kids felt even less need to see him or check on him with me here to watch over things. In that respect, I feel a tad guilty, but in all honesty... I'm better for him since I can be here all the time. His kids in different cities can't do much just because of distance.

Still, it's shitty they don't just call him more. Talk about things he'd like to talk about rather than being so self-absorbed they only talk about themselves.

So very weird to think about how dysfunctional I was but a few short years ago with my own family. Now I enjoy very tight bonds with my mom and Liz, while Oley barely has any relationship and Bernard chooses to keep his very simple and light.

We all have our tribulations though, I guess.

CHAPTER 45

Hazel

I N THE OVER three years since my divorce, I wonder how many first dates I've been on.

It's a far greater number than second dates, with third dates being almost unheard of.

I dated a man last year for almost eight weeks. Granted, that was basically once-a-week dinners as we were both really busy, which only told me that neither of us liked the other enough to make room in our schedules.

Tonight's date seems to be going well. His name is Lee, and he's a chiropractor. This is a setup by Marsha as he goes to her yoga class on Sunday. Marsha told me he had hit on her on the very first day, not realizing she was gay nor that her partner was sitting right beside her and would have gladly removed his testicles as she was a jealous woman.

They've since become yoga friends, and Marsha wanted me to meet him.

Tonight's date is at a big chain steakhouse over on the Western Blvd extension, whereby Lee orders salmon. Not that it's not a legit order, but I never understood people that ordered fish in a steak restaurant. I had the petit filet. It was so delicious I sadly have no leftovers to take home to Atticus.

As far as dates go, this one is shaping up well. I learned long ago to have them knock on Oley's door rather than my apartment when picking me up, because it is far too much of an ordeal to go through Atticus' charade of acting like a rabid killer dog when a man comes to the door. He snarls and lunges at the cage door of his kennel with foam and slobber flying all over the place. The few men who saw that happen were duly intimidated, but they failed to see the smug look on Atti's face just as I'd close the door behind us.

Little asshole.

God, I love him.

Lee escorted me down Oley's porch and to the passenger side of his car, which was a Mercedes. I was duly impressed. He held the door open for me and shut it after I was tucked in.

At the restaurant he held the door open for me, and pulled my chair out for me to sit. More importantly, the conversation isn't one sided and has flowed freely back and forth between us.

If I had to take any bonus points from him, it would

be his lack of enthusiasm for wanting to know more about Atticus. He was completely unintrigued by my story of how I found him in the ditch, and I know this because he didn't ask a single follow-up question. When I pulled my phone out to show him a picture, he smiled politely and said, "Cute dog".

It was the same exact thing Darren had said to me those years ago when he first met Atticus.

Ridiculous really.

But I overlooked it. Maybe people can't understand the charm of Atticus until they interact with him. Maybe the pictures without context are nothing more than just a "cute dog". I decide to give Lee the benefit of the doubt.

After dinner, we share a dessert—both of us having in common an unhealthy desire toward cheesecake. When he pays, I try not to notice, but I look anyway, and am pleased to see that Lee is a big tipper. Our waiter was fantastic, and I believe in tipping well, which goes back to my bartending days.

By the time he has me settled back into his Mercedes and we're heading back out to the farm, I've pretty much decided I'll say yes to another date if he asks.

"Have you ever done yoga?" he asks.

He's kind of a buttoned-up type of individual, driving with his hands on the ten and two o'clock positions on the wheel. His hair is cut short and styled meticulously, not a strand out of place. His clothes were almost overly pressed, but I'm not going to let that worry me. I can't be worried about whether he'd freak out over the amount of hair Atticus sheds at this point. We haven't even discussed a second date yet.

"I haven't," I say with chagrin. Marsha's tried to get me to go, but frankly... I'm a little intimidated by it.

"You should come tomorrow if you have some time," he says, daring to risk a quick glance at me before looking back to the road.

"I could possibly be convinced to try it," I say flirtatiously, thinking... this guy might have some potential. I mean... I'm not sure how I feel about a guy who does yoga. I know my dad would be rolling over in his grave right now if I thought it was cool. But I do respect he's a progressive man who tries things like that.

He starts to tell me about the different kinds, and I immediately get overwhelmed. He's telling me all about hot yoga—which sounds positively awful—when we're pulling back up in front of Oley's house.

This is always the awkward part. Does he walk me to the door or not? Is there going to be a kiss, and if so, when? Is it going to be a peck, or will there be tongue?

Lee turns off the car before shifting in his seat to face me. His hand goes to the seat behind my head. I smile in a way that hopefully conveys I want to see him again, so I would probably be open to a kiss.

He must understand the expression on my face because he leans slowly toward me. I reciprocate, willing to meet him over the center console. His hand slides to the back of my neck, and my mouth parts slightly.

His mouth, in turn, opens so wide I think I get a glimpse of tonsils. He pushes in for the kiss, mouth gaping to the extent he almost pulls my damn nose into his mouth. His lips fasten onto my face—yes, that area just beyond the edge of my lips because his mouth is so big when it opens. His tongue slides in, and then flops all around my mouth like a dying fish. It's wet and gross, and I involuntarily push back against his shoulders.

It's not a sexually charged kiss despite the tongue he's trying to jam down my throat. It's that this man doesn't know how to kiss. He easily takes my hint to move away, but then gives me a charming smile.

"Wow," he says all swoony like with his eyes twinkling. "What a kiss."

Forcing myself not to grimace, I have to dig my nails into the palms of my hands not to wipe the drool off my face.

"Yeah… what a kiss," I murmur.

"Come on," he says softly. "Let me walk you to the door so you can get some sleep."

I cringe as he helps me out, wondering how one awful, horrible kiss can absolutely kill dead every bit of like and attraction for a man. He starts to steer me toward Oley's door, and there is no doubt in my mind he's going to ask me out again.

Maybe even try to kiss me again.

There is no doubt in my mind I'd rather have a colonoscopy without any drugs.

I pull toward the side of the house, telling him. "Actually... I live above the garage."

When we get to the staircase, he gallantly sweeps an arm out and says in a faux—and really bad—British accent—"Milady".

I trot up the stairs, making as much noise as I can. By the time I reach the top, I can hear Atticus whining inside his kennel, knowing his mom is getting ready to walk through the door.

I quickly unlock the door, step in over the threshold, and then turn to face Lee.

He's directly in Atticus' line of sight, who stops whining and starts snarling.

His lips peel back, showing wickedly long, sharp canines. He pins his fierce gaze on Lee and starts lunging at the door, issuing big booming barks that speak to ripping Lee's throat out if he can get out of the cage.

I feign surprise and hold my hand to my chest. "Atticus... what in the world has gotten into you?"

Lee takes a step back from the door.

I turn to face him. "Honestly… he's usually a sweet boy, and when he bites, it's usually only if he thinks I'm threatened in any way. I'm sure he just needs to get to know you. Would you like me to let him out?"

Lee's face goes white with terror and his eyes bug out. He holds his hand out while taking another step back. "Actually… it's getting really late and I should be going. But thank you for a lovely evening."

"No, thank you," I say sincerely. "It's been very lovely."

"Yes, lovely," he mutters as he's halfway down the staircase while Atticus continues to call for his blood.

When Lee gets in his car, I turn to face my dog. "He's gone. You can stop now."

The barks cease immediately, and Atticus starts clawing at the plastic flooring, eager to get out to see. Gone is the ferocious, rabid dog of nightmares that wanted to disembowel Lee for having the temerity to walk his mom to the door.

In its place is ninety pounds of furry, lovable beast that only wants a hug from me.

I let Atticus out, barely bothering with the feeble "sit" commands, knowing he won't listen. He simply has to get his excitement out, which means paws to my shoulders and my arms wrapped around him for a hug while he pelts my neck and face with slobbery kisses.

When he finally calms down, I ask him, "Want to

go say hi to Oley and get some ice cream?"

Atticus barks. I'm not sure if it's because I said *Oley* or *ice cream*, two things he dearly loves.

We make our way back down the stairs, pausing long enough for Atticus to take a short pee. He still squats, although once in a blue moon he'll lift his leg to mark a bush. If I thought it made my dog in any way a sissy to squat when he pees, I only have to remember the look on Lee's face tonight as he confronted my own personal Cujo.

It's not even eight yet, so I have no qualms walking right into Oley's back kitchen door. He usually stays awake until the eleven o'clock news and keeps the door unlocked until then in case I want to come visit. It's so funny I just walk in and out of Oley's house like I own it, but anytime I go to visit my mom or Liz, I still knock at the door.

Oley calls from the living room, "That you, Hazel?"

"No. It's a gang of violent trolls coming to steal your virtue," I call back. Atticus goes trotting in there to say hello, and I pull out the container of vanilla ice cream from the fridge. "Want some ice cream?"

"No, thanks," Oley returns.

I frown. Oley never passes up ice cream, which is why he always has several containers in his freezer. I scoop out a small bowl for Atticus and call him. He comes running back in with his toenails clicking on the tile floor. It reminds me they need a trim.

I set his bowl on the floor. He doesn't get this treat often and he only gets a tiny bit, which is why he has it completely wolfed down before I can even turn to scoop my own bowl. Thereafter, he sits at my feet and begs me with imploring eyes for more.

Ignoring him, I take my bowl into the living room where Oley turns the volume down as soon as I sit on the couch. I sit Indian-style and rest the bowl on my lap. I'd worn jeans and a loose blouse tonight as it was mild outside for a mid-April evening but the chill from the bowl of ice cream makes me shiver.

"How was your date?" Oley asks.

I try to imagine having this conversation with my dad when he was alive, and I can't for the life of me. He was a good dad, but he wasn't the type I could have sat around after a date and chatted about it with. I always got the impression my dad wanted to shoot any boy who came sniffing around me.

I know he most definitely wanted to shoot Chris for luring me away from high school. My parents never knew I'd gotten pregnant and because I miscarried so soon, it was a blessing I never told them. Had my dad known, he would have for sure killed Chris for getting me pregnant and then leaving me.

But with Oley, it's completely natural talking about these things, as long as they don't get too overly personal.

"Let's just say there won't be a second date." I dip my spoon down into the ice cream. Atticus jumps up on the couch and lays his head on his paws, right by my thigh. He stares up at me from under those brown eyebrows, silently begging for a taste. If I were to turn my head away for a moment, his face would be all in it.

"A jerk?" Oley guesses.

I grimace. "Worse. A really bad kisser."

Oley snorts and looks back to the muted TV.

"What are you watching?" I ask. It's on a commercial right now.

"Some movie," he says vaguely.

"Some movie?" I ask with a laugh. "That's original."

He doesn't reply, and the silence seems ominous. The hair rises on the back of my neck, and it doesn't have anything to do with the chilliness from the bowl on my lap.

"Oley... is something wrong?" I ask him tentatively.

His neck twists so he can look at me on the couch. "I think there's something wrong with me."

My stomach clenches tight. Oley never complains about anything. Not even his damn hip, which I know hurts like hell sometimes. "What do you mean?"

"I'm tired, Hazel," he says quietly. "Like really tired lately. It's a real effort some days to get out of bed. I've never felt anything like this before, and at first... I thought it was just a part of getting old. But I don't think that's it."

"What do you think it is?" I ask him hesitantly.

"I don't know," he replies, his voice feather soft and fatigued. "But I think I need to get a checkup."

I lean forward and put the bowl on the coffee table, uncrossing my legs. Atticus starts to make a move for it, and I say, "Don't you even think about it."

My tone is cold and cutting, and for the first time I can ever remember, Atticus sort of shrinks down into himself and lays his head back on his paws. He actually obeys me where food is involved, and he doesn't move a muscle.

This doesn't surprise me as it's obvious he can feel the tension in the room right now.

To Oley, I say, "First thing tomorrow, I'll call and get you an appointment."

Oley nods, and there's no mistaking the relief in his eyes. He gives a tiny laugh. "I don't even have a primary care doctor."

"I'll find someone good," I assure him. "And I'm sure it's nothing to worry about. Maybe just need some vitamins or something."

"Or something," Oley mutters, and his gaze goes back to the TV. He lets his head fall back to the recliner with a sigh, turning the volume back up.

I silently eat my ice cream, although it feels like it's

curdling in my belly. The fact Oley is asking to go see a doctor makes me want to vomit. He's a tough, old country man, and I sort of convinced myself he was invincible because of how hard he works day in and day out at his age.

My nose stings as tears prick at my eyes. I blink them back and offer my bowl to my dog, not hungry anymore. Atticus gently licks my bowl clean.

CHAPTER 46

Hazel

"T HIS ISN'T UP for discussion," Oley tells me as his hands curve around the cup of coffee before him. My own coffee sits untouched and unloved. I don't feel like drinking it. Or anything for that matter.

I want to rail at Oley. Everything should be up for discussion. Opinions matter, particularly mine.

He's being shortsighted.

He's not in the right frame of mind to be making such decisions without truly considering all angles.

Too much has fucking happened the last few weeks, and he's reeling. I'm reeling. We need to take a step back, take a deep breath, and we need to make good decisions.

Except Oley isn't willing to accept that there's a "we" in all this.

There's only him, and his opinion.

"Oley," I say placatingly, hoping to gently poke around his defenses.

"No," he says sharply, holding a hand up. "My decision is final."

"But—"

"Hazel," he says. He slams his hand down on the table, making my coffee cup rattle and me jump a few inches out of my chair. His angry expression only holds for a moment, before it relaxes into contrition. "I'm sorry, Hazel. I know this is hard. But I need you to respect my wishes."

I burst into tears.

He's so very fucking right about all of it, and I hate him for it. I bury my face in my hands, ignoring Atticus as he ducks his head under and tries to push into my neck.

"Get away," I mumble as I shoulder him away. He starts to whine with the need to try to make me feel better, and I'm such a bitch because I won't let him.

I want to feel bad.

I need to feel this pain, so I can possibly shoulder some of it for Oley.

You see, we found out last week that he's going to die.

I just found out moments ago from Oley that he's choosing to die sooner rather than later.

The last few weeks have been a blur for me, and I can't even begin to imagine how Oley's been feeling about all of this. When he'd told me he wasn't feeling well, yeah… I was apprehensive, but I never imagined I'd be sitting here at his kitchen table having this discussion.

I was able to get him in fairly quickly to a doctor, and it was easy enough with some bloodwork to figure out his fatigue was from an iron deficiency. But that led to a colonoscopy, and I was not prepared for the gastroenterologist to call Oley one night while we were having dinner to give him the results.

Colon cancer, which was also in his lymph nodes.

It only went downhill from there. Within days, he was having a CT scan, which showed the cancer had metastasized to his liver. Several spots there, in fact.

It's a fatal diagnosis, but with the advancements in medicine Oley had options. Surgery to remove the mass, and then aggressive chemotherapy and immunotherapy to shrink the disease. If the stars and moon were aligned, it could potentially even buy him a few years.

It was a small ray of hope that could actually drive away the darkness for a bit.

But Oley snuffed the golden light out when he told me a bit ago, "I'm not going to have treatment."

I went on a ten-minute rant and when I wound down, Oley asked me for a cup of coffee. I seethed while I made it, and when I set it down on the table in front of him, he'd told me. "This isn't up for discussion."

I let my eyes roam over Oley's face as I wipe away

my tears. He looks exhausted from our discussion, and it makes me feel terrible. I don't want to sap what little bit of life he has left on stupid arguments.

But it's not stupid.

It's about one of the most important lives I've ever known.

"Hazel," Oley says again, interrupting my thoughts. I blink at him… blink away more tears. "I need you to be strong for me. I know it's not fair to ask you, but you're the one I'm going to lean on. I know you can do it. You're one of the strongest women I know. But I need you to let go of the idea that I can be saved, because I can't be, nor do I want to try."

My chest burns with the need to argue. It's like I'm filled with the Holy Spirit, and I want to preach a fiery sermon on the preciousness of life and how he should respect it.

How he should respect me and what I want.

But I swallow it down until it's a low flame deep in the pit of my stomach.

It takes great effort and force of will, but finally I nod at him. "Okay. It's whatever you want, and I'll be here for you every step of the way."

Oley extends a hand and covers mine. His grasp is warm and strong, and it's hard to believe he's going to die. The doctor said six months or less without treatment.

"I need to make a plan," he says softly.

I twist my hand, turn it palm up, and spread my fingers. Wrapping mine around his, I clasp it hard. It's my turn to squeeze. "We need to make a plan. It's a "we" thing, Oley."

His blue eyes look positively ancient as they well with tears. He nods back at me. "Okay. *We* need to make a plan."

♦

THAT NIGHT, I sit out on Bernard's trailer steps. We huddle close, our shoulders pressed to each other.

Bernard and I sip on expensive micro brews I'd picked up on the way over here.

Part of the plan was for me to come tell Bernard Oley's decision. I left Oley back at the farm, so he could call Tara and Cameron to tell them. They had no clue any of this was going on, as Oley wanted to wait to tell them until he knew everything about his condition.

Bernard was a little different. Oley had told him as soon as the pathology results came in from the colonoscopy. It was my job to tell him that Oley was choosing not to fight it.

Tipping my head back, I take in the velvety night sky thick with twinkling stars. I wish Atticus was here with me, so I could bury a hand in his fur and ponder life's mysteries as I stare upward. But I left him with

Oley because I don't want Oley ever left alone again.

"You know this is all going to fall on you," Bernard says thoughtfully.

"I know." Oley seems to think my shoulders can handle it. There's no way Tara and Cameron will uproot their lives to come watch their father die. I bet they come to visit soon, though. They'll want to assess the situation. They'll pull me aside for a frank talk about what's needed from them. They'll act concerned—and I'm sure they will be—but they'll expect me to deal with it all, just as I've always done where their father is concerned.

"What kind of help do you need from me?" Bernard asks.

I give a bark of a laugh. "You know what that crazy old coot wants to do?"

"What's that?"

"He wants to build a chicken coop." It comes out with a maniacal kind of laugh. I thought coming up with a plan would be about funerals and such, but Oley apparently has a bucket list. "Says he's been wanting to build one for years, but he just never got around to it."

Bernard chuckles. "No kidding?"

"You can help build the coop," I say as I turn my head to look at him.

Bernard smiles, tapping the neck of his beer bottle against mine in a silent toast. We take sips as we stare out into the darkness.

"Be there for him as much as you can," I finally answer his original question in a serious way. "We need to make the most of his time left."

Voice thick with emotion, Bernard says, "I'll spend all my time with him, Hazel. Move into the damn farmhouse if I have to. We'll make the most of it."

"He'll get sick of you and bark at you to leave," I say with a grin on my face. We'll definitely see some of Oley's crankiness, I'm sure.

"He's got cancer," Bernard teases. "He won't be strong enough to make me leave."

My laughter is genuine. I imagine Bernard and I will do a lot of double teaming on Oley over the next several weeks.

"What can we expect?" Bernard asks hesitantly, and my laughter dies flat.

Not even trying to stop the tears that flood my eyes, I just blink and let them roll down my face, sniffing hard at the snot that starts to form in my nose. Bernard gives me a comforting nudge with his shoulder.

"It's called failure to thrive," I say in a flat voice. "The cancer will just eat away the good cells. His liver will start to fail. He'll get weak. Won't want to eat. And just little by little, his body will just give up."

"Will he be in pain?" Bernard asks. His voice is husky and quavers with emotion. I risk a glance at him to see shiny paths of wetness coating his own scruffy cheeks.

"No," I assure him. "There will be plenty of medicine to make him comfortable in the end."

"A blessing," he murmurs.

"Yes," I agree.

CHAPTER 47

Atticus

OLEY HAS SMELLED funny for a while now. He's always smelled different from Hazel. A little dusty in the bones is the best way to describe it, but it's a smell I love because I associate it with Oley, and I love Oley.

But now, there's an underlying scent. Of something rotten deep inside of him. I don't know what it is, but I know it's making Oley sad.

It's also making Hazel sad, and I feel helpless. I don't think giving me rubbins is going to chase away this type of sorrow.

She left me a bit ago to go see Bernard. Normally, I want to go everywhere with Hazel but when she told me to stay with Oley, that seemed right.

He's sleeping in his recliner while I lay on the floor beside him, keeping watch. I had listened earlier while he called Tara and Cameron. They're nice enough people the few times they've visited and they like dogs, so I get lots of attention. But those phone calls took a toll on him, and he fell fast asleep after settling in his chair.

Its good Hazel left me behind. I can keep watch over Oley, and I'll be certain to offer my head for scratches as soon as he wakes up.

CHAPTER 48

Atticus

W E PARK AT the end of the block and after Hazel has me hooked up to my leash, we take a leisurely walk to the hardware store.

Normally I don't go on store runs with Hazel, but she said this one allowed dogs inside, so it's a special day indeed. I'm high stepping with my chest puffed out. People pass us and smile. A few ask to pet me, and I let them as I sense no danger to Hazel.

We've never been to this area of town before. Hazel said it was the "original" downtown, and that they are trying to refurbish it with small businesses. There are quite a few that sell food because I can smell all sorts of delicious things that make my belly rumble.

And wait... *that* smell is familiar.

Not food—and it's weird I'd even pay much attention to something that wasn't food, but yes... I know that smell.

It's of man and fun and kindness.

It's a smell that made Hazel very happy once, and I must inspect this further. Hazel's had a very heavy heart of late because of Oley.

I can't very well tell Hazel we have to go on an adventure to root out what's piqued my interest, so I do what any bad dog with a strong head and stubborn mind would do.

I bolt.

Poor Hazel, who is so trusting of me being obedient on my leash, lets it slip easily through her fingertips. Her cry of surprise causes me a tiny pang of guilt.

But I'm on a mission. I stretch out into a flat-out run, my leash bouncing along beside me as I traverse the concrete sidewalk. I almost get sidetracked by the smell of hot dogs from a cart I pass by, but for once, something is more important than food to me.

Right there.

Up ahead.

In that building that has a few tables with chairs outside of it. The door is propped open, and I come to a skidding halt as a woman walks out of it holding a cup of coffee. I give a deep inhale at her legs, and she shrieks in surprise.

No, that's not what I'm looking for.

"Atticus," Hazel calls at me sharply. I see her running my way, and I make a command decision.

I jet into the building, immediately getting overwhelmed by the smell of coffee. It's everywhere, and I lose the scent that drew me here.

People are sitting around at tables with cups of fragrant coffee in front of them. I'm immediately noticed, and people point and laugh as I look wildly around.

Hazel comes bursting into the shop behind me. I take another deep breath, lifting my nose as high into the air as I can possibly extend it.

I capture the scent just as Hazel makes a lunge for my leash, and I dash away from her once more. Weaving my way through tables, I hear someone yell out, "Hey… get that damn dog out of here."

"Atticus," Hazel yells sharply, and I know I'm in big trouble.

But what's done is done. I must press forward.

Right to a table where a man sits, grin wide and laughing as I approach. Another man wearing a uniform and smelling strongly of coffee stomps up with a very angry expression on his face just as Hazel catches up to me.

"Is that your dog?" he demands of Hazel.

She stares at him as she grabs my leash, face as red as the begonias she planted around Oley's front porch this spring. "I am so sorry. He got away from me. He's never done anything like this."

If dogs could snort, I would so snort. I do bad stuff like this all the time.

Hazel continues to stammer apologies to the coffee man without once bothering to look at the man whose smell led me here. I give a loud bark to get her attention, and she turns to glare at me.

"Let's go," she says sharply, giving a tug on my leash. She is really, really mad.

I bark again... defiant as ever.

And then the man sitting at the table speaks. "Hazel?"

She turns her head slowly, and then a huge smile breaks out on her face. I don't remember the last time I've seen her smile like that because Oley has made her so sad lately.

"Jack?" she exclaims. "Oh my God. Small world."

Yes! Jack! That's his name. From when I played with his dog Scout some time back.

"Will you please get that damn dog out of here?" the coffee man says in a voice that makes me want to growl at him and take a little nip.

"Do you drink coffee?" Jack asks Hazel as he stands from the table.

She's flustered because the coffee guy is a jerk, and she backs away while pulling me along. "Um... yeah, I do."

"What kind?" Jack asks.

"The dog," the guy snarls again, and I would really love to poop in his shoes.

"Come on, Jud," Jack cajoles. "She's leaving, but I want to buy her a cup of coffee."

Jack then turns to Hazel. "Tell me what kind and we'll sit at one of the tables outside."

Hazel tilts her head to the side, perplexed at this chain of events. She only hesitates a moment. "Regular coffee with some cream and sugar."

"Got it," Jack says with a grin.

We head toward the door, weaving our way back through tables as people smile and laugh at me. I high step it the entire time.

Hazel chooses a table outside furthest from the door. When she takes a seat, I sit down right beside her.

"Did you know he was in there?" Hazel asks me, her voice filled with wonder as her hand scratches at the back of my neck. My lips are all pulled back in full doggie smile as I pant and puff out my chest with pride over what I've done.

"Of course you knew he was in there," Hazel breathes out softly. "You're a wonder dog."

Yes. I. Am.

CHAPTER 49

Hazel

I DIDN'T THINK it possible, but Atticus continues to surprise me. Of course he knew Jack was in there. He ran right up to him.

I'm beyond astounded he could smell him, or that he would even remember his smell. I seem to remember a really amazing cologne he'd been wearing, but I didn't smell it just now.

I'd thought about Jack a few times here and there following our meeting, but it's been a long time since he's crossed my mind. Mostly because it's filled with a lot of other stuff surrounding Oley's diagnosis, but also because there was no need to dwell on someone I'd never see again.

"Here you go," I hear Jack say, pulling me out of my thoughts. I glance up and just damn... he's even more attractive than I remember.

Jack sets the coffee before me, rubs Atticus' head as he passes, and takes the chair opposite of me. He leans back casually and props an ankle on top of his knee. Resting his cup on his jean-covered thigh, he just stares at me with an amused smile.

I stare back because he's so pretty and why bother with words?

We just look at each other until it becomes awkward. I finally snort, and then we both start laughing.

"I can't believe I'm running into you like this," he finally says still chuckling.

"Well, in fairness… Atticus did the running," I point out.

"Did he know I was in that shop?"

"I kind of think he did," I tell him, wondering if that makes my dog sound weird. Speaking of dogs… "And how's Scout?"

Jack's expression turns soft. "He's good. He's actually with my ex-wife this week. We split custody."

My jaw drops open. I've never heard of such a thing, and whoa… he was married?

"Oh," I mutter, not quite knowing what the proper response is to that. I decide to indulge curiosity instead. "Do you have kids? You know… I mean, human kids?"

"Nope." His eyes get a little wistful. "But God knows, Scout is just like a kid. I'm sure you know what I mean by that."

"Sure do," I say with a laugh. Atticus is my child.

"So what are you doing here?" he asks, waving a

hand at our general surroundings. "I just sort of assumed you lived in Wilmington. Never thought I'd run into you here."

"I live here," I answer with a nod before picking up my coffee. I take the lid off to blow on the top. It smells wonderful. "And you?"

"Yup," he says with a grin. "Born and raised."

"Totally a small world," I say before risking a sip of the hot beverage. It's divine and Jack doctored it up with the perfect amount of cream and sugar for me.

"What are you up to today?" Jack asks me.

I throw my thumb over my shoulder. "Heading to the hardware store."

"It's not open right now," he says.

"Well, crap." I crane my neck over my shoulder at the business. It's two doors down from the coffee shop and dark inside. "The website said it opened at nine."

Jack shrugs. "That's what you get with a small business owner."

"I guess," I reply as I turn back to face him. "Oh, well… hopefully they'll open soon."

"They'll open whenever you want them to open," Jack tells me with a mischievous grin.

I cock an eyebrow at him. "What's the inside joke?"

"I own the place," he says with a laugh. "It's a family business, and I took over for my dad when he retired a few years ago. I was just having my usual morning coffee before heading in."

"Oh, Lord," I say as I start to stand from my chair. "I'm keeping you."

"You're not," he assures me, but he stands as well. "But let's head over, and I can help you with whatever your hardware needs are."

Coffee in one hand, dog leash in the other, I head with Jack over to his store. It's called Main Street Hardware, although we aren't on Main Street. I ask him about it.

"It used to be on Main Street, which is a few blocks over," he says, pointing in that direction. "We moved over here when they started refurbishing the area."

"To expand?" I ask.

"To downsize, actually," he says as we reach the front door. The whole front of the store is glass, and there's a pretty green awning over the exterior. "It's hard to compete with Home Depot and Lowe's these days. But they were offering great leasing deals on the retail space here, so I decided to make the move."

Jack pushes the door open, and motions for me and Atticus to precede him in. As I brush past, I don't smell the cologne he'd been wearing before, but I can smell a fresh, woodsy sort of scent I assume is his soap or shampoo. It's delicious.

Atticus and I mill around while Jack turns on the lights and boots up a computer at the checkout counter.

It's a cute little store with only a handful of aisles. Each product is beautifully displayed, and there are only a few of each item. He doesn't have the big-ticket items like doors, cabinets, lighting, and lumber that the bigger stores do. But he sells paint, along with small hardware like hinges and hand tools and such. One wall is devoted to gardening supplies.

"So what do you need today?" Jack asks as he comes up behind me.

I dig down into my pocket to pull out the list that Oley had written out. It's for the chicken coop he and Bernard will be starting soon. He's using some old reclaimed lumber he had stored in the barn.

Jack peruses the list, silently reading out the words. He looks up to me and says, "I've got most of this, but I'll have to order roofing shingles and possibly the flashing, although I might have some in the back."

"Sweet," I say, rocking onto the balls of my feet and nodding.

"What are you building?" he asks as he grabs a handheld basket and heads down an aisle.

"A chicken coop," I answer as Atticus and I follow along.

"You're a handy girl," he says with a laugh.

"Oh, I'm not the one building it. My friend Oley is."

"That wouldn't be Oley Peele by any chance, would

it?" Jack asks as he turns to look at me.

My jaw drops. "Yeah. How did you know?"

Jack laughs, turning to start pulling boxes of various sized nails off the shelf. "Well, Oley's not a very common name. He and my dad know each other well. He would treat our family's animals, and Oley always did his hardware shopping with us."

So that's why Oley recommended this place. He didn't tell me I had to come here, but he suggested it. I hadn't been down to this area of town since they started opening new businesses. It used to be loaded with bars and hookers, but now it's all cleaned up and with pretty storefronts.

"So how is he doing these days?" Jack asks amiably while he loads up the basket.

I swallow hard, take a deep breath, then say, "Not well. He's got cancer."

Jack's head snaps my way, his gaze sorrowful. "What's his prognosis?"

I shrug. "A few months. Maybe longer. This chicken coop has been on a project list for a long time. Years, he says. And he's bound and determined to build it before he dies."

The last words come out a little choked up, and Atticus pushes his head into my hand for a good dose of puppy serenity.

Jack takes me by the elbow, and I don't question it

as he leads me up to the checkout register. He lets me go and walks around the counter, grabbing a stool that sits there. He brings it back around, tapping his finger on the padded seat.

I sit down, holding Atticus' leash loosely in my hand. He drops to the cool cement floor and puts his head on his paws, staring up at me from under his eyebrows.

Jack jumps up on the counter, sitting adjacent to my stool. "Start from the beginning."

I blink at him in confusion. "Excuse me?"

"Start from the beginning," he repeats. "Tell me everything."

What exactly is the beginning? When did Oley become so dear to me that I know his death is going to crush me hard?

"A few weeks ago, I took him to the doctor."

He shakes his head. "No… start at the very beginning."

My gaze drops to Atticus for a moment before coming back to Jack with a smile. He wants to know it all.

"Okay," I tell him in fond remembrance. "Once upon a time, there was this puppy in a ditch, wrapped in barbed wire, freezing and starving…"

♦

I PULL INTO Oley's driveway, giving a short glance in

my rearview mirror. Jack's white truck pulls in behind me.

I'd spent far too long at the hardware store, talking to Jack, but Oley would never begrudge me that. I started at the beginning as he'd asked, ending up a blubbering mess by the time I told him about Oley deciding not to fight the cancer.

When I'd finished and my tears were dried, Jack simply said, "Let's get the rest of your supplies and head out to Oley's."

This came about because I'd lamented the fact Oley and Bernard were going to build this coop together, and neither of them knew what the hell they were doing. They were going to follow some plans I'd found on the internet, but Oley's expertise was in refurbishing old cars and I don't think Bernard had ever wielded a hammer in his life.

I pull in beside the Impala, and Jack parks behind me. After I unclip Atticus from his leash, he jumps out of my Jeep and takes off around the back of the house. I'd left Oley and Bernard there mulling over the plans and sorting out the stacks of wood they had on hand. I didn't think much in the way of actual building was going to be accomplished, and I'm glad Jack is here to lend an expert eye.

"This is a beautiful piece of property," Jack comments as he looks around.

"I know," I reply wistfully. I've come to think of this as simply "home" to me. I point out to the right. "There's a pet cemetery out there. And he leases out some pastures, so there are cows around back."

"Why does he want a chicken coop?" Jack asks.

I shrug. "I think they had chickens when he was a boy. I guess a nod to his childhood or something. Plus… yum. Fresh eggs."

Jack tips back his head and laughs. "There's that."

God, he's got a great laugh.

A wonderful smile.

And his arms… they're really nice, too.

I grin on the inside, having no regrets or guilt over being appreciative of how handsome Jack is. I'm living in a dire world right now with Oley's diagnosis, but I know better than to turn my nose up at something good.

And by good, I mean Jack is going to be a good friend. I can tell. He was clearly put in my path, and his readiness to jump in to help a woman who is a virtual stranger, and a man who's nothing more than an acquaintance, speaks volumes for the type of man he is.

CHAPTER 50

Atticus

I DON'T EVEN know what to do with myself. So many people in Oley's house.

So much potential for people to sneak food to me or scratch behind my ears.

Where to start?

I pad into the living room to assess the situation. Most everyone's stopped eating, but Carl still has a slice of pizza in his hand.

Carl is Jack's dad. He came out to visit not long after Jack started helping with the chicken coop last month. Since then, he and Jack have joined the Friday night pizza and baseball crowd. I have to cross in front of the TV to get to him, and Oley calls out to me, "Come on, Atticus. You make a better wall than a window."

He rolls slightly in his recliner, trying to see around me. His beloved Braves are playing.

Oley smells worse. The scent of rot overpowers the

dustiness and that's not good. He spends a lot of time these days in his recliner.

I move out of his way to sit beside Carl. He spares me a glance and a pat to the head. I stare hungrily at the pizza in his hand, but he doesn't get the hint.

I lean my head toward the hand holding the gooey goodness, and my nose twitches over how good it smells. Carl's eyes are glued to the TV, the pizza just hangs there limply. I part my mouth and lean in just a bit further—

"Dad, you better watch, Atticus," Jack says from the couch with a laugh. He's in the middle between Trey and Bernard. "He's going to get your pizza and quite possibly your hand by the look in his eye."

Busted.

Carl pulls the slice toward his body while giving me a disapproving look. I tilt my head, soften my eyes, and give a tiny chuff of hope.

Carl grins and relents. He breaks off some of the crust, then tosses it at me. Because I suck at catching things, it bounces off my snout and falls to the floor. I pounce on it before anyone can think to stake claim.

It's too yummy to even chew so I swallow it whole, sending another pleading look at Carl.

"No more," he says sternly.

That sounds pretty adamant, so I decide to hunt elsewhere.

I cross—quickly this time—back in front of the TV and head toward Trey. He sees me, already shaking his head. "Don't have anything for you, buddy."

When I cock my head at Jack and Bernard, they both smirk at me. I've struck out there, too.

Oh, well… to the kitchen. Normally, Benji's good about tossing me scraps, but he's with Alicia tonight. Ever since Oley got struck with the rot inside of him, Liz and Trey joined the Friday night festivities. I think Hazel's intent is to surround Oley with as much love and camaraderie as possible before he goes, and it's a brilliant plan. I can feel the happiness roll off Oley when people show up to see him.

Hazel and Liz are in the kitchen, standing on opposite sides of the kitchen counter while sipping beers. Their heads are in close, and they're talking quietly.

My ears perk and I shamelessly eavesdrop, because I have superior canine hearing.

"Seriously, Hazel," Liz says with a tsking sort of sound. "Is he ever going to make a move?"

"I don't know," Hazel replies softly. "At this point, I'm beginning to think he just wants to be friends."

Aha.

They're talking about Jack.

He and Hazel have been hanging out some this past month since they reconnected. He's even brought Scout over a few times. We run all over the farm, chase the ducks in the pond, and bark at the cows together. He's a lot of fun.

But I'm not sure what more Hazel wants. He's a friend to her. The way Bernard is. Or Charmin.

I'm not sure I understand the tone of her voice, which is slightly wistful with a little bit of frustration laced in.

"I don't get it," Liz murmurs. "You guys go out to dinner and movies. He comes out to hang out on the farm. You drop by to see him at the hardware store. But he hasn't even tried to kiss you once. Do you think he's gay?"

"He was married before," Hazel points out.

"Means nothing," Liz counters. I don't know what gay is, but I hope it's not something bad. I don't want anything to cause Hazel more sadness. Her plate is full enough with that already.

I understand Oley is dying. Technically, I don't really understand the exact consequences of such an event, but his body is failing. I can smell it. I can also see it.

I think it means he'll be gone one day, and then he'll be no more. That makes me terribly sad, too.

Hazel has been a trooper, though. She manages to keep the clinic going with Marsha, running back and forth to the house during day to make him lunch or check on him. I stay with Oley while Hazel works, and I don't even mind not being with her at the clinic. I think my job right now is to be vigilant and protective of Oley.

Hazel keeps a bright smile on her face all the time. She tries to cook the most tempting meals for Oley, even though he doesn't have much of an appetite these days. She runs him to doctor's appointments, and they sit on the patio some nights and have conversations that are so deep and long I always fall asleep. The only time she leaves is if Jack takes her somewhere for a little bit, but other than that, she's devoted to Oley.

Trotting up to Hazel, I head butt her in the hip.

I give her *the* look. *Give me food, woman.*

She gives me a head scratch instead, and that's fine. Not quite as satisfying to my belly, but totally fills my soul up.

"Maybe you should make a move on him," Liz suggests.

Hazel's eyes shine with amusement, but she gives a firm shake of her head. "It's not the right time. I've only got enough room in my life to care about one man right now."

Liz's face goes soft, and she reaches out to squeeze Hazel's hand. "I know it's hard."

"It's fine," Hazel says in that way where she always tries to be strong.

Only I know, though.

When Hazel goes to bed, many nights she does so crying into my neck with her arms wrapped tightly around me.

CHAPTER 51

Hazel

GOD KNOWS I'M happy to see Oley's kids and grandkids come in to visit him, but did they have to pick the weekend of my dog's birthday? Well, his half birthday. Ever since we celebrated his six-month birthday on that July 4th four years ago, Atticus has been the recipient of two birthday parties each year, and having Oley's family here kind of takes the specialness out of it.

The minute that wretched thought enters my head, my skin flushes with guilt. That's incredibly selfish of me. It's not about Atticus or me, but about Oley.

Except... I know he's had his fill of them and can't wait until they leave after the party. I know this because he told me so. He loves his family, but they also don't fit very well into his life. I watched them putting their father off with one excuse or another for years, and now that he's dying, they're hovering is kind of oppressive to him. This is the second time they've visited since his diagnosis.

Regardless, Oley and I decided to move forward with our birthday plans for Atticus despite his kids dropping by very unexpectedly. As in, Tara called as they were leaving Raleigh. I had to rush out to the grocery store and buy more chicken for the grill.

"What can I get you, Oley?" I ask as I bend over his rocking chair. It was a terribly hot day, but at least now that the sun's gone down it's just a tolerable mugginess. The ceiling fans on the patio help.

We're having the party out here because there are too many people to fit comfortably inside Oley's house, but also because Oley gets cold sometimes. He says the Carolina heat makes his bones feel better.

"I'm good, Hazel," he says, keeping his eyes on the kids running around the backyard with Atticus and Scout. Benji, Monica, and Tyrone, Jr. are wearing their butts out, but what dog doesn't love chasing kids and playing tug-of-war?

"I'll take another beer when you get a moment," Bernard says from beside Oley. He's rocking his chair to the exact same cadence as Oley's.

"Gotcha," I tell him with a smile.

Glancing around, I try to see if anyone else looks like they need anything. The barbeque was a success. I served grilled chicken, mounds of my potato salad, and a huge pot of baked beans.

Tara, Cameron, and their brood sit at one of the picnic tables under a nearby oak tree. Jack and Carl are playing a game of horseshoes with Tyrone and Trey. Liz, Carina, and my mom are sipping margaritas at a folding table I'd set out. The only ones missing are Charmin and Shane, but her due date is next week, and she didn't want to risk being away from the hospital and their doctor this close, which is totally legit. She did send a gift for Atticus, though, and I let him open it this morning.

It was a new super-sized Kong I immediately filled with peanut butter. He went to town on it while I took a shower and got ready for the day.

My heart swells, taking in all of Oley's friends. Some who are newer than others, but all came out to celebrate my dog's half birthday not for my dog, but for the man who once saved my dog and me.

I step inside the kitchen, wanting a cooling respite from the heat. In a bit, I'll pull out the doggie cake I'd made for Atticus along with the people cake I'd also made, and we'll make a big deal out of the birthday boy for a bit. He's officially four and a half years old. I'm not sure if it's because Oley's got a limited number of days left on this earth, but I find myself worrying about my dog's own days more than usual.

The french door opens, and I turn to see Jack stepping inside. I might be all kinds of a fool, but I can't help that my pulse always quickens just a bit when I'm close to him.

He gives me a big smile as he shuts the door. "It's hot as hell outside."

"Not so bad under the fans," I reply as I lean back against the counter.

"Came to get a few more beers." Jack says, but he comes to stand beside me. He reaches a hand out, tucking a lock of my hair behind my ear, which gives me goose bumps and an unbearable need to shiver.

He stares at me a long moment before he asks, "You doing okay?"

"Yeah," I murmur.

"No." He turns, steps in front of me, and moves his face in closer to mine. "Seriously… are you doing okay? And for once, be honest when I ask that question."

Jack does ask me that a lot. We see each other once or twice a week, and we talk on the phone or by text in between. He's the only one—besides perhaps Atticus— who keeps an eye on my mental health.

"He's going downhill," I finally manage to breathe out.

"Yeah," he says with a heavy sigh. "He's not looking good."

It made me think about when Tara showed up yesterday. She'd hugged her dad and told him how good he looked. And maybe he did in that moment because he was happy to see his kids.

But she doesn't see how he eats barely enough food to sustain a toddler each day. Or how he gets cold, and then really hot. Or how he's constantly thirsty, but nothing seems to satisfy him.

She certainly hasn't made mention of the fact his skin is yellowing with jaundice as his liver is being killed off by the cancer.

Jack brings his hands to my shoulders, and for a moment, I stiffen involuntarily. He's never touched me like this before. Every time we get together for a meal or to go see a movie, it's totally in the friend zone. Sure… I get a hug from him in greeting or in farewell, but it's always brief and brotherly.

His hands feel warm and heavy on me, and so very comforting. "What can I do to help you?" he asks.

I bite down hard on the inside of my cheek to keep from saying, "Kiss me."

God, that's inappropriate.

"Just continue being a good friend, Jack," I say. I bring my hands up to circle his wrists, giving him an affectionate squeeze.

He smiles, but then dips his head a little closer. "That I will always do for you. But you do know, Hazel…" His voice goes deep and low, sending a shiver down my spine when he finishes. "That I want to be more than your friend, right?"

I blink and blink and blink while I try to process those words. Things seem to go all slo-mo on me.

"But it's more important that you get through this with Oley," he explains. "You have the world's biggest burden on your shoulders, and I don't know how you do it. I'm in constant amazement at the way you just so effortlessly handle things."

More blinking.

His gaze grows softer. "But I know it's not effortless to you. It's taking a toll. So whatever you need, I'm the person you call first, okay?"

Three more blinks.

"Hazel," he chides. "Okay?"

"Okay," I whisper.

"Good," he says with a satisfied smile, cupping the back of my neck with his strong hand. Leaning in while tugging me closer, he touches his lips to my skin for the very first time.

Right on my forehead, and it's the best first kiss I've ever had. My hands tighten on his wrists, and I want to keep him there forever.

The kitchen door opens, and Bernard calls out, "What happened to my beer, Hazel?"

Jack doesn't jump away from me, but rather releases me slowly with an added wink before he turns toward the fridge.

Slow motion is gone now, the world back to real

time.

"What you drinking?" Jack asks Bernard as he opens the refrigerator.

My mom comes in behind Bernard, gently pushing him to the side as he just stands in the doorway. She beams at me. "Want to get the cake served, honey?"

"Yeah, sure," I answer. "I've got them locked upstairs in the guest bedroom."

No way in hell was Atticus going to get into them before we were ready.

Liz and Carina walk in, carrying their empty margarita glasses. "Any left?" Liz asks.

I nod toward the fridge, then Jack is pulling the pitcher out and handing it to them. "You ladies better watch it. I don't want you getting crazy on us."

Everyone laughs.

There's chatter.

Mom pushes me toward the hall that leads to the cakes. I take one last, lingering look at Jack, but he's talking to Bernard as he hands over a beer.

For the first time in a long time, my heart feels really good, and I'll take that feeling for however long it may last.

CHAPTER 52

Hazel

THE CHICKEN COOP has long been finished, thanks to Jack's guidance with Bernard and Oley, as well as his patience. Oley even insisted on stocking it with actual chickens. I dutifully collect eggs each morning, keeping a few for myself, but giving most away to either Bernard or the staff at the clinic.

The mood there has been somber. Things have been tidied up nicely with Marsha buying the practice. It was one of the first things Oley did after he decided almost four months ago not to fight the cancer. They agreed upon a fair price, and had a lawyer draft up the documents. While I didn't think it was any of my business, Oley had me involved so I understood very clearly that part of the sales agreement included a condition I remain employed there for at least three years after his death.

I didn't foresee that as a problem. Marsha and I get along very well, and she's as dependent on me to run the business side of things as Oley was. Still, it was a very sweet gesture from a man who has infinite sweetness inside of him.

Oley moans, his face screwing up in pain. It's amazing how efficient I've become at caring for him. The hospice nurses have been wonderful in teaching me the mystic arts of helping someone die.

It's been almost a week since Oley stopped communicating. He's in what appears to be a deep sleep most of the time, but there's also pain and discomfort. I have to gauge how much by sounds and movement.

Within moments, I have a dose of morphine delivered to him subcutaneously as I was taught by the nurse. There are no IVs because Oley didn't want any hydration to prolong the process. When he was awake and had more strength to swallow, I could dribble the medicine in his mouth with an eye dropper. Now he can't be depended on to swallow the grace morphine gives, so I inject it under his skin.

While I'm up and attending him, I check his diaper. It's dry, which is not surprising. No food or hydration will do that. I step over Atticus who spends most of his time lying beside Oley's hospital bed. We'd put it in the living room, so he could watch TV on his better days. I still put the Braves on any time they're playing, and I'd like to think some part of Oley knows and appreciates it.

Grabbing an oral swab, I start to dip it into a glass of cold sweet tea that's always sitting by his bed. It's right next to a sealed letter. The envelope has my name written on it, and it's from Oley. When he started the downward spiral and became bedridden, he made me promise not to read it until he died. Of course, I agreed.

Oley's mouth is open, as it usually is, with his tongue slightly peeking out. I gently pull down on his chin to get it a little wider and with great care, I swipe around the inside of his mouth to moisten it. I doubt he can taste it, but it makes me smile to know he's getting his beloved sweet tea right until the end.

This past week as been tough. I've been by his side the entire time, sleeping on the couch for stolen snatches. I'm able to shower and have an hour to myself when either Jack, Bernard, Liz, or my mom comes by to sit with Oley.

He has all the signs that death is bearing down on him that we were taught to be on the lookout for. First, it was weakness and disorientation. The agitation was terrible to watch, but they have drugs for that. The cocktail that seems to give him the most relief is a mix of Ativan and Morphine.

He lost consciousness for great periods of time. All the while, I'd sit by him and talk, hold his hand, or rub his arms. I called Tara and Cameron to come, as I thought we were getting very close. For three days they sat by his bed while I did the medical care as hospice had taught me. Swabbing his mouth when asleep, encouraging ice chips when he was awake. Changing his diaper and bed linens—usually when the hospice nurse came by as it was easier with two people. Rubbing lotion on his dry skin and combing his hair.

On the fourth day after Oley had stopped communicating, Tara and Cameron left. Cameron had work duties, and I think Tara couldn't take it any longer. I didn't hold that against either one of them. The business of watching a loved one die is truly the most horrific experience ever. I felt bad for them, seeing years of regret etched upon their faces.

I hugged both and promised I'd call them as soon as he was gone. They both love me dearly right now.

Over the last two days, Oley's gotten worse. The hospice nurse was just here a few hours ago, and she doesn't seem to think it will be much longer. He's got fluid sitting at the back of his throat because he can't swallow. It makes an awful gurgling sound when he breathes, and I was terrified he was drowning. The nurse assured me he was not, but gave him some Atropine to help dry it up some. We also elevated his torso to help. His breathing is erratic. Cheyne Stokes, the nurse called it. He'll breath fast for a while, then it will slow until he's barely breathing at all. I'll sit poised by his bed, gripping his hand, thinking it's the end.

Then he starts breathing normally—albeit shallow-ly—again.

It's pure torture just waiting.

I run my hand down Oley's arm. It's getting colder to the touch. Another sign. His skin is paler today with almost a bluish cast to it.

I lower the bed rail, sitting down by Oley's bum hip. That stupid hip I thought was the bane of his existence when it was really cancer.

Atticus pushes from the floor and rests his head on my leg, regarding Oley with soulful eyes. I'd read there was an old Indian legend that dogs with bi-colored eyes were said to be able to see both heaven and earth. I wonder if that's true. I know the truth teller sees things that normal beings don't, so maybe.

Atticus gives a baleful whine.

It makes me smile. "Want to come up here?"

He chuffs. With a gentleness that I didn't know this big, goofy dog possessed until Oley became sick, he gets his front legs up and over my lap, resting most of his weight on me but lets his head go to Oley's stomach. I reach over, taking Oley's arm to pull it so it's in reach of Atticus' face. His tongue comes out, and he licks the back of Oley's hand.

I'm startled for a moment when Oley's eyes flutter and then open. His eyes are watery, the color of his irises lackluster. In the mounds of literature I'd read from the hospice people, I learned patients can sometimes have a surge of energy or a moment of supreme clarity before the end.

I lean forward slightly, and Oley's gaze clears a bit before focusing on me.

"Hey, Oley," I say softly, my voice barely able to squeak the words out. His expression glazes for a moment, and I think he might slip back under.

But then it clears again, and his mouth moves ever so imperceptibly into what might be an attempt at a smile.

Then he looks down his body at Atticus, the dog's own eyes focused with an almost scary intensity back at Oley.

His hand moves. He gives Atticus a pat so weak it barely touches the fur at the side of his head.

I'm stunned when Oley's mouth opens and closes a few times as if he's trying to push words out. I think about getting a swab to moisten again, but then he talks.

The words are stilted, raspy, and barely audible. But I understand him perfectly.

"Thank you, Atti. For bringing Hazel. Into my life."

Tears fill my eyes, flowing freely down my face. Another roundabout way that Oley gives me a compliment.

He manages another weak pat before his eyes slowly close. When he pulls in a watery-sounding breath, it comes out as a relieved sigh.

Oley then slips away from us.

Atticus and I sit there a while, immersed in a mutual grief. I've cried a lot this past week, but there's still tears aplenty for me.

But I also have a sense of peace within me. Oley's not suffering anymore, and has moved on to a better place. I'd like to think Atticus can see him in heaven, hopefully waiting for us one day.

We finally get off Oley's bed. Pulling the sheets up to his chest, I tuck him in. I call the hospice nurse who will come over to verify his death, then she'll work with the funeral home to come get him.

My next calls are to Tara and Cameron, as is their right.

I call Bernard next. He weeps quietly for a few moments. But as we had planned, he starts the call chain to inform Tyrone, Liz, my mom, and Charmin.

Lastly, I call Jack. He tells me that he's on his way.

I grab the envelope with my name on it, heading to the couch. Atticus curls up beside me without his usual need be all over me. I think it's enough for us at this point to just have each other close. It's like he understands the solemnity of the moment.

Breaking the seal, I pull out a handwritten letter from Oley. It's in print as that was how Oley wrote. It appears shakier than normal, but isn't a struggle to read.

Dear Hazel,

You know I'm a man who has difficulty coming out and saying what's in my heart. But I couldn't leave you back here on earth without telling you something very important.

I love you.

I love that hellion of a dog, too, and will always be thankful to Atticus for bringing us all together.

With that said, I have a few things for you. My lawyer will be reaching out to all my heirs soon, which includes you.

I'm leaving you the farm. The reason I'm telling you this now in a letter rather than face to face before I died is because I knew you'd argue with me about it, and I don't like arguing with you. I've also set up an account for you, in which I put the money Marsha paid me for the practice. You deserve that because you're the one who helped me build up a business that was actually worth something.

I'm sorry if you catch any wrath from Tara and Cameron about this. They aren't going to be happy I've left these things to you, but I've given them all my life insurance so they can't quibble too much. Besides... I knew who would be sitting by my side when I died.

Hazel… you've been such a blessing and a joy to me. It's with great meaning when I tell you that I considered you to be my daughter in all ways.

Tell the gang I love them, and how much I appreciate the way they all rallied around me these last few months. Keep Friday night baseball and pizza a tradition. That's now a family thing that you own.

Lastly, after you finish this letter, I'm sure you'll have a good cry. But then no more tears for me. I'm ready, and I don't fear where I'm going.

Love,
Oley

The words blur as I go ahead and have my good cry. Atticus shifts his head to put it on my lap. My fingers go to his fur, and I let it all out.

When the tears dry up, I look back down at the letter again and see there's a postscript.

P.S. I foresee a beautiful and happy relationship between you and Jack. I can't wait to see my "grandkids" from heaven above.

I burst out laughing, pulling the letter to my chest where I hug his words to me.

CHAPTER 53

Hazel

WE SAY OUR final goodbyes to Oley on a mid-August Saturday morning. There was no big church affair or tearful farewell over a grave. Instead, we spread his ashes over his beloved pet cemetery, which represented the type of man he was.

The turnout is a little overwhelming. It is the most beautiful type of validation of how loved and revered he was. When we posted his obituary and invited all friends to join us in a remembrance celebration at the farm, we invited humans and pets alike. There were almost as many animals as there were people who came to pay their last respects.

The gathering at the pet cemetery is informal. Cameron speaks of his father as best he can, but sadly... he really didn't know the man Oley had grown to be later in life. Bernard also speaks about his friend, about the Oley that I knew. He gets choked up several times, but I adhere to Oley's wishes and don't cry for him anymore.

Instead, I let myself be filled with the light and peace the man gave to me when he left this world.

When he left me a better person for knowing him.

After Bernard finishes, Tara does the honor of sprinkling his ashes. Her daughter Abigail, who has an incredibly lovely voice, sings one of Oley's favorites, *Amazing Grace*. That song never fails to make goose bumps prickle along my skin.

The short ceremony complete, I invite everyone up to the farmhouse where I had the foresight to have some food catered. This was probably unnecessary because practically everyone showed up with food, which is a very southern thing.

What I like best as I mill around and talk to people is there's a lot of laughter going on. People telling their best Oley stories, and I know that's exactly how he would have wanted this to be.

I glance over at Jack. He's got Atticus by his side, holding tightly to his leash. While he's being such a good boy today, because I think he truly understands what's going on just by reading the heaviness of emotion here today, Jack's not taking any chances that my dog will break away and do something crazy.

Jack has been a rock. My personal strong pillar to lean against.

As Oley had said would happen, his lawyer did in fact reach out to me as well as Tara and Cameron. I guess timing was of the essence because his wishes for cremation were within his estate documents, as well as how he was dividing his assets among his loved ones.

Tara was not happy about me getting the farm. Surprisingly, Cameron had pulled me aside this morning and told me he was happy about it. He knew I'd care for and love this place in ways he and his sister wouldn't. He even admitted that had they been left the farm, he was sure they would have sold it for the money since their lives were established away from here.

Regardless of his kind words, Tara felt the need to deliver some unkind words to me about it. Unfortunately for her, Jack happened to be standing beside me when she approached, and he gave her a very subtle but pointed dressing down that made her snap her mouth shut. She's been polite but distant since then, and that works for me.

My mom comes up beside me, wrapping an arm around my waist. I lean my head on her shoulder.

"You okay, baby?" she asks softly.

"Actually, I am," I reassure her. She's not begrudged my sorrow or the strong relationship I had with Oley, especially since it had become more than what I was ever lucky enough to have with my dad.

She knows what I know deep in my heart.

God gave me Oley as my second chance. He gave me another father to guide me and love me.

Oley didn't say he loved me until the letter I'd read after he died. And that was fine. I always knew it because Oley was more about the action over the word.

But I didn't hesitate to tell Oley my feelings. I told him I loved him on that very first day he got the cancer diagnosis, and every day thereafter. He was so cute about it at first, sort of grunting and then stammering with embarrassment.

After that, my words would just make him smile with a special sparkle in his eyes. Usually, his response was a hug or a squeeze to my hand.

It was beautiful, and it was perfectly enough for me.

My gaze sweeps across the yard, and I spy Bernard over at the fence looking over the cow pasture. He's got his forearms resting across the top of one of the posts as he leans his weight against it, one leg crossed over the other.

"I'm going to go talk to Bernard," I tell my mom.

She gives me a squeeze and releases me.

It's difficult maneuvering over turf in high heels, and I know to anyone watching, I probably look ridiculous.

When I reach Bernard's side, I slip my arm around his waist. He startles for a moment, turning his head my way. When he sees it's me, he gives me a bright smile and pushes off the post to put his arm around my shoulders. He pulls me in close, and we stare out over the rolling green hills for a long silent moment.

He looks great today. Tyrone lent him one of his suits. He shaved and got a haircut, although I know Oley wouldn't have cared how he dressed.

"Your words were lovely, Bernard," I tell him.

"From the heart, Hazel," he replies gruffly. "Can never go wrong when they come from that place."

I smile, leaning my head onto his shoulder. "You were such a dear friend to him. You enriched his life so much. I hope you know that."

"I do," he says softly. "He gave it back tenfold, though."

A tiny laugh bubbles up inside of me. "Just think about what a trio we made. A cranky old veterinarian, a worthless bartender, and a homeless guy."

Bernard chuckles, but his voice is tender when he says, "You were never worthless, Hazel."

"Maybe not to you and Oley, but I was to myself."

"Well, I hope you know what you meant to that ol' coot," Bernard says as he releases his hold on me to turn to me. "You made his life a very happy one, if only for a few years."

"I'm glad," I say. For the first time today, I can feel the threat of tears. An overwhelming longing for Oley hits me, and I have to fight it back.

Bernard glances over his shoulder at the farmhouse, at the multitudes of people and animals standing around. Eating, drinking, and laughing.

"Quite the turnout," he murmurs.

"Yup," is all I say as I take it all in.

"I'll help you clean up after everyone leaves."

"You're a dear, sweet man, and I'll take you up on it."

"Let's head back," he says as he clasps my hand in his. "There's apparently socializing we need to be doing."

My responding laugh is all he gets. We walk in silence for a bit, Bernard letting me lean on him as my heels sink into the soft ground.

Just before we reach the edge of the crowd, he leans his head toward me and asks, "We on for pizza and baseball Friday?"

"You betcha," I reply.

◆

I YAWN AS I walk Tyrone and Bernard to the door. Carina had left with the kids long ago while we cleaned up. Tara, Cameron, and their broods also took off for Raleigh and Charlotte even though I begged them to stay, but I think ultimately it was awkward for them to sleep in a home that wasn't theirs anymore.

Hard hugs are exchanged, and I get an extra kiss on the cheek from Bernard. I lock the front door before heading back into the kitchen. I find Jack wiping down the kitchen counters. Atticus is on the floor, sound asleep. He doesn't even open his eyes when I walk in.

Jack glances at me, gives me a big smile, and goes back to running the wet cloth over the granite surface.

"I'm tired," I say as I blow a breath out. After I pull a chair away from the table, I sit down heavily.

"It's been a long day," he replies, turning to the sink and draping the cloth over the faucet.

He turns back around, tucking his hands in his pockets. Jack is a jeans and t-shirt kind of guy, and it's the way I prefer him. But I have to say he looks mighty damn fine in a suit. He's currently got the jacket and tie hanging on the knob of the back door.

"What are your plans tomorrow?" he asks.

"Charmin and Shane are going to come out to hang for a bit before they head back to Raleigh."

"Need your baby fix, don't you?" Jack asks with a knowing twinkle in his eye.

"Is it that obvious?" I ask. Charmin just had the baby—a girl named Felicity—two weeks ago. I hadn't been able to see her before the funeral. What with Oley becoming bedridden and then dying.

"Well, you did pay more attention to the baby than you did Atticus today, so that says something."

From deep within his slumber, Atticus hears his name and raises his head, looking around blearily. I tell him honestly, "You'll always be my number-one baby, buddy."

This seems to satisfy him, and his head drops back down. His eyes close, and he's out.

"What are you plans the day after then?" Jack asks. "And if you're doing something then, what about the day after?"

"What are you getting at?" I ask with a smile.

"I'm trying to ask you out on our first official date." His grin is charmingly devilish, and it makes me ridiculously happy.

I don't let him know that, though. Instead, I cock an eyebrow. "You do understand, don't you, that we've been out to dinner many times as well as the movies? I think we've already had a date."

Jack shakes his head. "Those weren't dates. They were friendship outings."

"What's the difference?"

"We'll be having our first kiss after our first date," he says smugly. "That's the difference."

"Oh," I murmur, feeling my cheeks flush. "In that case, the day after tomorrow I'm totally free."

"And hopefully the days after that." His eyes are soft and yearning as he searches my face for the answer.

"And all the days after that."

EPILOGUE

Atticus

"Love isn't something you find.
Love is something that finds you."

—Loretta Young

Three years later…

MY BODY IS getting weary and my bones are aching, which is why my favorite place to rest is right here on the couch with Hazel. Of course, we have to share space with Jack, but that's okay. Next to Hazel, he's my favorite human, just barely edging Bernard out—only because Jack lives with us and sneaks me food all the time.

I'm curled into a circle with my head pressed against Hazel's hip. I can't put it on her lap because it's huge now… like there's a big round ball inside. It's not a ball, but a tiny human she's carrying around.

Jack sits on the other side of Hazel, with a big book spread out across his lap. Hazel's leaning against him looking at it, but she has one hand buried deep in the fur at my neck to give me rubs.

"Oh my gosh," Hazel says with a laugh as she points at a picture in the book. I don't bother raising my head to see. I'm too comfortable. "Remember when you took that picture at the Grand Canyon?"

Jack laughs. "It was the most perfectly timed picture ever."

Okay, curiosity gets the better of me. I lift my head up, stretching my neck. Jack holds the book up so I can see. "Remember that, Atti?"

I do indeed. Me sitting beside Hazel when we visited the Grand Canyon. She was laughing at something Jack said. I was sleepy because we'd been hiking all day, and I was in the middle of a huge yawn. When Jack took the picture, it looked like Hazel and I were laughing in sync at something the both of us found funny.

Those were some good days, although there's no way I'd have the stamina to go on another grand adventure like we did then.

After Oley died, Hazel took an opportunity to write for a travel blog that was focused on traveling with pets. For an entire year, Hazel, Jack, and I traveled around the United States together. Jack's father watched the store, and Marsha assured Hazel she'd survive without her at the clinic.

We saw everything there was to see. My favorite was

the places that had snow for me to romp around in.

I think Hazel's favorite was on the beach in California where Jack proposed to her. He had the ring in a box tied to my collar, but then I got too excited and chased after a seagull with the ring still tied to me. I've never heard Jack yell so loud as when he chased me, or Hazel laugh so hard.

"Ouch," Hazel exclaims, and I go on high alert with my ears perked forward. I stare at her intently, waiting for her to tell me her troubles so I can solve them.

She rubs the lower part of her belly with a laugh. "That kid is going to be a soccer star."

Oh… okay. Just the tiny human moving around inside of her. No biggie as that happens a lot lately.

I'm sure Hazel and Jack are aware, but I know that baby is going to be making an appearance very soon.

It's a special baby, too. They worked long and hard to get it. Hazel had to see the doctor a lot. Even had to get a lot of shots in her legs and stomach and butt. Jack helped give them to her, and I provided the doggie Xanax fix each time because she's scared of needles. She once told me after one of her shots that the baby was a team effort, and she couldn't have done it without me.

That made me proud.

I'm not sure how I feel about the little human, though. Deep down, I know it will take Hazel away from me. Not completely, but to a great extent.

What I also know within my soul is this will make Hazel happier than anything has ever made her in her existence. Happier than even me.

I've pondered this for months, and I finally figured out this is okay by me. It's a sacrifice I'll gladly make for her.

After all, I'm pretty sure I was put on this earth for the sole purpose of making Hazel who she's supposed to be. When the tiny human is born, Hazel will have completed her journey.

Then my work here is done.

About the Author

S. Bennett is the pen name for New York Times, USA Today and Wall Street Journal bestselling author Sawyer Bennett.

Under the name S. Bennett, Sawyer writes general, young adult and women's fiction stories that deal with the realities we face on a daily basis such as love, loss, personal growth and all things in between. She tackles difficult issues with grace, while adding her signature humor along the way. Because Sawyer is a romance writer at heart, you're likely to find a love story within each of her books, though it's not always a guarantee.

When she isn't writing as S. Bennett, she's writing contemporary romance as Sawyer Bennett, and sweet romance under the name Juliette Poe.

Go here to see other works by S. Bennett
sawyerbennett.com/bookstore/s-bennett-books

S. Bennett also writes sexy, contemporary romance as
Sawyer Bennett! Click here to see her books.
sawyerbennett.com/bookshop

Don't miss another new release by Sawyer Bennett!!!
Sign up for her newsletter and keep up to date on new
releases, giveaways, book reviews and so much more.
sawyerbennett.com/signup

Connect with Sawyer online:

Website: sawyerbennett.com
Twitter: twitter.com/bennettbooks
Facebook: facebook.com/bennettbooks
Instagram: instagram.com/sawyerbennett123
Book+Main Bites:
bookandmainbites.com/sawyerbennett
Goodreads: goodreads.com/Sawyer_Bennett
Amazon: amazon.com/author/sawyerbennett
BookBub: bookbub.com/authors/sawyer-bennett

The Ladies Who Write Are Here!

I am part of a fantastic group of romance authors called the Ladies Who Write (LWW), and we have created a fun, sexy world just for you! Join me, along with Marina Adair, Emma Chase, Melissa Foster, Jennifer Probst, Kristen Proby, and Jill Shalvis, as we bring a whole new group of characters to life. In *ATTICUS*, we got our first look at the ladies of LWW with the introduction of Aubrey Stewart. Be sure to keep your eyes peeled for future appearances by Aubrey and others in the LWW world across books from all seven of the Ladies Who Write authors!

For more information on our group, and to stay up to date on the release of LWW books, visit www.LadiesWhoWrite.com and sign up for our newsletter.

ladieswhowrite.com/newsletter

CPSIA information can be obtained
at www.ICGtesting.com
Printed in the USA
LVHW02s1654040918
589112LV00002B/337/P